Bombshell

"Sesily, what did you do?"

"What makes you think I did anything?" Later, Caleb would be impressed by her lack of hesitation. By the way she grabbed his hand, as though it was the most ordinary thing in the world, and yanked him into the darkness beneath the nearest tree.

Later, he would take himself to task for not resisting. But how was he supposed to resist as she pressed herself to him, her hands sliding up over his chest, her fingers finding purchase in his hair? He was only human, after all.

One of his arms wrapped around her waist, pulling her tight to him. Only to make sure they kept their balance.

Not for anything else. Not because he wanted her there.

"I swore I'd never do this," she whispered, distracted as she moved impossibly closer, aligning their bodies in a way that made him think violent thoughts about fabric.

He meant to resist. "Do what?"

"Kiss you," she said, and for a moment the matter-of-fact words sizzled through him. "Unfortunately . . . circumstances dictate . . ."

He meant to stop her.

Except there was no stopping Sesily Talbot.

By Sarah MacLean

SARAH MacLEAN

BOMB SHELL

HELL'S
BELLES,
BOOK 1

AVONBOOKS

An Imprint of HarperCollinsPublishers

BOMBSHELL. Copyright © 2021 by Sarah Trabucchi. All rights reserved. Printed in the United States of America. No part of this book may be used or reproduced in any manner whatsoever without written permission except in the case of brief quotations embodied in critical articles and reviews. For information, address HarperCollins Publishers, 195 Broadway, New York, NY 10007.

First Avon Books mass market printing: September 2021
First Avon Books hardcover printing: August 2021

Print Edition ISBN: 978-0-06-305615-2
Digital Edition ISBN: 978-0-06-305584-1

Cover design by Amy Halperin
Cover art by Alan Ayers
Chapter opener art © Peter Hermes Furian / Shutterstock, Inc.

Avon, Avon & logo, and Avon Books & logo are registered trademarks of HarperCollins Publishers in the United States of America and other countries.

HarperCollins is a registered trademark of HarperCollins Publishers in the United States of America and other countries.

FIRST EDITION

Printed and Bound in Barcelona Spain by CPI BlackPrint

21 22 23 24 25   CPI   10 9 8 7 6 5 4 3 2 1

*A week before I finished writing this book,
my seven-year-old daughter told
me I should dedicate it
"to the people helping during the pandemic."*

I know a good idea when I hear one.

*For frontline workers in health care,
education, farming and food service,
shipping and delivery, and for everyone
working to keep us all healthy.*

Thank you.

Sesily

When the stilt-walker approached, Sesily Talbot realized someone was toying with her.

She should have noticed immediately, when she'd stepped off the boat and through the river gates of the Vauxhall Pleasure Gardens, when the dancer dressed as an enormous peacock, brilliantly colored tailfeathers spread wide as a Marylebone rowhouse, caught her on her way off the beaten path and pulled her, instead, to the dancing grounds.

"Not this path, lady," the beautiful bird had whispered before tugging her into a wild, spinning reel. Sesily had never been one to refuse a dance, and she'd happily followed her new, feathered friend.

When the jig left her breathless and heated despite the cool October night, she'd peeled away from the entertainment and headed for somewhere quieter. Somewhere to hold her solitude. Keep her secrets.

Sesily hadn't made it more than a minute into the darkness when the fire-eater found her, blocking the path that twisted and turned beneath a web of tightropes high above, luring revelers further into the salacious extravagance of the gardens.

Red paper lanterns glowed with delicious temptation behind the performer who blocked Sesily's way, her face painted white like a clown's, bright blue eyes twinkling as she drew close to her torch and set the inky black night aflame.

Sesily knew her role and didn't hesitate to ooh and ahh, letting the fire-eater take her hand with a deep curtsy and a charming, "Not this path, lady." She led Sesily back to the light, away from the route she'd sought.

Sesily should have noticed then, that she was a pawn.

No, not a pawn. A queen. But played, nonetheless.

She didn't notice. And later, she would wonder at her ignorance in the moment—rare for her twenty-eight years. Rare for someone who reveled in knowing the score. Rare for someone who had made a life's work of winning the room, spinning the spinners.

Instead, Sesily Talbot spent the next hour being spun herself.

Lured by a fortune-teller.

Entertained by a pair of mimes.

Amused by a bawdy puppet show.

And every time she tried to find a new path, one that led deeper into the gardens, away from the formal performance and toward the kind of entertainment that made for gossip and scandal and something to keep her mind from the emptiness in her chest, she was intercepted— ever waylaid from more reckless adventures.

Adventures more suited to her reputation: Sesily Talbot, walking scandal, buxom beauty, untethered heiress, and queen of recklessness, whom most of London called *Sexily* when they thought she wasn't listening (as though it was a *bad* thing).

At twenty-eight years, Sesily was the second oldest and only unmarried daughter of wealthy, baseborn Jack Talbot, a coal miner who'd pulled himself up through the soot to win a title from the Prince Regent in a game of cards. As if that weren't enough, the newly minted Earl of Wight set about wreaking common havoc on the aristocracy, his flamboyant wife and five dangerous daughters in tow. Daughters who'd scandalized society right up until they'd made enviable society matches: Seraphina, Sesily, Seleste, Seline, and Sophie—the Soiled S's, named for the coal dust they'd been born into, now reigning over London as a duchess, a marchioness, a countess, and the wife of the wealthiest horse breeder in Britain.

And then there was Sesily, who'd spent a decade flouting tradition and title and rules and—the most dangerous of the daughters. Because she had no interest in the games the aristocracy played. She did not concern herself with fabricated opponents who glared at her from the opposite ends of ballrooms. She did not have the same goals as the rest of society.

Reckless Sesily.

She did not relegate herself to the shelf of spinsterhood, nor to the outer edges of Mayfair, where the aged and ruined lived out their days.

Wild Sesily.

Instead, she remained rich and titled and merry, with seemingly no interest in the opinions of those around her. Unwilling to be tamed by mother, sister, companion, or community.

Scandalous Sesily.

Censure did not take. Nor contempt. Nor disapproval. Which left the aristocracy no choice but to accept her.

Bored Sesily.

Not bored. Not that night. Boredom might have brought her to Vauxhall, but not alone. She'd have come with a friend. With a dozen of them. She'd have come for raucous entertainment and a whisper of trouble, but nothing like what she wanted that evening. Nothing like what clawed at her, making her want to seek out the worst kind of trouble. Tempt it. Scream at it.

Frustrated Sesily. Angry Sesily.

Embarrassed Sesily.

In the worst possible way. By a *man*. A tall, broad, green-eyed, irritating man in shirtsleeves and waistcoat and maybe a silly American-style hat that didn't at all suit in Mayfair but was distractingly good at revealing the angle of an altogether too-square jaw. Far too square. Unrefined in the extreme.

The only man she'd ever wanted and couldn't win.

So much for Sexily.

But she absolutely refused to suffer her disappointments in public. That was the kind of thing other people did, not Sesily.

Sesily Talbot picked herself up, painted her face, and went to Vauxhall.

Of course, if she weren't so busy suffering that particular evening's disappointment in private, she would have noticed that she was being watched, and maneuvered, and guided long before the stilt-walker stepped out of the shadows of the tall trees lining the path that led to the rear section of Vauxhall. The Dark Walk.

In the decade that Sesily had attended Vauxhall, the majority of visits had involved slipping the notice of parent, chaperone, sister, or friend and darting down the ever-darkening path to the place where events moved from performed to private. Away from fireworks and circus acts and hot air balloons to something more improper. Something that might be considered sordid.

In all those years, she'd never once seen a performer this far along the path. This deep into the darkness.

Certainly not as the clock neared midnight on the last week of the Vauxhall season, when the lateness of the hour did nothing to lessen the number of people in the gardens, and performers should be occupied with entertaining throngs of revelers marveling at the sheer, lush temptation of the place.

And yet, there'd been a dancer, and a fire-eater, and now there was a stilt-walker, with her enormous wig and her extreme maquillage and her delighted smile and, "Not this path, lady!"

And that's when Sesily knew.

She pulled up short, tilting to look up at the performer high above her, somehow, impossibly, dressed in massive, magnificent skirts—skirts that would threaten to fell a perfectly ordinary woman on her own two feet. "Not *any* path tonight, though, is it?"

A big laugh, made bigger as it rained down upon Sesily in the darkness, carried on the cool autumn breeze and punctuated by the bright fireworks that had begun in another part of the gardens, summoning the masses to marvel at them.

Sesily was not interested in the sky. "Or is there a *different* path for me tonight?"

The laugh became a knowing smile, and the stilt-walker turned away. There was no question that Sesily would follow, suddenly imagining herself an arrow loosed from a bow, away from the target she'd chosen, and instead, aimed for somewhere else. Something else.

And though anger and frustration and that thing she would not ever admit to feeling still burned hot in her breast, Sesily could not help her own smile.

She was no longer bored.

Not as she followed the giantess through the trees to a light in the distance that flickered and glowed brighter and brighter, until they came upon a clearing where Sesily had never been before. There, on a raised platform, stood a magician, and one with no small amount of skill, considering the way she defied the fireworks in the sky and held the rapt attention of the audience clustered tightly around her as she levitated a hound before their eyes.

The magician's gaze found the stilt-walker and slid instantly to Sesily, not a flicker of surprise in her eyes as she completed the trick and released the hound with a wave of her hand and a bit of dried meat.

Wild applause exploded through the clearing as she took her bow, deep and grateful, honoring the truth of all artists—that they were nothing without audience.

The audience returned to the evening, their rush to find another spectacle more urgent than usual—driven by the knowledge that they had scant hours before the gardens closed for the season.

Within moments, Sesily was alone in the clearing with the magician and her hound, the stilt-walker somehow disappeared into the night.

"My lady," the magician said, her easy Italian accent filling the space between them, the honorific clear as the night sky. She knew who Sesily was. She'd been waiting for her, just as they all had that evening. "Welcome."

Sesily approached, curiosity consuming her. "I see now that I've not been making the night difficult;

you've been holding me at bay. Until you had time for me."

"Until we could give you the time you deserved, my lady." The magician bowed, extravagant and low, collecting a small, gilded box from the ground and setting it at the center of the table between them.

Sesily smiled, looking to the dog at the magician's feet. "I was very impressed with your performance. I don't suppose you'll tell me how the illusion works?"

The woman's gold-green eyes glittered in the lanternlight. "Magic."

She was younger than Sesily had first believed, a dark hood having hidden what she now recognized as a pretty, fresh face—the kind that most definitely turned heads.

As someone who prided herself on her own ability to turn heads, Sesily admired the woman's unique beauty.

Of course, she hadn't been able to turn the only head she'd ever really cared to turn.

She'd so failed to turn that head, it was on a boat to Boston that very moment.

She pushed the thought out of her mind. "You had them all enraptured."

"The world enjoys a spectacle," the magician replied.

"And in the spectacle, they fail to see the truth." Sesily knew that better than most.

"Therein lies the business," the woman said, opening the box, a collection of silver rings winking at her. "Shall I show you another trick?"

"Of course," Sesily replied, flashing a bright smile to hide the immediate pounding of her heart. Earlier that day, she'd felt herself on a precipice, at one of the rare moments in life when a body knew there would be a *before* and an *after*.

But that had been a feeling in her heart. One that would wane. Quiet. Until the moment would fade and she'd struggle to remember the details.

That had been emotion.

This . . . this was in her head.

This was truth.

She did not hesitate, putting her hand into the empty box, her fingers brushing across the firm, smooth oak within. Extracting her hand, she said, "Empty."

The woman's brows lifted in a charming flirt and she closed the wood top with a firm snap, then passed a hand over the top before opening it again. "Are you certain?"

Delighted and curious, Sesily reached inside, her breath catching as she removed the small silver oval inside. Turning the portrait over in her hands, she tilted it to the light.

Surprise came. "It's me."

The magician inclined her head. "So you know it was meant for you."

The interception. The machination. The maneuvering. The way her path had been charted that evening. Her fingers tightened on the little portrait, the silver frame biting into her skin.

But why?

As though she heard the question, the magician passed another wave over the empty box. Tilted it toward her. Sesily reached inside, heart in her throat, breath coming fast.

Here, now, everything was to change.

At first, she thought it was empty again, her fingertips stroking over the smooth wood, seeking. Finding.

She extracted a small ecru card. Held it to the light.

An ornate bell inked on one side, a Mayfair address in the lower left corner.

She flipped it over, the strong, sure script searing through her.

Not this path, Sesily.
We've a better one.
Come and see me.
Duchess

Chapter One

South Audley Street, Mayfair
The London Home of the Duchess of Trevescan
Two Years Later

It's as though one is watching a carriage accident."
Lady Sesily Talbot stood behind the refreshment table at the Duchess of Trevescan's autumn ball, contemplating the teeming mass of aristocrats and happily commentating for her friend and hostess. Indeed, Sesily had trouble looking away from the throngs of frocks— each one unique and dreadful in its own way.

It was 1838, and while ladies of the aristocracy had at long last been blessed with unabashedly plunging necklines and tight, boned bodices—two of Sesily's favorite things—anyone in a dress was simultaneously cursed with lace and frippery and haberdashery, brightly colored ribbons and flowers piled high, like a tiered cake at court.

Sesily nodded toward an unfortunate debutante lost in a sea of patterned grenadine gauze. "That one looks as though she's been upholstered in my mother's bedchamber curtains." She tutted her disapproval. "I take it back. It is not *one* carriage accident. It is a ballroom full of them. History will surely judge us harshly for these fashions."

"Would we say *fashions*?" At her right elbow, the Duchess of Trevescan, Mayfair's most beloved hostess—though not a single member of the aristocracy would ever admit it—brushed an invisible speck from her stunning, fitted sapphire bodice (fully lacking in frippery), pursed her boldly stained lips, and surveyed the crush of people with a discerning eye.

"The only explanation is that the new queen loathes her sex. Else why would she choose to make *these* the styles of the day? The goal is clearly to make us all look atrocious. Look at that one." Sesily pointed to a particularly unfortunate bonnet—an oversized oval creation that encircled a young woman's face in an effect that could only be described as clamlike, complete with layers and layers of pink lace and feathers. "It's as though she's being reborn."

The duchess coughed, sputtering her champagne. "Good God, Sesily."

Sesily looked to her, the portrait of innocence. "Show me the untruth." When the duchess could do no such thing, Sesily added, "I'm going to have my modiste send that poor thing something that makes her look *gorgeous*. Along with an invitation for a bonnet burning."

A chuckle, followed by, "Her mother will never allow you near her."

That much was true. Sesily had never been beloved by aristocratic mothers, and not only because she refused to wear the fashions of the season. Her beautiful mauve silk aside, Sesily was universally terrifying to the aristocracy for additional, hopefully much more unsettling reasons.

Yes, she was the daughter of a coal miner turned earl and a fairly crass and somewhat difficult woman who'd never found welcome in London society. But that wasn't it, either. No, Sesily's particular fearsomeness came with being thirty years old, unmarried, rich, and a woman. And worse, all those things without shame. She had never taken herself up to a high shelf to live out her days. She hadn't even taken herself off to the country. Instead, she took herself to *balls*. In low-cut, boned silks that looked decidedly unlike pastry. Without bonnets made for either debutantes or spinsters.

And that made her the most dangerous of all the Dangerous Daughters of the Earl of Wight.

What an irony that was, as Queen Victoria sat upon her throne not a half mile from Mayfair, all while the aristocracy trembled in fear of women who refused to be packed up and sent away when they grew too old, refused to marry, or showed no interest in the rules and regulations of the titled world.

And Sesily had no interest in the proper, prescribed universe of the aristocracy. Not when there was so much of the rest of the world to live in. To change.

Perhaps, years ago, when she and her sisters had arrived in London with soot in their hair and the North Country in their accent, she might have been able to be shamed. But years of scornful looks and cutting remarks had taught Sesily that society's judgment either snuffed the light from its brightest stars or made it burn brighter . . .

And she'd made her choice.

Which was why the Duchess of Trevescan had summoned her here, to South Audley Street, two years earlier, and offered Sesily something more than a pressed silk frock and a perfect coiffure. Oh, Sesily still had those things—she knew armor when she saw it—but when she donned that dress, it was as likely that she was headed to a dark corner of Covent Garden as it was that she was headed to a glittering ballroom in Mayfair.

It was in the dark corners, after all, that Sesily made her mark, alongside a team of other women she'd soon counted as friends, brought together by the duchess.

Married too young to a hermit duke who preferred the isolation of his estate in the Scilly Isles, the Duchess of Trevescan refused to while away her youth in similar isolation, and instead chose to live in town, in one of London's most extravagant homes. As for what she did there, what the duke did not know would not hurt him, she liked to say.

What the duke did not know, the rest of London did, however . . . When it came to scandal, the woman referred to simply as *The Duchess* outranked them all.

The promise of scandal brought London's finest to the duchess's parties. They adored the way she wielded her title and offered the illusion of propriety, the promise of gossip to be whispered about the following morning, and the hope that those in attendance might be able to claim proximity to scandal . . . humanity's most valued currency.

But valuing scandal did not mean mothers liked their daughters too close to those who caused it, and so Sesily would never have the chance to burn the bonnets of the battalion of debutantes twirling through the massive gilded ballroom.

"It's a pity, that," she said to her friend. "But never fear. I shall send the gift anonymously. I shall be fairy godmother to the hideous fashion plates of 1838, whether or not their mothers have me round to tea."

"You've your work cut out for you; every fashion plate of 1838 is hideous."

"Then it is lucky I am rich. And idle."

"Not so idle tonight," came the soft reply, and Sesily's gaze was instantly across the room, where a blond head stood above the rest of the revelers. No bonnet, but deserving destruction nonetheless.

"How long before the message is delivered?" Sesily asked.

The duchess sipped at her champagne, pointedly avoiding Sesily's focus. "Not long now. My staff knows its business. Patience, friend."

Sesily nodded, ignoring the tightening in her chest—the excitement. The adventure. The promise of success. The thrill of justice. "It is the least of my virtues."

"Really?" the duchess retorted. "I would have thought that was chastity."

"I confess." Sesily cut her friend a wry smile. "I'm better with vices."

"Good evening, Duchess, Lady Sesily." The greeting came from behind them, on the meek, barely heard voice of Miss Adelaide Frampton, shy, retiring queen of wallflowers, who was followed by pitying whispers. *An ugly duckling who never became a swan, poor thing.*

While Mayfair's whispers would wound another, that particular perception suited Adelaide down to the ground, allowing her to go unnoticed in society, few noticing the way her warm brown eyes remained ever watchful behind thick spectacles, even as she disappeared in a crowd.

Even fewer noticing that in disappearing, she saw everything.

"Miss Frampton," the duchess said, "I take it all is well?"

"Quite," Adelaide said, the words barely there in the cool breeze that blew in from the large open windows behind them. "Terribly warm in here, don't you think?"

Sesily reached for the silver ladle in the enormous crystal punch bowl, swirling it round and round as she gathered the courage to pour herself a cup of the tepid orange punch within. "This looks gruesome."

"Events welcoming young ladies require ratafia," the duchess replied.

"Mmm. Well, as I haven't been a young lady requiring ratafia in . . ." Sesily paused. "You know, I'm not sure I've ever required ratafia."

"Born able to hold your liquor?"

Sesily smiled at her friend. "Like finds like, one might say."

The duchess sighed, the sound full of boredom. "There's a footman somewhere with champagne." Of course there was. Champagne flowed like water at Trevescan House.

"I must say, Lady Sesily," Adelaide interjected, "it is *quite warm.*"

"I see," Sesily replied, her gaze tracking the crowd, noting that the blond head she'd been watching before was now closer to the doors leading into the dark gardens beyond.

There was no time for champagne. The missive to the Earl of Totting had been received.

Sesily poured a glass of the unpleasant-looking punch. Before she could return the ladle to the bowl, however, a newcomer jostled her arm, sloshing an orange blossom right over the rim of her glass and onto the brilliant white tablecloth.

"Oh no! Let me help with that, Lady Sesily."

Lady Imogen Loveless extracted a handkerchief from her reticule, or at least attempted to. She had to dig, first haphazardly displacing a pencil and a slip of paper onto the table next to the punch bowl, dropping a small shell-shaped box with a gold clasp to the plush carpet below—"Only smelling salts," she rushed to explain. "Don't worry—they'll keep!"

Sesily turned raised brows to the duchess, who watched Imogen's hurried movements with equal parts amusement and amazement—the latter winning out when Imogen pulled three hairpins from her bag. She seemed to know she shouldn't put *those* on the table, however, and instead shoved them directly into her disheveled coiffure, wild and precarious as it was. *Then*, she extracted the handkerchief, brandishing it in triumph. It was wrinkled and embroidered in a wild riot of extremely crooked stitches in the vague shape of a bell. Sesily had never seen anything so well matched to its owner.

She set her punch down on the table and accepted the fabric with a smile. "Thank you, Imogen."

"Don't stare, my dears." This from an elderly doyenne on the far side of the table, flanked by two hideously-frocked, pale-faced young ingenues, who had apparently never witnessed quite this flavor of chaos.

"Oh dear," Imogen said, her wide-eyed gaze falling to one of the girls. "Truly that bonnet is . . ." She trailed off, then said, "Awesome."

Adelaide gave a tiny, barely-there snort of amusement, and Sesily feigned deep interest in her glass.

"I particularly like the . . ." Imogen searched for a word, moving her hand in a large oval in front of her own face. ". . . ornamentation."

The girl's grandmother harrumphed.

"Lady Beaufetheringstone," the duchess said, leaning over Sesily's arm toward the punch bowl. "May I serve you and your—"

"Granddaughters," the lady barked. "That would be fine, Duchess, as we should like to be on our way." She lowered her voice to a still very audible whisper and said to the young ladies, "Obviously, I wouldn't like you two to be painted with *this* company."

Sesily refrained from pointing out that the poor pale girls could do with some color. Instead, she cleaned her sticky hand and stared directly at the older woman until the trio scurried off, no doubt to whisper about the unfortunate souls lurking at the refreshment table.

"Do try not to cause trouble," the duchess said under her breath.

"I would never," Sesily replied, casually. "I was merely resolving to begin my fairy godmothering with those two girls. I shall have them round to tea."

The duchess raised a brow. "You don't drink tea."

Sesily grinned. "Neither will they, when I'm done with them."

"Sesily Talbot, be careful, or what they say about you will be true."

Of course, it was already all true. Or, most of it. At least, most of the best bits. Which, sadly, were considered to be the worst bits to most of society. There was no accounting for taste.

Adelaide leaned back and looked to the floor between them, where Imogen's mint green skirts were all that could be seen. "Why is Imogen beneath the table?"

The duchess sighed to the roomful of her guests. "Can you blame her with this company?"

Sesily swallowed a chuckle. "Any news, Adelaide?"

"Oh, yes," Adelaide replied. "Your retiring room is the nicest in London, Your Grace. Very conducive to conversation."

"Is it?" the duchess asked, as though they discussed the weather.

"Seems that Viscount Coleford is in attendance with his new bride." Bystanders might miss the edge in Adelaide's voice, but it was clear as crystal to her three friends.

Sesily slid a surprised look at their hostess. "Is he?"

Coleford was a monstrous bully of a man, pickled in venom and willing to take it out on anyone who drew close—as long as they were weaker than he. He had just married his third wife, forty years his junior, all of London looking the other way despite the mysterious deaths of two prior viscountesses—the first after the death of his grown son and only heir, and the second after two years of marriage without issue.

Like too many of his peers, the old viscount had been allowed to relish in his power for too long. Which was why, like so many of his peers, he was on their list.

But his was not the box that would be ticked tonight.

"Enemies close," the duchess replied beneath her breath as she flashed a bright white smile in the direction of a couple dancing by—the publisher of several of London's most popular newspapers and his beautiful wife, whom Sesily knew from her regular attendance at the city's most exclusive gaming hell.

A clever addition to the evening's play, which was about to begin.

"Seems, also, that the Earl of Totting escorted Matilda Fenwick this evening." Adelaide pushed her spectacles up on her nose and shook her head, her red ringlets bouncing. "They say she's to be a countess soon enough."

Tilly Fenwick, eldest daughter to a very rich merchant on the hunt for a title, doomed to a life married to a man drunk on power, who destroyed women for sport.

Which was why the future countess had come to them.

Sesily considered the ballroom, easily finding the set of broad shoulders she'd been watching all evening. Across the room, the Earl of Totting, one of the handsomest men in all of London—who also happened to be one of the worst men in all of London—moved with slow, even grace toward the open doors.

A breeze blew in, bringing a brisk November chill with it.

"Brutal heat in here," Adelaide said.

Sesily shivered and met her friend's keen gaze. "I was just noticing it. Positively cloying."

Totting drew nearer to the exit.

Imogen came out from beneath the table, brandishing the pillbox. "Found it!"

"Wonderful news," Sesily said, pressing the handkerchief back into the other woman's hand. "Thank you."

Imogen shoved the handkerchief into her reticule and began to collect her dispersed items, hands flying across the table. Were anyone watching, they'd see nothing amiss, at least, nothing that was not to be expected from Imogen.

They wouldn't see the pill she dropped into the glass of ratafia.

Nor would they think twice about Sesily lifting her madcap friend's pencil and paper, casting a glance at the text scrawled there.

7-out
10-down

Seven minutes, then ten more.
Sesily's brows rose at Imogen. "That's it?"
It wasn't much time.

Imogen blinked. "Do you know Margaret Cavendish? The author?"

"What?"

Her madcap friend smiled. "*The Contract*. It's lovely. *I shall make thee a meteor of the time*, she writes. So poetic."

Imogen would not know poetry if Byron himself kidnapped her in the dead of night. Sesily tilted her head, irritation coursing through her. "Yes, well, first I'm not certain that Cavendish was referring to actual speed. But more importantly, I'm supposed to—" She stopped herself, lowering her voice so no one else would hear. "In seventeen minutes?"

"I tell you, Sesily," Imogen said. "If anyone can do it, it is you. I believe in you."

In and out in seventeen minutes.

"Well, no one has ever said I'm not fast," Sesily said, dryly.

A trio of snickers replied.

"A meteor of the time, you say?"

"To be honest," Imogen said, collecting the paper and pencil, "I didn't get much further in the book. Any more than ten minutes of reading and I'm absolutely *dead* asleep."

"Terrible, that," Adelaide commiserated.

It was an understatement. The last thing they needed was a corpse in the gardens.

But there was one thing that would be worse, for Sesily, at least. "Imogen, are you able to remember *anything* you read that close to bedtime?"

Imogen looked absolutely delighted when she proclaimed, "Not a bit of it! Isn't it wonderful?"

Sesily, Adelaide, and the duchess exchanged a look. Sesily had seventeen minutes, but she'd be the only one who would remember them.

Excellent.

It was incredible that Imogen was known throughout society as an absolute lost cause. Society rarely saw the truth when it came to women.

Sesily looked toward the doors. The broad shoulders had disappeared. "Can't suffer the heat any longer."

On cue, Adelaide stepped around the edge of the refreshment buffet, tripped on the edge of the tablecloth, and fell to the ground, drawing a cry of surprise from Imogen, an "Oh! My dear Miss Frampton!" from the duchess, and the attention of the entire room.

As planned.

Well, *almost* the entire room.

Chapter Two

High above the ballroom, watching from the upper gallery, Caleb Calhoun took a glass of champagne from a passing footman's tray and watched the play below. Sesily whisked her ratafia from the table and, without even a glance at the commotion her friends caused at the end of the table, slipped into the dark gardens.

He resisted the urge to follow her.

Another man would, of course. Another man who was in business with Sesily's eldest sister, who had bought horseflesh from her brother-in-law and books from her sister, and dandled her nephew—his godson—on his knee, would feel a moral obligation to follow her into the gardens and keep her safe from whatever trouble she was courting.

This other man, this paragon of nobility, would pledge his sword to the lady.

But there was nothing noble about Caleb Calhoun.

Oh, he'd played the part, pretending not to notice the way she filled a room with her bright smile and her brazen charm and her absolutely wild beauty. Pretending not to notice the way her vividly-colored dresses pulled tight around her ample breasts and her curved waist and her hips—full of sin and promise.

Pretending not to notice *her*.

And still, there he was, above the rest of the revelry, noticing her, not six hours after returning to London for the first time in more than a year, during which the Atlantic had made it impossible to notice her.

It had not, however, made it impossible to think of her.

He gritted his teeth, and returned his gaze to where Miss Adelaide Frampton limped across the ballroom making a proper meal of her turned ankle—though nothing close to the meal Lady Imogen Loveless was making with her frantic waving and repetition of *clear a path, please!*

And a sea of London's ostensibly best and brightest, gobbling up the spectacle.

Caleb drank deep from the glass of champagne, wishing it were something stronger. Wishing he were anywhere but here, at a silly ball hosted by a duchess, where he would never have been welcome, if not for the fact that the Duchess of Trevescan thought it was a lark to welcome rich Americans into her absent husband's Mayfair home to scandalize society.

She hadn't hesitated when he'd turned up without an invitation.

Thirty-five years old, Caleb had lifted himself out of poverty on the streets of Boston and become an exceedingly wealthy man. He liked to think that his success came from his being happy with what he'd been given—money and power on the western shores of the Atlantic had been enough for him. He was a king in Boston, and had no aspirations of assuming such a crown here.

For his part, Caleb knew his mere presence in a ducal home was a coup, though he alone understood just how much of one.

That, and it gave him a chance to not notice Sesily Talbot, which had been harder to do in the days when she'd leaned over his bar, helping herself to a bottle of her favorite bourbon.

Not that she did that anymore.

She rarely frequented the tavern now, he was told.

Not that he cared. He was on the other side of an ocean. She was a grown woman. Well able to take care of herself.

Not his concern.

He cursed under his breath, his attention returned to the open glass doors leading out into the dark gardens beyond.

Who was she meeting?

He placed his empty glass on a passing footman's tray.

His teeth clenched at the thought, the muscle in his jaw already aching with the knowledge that any man lucky enough to find Sesily Talbot would not remain a gentleman.

But Caleb had known Sesily Talbot for two years, and if he knew one thing about the woman all of London called *Sexily* behind their waving fans and in their secret card rooms, he knew she could hold her own. She knew her power and wielded it with precision—with men and women alike. He'd never seen her in a scrape she could not avoid. Never seen her lose.

Never seen her properly matched.

He could match her.

He wouldn't, but he could.

Still, he made for the stairs, casting a look over the crush of toffs below—recognizing a handful who liked smuggled bourbon and a few more who could throw a sound punch. Not all of them without purpose, he supposed.

Christ. He hated London. Hated the way it hung about his neck when he was here, full of the past, and his sins, and the threat that they might all be revealed if he stayed too long.

And Sesily Talbot, a temptation that made that threat all the more real.

Minutes later, he was out in the November air, hunching his shoulders against the brisk wind whipping through the fabric of his topcoat.

She hadn't been wearing a cloak, or even a shawl, and the cold chill would be uncomfortable for her, chafing her bare skin.

Doing his best to put her bare skin out of his mind, Caleb made his way down the steps leading away from the balcony and into the dark gardens. He stilled to listen for any sound—knowing that it was unlikely she would be easily heard. Even if he could hear her, the rough wind in the leaves above made it impossible, requiring him to rely on instinct and knowledge of Sesily Talbot if he was going to have a chance at finding her.

Which wouldn't be difficult, as Caleb had spent the last two years unwillingly consumed with all he knew about Sesily Talbot.

She'd be in the labyrinth.

And there was only one reason why a woman like Sesily entered a labyrinth on a cold November evening—she was with someone who would keep her warm.

He tensed at the thought, even as he reminded himself that Sesily's late-night assignations had nothing to do with him . . . or with anyone else for that matter. Over the years, her scandals—along with those of her sisters—had graced every gossip rag in London, making her the object of public scorn and private admiration. There were equally as many homes that shunned her as there were that welcomed her with delight.

Where Sexily went, attention followed.

Even in the Trevescan labyrinth, Caleb thought with no small amount of irritation. He didn't care to discover Sesily in the arms of her latest paramour.

He certainly had no interest in hearing the sounds of her pleasure, or seeing the flush that chased over her skin when she took that pleasure.

He relaxed the fist that had somehow formed at his side.

No interest at all.

It mattered not a bit to him whom the woman was meeting, or what she was doing deep inside this hedge maze. He should turn around, in fact.

He stepped through the magnificent arched entrance.

Dammit. He wasn't going to turn around.

And then, to his left, down a dark path, barely seen in the faraway light of what he assumed was a torch designed to lure would-be scandal-makers to the destination of their choosing, Caleb detected movement.

Not just movement. Speed.

Sesily was headed out of the darkness, straight for him.

She didn't notice him right away, too busy fiddling with her elaborate skirts. Once she was through with that, she tossed something into the hedgerow, the item flashing in the light of a nearby torch. The punch glass.

She came up short when she noticed his presence, her breath harsh and quick. Not excitement. Exertion.

Her hand flew to her breast, to the line of her dress— was it lower than before? Frustration tumbled through him at the recognition—at the possible activities that she'd engaged in to look so flushed.

"Caleb," she said, quick and surprised, and he hated the ease of it on her tongue. The familiarity of it, as though she owned it. As though she owned him, even after a year apart. And then she smiled, as though they were anywhere but here. As though she was happy to see him. "What are you doing here?"

He wasn't about to answer that. "I could ask you the same."

"Are you surprised to find me lurking in the gardens?" she quipped, the flirt in the words pure Sesily, but tinged with urgency, as though she had somewhere to be. "Surely you'd be the only one." She looked over her shoulder, then back at him, and smiled, wide and winning, and offering a dozen things he'd happily accept if he were a different man. If she were a different woman.

If he were a different man, however, Caleb might have missed the flash of emotion that preceded the sultry seduction, the delight, and the wild promise of fun.

He would have missed the fear.

He was on alert, looking past her into the darkness, hoping his casual tone masked his instant anger. "Short tryst."

She ignored the observation, all hint of nerves missing from the words, even if she moved toward him, making to pass him in the aisle of the maze. "Were you inside?"

"Is there another option?"

"With you, just returned?" She paused. "Surely it's possible you were so destroyed by our time apart that you bypassed the party altogether and came straight to find me."

He pressed his lips together, ignoring the way the words thrummed through him. "Lingering in the darkness in the wild hope that you might turn up?"

"I'm very good at turning up for trouble."

"I don't think I'm the trouble you turned up for tonight."

"And thus, my girlish dreams are dashed." She extracted a watch from the reticule, checked it in the light from the ballroom beyond, and then made to pass him. "Are you for your own tryst?" She tutted her disappointment. "I shall endeavor to keep my heart from breaking."

He ignored the tease and moved into her path, forcing her to pull up short. "Who were you with?"

"Why Mr. Calhoun," she said, feigning shock. "A gentleman would never ask such a thing."

"I never claimed to be a gentleman."

She made a show of assessing him, her heated gaze sending fire straight through him. "And yet, I have never seen proof otherwise."

"Sesily . . ." He growled a warning.

"So sorry, American, but I'm short on time."

He turned as she passed him and headed for the arched entrance to the maze. "Somewhere to be?"

"Somewhere *not* to be, as a matter of fact," she replied, increasing her pace, heading for the gleaming lights of the ballroom beyond.

He followed, easily catching up. "What were you doing in there?"

She did not slow, even as she cast him a full, practiced smile that would have dazzled a lesser human. "A lady must be allowed her secrets."

He was meant to think that she'd been trysting in the darkness. And others might. But he'd seen the truth in her eyes. She didn't want anyone knowing what she'd been doing in that labyrinth.

Which meant that Caleb was going to have to find out.

"Fair enough." He stopped and turned on his heel, aiming for the maze once more.

"No!" She squeaked, looking down at the watch in her hand again.

He looked, too. "What are you worried about missing?"

"On the contrary," she said, glancing toward the maze. "I'm worried that I *won't* miss it."

"Sesily."

There was just enough wash of golden light from the ballroom for him to see her, to *really* see her. He bit back a frustrated curse at the way his chest tightened. No matter what he had hoped, a year away had done nothing to stop his reaction to this woman. And truly, it should not be such a surprise. Because Sesily Talbot had been sculpted by angels. Smooth golden skin, dark hair gleaming like the night sky, and a full, beautiful face that threatened to lay a body low even now, as she pursed her lips and considered her next move.

He nearly turned on his heel and made for Southampton again—back to Boston. At least with an ocean between them he couldn't be tempted by her.

Lie.

He was saved from having to linger on the thought when he heard the sound behind them. Movement in the labyrinth. It would be impossible not to hear it, as it did not sound graceful or mincing or delicate or clandestine. It sounded like someone had loosed a large animal inside. A bull or an ox—something that lumbered.

And groaned.

He looked to her. "What did you do?"

"What makes you think I have anything to do with it?" Later, he would be impressed by her lack of hesitation. By the way she grabbed his hand, as though it was the most ordinary thing in the world, and yanked him into the darkness beneath the nearest tree.

"Does my sister know you've returned?" The question was perfectly ordinary, as though they were inside the ballroom at the refreshment table where her friends no doubt continued to wreak havoc.

"She does. I went to the Sparrow first." The Singing Sparrow, the Covent Garden tavern jointly owned by Caleb and Sesily's eldest sister, Seraphina Bevingstoke, Duchess of Haven.

"And me, always the last to know," she said, quietly, pivoting to push him back to the trunk.

Later, he would take himself to task for not resisting. For not even lasting twenty-four hours in this godforsaken country before he failed to resist.

But how was he supposed to resist Sesily Talbot as she pressed herself to him, her hands sliding up over his chest, her fingers finding purchase in his hair? He was only human, after all.

"I was not aware that I was to apprise you of my comings and goings." One of his arms wrapped around her waist, pulling her tight to him. Only to make sure they kept their balance.

Not for anything else. Not because he wanted her there.

"Why start now?" she said, the question punctuated by another groan from the maze, and she moved impossibly closer to him, aligning their bodies in a way that made him think violent thoughts about fabric. "I swore I'd never do this," she said, her fingers clenching in his hair, tugging his face down toward her.

He meant to resist. "Do what?"

"Kiss you," she said, and for a moment the matter-of-fact words sizzled through him.

He meant to stop her.

Except there was no stopping Sesily Talbot.

She continued in a low whisper, more to herself than to him, it seemed, even as she rose on her toes, the movement sending his hand sliding over the stunning swell of her bottom. "You don't deserve it."

Why in hell not?

He absolutely didn't deserve it. But he still wanted to know why *she* thought he didn't. She had no reason to think such a thing.

"Unfortunately . . . circumstances dictate . . ."

No. He wasn't going to kiss her. That way lay madness. It did not matter the feel of her bottom or the swell of her breasts or the way her lips curved like promise or the fact that she'd never met a scandal she didn't like.

It mattered that she was sister to his business partner and the closest thing he had to a friend. It mattered that she was an English lady. That she was daughter to an earl. Sister-in-law to four of the richest men in Britain, three of whom held venerable titles.

It mattered that she was a goddamn hurricane.

Hang on . . . *unfortunately?*

"What circumstances?"

The animal in the labyrinth cursed, angry and pained. Caleb made to look, but she was there, her fingers at the curve of his jaw, tilting him back to her.

She was right there. A breath away.

Shit. He wasn't going to kiss her.

He was almost sure of it.

And he didn't. She kissed him first.

But then it didn't matter who'd kissed whom, because the only thing that mattered was Sesily's full, soft lips on his, hot and sweet and perfect, and how was he to deny himself? She was *right there*, in his arms like a gift that he did not deserve. A gift he could not accept.

But he wasn't a fool. He'd open it. Look at it. Taste it.

Just for a moment.

And then he'd do what was right.

Her lips softened, opening on a little sigh, and he did taste then, his tongue sliding against hers as she pressed herself closer. She was delicious. The sounds of her. The sight of her. The feel of her. And he didn't want to stop, because he could not remember the last time that he'd felt like this.

Like everything was right.

Of course, nothing was right.

"Oy!"

She broke the kiss at the sound, loud and affronted and near enough to distract Caleb from his newfound goal—to kiss Sesily Talbot again. Immediately. But in order to do that, he required solitude, which meant responding to the man who'd stumbled out of the labyrinth, hand to his head as though he had a banger of a headache.

Before he could turn his head, Sesily whispered, "Don't give him any reason to stop."

She didn't want to be seen.

Curiosity flared, but he knew better than to press her. Instead, he pulled her tight against him, turning just enough to ensure she was hidden in the shadows. "What happened?"

She shook her head.

Whatever it was, she needed his help.

"Alright," he whispered, looking over the top of her head at the man headed back to the ballroom.

"Is that you, Calhoun?" the man slurred. "I thought you'd decided to stay on your side of the pond. Bad luck for us, I suppose." Lewdness slid into the snide words. "Does that girl's family know she's climbed down into the American muck?"

Caleb turned to stone, recognition flaring.

Jared, Earl of Totting, was a bastard through and through. Rich and entitled, with enough size behind him to make him dangerous when he chose to terrorize. And he did. He'd been banned from Caleb's tavern almost as soon as they'd opened for business; the earl was the kind of man who never left a pub without starting a brawl, and that was on his good nights. His bad ones were why half the brothels in Covent Garden wouldn't see him through the door.

And Sesily had been in the maze with him.

Caleb didn't like that. In fact, he was about to show this rich, entitled horse's ass just how little he liked it.

Sesily's fingers tightened on his forearm, now steeled for battle. "Caleb," she whispered, his name soft as silk on her lips. "Please."

He might not have listened.

He might have ignored the plea and the warning, and allowed his misguided sense of honor to put the bastard into the ground. But at that precise moment, the earl stepped from darkness into the pool of golden light that spilled from the wall of windows that lined the outer edge of the Trevescan ballroom . . . giving Caleb a clear look at his face.

And the proof that whatever he could do to Totting was nothing compared to what Sesily had done.

Caleb looked down at her, careful not to let his shock into his eyes.

"Please," she said, her fingers tight like a vise on him. The word barely sound. He heard the rest like she'd shouted it. *Don't say anything.*

He couldn't quite agree to that bit. Instead, he offered the earl his broadest American devil-absolutely-don't-care grin, and said, "Enjoy your evening, Totting."

The earl told him exactly what he thought Caleb could do with the pleasantry, and listed his way back toward the ballroom.

Once the man was out of earshot, Caleb leaned down, close enough to feel the heat of her. To delight in the scent of her—like sugared almonds. But he wasn't about to dwell on either of those things.

He was too busy being shocked. "You're going to tell me everything," he whispered, low in her ear. "As payment for keeping your secret."

She turned to face him, the warm golden light diffused to silver on her face. "I think we both know that's not going to happen," she said. "Besides, I let you kiss me, and that should be payment enough . . ."

"You kissed me."

She gave him a little half smile. "Are you sure?"

"Sesily, what in hell are you up to?"

She was back to playing games. "What makes you think I had anything to do with it?"

"Because you're rich and beautiful, with the freedom that comes with both of those."

"You think I'm beautiful?" she asked, as though everything was perfectly normal.

"I think you're fucking fearless, which makes you incredibly dangerous."

She peered around him, watching as the unsuspecting earl climbed the steps to return to the ballroom. "Dangerous to whom?" she asked, casually, as though they were anywhere but here.

To me. Caleb swallowed the response. "To yourself."

She cut him a quick look, then returned her attention to the earl. "Nonsense. I did exactly what any good girl should do when she gets herself into trouble."

"And what's that?"

She smiled. "I found a proper hero to protect me."

She wasn't just dangerous. She fairly guaranteed his demise. "Christ, Sesily. You think he won't come looking for you when he—"

"He won't remember anything about the last seventeen minutes," she whispered, waving a hand to silence him. "Look."

Her face was turned fully to the ballroom now, her pure, unabashed excitement undeniable in the candlelight.

"It's happening," she said, quietly, as Caleb followed her gaze as Totting pushed back into the crush of people. "Watch."

Within seconds, fans began fluttering, attention turning to Totting from all over the room. Then the whispers started—heads bowed in serious conversation around the room. And then . . . the laughter.

The pointing.

The evisceration.

And Totting, the arrogant sot, had no idea that the attention was directed toward him. He was so confused that he even turned around at one point, seeking the person who was surely behind him.

That's when Caleb saw Sesily's work in full, glorious, horrifying light.

There, across the earl's broad forehead, in dark, indelible ink, the lettering impeccable, was a single word.

ROTTER.

Six letters, and nothing that London didn't already know. Nothing London did not turn from, averting its collective gaze, because money and name and privilege made for unbeatable, undeniable power when it came to titled men.

But that evening, Sesily beat it. Sesily denied it.

And gave permission to the rest of the aristocracy to do the same.

He looked back at her. Saw the emotion on her face. Felt it in his own chest—not that he'd ever admit it. *Pride*.

· "Sesily Talbot, you court trouble."

"You disappoint me, Mr. Calhoun," she said, the words distracted as she watched the play unfold on the stunning stage laid out before them. "I would have thought that after what you'd witnessed tonight, you'd know that I've no need to court trouble."

He should leave her there. Leave her in the darkness to find her way back inside, or back home, or wherever it was Valkyries went to when they were done with their battles.

He should walk away from that woman who had been a danger to him from the moment he met her.

He certainly shouldn't ask her, "And why is that?"

But he did, and then he watched her full, red lips curve before she turned to reply, the pure, unadulterated satisfaction in her eyes a punch to the gut. "Haven't you noticed, American? I *am* trouble."

Chapter Three

The Place
Covent Garden
Three Nights Later

There weren't many locations in London where a known scandal could drink and socialize unnoticed, but The Place, tucked deep in Covent Garden and accessible only to those who knew the tangled web of streets between Bedford Street and St. Martin's Lane, was one of them.

Which made the pub Sesily's favorite haunt.

Yes, there were several casinos that received women (one that was women-exclusive), a handful of pubs where women were protected (including the one owned by her sister), and 72 Shelton Street—a ladies' club that threw some of London's best parties and specialized in women's pleasure of all kinds. While discretion was guaranteed at every one of those places, however, those who frequented them were often there to be seen. In the rare instance that they *weren't* looking to be recognized, no one could escape it—and recognition made things complicated.

Doubly so when you might be overheard discussing the destruction of society's worst.

The Place wasn't for being seen. It was for living. For drinking and dancing and laughing and being welcomed without hesitation.

The kind of place that felt like home to someone who spent her days under the stern censure of society. The kind of place that would tell society precisely what it could do with its censure . . . if only society could find it. Which it couldn't.

The perfect haunt for four women who made it their work to bend the rules society and the world insisted they follow, and who did all in support of anyone who wished to do the same.

No one at the place cared that Sesily was a scandal, or that Adelaide was a wallflower, or that Imogen was odd, or that the duchess lived her life as though she'd never been married in the first place. And because of that, the foursome made it their haunt.

"I heard from Miss Fenwick this morning," the Duchess of Trevescan said as Sesily slid into the chair next to her at the table in a back rear corner of the large central room of the pub—one of the only spots in The Place that wasn't aglow with lamplight refracted through brightly colored glass and filled with a riot of laughter and good-natured shouts and raucous music that would soon tempt half those assembled to dancing.

"Happy with our work, I hope?" Sesily said, blowing quick kisses across the table to Imogen and Adelaide. She smiled up at the barman who appeared at her elbow. "Good evening, Geoffrey."

"Whiskey tonight, luv?" He winked and Sesily imagined for a moment that she might find him handsome in another place, at another time.

Four nights ago. A year ago. Two.

She nodded. "I'm a crashing bore, I know."

"Impossible," he replied, and was off to fetch her drink.

Adelaide blinked from behind her enormous spectacles. "How is it that we waited three quarters of an hour to be noticed, and you arrive at the height of the evening and receive attention in mere seconds?"

"My ineffable charm," Sesily said with a grin as she reached across the table and snatched a roasted carrot from Adelaide's plate.

"That, and half of London wants to swiv you," Imogen pointed out.

"Only half?" Sesily retorted, removing her cloak. "You wound me."

"With that dress, perhaps more than half."

Sesily looked down at the wine red silk, brand new and cut low and tight enough to display ample breasts. When she stood, it would flatter every swell and curve. As well it should. It had cost a small fortune.

"You're damned right more than half," she quipped. She looked *excellent*.

Imogen snorted, Adelaide shook her head with a laugh and returned her attention to her gossip rag, and the duchess drank her champagne as though she were at court, which Sesily imagined she was. In the two years Sesily had worked alongside her, the duchess had used her wide-reaching influence to solve scores of what she referred to simply as *problems*—many for the women in this room.

Brutal husbands with heavy hands, fathers and brothers who treated daughters and sisters like chattel, business owners who mistreated their employees, brothel owners who didn't respect their girls' work, men who didn't take kindly to the word *no*.

Memory flashed—a long ago meeting at Trevescan House, when the duchess had invited Sesily to join her.

Proposing a new kind of partnership. One for which Sesily was uniquely qualified. The reckless scandal, who was never taken seriously, and so could move about in full view of the wide world.

Sesily could still feel the way her heart had pounded at the offer—to be part of something bigger than herself.

To trod a new path that had led her here. To this table, three days after she'd given Tilly Fenwick freedom from a marriage that would have destroyed her . . . or worse.

"What did Miss Fenwick have to say?"

The duchess smiled and tipped her glass in Sesily's direction. "Well, it began with effusive thanks."

Pride burst in Sesily's breast. "The betrothal?"

"It seems Mr. Fenwick has decided that there is little value in having a daughter who is a countess if everyone will call her Countess Rotter behind her back."

"To her face, at this point," Sesily said. Society might not be able to remove the title from Totting, but they could eliminate its value for a generation or two.

"And so poor Tilly lives to be married off another day," Adelaide said from behind her newspaper.

"Well, now that Tilly Fenwick has such a committed group of benefactors . . . her father may be required to think twice next time."

"Lucky girl," Sesily offered, casually.

It was the truth. While many of the motley, raucous crowd at The Place marveled at the duchess's immense power and how she did her best to use it for good, far fewer recognized that she'd aligned herself with a far-reaching network of some of the most fearsome women in London . . . including the trio who joined her that night.

Virtually no one knew that, and those who did would never tell.

The quartet had come together in circumstances born of serendipity and necessity. The duchess had been looking for brilliant women who had little to fear from society, and she'd found them in Imogen, who came with an expertise in things both extremely useful and extremely dangerous; Adelaide, whose meek exterior made her a superior thief; and Sesily—scandalous Sesily—who had shocked society so many times that few even noticed when she disappeared from a ballroom, scoundrel in tow.

Hadn't she done just that three nights earlier? Left the ballroom, no one the wiser, under cover of scandal— invisible in it?

Not invisible to everyone.

Caleb had seen her.

Caught her.

Protected her.

She drank, willing the thoughts away. Now wasn't the time for the man and his ridiculous broad shoulders and his unreasonably handsome face and the way he kissed her like he'd been waiting his whole life to do it.

He clearly hadn't, or he wouldn't have made a habit of *leaving the country* every time he saw her.

She cleared her throat and returned to more important matters. "If you ask me, Lord Rotter received an absolute gift. He could have had it far worse. Frankly, I'd have preferred him to have it far worse."

"I offered to take care of the problem," Imogen said. "You all told me, *categorically*, that he had to awaken."

The duchess gave a little snort of amusement. "He did have to awaken."

When Imogen did not reply, Adelaide lowered her paper. "You understand that, don't you, Imogen?" In the silence that followed, Adelaide prompted, *"Don't you, Imogen?"*

"Yes of course," Imogen said, finally, cantankerous.

"Good."

Imogen crossed her arms in silent defiance as the barman returned with Sesily's whiskey. She waited until he disappeared, flushed with pleasure at Sesily's grateful smile, and then added, "I'm merely saying that if he *hadn't* awakened—"

"If he hadn't awakened," Sesily interjected, taking half a potato from Adelaide, "we'd have had a dead body to contend with."

"It's not as though we don't have ways of dealing with those," Imogen said.

"Well, I'm most certainly not going to ask what ways you have for dealing with those," Sesily said, "but I'm certain that even if we had *dealt with* it, I'd be on a boat somewhere, running from Peel's boys just to be safe."

Robert Peel's Metropolitan Police made for a more formidable foe requiring more creative solutions to the *problems* the quartet agreed to solve. No, Scotland Yard most definitely would not take kindly to the death of an earl.

But the earl wasn't dead. He was worse, destroyed by the truth—the truth that had only ever been acknowledged in knowing looks shared between men, and quick about-faces by young women who had had the benefit of privilege and warning.

The truth, which had been ignored, as long as he didn't harm one of their own.

They'd all known the truth about Totting, and not one of them had done anything to stop him, so Sesily, Adelaide, Imogen, and the duchess had done what the others would not. And Sesily didn't mind in the slightest that it was by her own hand.

Now, the whole of the aristocracy could finally turn its back on the Earl of Totting, full of cowardice, relief, and the sheer delight that came with watching the fall of power.

"*The Scandal Sheet* is already reporting it—consumed with what it calls *A Rotten End*," Adelaide said.

"Of course they are calling it that. Ever on the nose," Sesily said, toasting the duchess with her whiskey. "I wonder how they had that gossip so quickly?"

"As it happens, the publisher was in attendance at the ball. Can you believe it? What luck," the duchess replied with a laugh. "Now, the work is protecting the rest of the city from the bastard. It wouldn't be the worst thing in the world for him to fall into the wrong hands somewhere in the East End."

Adelaide looked up. "God knows there are plenty of wrong hands who'd be happy to catch him."

"And *I'm* the dangerous one," Imogen said.

"You enjoy setting things aflame."

"With chemicals," Imogen retorted. "Not my own anger."

Adelaide smiled and gave a little, innocent shrug. "Really, Imogen. I don't know what you're on about."

Sesily couldn't help her laugh. Adelaide might be considered tepid and meek by most of Mayfair . . . but she had a wicked sense of justice and a willingness to do anything to mete it out.

"Well, either way, neither of your particular brands of justice shall be meted out," the duchess said. "I have it on good authority that Totting has a number of debts coming due in the next few days from less than accommodating lenders. Bad luck, that."

The Duchess of Trevescan had a vast network of informants that spread from royal palaces to dockside taverns. She knew every noble scoundrel in London, and a fair number of the less-than-noble ones. Totting would need more than luck to escape the dark corners of London unscathed.

"If the rotter wasn't an absolute maggot, I'd feel sorry for him," Sesily said.

"The state of his person aside, everyone is wondering who could have done the damage to his reputation," Adelaide said.

"Would we call it a reputation?"

"A half dozen names bandied about in this column alone."

"Oh?" Sesily said, casually, indicating her friend's plate. "What is that, turbot? Are you going to finish it?"

Adelaide snapped the paper down. "Would someone summon one of her adoring masses and get her fed?"

The duchess waved a hand toward a passing barman. Once additional food was ordered, Adelaide said, "The most likely culprits appear to be a parliamentary rival—"

"Please," Sesily said. "Not one man in Lords has the nerve."

"—a bet-taker to whom he apparently owes a fair amount of money—"

"Illogical. A bookmaker would have done worse to his face."

"But not to his title!" Imogen proclaimed happily.

Sesily grinned with pride. "No. Certainly not."

Adelaide continued. "And an ex-lover who was apparently devastated by the loss of his companionship."

Sesily scoffed. "Well, that's absolutely a suspect named by Totting himself, because anyone with half a brain can understand that no one would ever be devastated by the loss of that man's verminous companionship." When she'd found the earl in the labyrinth that night, he had been less than gentlemanly. She'd been lucky that he'd been willing to take the drink she'd proffered, so she hadn't been required to free the blade sheathed beneath her skirts.

Sesily and the others' nocturnal activities aside, women of sense did not leave the house without a weapon. Not in London in 1838, at least. A queen on the throne had ensured that too many men had taken entire leave of their senses.

"Careful, Sesily," the duchess said, "you're beginning to sound put out that your name isn't on the list."

"You must admit there's a distinct lack of creativity in it."

"I will admit no such thing as long as it's keeping eyes off the true culprit, and ensuring that the truth shall be the best kept secret in London."

"I suppose that's fine," Sesily replied. "And so? What's next, now that we've closed the book on Rotting?"

"There's a moneylender preying on widows in St. Giles," Imogen said. "I wouldn't mind seeing him the victim of bad luck."

"And Coleford," Adelaide interjected, cool loathing in her voice as she invoked the viscount from the ball. "I am not ashamed to say I'm willing to do fairly anything to destroy him."

Rumor had it that Lord Coleford was using his position as a benefactor of the Foundling Hospital to help a pair of monstrous brothers take clothes from mothers' backs with the promise of finding the children they'd long-ago surrendered to the orphanage.

"It just so happens that I've something arranged for you on that front. I believe you'll be receiving a dinner invitation from the new viscountess. I urge you to accept," the duchess said, before adding to Sesily, "You, as well."

Sesily nodded, more than agreeable to whatever plan would bring down the awful man. "Any news on the raids?"

In the last several months, there'd been a number of raids around London—gaming hells, taverns, pleasure clubs, and more, all with a common thread: they were largely owned and frequented by women.

What had begun as a handful of brawls, a rough-up here and there, had become more serious in the last few months. A secret, high-end brothel in Kensington, owned and operated by the women who worked it, had been burned to the ground. Even 72 Shelton Street— one of the best protected clubs in London—had been raided and wrecked, and was now in the process of being rebuilt. The same had happened to a nearby casino with a women-only membership.

They were places where women held power. And wherever women held power, be it a throne, a club, or a labyrinth, there were men wishing to seize it.

"Brutes are easy to hire," said the duchess with a shake of her head, "but their heads grow back when they are severed from the body. Right now, the muscle appears to be The Bully Boys."

Sesily grimaced at the name—street thugs who hired themselves out to the highest bidder. "They're not the money."

"No," the duchess agreed. "I expect there's money from the House of Lords in the mix. No one likes the freedom a woman on the throne inspires—least of all the men who benefit from keeping women under their thumbs. We're working on it."

Sesily groaned her frustration. The foursome had been tracing the source of the raids for months, and she was growing impatient for a proper lead on the identity of the men terrorizing the city.

In the meantime, they busied themselves with men like Totting, who deserved his own punishment.

"Sesily," the duchess said, as though she could hear Sesily's thoughts.

She looked up. "Yes?"

"It is only the four of us who know what happened in my gardens, is it not?"

Sesily's heart began to pound. The duchess was concerned about their identities being revealed. She drank, ignoring the thrum of memory that came with the question. Caleb Calhoun, tall and broad, putting himself between Sesily and danger.

"Well. Us and Miss Fenwick."

Silence fell, punctuated by shouts and laughter beyond, somehow quieter than the sound of her friends' gazes, rapt upon her.

She looked away, toward the rest of the room. "Oh, there's Maggie," she said, brightly, knowing that it was a properly ridiculous observation. Of course there was Maggie.

To be at The Place was to be with Maggie O'Tiernen, owner and proprietress—a Black woman who'd left Ireland for London the moment she was able to build a new life, where she could live freely and embody her authentic self. In doing so, she had built one of London's most welcoming spaces. Whoever you were, whomever you loved, whatever your journey to yourself, there was a seat for all women at The Place.

Sesily desperately attempted to catch the eye of the bold and boisterous Maggie, who would absolutely come to rescue her from the prying eyes of her companions—if she wasn't busy recounting one of her delicious stories to a rapt audience.

"Hang on, now." Imogen had noticed something was off in the conversation, which meant something was *very* off in the conversation. "What's happened?"

"Tell us," the duchess said, casually and not at all casually, helping herself to another glass of champagne. "How *did* you avoid discovery in my gardens?"

"Well," she hedged. "It was dark."

Three sets of brows rose around the table.

"You are, and I say this with all affection, the worst liar I've ever known," Adelaide said.

"We can't all spend our lives lying to nobs and stealing their secrets, Adelaide."

"And why not?" Adelaide retorted.

The duchess sighed. "Who knows, Sesily?"

Sesily looked to the other woman—the woman who had brought them all together. "I have a feeling you are asking that question for effect."

The other woman's red lips curved. "Of course I am. You think I sent you off to deal with that particular problem without ensuring your safety?"

Irritation flared. "You had watchmen in the garden?"

"Had I known you'd be so . . . well taken care of . . ." The duchess trailed off, but Adelaide and Imogen leapt upon the tail of the words like cats with a mouse.

"Hang on!"

"Taken care of, how?"

Dammit. She'd have to tell them. They were relentless. "Nothing!"

"I wouldn't call it *nothing*," the duchess replied.

Sesily shot her a look. "He'd never tell anyone what happened."

"*Who'd* never tell?"

"And what happened?"

Sesily flattened her lips at the duchess idly tracing the rim of her champagne glass. "Everyone *thinks* you're above gossip and excitement, but you *positively thrive* on it."

The duchess's face broke into a wide smile. "In fact I do." Sesily groaned. "And you'd best tell them the truth, before Imogen decides to deploy whatever weapon she's most recently concocted to hurry you along."

On cue, Imogen replied, "Did you know that if you set a handkerchief aflame once it is properly inserted into a bottle of alcohol, you've all you need for a lovely explosion?"

"I did not, as a matter of fact," Sesily said.

"Might be useful in dealing with whoever saw you in the garden, is all I am saying."

"There is no need to explode him," she said. "Caleb Calhoun is in business with my sister. And if he weren't, he'd still be her friend. That alone ensures that he'd never reveal what he saw in the gardens."

"He didn't see *her* in the gardens," Imogen pointed out.

"We barely know the man," Adelaide added.

Sesily didn't like how defensive she was feeling about Caleb, who hadn't really done much to deserve her defense in the last two years. He was barely ever in London, and when he was, he seemed to do all he could to avoid her, which grated, if she was honest. But some men were simply decent. And he was one of them.

He didn't kiss like he was decent.

She pushed the thought away as the duchess said, "I don't care for relying on theoretical loyalty for silence. I require proof of the first, or insurance of the latter." She leaned back in the chair, a stunning diamond necklace gleaming at her neck. "Caleb Calhoun is not stupid, and if he's paying attention to you—"

"He's not."

The duchess cut her a disbelieving look. "*If he's paying attention to you*," she repeated, "that means he's paying attention to *us*, and it won't take him very long to put it together that our nights of debauchery at The Place aren't exactly what they seem. We need insurance. Which means it's time to discover the American's secrets."

"I told you, he won't say anything. Even if he weren't Seraphina's friend . . . even if he didn't have tens of thousands of pounds tied up in business with her on both sides of the Atlantic, he's not exactly beholden to the aristocracy."

"And you know that because . . ."

"He's American."

The duchess considered the words. "Well. American or not, he does enough business on this side of the Atlantic that I'd like to be absolutely certain where his loyalties lie. And I'd like them to lie with us."

"Information." It wasn't a difficult leap to make. The duchess had made a life dealing in that particular currency and in the last two years, Sesily, Adelaide, and Imogen had joined her. Between them, they held some of the city's most prized secrets, understanding what too many did not: that kept secrets were more powerful than those that were revealed.

But one had to have a secret for it to be uncovered. Sesily shook her head. "There's nothing."

"Mmm."

"You think that in two years I haven't scrutinized the man in business with my sister?"

"Well, first, I don't think your scrutiny has anything to do with your sister." Sesily didn't care for the duchess's casual statement, but she bit her tongue. "And if the events in my gardens are any indication, you most certainly have . . . scrutinized him."

"Hang on!" Imogen's eyes went wide.

"What happened in her gardens?"

"Nothing!" Good Lord. Was she *blushing*? Awful. This was awful. "I did what I had to do to keep myself from discovery." The duchess smirked and drank more of her champagne. "Who drinks champagne in a tavern, anyway?"

The other woman shrugged. "Duchesses."

"Did you . . ." Adelaide paused, then lowered her voice to the loudest whisper Sesily had ever heard. "*You know*?"

"She means did you swiv him," Imogen said, matter-of-factly.

"Yes, Imogen, I gathered as much." Sesily paused. "No. I did not. Believe it or not, Caleb Calhoun is not a part of the half of London that desires to swiv me." She paused, then added, "Also, it would do us all well to find another word for the act. That one is . . . not pleasant."

"What would you prefer? Did you *discuss the weather*? Did you *play croquet*?"

Adelaide laughed.

Sesily cut her a look. "Do not encourage her."

"Did you *prune the hedge*?"

"Really, anything sounds salacious when you say it that way, Imogen," Adelaide pointed out.

Imogen grinned. "It does, doesn't it?"

Duchess blessedly chose that moment to enter the fray. "There was no weather discussing, croquet playing, or hedge pruning. Sesily did what was required to keep herself from being found out."

"Which was?"

"I kissed him."

"He must have enjoyed that," Adelaide said.

"We could use that against him," Imogen said. "Your sister won't like that he compromised you."

Seraphina was far more likely to think Caleb had been the one compromised, but before Sesily could point that out, the duchess said, "It's not enough," as though they were having a perfectly ordinary conversation rather than discussing blackmailing the man Sesily had kissed three nights earlier.

"We are not using that against him!" Sesily said, riddled with embarrassment. "I'd prefer everyone forget it happened."

"Ah," Imogen said.

"What does that mean?"

"You *didn't* enjoy it."

Except she had. She'd enjoyed it very much.

"Oh, no." This, from Adelaide. Damn Adelaide, who always saw everything. "You *did* enjoy it."

"I did, in fact," Sesily grumbled.

"And he—"

"He appeared quite unmoved by it," she said, hating the sulk that edged into her words.

All three women sat forward in their chairs.

"What in—"

"Hang on!"

"He's clearly a horse's ass."

They might drive her up the wall, but in that moment, Sesily couldn't have asked for better friends. They all looked absolutely insulted on her behalf, and Sesily couldn't help but feel a little better about the whole thing.

A very little better.

Because Sesily had been waiting two years to kiss Caleb Calhoun and in all the dozens of hundreds of ways she'd imagined his response to such a thing, she'd never once imagined that he'd be unmoved by it.

She'd imagined him devastated by it. Destroyed by it. From time to time she allowed herself to imagine the great brute sinking to his knees and thanking his maker for it.

But she'd never imagined him unmoved.

Dammit.

For a heartbeat, that night, under the linden tree in the duchess's garden, as his hand had come around her waist and held her tight to him and the heat of him blazed against her chest, and he smelled—and tasted—like the smoke from a Highland scotch . . . for a moment, she'd thought he was moved. She could have sworn his lips had softened. Could have sworn she'd heard a slight groan at the back of his throat.

But then Totting had come out of the labyrinth and Calhoun had looked at her the same way he always did, in the fleeting moments when he was on British soil and found time and inclination to look at her—his eyes devoid of emotion, as though he'd just as well have been kissing the linden tree instead.

The disinterest was the worst bit. In thirty years, Sesily Talbot had engendered many, many emotions from the world at large. She'd entertained and tempted, won friends and wooed strangers, been cause for delight and, now and then, disgust. But she'd never, ever, been forgettable.

That was the worst bit.

Made that much worse by the fact that she quite desperately wanted Caleb Calhoun to remember her.

Though, to be honest, she was rarely sure if she wanted to be remembered for a passionate embrace or for a passionate punch in the nose. Perhaps they weren't that much different.

"Are you very sure you wouldn't like me to test my gin explosion on him?" Imogen said, interrupting her thoughts.

"It's not the worst idea I've heard," Sesily said.

"It would solve the problem of the man knowing more than we'd like," the duchess said. "Though truthfully, it might be too kind. I am now doubly interested in his secrets. For our security, and your honor."

"You can't punish the man for not wanting me."

The duchess's gaze narrowed. "Why not?"

Sesily laughed again. "Anyway, there's nothing to find." When he was in London, Caleb was either at the pub he owned with her sister or in the town house he kept in Marylebone, doing whatever it was men did alone in their homes. "He doesn't drink or gamble to excess. He doesn't even have a club here."

"None of the St. James's spots would welcome an American," Imogen said.

"The Fallen Angel would welcome him," Sesily pointed out, referring to the casino on St. James's that made the rest of the gentlemen's clubs on the street look excruciatingly boring. "But he doesn't wish it; I'm telling you, he's uninteresting."

At least, that's what she told herself.

"Mmm," the duchess said again. "And you don't think that's strange? No secrets?"

"Everyone has secrets," Adelaide pointed out. "That's the only truth."

"Are you offering to lure them from him?" Sesily hated the taste of the jest in her mouth.

"No. But truly, Sesily. If a man like Calhoun lives the life of a monk, that's absolute proof that he's hiding something." A pause. "Probably something *good*."

She was right, of course. If it was anyone else, she'd feel the same way.

"Well, it's not in London; it's probably in America," she said. "That's why he's always there and never here." Not that Sesily cared where he was.

Lie.

The duchess nodded. "But in the best of circumstances it would take three months to get answers from the other side of the world. We need to act now."

Sesily swallowed back her irritation, knowing that she should agree with the duchess's plan. Caleb had witnessed their work. She should be concerned with ensuring his silence, just as her friends were. But she didn't *want* to know his secrets. She didn't want any more reason to think about the man.

And still, she didn't want anyone *else* to know his secrets, instead.

"I imagine your sister has some ideas," the duchess said, matter-of-factly. "Perhaps I'll pay her a visit."

"No." Three sets of eyes widened at the sharp retort. She cleared her throat. "What I mean to say is, I'll do it."

The duchess's brows rose. "I don't think that's a good idea, Sesily."

"Why not?" Adelaide asked, ever keen, eyes enormous behind her spectacles.

Imogen even mustered some curiosity, finally interested in the conversation. "Yes, why not?" She looked from the duchess to Sesily, who did not flinch from the duchess's attention.

"No reason."

The duchess sat back in her chair, her expression clear. *You tell them, or I will.*

Sesily sighed, then grumbled, "Fine. Because once . . . a very long time ago . . ."

"Not *so* long ago," the duchess interjected.

If only murdering a duchess weren't a capital crime. "*Two years* ago . . . I thought perhaps he was . . ."

The one.

Silence fell at the table, as though she'd spoken the words aloud.

"Oh."

Sesily winced at Adelaide's soft, understanding reply. "As I said, it was years ago."

"Only two years, though," the duchess said. "And it was something of a heartbreak, if I recall."

"It wasn't a heartbreak," she replied. "It was—a rejection. We are all rejected at some point or another."

"You aren't," Imogen said.

"Well, I was then. And anyway, I was wrong."

"*Either way,* I suggest we try out my new explosive on him."

"How?" Adelaide asked.

"Well, I think we'd do it at his home, because I doubt Seraphina would like it if we exploded her tavern."

"Not how do we explode Calhoun, Imogen," Adelaide said. "How did he break Sesily's heart?"

This was mortifying. "He—" Sesily hesitated. "Truthfully, the term *broke my heart* is really an overreach."

"He refused her advances and left the country. That day."

"Dammit, Duchess!"

The other woman's eyes went wide, her diamond earrings winking in the candlelight. "I'm simply trying to get through it!"

"Did you *tell* him? That you thought he might be—"
Don't say it.

She cut Adelaide off. "I did."

"Oh dear. How mortifying."

"Not more mortifying than this recounting," Sesily said.

"What did he say?" Imogen asked.

He hadn't said anything. He'd just—"As I said, he left."

"Well, he's back now, so I remain in favor of exploding him."

Sesily sighed her exasperation. "Can we be done now?" No one pressed for more information, thank God, and she added, "I'm telling you, he's not a worry. It's not as though he's summoning Scotland Yard to investigate the events in the gardens."

"You're sure?" Adelaide asked.

"Quite."

"Hmm."

Sesily's brows knit together. "Why?"

"I'm sure it's nothing," Adelaide said, "but Mr. Calhoun just walked in the door."

It took all Sesily had not to turn and look. "Why on earth would he be here? He's got a perfectly nice pub of his own not five minutes west of here."

"I don't know, but I don't like it." Adelaide's eyes narrowed behind her spectacles.

"Why not?" Sesily's stomach dropped.

Don't look. Don't look.

"He's with Thomas Peck."

She did look, then, finding Caleb instantly. Ignoring the way her heart thumped in her chest, she considered his bearded companion, taller than him and equally wide. Thomas Peck, the pride of Bow Street, and now one of the best-known faces of the Metropolitan Police.

"If this is the company he keeps," the duchess said,
ever world-weary, "it seems we shall require Mr. Calhoun's secrets after all."

And so it was decided. Sesily stood, knowing what
she had to do. "I'll get them."

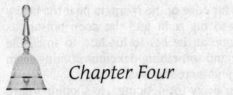

Chapter Four

What was she doing there?

Not that he should have noticed her. There were dozens of women in the tavern—it felt like a hundred of them, with the wall of heat and perfume that struck when he stepped through the door from the cool night beyond.

Maggie O'Tiernen's place always teemed with women, understandable as it promised safety, security, and a lack of censure to women of all walks, allowing them a level of privacy and privilege they were rarely afforded in other taverns.

Caleb had spent his life in taverns. He owned twelve of them, and he'd worked hard to build them into places that welcomed women. But where his pubs worked for that welcome, The Place came with it built in.

So, on any given evening, Maggie's place was full. Full of women who danced and drank and laughed—enough to make it difficult to single one from the whole crowd. Many with wide smiles and unbridled laughter. Many with smooth skin and wild curves. Many of them brunettes. Many of them beautiful.

He shouldn't have noticed one among the rest.

Of course, he did. He'd barely had a chance to look over the crowd, to register the group that danced in the lamplight on the far edge of the room, to hear the heavy clink of glasses to his right and the deep boisterous laugh from Maggie at the bar to his left, to smell the perfume and ale and something delicious coming from the kitchens . . . and there she was.

She was too far away for noticing. He shouldn't have been able to see her dark hair, gleaming in the orange light of the pub as she turned to face him. He shouldn't have been able to detect the stain of red on her lips or the low dip of the line of the dress she wore that had clearly been purchased from the devil himself. Not that Caleb should have been able to see the sinful garment, nor the way it framed the rise of her breasts, the swell of her hips. Nor should he have been able to hear her laugh over the scores of others, or smell her, warm and rich like almond tarts.

But he did. Instantly.

Because he'd always been able to see those things. Hear them. Scent them. From the moment he'd met her, two years earlier.

"Fucking hell." What was she doing there?

At his shoulder, Thomas Peck, one of London's best detectives, stiffened. "Do you see something?"

Always. If she was there, he saw her.

"No." Caleb pushed into the room, keenly aware of the attention they drew from a tableful of women nearby. He wasn't a fool; he knew he was the kind of man people noticed, and it was doubly true when he was one of only a handful of men in a room. He didn't like being in The Place when it was full—didn't like feeling like he was trespassing. "Let's get to Maggie and get out."

Doing everything he could to ignore Sesily, Caleb redirected his attention to the proprietress of The Place, who towered above everyone else, black hair twisted high on her head, reigning over her subjects as she poured ale, flirted indiscriminately, and watched the crowd. She was bent over the bar, in close conversation with an Indian woman, when she met Caleb's eye. Surprise flashed in her dark eyes—men weren't regulars at The Place, and especially not at that hour—and Maggie's attention slid to his companion, recognition flaring, along with distaste. Raising a single brow in his direction, she indicated the far end of the bar, where it was quieter.

Though, with Sesily Talbot close, it wouldn't be quiet for long.

Setting his jaw, Caleb followed Maggie's instructions as she returned to her conversation. He led Peck through the room, trying not to notice the keen blue gaze that followed his movements from the table tucked in the corner.

As they made their way, Peck asked, "You're sure that O'Tiernen will talk to us?"

"She'll talk to *me*," Caleb said, "but I'm guessing you knew that, or you wouldn't have had to strong-arm me into joining you."

"I didn't strong-arm you, Calhoun. I asked you for a favor."

"Right," Caleb retorted. "And I said yes because I'm a giving kind of man, and not because you're one of Peel's boys."

Peck didn't like the casual descriptor, but Caleb didn't trust uniforms in general, and so he wasn't about to play charming. Still, Peck knew he wouldn't have made it through the door without Caleb to vouch for him. "You can't deny that my owing you a boon isn't the worst thing in the world."

Caleb couldn't think of many things worse than being in close quarters with an officer of the law, but he supposed that, as they came, Thomas Peck wasn't the bottom of the barrel. He was a decent sort who'd made a name for himself before the formation of the Metropolitan Police Force as being one of the few Bow Street Runners who cared about honest justice rather than lining his pockets.

When Peck came knocking at The Singing Sparrow earlier in the day, it had been with justice in mind. In recent months, a half dozen locations across the East End, every one owned or operated by women, every one tossed over in a riot or a raid or a robbery—not one of them reported. Peck wasn't a fool, and he knew there was something going on. And he wanted to get to the bottom of it.

But that required finding someone willing to talk. Which he wasn't going to get at most of the joints— exclusive clubs with private membership rolls featuring some of the wealthiest women in London. Rough and tumble Thomas Peck, who barely knew how to tie a cravat, wasn't going to get in those doors.

The Place, however, had a door that opened, even if men were rarely welcome there. The policeman had known better than to come to The Place on his own, however—his weren't the kinds of questions answered easily, because Scotland Yard wasn't the kind of place anyone here, deep in the winding streets of Covent Garden, trusted. And rightly so.

If Peck was going to gain more information about whoever was so full of anger and vengeance that he was coming for every place made safe for women, the policeman was going to need someone Maggie knew. And, though Caleb would rather gnaw off a limb than linger with a member of the Metropolitan Police, he wanted whoever was shaking down places in the Garden caught, and not only because The Singing Sparrow welcomed women and was owned by one.

That, and refusing Peck's request would draw the wrong kind of attention from Scotland Yard, and Caleb couldn't risk that.

Which meant he was there for business, and not for the woman draped artfully against the bar not ten paces from where Maggie waited for him. He met her blue eyes for a heartbeat, and looked away.

He had his own trouble to sort out that evening. Sesily Talbot would have to wait.

Haven't you noticed, American? I am *trouble.*

As though anyone with a pulse could notice anything different.

Maggie met them at the far end of the bar. "Have you forgotten to change your watch, American? You should know better than to darken my doorway at this hour. And with such unsavory companionship." Gone was the easy smile she had for the rest of the room. She tilted her head in the direction of the police detective. "He's bad for business."

Caleb nodded, turning his back squarely on Sesily, who had settled in, unabashedly watching the show. "Mine, too."

"Aye," she replied, Galway in her voice. "But that's less of my concern. Ale?"

"What are you pouring?"

Her gaze narrowed and she turned away, filling a pint from a small cask nearby. Setting it on the bar, she said, "Beggars can't be choosers, American."

Caleb lifted the glass and toasted her. "Fair enough." He drank deep, anticipating the normal swill found in any tavern in London, but finding, instead, something potent and unexpected. Pulling back, he inspected the glass, then looked to the proprietress. "What is that?"

She smiled. No one liked a secret like Maggie. "It'll knock you back, no?"

"It certainly will. Where'd you get it?"

"There's a new brewer in town."

"I'd like to meet him."

"We'll see. I'm not feeling a very giving mood with you now, American, bringing the Yard into my place." She looked to Peck.

"I'm not here for ale," he said.

"Imagine my surprise." The retort was dry as sand.

The detective inspector leaned far enough over the bar to ensure that they could not be heard above the din of the tavern. "I'm on the hunt for the boys who tossed over The Place a few weeks ago."

It was the wrong thing to say, but Caleb wasn't about to help Peck fix it. Not when Maggie cut him a look and pulled a length of linen from where it hung at her waist to make a show of cleaning the shining mahogany. "Tossed over which place?"

It was a deliberate misunderstanding. Caleb had heard of the damage done to The Place. Chairs and tables destroyed, lamps and curtains pulled from the walls, a roomful of casks hacked to bits, the two windows onto the street smashed before Maggie and a few regulars had chased away the offenders with, if reports were to be believed, a shard of broken mirror and a meat cleaver.

"Miss O'Tiernen, you were closed for a week afterward," Peck said, the disbelief in his tone making it even less likely that she'd give up any worthwhile information.

She turned her cool, midnight gaze on him. "Renovations."

There were a thousand reasons why she wouldn't want Scotland Yard in the mix with whatever she knew, and Caleb recognized at least a dozen of them behind her eyes. Including one he didn't care for: fear.

Peck lowered his voice. "I believe the men who raided you are members of a known gang perpetrating crimes all over London, called The Bully Boys—and I'd like to help you."

She did look at Peck then, disbelief on her face. "You'd like to help me." A pause. And then, "Detective Inspector . . . you walk in here and tell me about The Bully Boys like I haven't known them since you were learning to fire that pretty pistol you've strapped to your side. The women in this room have forgotten more about The Bully Boys than your men have ever learned."

"I want to learn," Peck said.

"And what . . . you'll play protector? Keep us safe?" Maggie scoffed.

"Yes," Peck replied without hesitation.

Maggie's lips twisted in a wry smile, wise with years playing her own protector. "Only till Mayfair calls, though, yeah?"

Caleb couldn't help the twist of his own lips. He didn't imagine Tommy Peck got this kind of set down regularly.

"Like I said," Maggie finished. "We were closed for renovations."

Peck stiffened in frustration, and Caleb stepped in before the policeman got them both barred from The Place. They weren't getting information from Maggie. Not tonight. And possibly not ever. He set a hand on Peck's shoulder. "Renovations it is."

"And unless the two of you are here to entertain my customers with a brawl"—she made a show of sliding her gaze over both men's broad chests, before meeting Caleb's eyes—"you *ain't* welcome during business hours. I suggest you go back to your pub, and *you*"—she looked to Peck with a false smile—"go back to doing Her Majesty's work. We've no need for you here. Unless you're going to give us a look at those muscles."

She raised her voice at the last, and Caleb gritted his teeth, knowing, without question, that at least one woman in the room would pick up that particular gauntlet.

"Are you to fight, American?"

Christ. Sesily appeared at his shoulder, close enough to touch. When had she moved? How hadn't he noticed? He turned and leveled her with his coolest look, willing his pulse steady. "You'd like that, wouldn't you?"

She made a show of inspecting him and then Peck. Lingering a bit too long on the other man. Long enough that Caleb seriously considered accepting the offer of a brawl.

What this woman could do to him.

"Tell me, Detective Inspector, whom do you think would win in this particular fight?"

Peck's brows rose in surprise at the brazen question. "I beg your pardon, my lady?"

"No need to stand on ceremony." She smiled, wide and warm, the full force of it dazzling the detective and setting Caleb to wondering how best one disposed of the body of a Metropolitan Police officer. "Please. Call me Sesily."

Like hell he would. "Don't even think of calling her that."

Her eyes went wide and innocent, as though such a quality were possible in a hellion. "Why Mr. Calhoun, I wasn't aware you were in a position to decide what others call me." With that set down, she turned her cheeky smile back on the detective. "Detective Inspector, you are more than welcome to call me Sesily, but only if you tell me who you expect would triumph in a match between the two of you."

Peck wasn't a fool and he wasn't a monk. Instead, he offered Sesily Talbot a winning smile of his own and said, "I expect it would be me, my lady."

The honorific was the only reason why Thomas Peck, pride of Scotland Yard, remained standing in that moment, especially when Sesily moved closer, sliding between Caleb and the policeman, like a vine. Or one of those snakes that squeezed its prey until it was dead and then ate it in one enormous gulp.

She tilted her chin up to look into Peck's face, which Caleb imagined some might find handsome if they liked beards and chiseled marble. "So confident!"

"Oh, are we wagering?" Imogen Loveless had arrived, her words forthright and bloodthirsty. "Will there be a bout?"

"A lady can dream," Sesily replied, all flirt. "Right now, we're discussing who will win."

"Not all of us are discussing it," Caleb grumbled, taking a step back when Lady Imogen pushed into the space next to Sesily and lifted herself onto her toes to get a better look at Peck's shoulders.

Peck's attention snapped to her, and something shifted in him, his spine going straighter, shoulders going broader. "Excuse me, miss."

"I've a bob on the American if there's a fight!" Adelaide Frampton called happily from a distance.

"There's no fight," Caleb grumbled, ignoring the sliver of gratitude he felt that someone was on his side in this non-existent competition.

"You appear to be quite strapping," Lady Imogen said to Peck.

He cleared his throat. "Er . . . Thank you?"

"Do you play croquet?"

"No?"

Caleb couldn't linger on the odd conversation. He had his own problems, however, as in the small space, Sesily was suddenly pressed to him, her beautiful eyes on his, her soft curves against all the hard planes of him as she and her friend sized them up like horseflesh.

He inhaled sharply and stepped back, putting space between them. Requiring space between them.

She met his eyes. "Mr. Calhoun, really. There aren't many reasons for men such as you to find themselves inside The Place—indeed the obvious reason is that you're here for an exhibition match. You needn't look as though you've scented something unpleasant."

It wasn't unpleasant, though. It was magnificent. Lush and beautiful and a scent that should have been impossible to find in a dark pub in the labyrinth of Covent Garden. Nevertheless, he raised a brow in her direction and said, "Remarkably like sulfur, actually."

Her eyes lit with laughter. As Lady Imogen replied offhandedly, "Oh, that's me, probably. I've been testing out new explosives."

Peck's wide eyes met Caleb's over the woman's wild hair. "Explosives?"

"Mmm," she said before nodding once, her inspection complete. "My money is on this one. He's a touch taller and he's received proper training."

Proper training was precisely why Caleb could fell Peck like a tree. There was no place for rules in a decent bout.

For his part, Peck didn't seem to know what to say, so he settled on another somewhat strangled, "Thank you."

"I hope I have not offended, Mr. Calhoun," Lady Imogen said, in a tone that suggested precisely the opposite.

"Oh, Caleb's not offended." Sesily waved a hand in the air. "It's merely a matter of facts, Imogen."

She was baiting him. And he knew better than to take it.

"We'll never know, as there won't be a bout tonight, ladies," Maggie interjected. "These two are too expensive a proposition. And they're leaving. *Now.*"

Sesily made a show of looking disappointed. "Another time, then," she said before stepping past him to the bar. "Maggie, I don't suppose you've any of those delicious pork pies of yours tonight?"

And like that, the men were dismissed, as though they'd never been there to begin with. Which was what Caleb wished whenever he encountered Sesily.

At least, it was what he *told* himself he wished.

"Who is she?" Peck asked, under his breath.

She's not for you.

Resisting the urge to put the thought into words, Caleb pushed past the detective with a terse, "Sesily Talbot. She's not a part of your investigation."

Even as he said the words, he had a sense they were not true.

"Not the Talbot girl. I've heard of her . . ." Caleb gritted his teeth. Of course Peck had heard of her. Sesily had made a life of being the kind of woman people had heard of. "I mean the other one. The one who thought I could knock you out."

"The one who was wrong, you mean? Imogen Love-less. *Lady* Imogen Loveless," he said, making sure to add the important bit.

"Lady?"

"Daughter of an earl, with a taste for explosives, I gather."

Outside, the street was quiet and the air was brisk, and before the door to The Place had even closed, Caleb was rounding on Peck. "I told you nothing good would come of a visit to Maggie's."

"Not true," the detective replied. "I got in the door. I spoke to her. She knows I know someone's after places like hers. And maybe, someday soon, she'll believe I want them caught."

Caleb slid him a look. "You understand that no one in the East End is likely to trust a Peeler."

Peck's jaw tightened at the slang. "I grew up here. I'm not the enemy."

Caleb had lived long enough to know that the former didn't prove the latter, but he stayed quiet. He wasn't friend or counselor to Peck, and he had no desire to get close to a police detective. That was the last thing he needed.

What he needed was to go back to America and never return.

Immediately.

"Detective Inspector!"

Dammit. She'd followed them.

Caleb tucked his chin and pulled his coat around him, refusing to turn to face the brightly lit tavern . . . and Sesily.

She hadn't called for him, which meant he could leave. She was Peck's problem now, and the other man had already responded to her friendly shout.

"Detective!" She was closer now, and a touch breathless, the sound just enough like sin to make a body imagine what it would be like to be the cause of Sesily Talbot's breathlessness.

No. He wasn't going to think about that. He was going back to his tavern. He had a business to run. Whatever trouble she was causing tonight wasn't his concern.

"Lady Sesily," Peck said, gracious and gentlemanly, as though he had all the time in the world for Sesily.

Good. Better Peck than him.

Caleb had just forced himself to take a step away from them when she said, happily, "You don't mind if I converse with your friend . . . just for a moment?"

Caleb pulled up short.

"I promise I shall return him before you've even noticed he's gone."

He looked over his shoulder. "We've nothing to discuss."

She smiled. "Don't worry, Mr. Calhoun, I shall do all the talking."

"I've no doubt of that," Caleb said, and her smile grew even wider. She was unflappable. It was infuriating.

"No need to return him at all, Lady Sesily," Peck interjected with a nod to the tavern. "I've work to do, and I've already been told that I'm bad for business."

"Oh, I wouldn't take it personally," she retorted. "Once you decided you weren't up for a bout, you were *both* bad for business."

Peck laughed at the jest and rubbed one hand over his jaw, smiling sheepishly. "I'll take comfort in that."

"Next time, you should try for a fight," she whispered. "You'd be amazed by how far that would get you."

"With Miss O'Tiernen?"

She shrugged. "Probably not, but *I* would like it very much."

The woman simply couldn't not flirt.

"I shall keep that in mind," Peck replied before tipping his hat at her, then Caleb, and heading off to wherever he had to be next, chasing information no one would give him willingly.

Sesily watched him disappear into the darkness before saying, softly, "He seems a decent fellow. Pity he's a Runner."

"What do you want, Sesily?" The question came out harsher than Caleb intended.

She looked to him, as though she was surprised he was there. As though she hadn't been the one to chase after him. "Right! Yes." She looked about for a moment before making her way to a dark doorway several yards away. When he did not follow, she turned back. "Mr. Calhoun. If you don't mind?"

He crossed his arms over his chest. "I do mind, in fact. I'm not in the mood to be strangled."

"Oh, is strangulation an option? If only I'd brought my garrote."

"After seeing what you can do to men, I'm surprised you don't keep it on your person at all times."

She shot a dangerous look in his direction. "Follow me."

Whether curiosity or self-preservation, he did, approaching the narrow space where Sesily had already pressed her back to the door. "You shouldn't be out here alone."

"I'm not alone."

"You would be, if I weren't here."

"But you are, and I am perfectly safe."

"Are you sure? I hear I'm a losing proposition in a fight," he replied without thinking. Without realizing how it would sound.

One side of her pretty mouth rose in amusement, making the quiet of the cold street ear-splitting. "You didn't like that."

Of course he hadn't. But he'd never admit it.

"I wasn't about to tell Peck he wasn't a winner," she said. "You catch more flies with honey. Not that you've ever tried that with me."

"I've no intention of catching you, Sesily."

"Yes, yes, you've made that abundantly clear," she said, and for a heartbeat he thought he heard an edge in the words, before she flashed him a bright smile. "Though I can't imagine why not. I'm a lovely fly."

Lord, this woman would try a saint. "And what makes you interested in catching Peck?"

"A body would have to be deceased not to notice Thomas Peck, Caleb. He's a legend."

Something hot and angry flared in him. "I should have guessed. Poor Peck, pegged for your favorite game."

"And what game is that?"

"Scandalous nonsense. What fate will he meet?"

"Whatever fate I decide for him. I rarely hear complaints."

It was too much. "I think the Earl of Totting might have one or—"

She reached out and placed her palm over his mouth, stopping his words with her soft skin. Why wasn't she wearing gloves?

"I'd be more concerned about your own fate, American," she whispered harshly in the darkness, "catting around with a Scotland Yardsman. I don't care for the idea of your Mr. Peck learning about what you saw the other evening."

She couldn't possibly believe he'd turn her over to Peck. Of course, he didn't tell her that. Instead, he waited for her to lower her hand and said, "I assure you, Peck is not interested in your nocturnal activities."

"Good. I suggest you follow his lead. They're none of your business."

It was his turn to be annoyed. "They're absolutely my business."

"How?"

"Leaving aside my responsibility to your sister, my friend—"

She rolled her eyes. "Spare me the misplaced masculine honor. I do not require it."

"She's also my business partner—"

"Which has nothing to do with—"

"Reputations paint wide swaths, Sesily."

She laughed at the ridiculous statement. "Even if we weren't discussing a *tavern* owned by my sister who *divorced and then remarried* the same man, I do believe the horse has left the barn on my reputation, Calhoun. The lion's share of London calls me Sexily."

He gritted his teeth at the name, full of lewd humor and loathsome disdain. "They shouldn't."

"And why not?" Was she . . . affronted? "Truly, you wound me."

"Why? I don't call you that."

"Yes. I'm aware. And what a pity, as it is the truth."

Of course it was.

"Which brings us back to the matter at hand."

What was the matter at hand? It wasn't the kissing.

It couldn't be the kissing.

A shout sounded in the distance, reminding him that they were out in the open on a London street, and he shouldn't be thinking about kissing.

"No one can know what happened. Not your friend Peck—"

"He's not my friend."

Surprise flashed in her eyes at his immediate denial. "You vouched for him when you walked through the door with him."

He sighed his frustration. "I didn't have a choice."

"Why not?" The question was too quick. Too curious.

He answered with a half-truth. "Because I'd rather have Scotland Yard owe me a boon than decide it owes me something else entirely."

She raised a brow at that. "Worried about your illegal bourbon?"

Every tavern worth its salt poured illegal bourbon, but it was a better answer than the truth. "Exactly that."

"I don't think so," she said, and a thrum of irritation coursed through him. "You are keeping truths of your own, Caleb. And if I have to learn them to keep mine safe, I will."

It was not bravado, but a promise, and Caleb didn't care for it. He didn't want her near any of his secrets. Proximity to his past was not a lark, and the idea of her tied up in it made him want to rage. But he could not show her the nerves she had made raw. It would be a red flag to a bull.

Instead, he forced a laugh and said, "I am an open book."

"You are the very opposite of that and we both know it," she replied, casually, "but there are worse things than Scotland Yard owing you a favor. And you're collecting boons this week, it seems."

"What does that mean?"

"I mean, I owe you one, too. For condescending to hide me in the gardens."

There'd been nothing condescending about that moment, when she'd wound herself around him and stolen his breath even as he collected her against him and took everything she offered.

She stepped closer to him. He did not back away, adoring the temptation of her even as he loathed himself for not being more responsible. For not remembering that she was his friend's sister. That she was off-limits. "Are you offering me a boon?"

"Name it." She settled one hand to his chest, and he wondered if she could feel his heartbeat through the wool of his topcoat.

He shook his head. "No."

"Shall I name it?"

"You think you know me well enough to know what I want?"

"I know precisely what you want. But I am willing to wait for you to discover it yourself."

"And what is it?"

She smiled, a cat with cream, and though she didn't reply, he could hear it nonetheless.

Me.

Forthright. Arrogant. Bold and perfect and true. Because he did want her. He'd wanted her for long enough to know that he'd likely never not want her.

He'd also never have her, and that was the truth that roared through him. Frustrated and angry and unwelcome and familiar. How many times had he heard that roar riot through him as he thought of this woman, who tempted him beyond reason, and whom he could never have?

Except this time, she heard it, too, her gaze sharp and clear on the tavern behind him, where the door had burst open, scattering women into the street.

The roar wasn't in his head. It was inside The Place.

And Sesily was already pushing past him, headed for it.

Chapter Five

Ignoring Caleb's shout—he couldn't honestly believe she'd listen, could he?—Sesily pushed through the crowd of women pouring out the front door of The Place, desperate to get inside . . . and to take on whatever she'd find within.

Inside, a half a dozen men with ugly faces and uglier clubs had entered the tavern through the rear entrance beyond the kitchens. They had destruction in mind—destruction aided by the absolute mayhem they'd caused when they'd come through the door.

She looked to the table where she'd been sitting with her friends. Empty.

A quick glance around the room found Adelaide and the duchess, tall above the crowd at the far end of the space, headed straight for a bruiser on the way to an oil lamp high on the wall. If he was planning to burn the place down, the duo were more than capable of stopping him.

"Imogen," Sesily whispered, looking for the last of her group. It didn't take long to find her—atop a chair at the center of the taproom, offloading items from her ever-present reticule.

Sesily couldn't be certain Imogen wasn't *also* at risk of setting the place on fire, but at least she wouldn't do it on purpose. Before Sesily could consider that possibility, a scream nearby had her reaching to extract her best knife from where it was strapped to her thigh, beyond the fake pocket in her silk skirts.

Before she could get into the fray, a heavy hand stopped her, fingers curling around her arm. She spun, eager to face her captor, knife already raised and ready to strike. Caleb wasn't a slouch, however, and he was ready for her, even as his eyes went wide at the sight of her wickedly sharp blade.

He caught her wrist, barely preventing the knife from slicing into his cheek. "We're going to talk about a few things when this is over. Not the least of them will be the fact that if I were any slower, you'd have taken out an eye."

"Hesitation in battle is for dramatic novels and play fighting," she replied.

He released her, admiration in his green eyes, and Sesily promised herself she'd savor the memory of that look the next time she was alone. More screams sounded, and Imogen cried "Ha!" from her tabletop, which meant she'd found whatever terrifying tool she'd been searching for.

"What else?" Sesily asked, as she considered her next move, her grip tightening on her knife.

"What else what?" he snapped, turning to face another man with a wicked looking club. He caught the blow and delivered a brutal one of his own.

Impressive.

"What else are we going to talk about when this is over? Besides my nearly taking out your eye?"

He kept fighting, as though it were perfectly ordinary to converse while under attack. "We're going to talk about the fact that you ran *into* the place *out* of which everyone else was running."

She watched as he landed a handsome uppercut. "Nicely done."

"Thank you," he replied. "Looks like I can win a bout after all, doesn't it?"

She swallowed her smile at his lingering affront. "What did you expect me to do, run away?"

"That's exactly what I expected you to do," he said as he caught his opponent's club-hand and smashed it against a wooden column twice, until it dropped to the floor.

It was a pity he was wearing a coat. Really. She'd like to see his muscles working.

She barked a little laugh. "Tell me, American, when was the last time you knew me to run away?"

"This isn't a horse loose in a barn, Sesily. This is serious."

"First, I would absolutely never run toward a barn." A mighty crash sounded behind her, along with a collection of screams, and Sesily turned away from Caleb to find an enormous man sending a table flying into a group of women huddled nearby.

Rage filled Sesily as she clutched the handle of her blade tight in her palm. "Second, if you think I can't see how serious these men are, you haven't been paying much attention."

She raised her voice in the direction of the melee. "Oy! Why not try someone who is armed, you great ox?" The man rounded on Sesily, who shot him her most dazzling smile and said, "Or are you afraid a woman might take you down?"

Her soon-to-be opponent came for her, tossing another table aside like kindling, but behind him, several of The Place's regulars leapt in to help the women he'd threatened. Mithra Singh, a brilliant lady brewmaster who was quietly taking the West End pubs by storm, hurried them from the building.

At the same time, Lady Eleanora Madewell and her beautiful Norwegian partner—known only as Nik to most of the Garden because she ran with the best smugglers in Britain—took to the far corner, where Duchess and Adelaide required reinforcements.

Sesily crouched, weapon in hand. "Shall we get on with it?"

The enormous man grunted, and she wondered if he had the capacity for complex language.

"Sesily—" Caleb warned, throwing another punch. "Don't you dare take on—" The words were lost as he took a blow with a heavy thud. "Goddammit."

He was in the fight again, which suited Sesily just fine, as she was watching the brute heading for her, waiting for the right moment to strike. What she lacked in muscle she made up for in unexpected skill, but the element of surprise was critical.

"You are an ideal-looking brute," Sesily said cheerily as her opponent approached. "Truly, Drury Lane ought to put you on the stage."

The man's brow knit in confusion.

"Sesily—" Caleb again.

"Honestly, Caleb, you should see him. Like a storybook ogre."

"I don't need to see him, dammit! Do not incite—"

The rest of the instructions were lost as her opponent threw his punch. Sesily ducked and, while he was off-kilter, struck, putting a long gash in his side. He shouted at the pain and she called out, "Sorry!" as she reached down, lifted a chair leg and, using the momentum of the movement, cracked him in the jaw before he could take hold of her.

His head snapped back and she turned away, knowing she'd done the job before he collapsed onto another table, the force of his body crushing the wood to the ground like a pile of matchsticks.

"Dammit," Sesily said. "Now I've broken a table, too."

"What did you do?"

She turned to look at Caleb, who was staring at her, his own opponent doubled over in pain. "Men never know what to do with women who fight. They always forget critical information."

"What's that?"

"That when we enter the fray, we do so to win." She lifted a chin in the direction of the man he'd been fighting. "Do you require assistance?"

His eyes narrowed. "Absolutely not. Goddammit, Sesily. This place is in danger. You're in danger. You ran toward it, like a madwoman. Without waiting for me."

"And if I had waited, would you have let me enter?"

"Of course not."

"Men are ridiculous."

"For wanting to keep you safe?"

"For believing that you aren't the thing from which we are most in danger." She spread her arms wide. "Look around you."

The words landed, but Caleb didn't have time to dwell on them, as his opponent righted himself and lumbered toward him. With a scowl, he turned away from her, shouting over his shoulder, "I'm calling in my boon. I want you out of here. I'm sure you know a half dozen ways to exit this building."

"I do, in fact," she said, "but I'm not going anywhere."

"So much for favors," he replied. "Infernal woman."

She couldn't help her laugh.

"Goddammit, Sesily—"

His retort was punctuated by a shout that was followed by a mighty crash. Her gaze flew to Maggie, tall and strong behind the bar, but outflanked—two men coming for her, menace in their eyes.

"Didn't heed the lesson we taught you last time, did you?" one of the thugs said, and Sesily could hear his loathing from the distance she was already closing. As she neared, she recognized him. Johnny Crouch, a local bruiser who ran with The Bully Boys. Word was that he'd been seen at several of the recent raids.

"Sesily!" Caleb shouted at a distance from the midst of his bout, no doubt wanting her to stop. To wait for him, or some nonsense.

"I never was very good at lessons, Johnny," Maggie retorted, reaching for a bottle of whiskey—the nearest weapon.

"Too bad, that," he replied. They were nearly on Maggie now. "This time, you won't have a chance to remember. Bringing Peelers into it weren't smart. Can't have the detective inspector sniffing 'round."

Sesily clenched her teeth at the words. The Bully Boys had been watching The Place. They'd seen Caleb and Peck enter earlier. And it didn't matter that Maggie hadn't said a word—she'd be punished for nothing more than the fact that her door had opened.

Anger flared, hot and full, as Sesily reached the trio. "Have you ever noticed, Maggie," she began, peeling back her skirts, revealing the trousers she wore beneath them, designed for ease of movement. She stepped up onto a chair and onto the bar without hesitation. "That the more a thug talks, the easier he is to take on?"

The villain in question turned to face her, his twisted nose revealing multiple breaks, alongside a wicked scar across one beady eye. She smiled. "Hello, Johnny."

Crouch's gaze lingered on her full chest. "Who're you?"

Resisting the urge to flinch beneath the disgusting inspection from the man who was clearly leader of this vile crew, Sesily said, "Truly, I'm disappointed you don't remember me. But never mind that. You were teaching Maggie a lesson?"

"Sesily!" Caleb's roar carried through the din of battle, and Sesily ignored it.

"You're damn right we're going to teach 'er a lesson. She'll think twice before opening this place again. Women ought to know their place." He reached for her slipper on the bar, his hand sliding over her ankle. "That includes you."

Close.

Swallowing down the bile that rose in her throat at the leering words, Sesily tested the weight of the table leg she held behind her skirts. "Has no one ever told you that you shouldn't touch women without their permission?"

"No one worth listening to," he said, his grubby fingers crawling up her leg, soiling the silk. She added ruining her new dress to the list of Crouch's punishable offenses.

Closer.

A crash sounded from the far edge of the room, along with a howl of masculine pain. "It sounds like your friend who was aiming to set the place on fire has been thwarted. You get yours next."

"And who is going to give it to me, kitten?" His hand curled around her calf. "You?"

She smiled brightly. "You're going to be so surprised at the sharpness of my claws." Without hesitation, she knocked him back with the table leg, sending him crashing into the casks behind him.

His companion, larger and clearly even less intelligent, shouted, "Johnny! Wot 'appened?"

"You bitch!" Johnny spat as he struggled to his feet, fury in his eyes.

A roar sounded from behind her, followed by another smashing table.

"Alright, Maggie?" Sesily asked.

"Alright." A flick of Maggie's wrist, and the bottle had smashed on the lip of the bar. She held up the neck and a wicked jagged edge.

Sesily tilted her head. "Impressive."

"I make do. We can't all have monogrammed blades," Maggie replied.

"I shall have one made for you."

"Cheers, luv."

And then there was no time for conversation, because Johnny had found his feet again and Sesily was leaping down from the bar, putting it between them. He didn't hesitate to follow—remarkably nimble considering he'd just taken a blow to the head—and Sesily backed away as he came for her, ready to punish.

Her heart began to pound, and she prepared to fight even as she heard a mighty crack and a shout behind her.

"That will be another one of your boys going down," she said. "You see, there's only one thing that American brute likes less than me being here, and that's *you* being here."

Nervousness flashed in the man's eyes, and his gaze slid past Sesily, searching for proof of her words. But, instead of finding reason for fear, he found something else.

A wicked, triumphant smile came over his face. "Not *my* boy."

Then it was Sesily who was nervous. She couldn't stop herself from turning to find the brute who'd been fighting Caleb tossing tables out of the way to get to the bar.

No Caleb.

Where was Caleb?

She hesitated, panic edging into her consciousness when she couldn't see him. And in the hesitation, the giant was on her, his hand wrapping around her left wrist, tight and uncomfortable. Unpleasant.

He was going to break it.

"Sesily!" Adelaide's shout came from the far side of the room, followed by an insistent, "Imogen!"

"I see!" Imogen replied, but it wasn't enough. She wasn't close enough.

Mithra was coming through the door. Nora and Nik were tossing aside broken furniture as they crossed the pub.

Everyone was too far away.

Sesily winced and bent with the force of the bruiser's grip, balling her right hand—not dominant, but still able to pack a punch—and letting fly, landing high enough on one of his massive cheeks to ensure he'd sport a bruise in the morning.

Not that this seemed the kind of man who owned a mirror, let alone looked into it regularly.

That, and it didn't seem to impact him. She went for him again, this time landing the punch just as she lifted her knee in a sharp blow to his groin. He doubled over, and she was already passing him, her gaze tracking to a body on the floor in the distance. "Caleb!" she shouted, making her way toward him.

Except the big brute grabbed her from behind.

She struggled, unable to loosen his grip, casting about for an ally, finding the duchess several yards away, moving quickly, reaching into her pockets for something sharp and dangerous.

Sesily shook her head. "Caleb needs help!"

The words were barely out when her captor's arm came round her neck, like steel. Tight. Too tight. She grabbed at the hand, scratching him. Squirming even as she knew that he was too big and too strong. He was going to kill her.

Had he already killed Caleb?

He would loathe having to die for her.

She couldn't breathe, but she could see the girls coming to her aid from all angles. And then she couldn't see much at all, but she could hear—shouts and crashes and a wicked roar, and she thought she heard Imogen talking about chemical reactions, and it all seemed so far away . . .

Chapter Six

"Goddammit, Sesily, wake up. Right now."

As far as awakenings went, it wasn't the most delicate one she'd ever received, but it worked. She had a cracking headache, and she gasped at the sharp pain. Her brow furrowed.

A wicked curse sounded, in that broad American accent that never failed to garner her attention. "That's right." Another insistent growl. "Wake up."

A bright light shone through her eyelids and she turned her face away, into ready darkness and warmth. "No!"

"Yes. Open your eyes, Sesily."

She lifted a hand to ward off the glaring light. "Make it stop," she said into the darkness. "It is too bright."

A hesitation. And then, "Fine. Open your eyes."

She didn't want to. She wanted to curl into the lovely warm cushion, scented with leather and amber, until the pain in her head subsided. "No."

"Oh, for—" The cushion moved. It wasn't a cushion. It was Caleb. And he was moving her, like she weighed nothing, to reveal her face.

She whined her displeasure, but the bright light subsided. Thank heavens.

"Sesily Talbot, if you don't open your eyes right fucking now . . ." The warning was full of fury and something else. Was it possible it was . . . fear?

She opened her eyes.

The lantern light remained bright enough to make her suffer. Her stomach roiled and she put her fingers to her brow as she groused at him. "There. Are you happy?"

"No," came the flat reply as he lifted the lantern, turned to the lowest setting, to look at her. "Look at me."

"You are *so* directive." She did as she was told, quickly discovering that the pain was not the only reason she was overcome with queasiness. They were in a carriage, and it was moving at an extraordinary clip. She swallowed around the lump in her throat.

"I wouldn't have to be if you were more biddable," he said, distracted, seizing her chin and tilting her face toward the light, his attention on her eyes. "Stay still."

"That might be . . ." She closed her eyes and took a deep breath. ". . . difficult."

Another curse and he shifted, adding a second motion to the first, offensive one. Her insides tilted, and she willed herself not to cast up her accounts. Not here. Not with him.

Horror warred with pain and embarrassment.

"Perhaps you could—" *Toss me from the carriage. Put me out of my misery.*

She wasn't sure what she was going to ask, but he found a third option, holding her tight to his chest, twisting their bodies to shield hers with his enormous one, and raising a heavy, booted foot to kick out the window of the carriage, sending glass exploding into the street beyond.

Surprise and something suspiciously like a thrill chased away nausea for a heartbeat.

The conveyance slowed in the wake of the explosion, the coachman shouting, "Sir?"

"Carry on," Caleb shouted back, pulling a handkerchief from his pocket and wrapping it around his hand, clearing broken glass from the edge of the now empty window frame before moving her into the breeze whooshing round the interior of the carriage. "Breathe."

She did, closing her eyes and letting the fresh air wash over her, the roiling in her stomach almost immediately subsiding. "Thank you."

"I can't have you retching in my carriage."

"Well then, we are both grateful for this turn of events." She took another deep breath. "I shall of course pay for the new glass."

"No need." His hand returned to her chin, but he did not reply. She opened her eyes to discover him directly in front of her. "It is payment enough to know that Athena can be laid low by a carriage ride."

"Athena?" She shouldn't like it. Certainly she shouldn't reveal how much she liked it.

"That's what you looked like," he said, staring into her eyes. No. Not into. Inspecting them. Searching, no doubt, for some evidence that she'd been harmed. "Leaping into the fight, like you were born on a battlefield." When he spoke, his voice was low and soft, and if she didn't know better, she'd think he cared for her. Which of course he didn't. Not an hour earlier, he'd made it clear. *I've no intention of catching you.* "But even Athena required warriors, you madwoman."

The last carried the edge with which she was comfortable, and Sesily was grateful for it, not knowing how to respond to the softness. He was never soft with her.

"Where are my friends?"

"The motley group of women who fought by your side?" She watched him as he inspected her, his countenance belying his soft words—lips pressed together, jaw set, nostrils flared in what she knew was frustration. "I suppose they are your warriors?"

"We are each other's warriors," she replied as he tilted her chin up, turning her toward the lantern light again. She allowed it, ignoring the shiver he sent through her when he set his fingers to her throat, stroking over the skin there. "Are they all well?"

"Can you breathe?"

"Yes. My friends. Are they—"

He pressed gently at her neck. "Is there any pain?"

She grabbed at his hand, her fingers wrapping around his wrist. Waited for him to look at her. "My friends, Caleb."

"The duchess saw us into the carriage, along with Miss Frampton. They assured me they would find their way out of trouble."

Sesily nodded. They'd never had difficulty escaping fights before. A vision flashed. Nik and Nora. Mithra. Maggie. "And the others? Maggie?"

"All safe. Lady Imogen put the man who harmed you to sleep with a mysterious concoction and a handkerchief."

"Ah, yes. She is very proud of that trick."

"She should be," he said, admiration in his tone. "I only wish she'd left him for me so I could have had the pleasure."

"You, too, have a deadly handkerchief?"

"I do not require a handkerchief to punish the man who did this to you."

The calm words sent another thrill through her, but before she could ask him to elaborate, he'd returned his attention to her neck. She watched and took the opportunity to study him. His brow furrowed, and there, at the edge of his hairline, where his mahogany curls were pushed back in disarray, a stream of dark red, down his temple.

Her hand flew to his face. "You're bleeding!"

"It's nothing," he said, dodging her touch and pressing the flat of his hand to the skin above the line of her dress, warm and steady. Safe. "Take another breath."

"I'm perfectly able to breathe, Caleb," she said, defiantly. "I live, do I not?"

"Remarkably, yes, considering you nearly got yourself killed."

"Only because I thought you were—" She stopped before she finished the sentence.

His eyes narrowed. "I was what?"

"You are bleeding. Let me—"

He caught her wrist. "You thought I was what, Sesily?"

She twisted in his grip. "I thought you were dead. I saw you on the ground. It . . . distracted me from the fight."

It was the wrong thing to say, he stiffened as though he'd been struck, releasing her. "You should not have been in the fight to begin with. Does your throat . . ." He cleared his own. ". . . does it pain you?"

She swallowed gingerly. "Not much."

"It will. Tomorrow you shall be hoarse."

"I shall be fine," she said, batting his hands away. "I *am* fine. But Caleb, you are bleeding. And you were knocked out, as well. Let me—"

He ducked her touch again, lifting himself onto the opposite seat, pressing himself into the corner, as far from her as possible. "I've no need of your assistance.

You should concern yourself with keeping the contents of your stomach within. We'll be there soon."

"Arrived where?"

"Your sister's home."

The nausea returned. "No."

"It's that or your parents' home."

"Then I choose Park Lane." The big, beautiful family home of the Earl and Countess of Wight.

He nodded. "I'm not exactly dressed for an audience with them, but I suppose they'll understand when I explain the events of the evening."

She cut him a look. "And how do you intend to explain them? Will you begin with the fact that I was perfectly safe until you turned up with your friend from Scotland Yard? Until you fairly summoned a gang of bruisers with your meddling in affairs that are not your own?"

Shock filled his eyes, followed by realization. "You think they were watching Maggie's."

"I think that anyone like Maggie—who prides herself on a place made safe for those who are used to feeling unsafe—is the enemy to those men and whoever funds them." She paused, turning to the fresh air, annoyed by the ache in her throat and the rolling of her stomach. "And I think you would have thought the same if you'd taken a moment to think at all."

He was silent for a long moment in the wake of her censure, and she wondered if he was simply never going to speak again. Perhaps he'd just find the nearest boat and head back to Boston.

No such luck. "That may be true, but there's no question you'd be much safer if your parents bolted the doors and windows to ensure you remain out of trouble."

"I'm not a child, Caleb."

"You think I don't see that?"

She continued as though he had not spoken. "I'm a fully grown woman. I think it's amusing you believe a little thing like a lock would keep me from living my life."

"I believe a little thing like a lock would keep you living. Full stop."

"You're being dramatic," she said.

His eyes went wide. "You were *unconscious*!"

"And now I'm perfectly fine!" Their gazes locked across the carriage, suddenly smaller than it had been. "There is absolutely no reason for you to involve yourself in my affairs. This is none of your concern."

He leveled her with a dark gaze. "Not an hour ago, I dragged you out of a destroyed tavern, Sesily, so I would say this is very much my concern."

She turned back to the window, though she did not think the possibility of being sick was from the motion of the carriage any longer. "I see you have painted yourself the hero here."

"Enlighten me with how this does not end with your entire family thanking me for coming to your aid and taking my—exceedingly reasonable, I might add—suggestion that you be sent to the country. Forever."

She smiled in his direction. "Oh, I've no doubt my mother and father would fall over themselves in gratitude," she said. "Taking their reckless daughter in hand. In fact, I would go so far as to suggest that their thanks would extend to offering you payment you've *no intention* of collecting."

He stilled, and Sesily found herself grateful to discover that Caleb Calhoun remained intelligent, despite all evidence to the contrary in the previous quarter of an hour. "You mean marriage."

Sesily hated the way the words came out, like an unpleasant scrape. A knife pressed too hard against a plate.

But she would never show it. Instead, she brazened it through. "Precisely! My mother would somersault the length of Hyde Park if you plucked me from my dusty shelf. And as for my father . . ." She paused for effect. "Well, consider the dowry carefully, because I'm certain he'd happily part with every hard-won farthing he has if it would encourage you to remove me from my place of honor round his neck."

Caleb's gaze narrowed. "Your parents would never force a marriage between us."

Force. Amazing how so much meaning could be packed into one small word.

She laughed, high and bright like broken glass. "I think my parents would host a wedding for the ages if you deigned to offer for my hand. And I think they'd make it impossible for you not to offer for my hand if you turned up at two o'clock in the morning with me in tow like this, skirts filthy, hair askew."

He watched her in the darkness for a long moment, the dim light casting shadows over his troubled face, the muscle in his jaw working at speed. "You're right."

She hated the words even as she knew that they were the ones she'd been aiming for. Hated her triumph, even as she knew that she didn't want marriage to Caleb any more than he wanted it from her.

But did he have to look so horrified?

She turned to face the breeze. "I know I'm right. But there is no need for you to worry. You are not destined for the parson's noose."

"Why not?"

She cut him a look. "First, as I said, I'm a grown woman, not some girl to be shoved down the aisle. And second, my parents are in the south of France until the spring."

On another night, with a different man, she might have enjoyed the wild play of emotions over his face, delighting in the guilt and surprise and shock and frustration and exasperation he could not hide from her.

But it was not another night. He was not a different man. And Sesily did not enjoy the fact that his final emotion was relief.

"So this was, what, toying with me?"

She flashed him her finest grin. "I told you I was trouble."

"God knows that's true."

"Drop me home, please."

"No." She turned her head, disliking the casual refusal, the way he'd crossed his enormous arms over his enormous chest and leaned back into the corner like this was an American stagecoach and not a perfectly reasonably sized carriage into which he did not fit.

"I beg your pardon?"

"I'm not leaving you alone at Talbot House in the middle of the night."

"Believe it or not, I have spent a fair number of middles of the night at Talbot House."

"Well first, considering your actions tonight, I'm not sure that's true." *Fair, but she wasn't about to admit to that.* "And second, if your parents are not here, you require a chaperone."

Her eyes went wide. "Did you miss the bit in which I am thirty years old?"

"No, Sesily, I've never known a woman so eager to tell me her age." He paused, then, "So we return to my original plan. I'm taking you to your sister."

"No." She'd rather leap from the damn carriage than be delivered to her sister.

He sighed his frustration. "Sesily."

"I don't require a chaperone!" she shouted.

"You do tonight!" he shouted right back.

Lord he was infuriating. "Well then, you'll have to drive me around London until it's safe for me to return to my home. I will not be brought to Haven House in the dead of night."

"Why in hell not?"

There were a thousand reasons. "My sister is not my keeper."

"Neither am I."

"And yet you cannot stop acting like one."

"Goddammit, Sesily, you were nearly killed tonight! In some . . . reckless bid for what . . . attention?"

She was feeling less nauseated at the moment. Indeed, her nausea had been overcome by rage. "A bid for *attention*?"

He had the grace to look away, apparently realizing that he'd misstepped. "I didn't—"

"But you did," she cut him off, her anger rising. "You *did* mean it. Ah, scandalous Sesily, at best a vapid bright eyes, and at worst a tragic lightskirt, but either way, bored and alone without a man or a family to keep her properly leashed. With nothing to do but while away her hours and descend into recklessness."

"I didn't say any of that." The words came on a grumble that might have sounded like guilt.

"Not tonight," she retorted, hating herself for saying it.

His gaze found hers and the air between them crackled like fire. "I've never said it."

"No, but you've thought it," she retorted. "You, like the rest of the world, thought it the moment we met. The worst kind of woman. A wild scandal. A threat. Christened Sexily by the men of London and leans into it, don't you know?"

He came forward like a shot. "Don't. Don't call your-self that."

"Why not? Is it not true?"

She would have laughed at the way he struggled to find the right reply in the darkness. If she weren't so furious with him. "You, like everyone else in London, think life happens to me. That I live by the swing of my skirts and the breeze in my hair. You think I ran into the fray on a lark. And now you return me to my sister, hoping that she will leash me. That she will keep me out of the next fray."

His lips flattened into an impossibly straight line.

"Bollocks that," she said, turning back to the window, the shops of Piccadilly flying by, her sister's home grow-ing ever nearer. "The Place is safety. It is a gift to those of us who don't have the life my sisters have. The one they chose. And when men came for it, I did what any decent person would do—what *you* did, I might add—I fought."

She returned her attention to him, then, anger and frustration rose in her breast, making her want to do more than shout at him. Making her want to shout at ev-ery man who had stepped into O'Tiernen's that evening and threatened that place she loved. "They came for my friends, and I fought. And it wasn't harebrained or mis-guided or a lark. And I didn't do it without thought. And it wasn't stupid and it wasn't reckless and I don't have to explain it to anyone—least of all my sister who *adores* calling me reckless—simply because you couldn't keep your hands off me long enough to walk away. That was *your* mistake. Not mine. And if you feel some false sense of responsibility or guilt or misplaced heroics be-cause of it, that's your problem. I won't pay for it."

The words fairly ran together at the end, trailing off into the heavy silence of the carriage, filled with the sound of wheels and hooves on the cobblestones outside. She watched him for long moments, wondering if he'd even heard her. Wondering if he'd reply, before deciding she didn't care.

She turned to the window as he said, "I was to leave you? Unconscious?"

She breathed deep, swallowing around the ache in her throat, before adding, "I wasn't alone. I had my friends. And I didn't ask for you to play the savior. Indeed, I would not have required a savior at all if not for—"

"—if not for my interference. Yes. You've made that clear." The words were like steel. He was angry.

Good. So was she.

Her stomach began to churn again.

And then, he finally, *finally*, said, "What then?" And there, in his tone, she heard it. He was ceding the fight.

"What then, what?"

"At some point, either under cover of darkness or during full light of day, you're going to have to exit this carriage."

"I don't see why."

"Because it is only a matter of time before you vomit all over it, or the horses require rest. So, where? Where can I take you, where someone will watch over you? Where you will receive the care you require, should you need it?"

She sighed. "I don't need it."

"Not an hour ago, you were nearly dead. I'm not taking you to an empty home to skulk off to your bedchamber as though nothing happened."

Irritating man. "Take me to Trevescan Manor." The duchess had a dozen guest rooms and a penchant for elaborate breakfast spreads.

"No." He shook his head firmly. "The rest of London might not see it, but you four are up to something and I'm not about to leave you to it. Not tonight." He paused, then added, "You took on an opponent who was stronger, larger, and crueler than you tonight."

She waved the words away. "Find me a woman who hasn't had to—"

"Yes, but that's the second time in a week. What in hell are you four up to?"

Shit. This was just what the duchess had feared. Caleb, a man who saw more than most, with a newly piqued interest in their activities. That meant two things: first, they would require information about him. Enough to buy his silence if necessary.

"You're not going to tell me, are you?"

Second, he had to be thrown off the scent. She put her fingers to the bridge of her nose. "Caleb, I have a raging headache, a roiling stomach, and I went head-to-head with a gang of brutes tonight. Please . . ."

He reached up and rapped thrice on the roof.

Instantly, the vehicle turned.

Inhaling sharply and grabbing the sill of the now destroyed window to keep her balance and her stomach, Sesily said, "Where then?"

"My home."

Her eyes went wide.

His home.

What an odd idea. That he had a home.

A place with a hearth and a kitchen and a bedchamber. And a bed. A place full of his secrets, and he was taking her there.

She turned to the window, grateful for an excuse to look away.

To breathe.

She was grateful for the fresh, cool air when he added, "But you shall owe me, Sesily Talbot. And I'm a man who collects."

Sesily could hear the truth in the words—even as they pooled inside her, less a threat, and more a promise, making her wonder at the way he might collect from her. With another man, in another place, at another time, she might have had the courage to ask him to be more clear.

With another man, in another place, at another time, she mightn't have cared so much about his response.

But she did, and so she remained silent—heroically silent, if she was being honest—afraid that if she pushed him, he'd return to his original plan, and take her to her sister.

The carriage turned off Piccadilly and up Regent Street, bypassing Mayfair altogether. She bit her tongue, refusing to speak as they entered the new neighborhood, where she knew he kept a home.

A home that had been open twice in the two years she'd known him.

Not that she'd noticed.

Not that she'd gone looking.

The carriage slowed, making several quick turns in succession into a web of the quiet streets of Marylebone, the silence within accentuating the turning of her stomach. When the vehicle stopped, she didn't wait for anyone to open the door, instead scrambling out onto the street. The fresh air in the carriage had helped, but nothing cured carriage sickness like solid ground.

Only then did she consider Number Two, Wesley Street—clean and well-maintained in three floors rising up from the quiet, tree-lined row. The carriage set off, and Sesily slid a look up and down the street. Not a soul to be seen.

"Inside," he commanded in a low grumble as he pushed past her, up the steps to the bright white door, and set a key to the lock. This was it. Caleb Calhoun's London home.

He stepped back from the door to reveal the darkness within, barely lit by the light from the single lantern left on a small table just inside the door, presumably by an enterprising servant before they'd taken to their bed.

"Thank you," she said, happily, enjoying the surprise and irritation on his handsome face as she pushed past him into the foyer of the home, which smelled exactly like him. Amber and leather and paper and scotch. She took a moment to breathe in the place—his London sanctuary—as he increased the light from the lantern, allowing just enough to make out the space he'd called his home.

There was a sitting room to her left, and in the dim light, she found a low settee and a large, leather upholstered chair, each facing a large, ornate hearth where a fire had been banked. Those invisible servants again.

A small table sat covered in papers—presumably related to the tavern that he and her sister owned. Or perhaps one of the dozen he owned in America.

"Your study?" she asked.

"No one comes here. The rooms all serve equal purpose."

She entered the room, and her slippers were lost in the thick pile of the carpet, lusher than any she'd ever trod before. She couldn't help her smile. Caleb Calhoun might play the simple American, needing little more than a crust of bread and a pallet of hay for survival, but he liked a decent carpet. A large chair.

"I apologize for the . . ." He trailed off, waving a hand at the papers before raking his fingers through his hair. Was he nervous? "I wasn't expecting you."

She gave him a little smile. "I wasn't expecting me, either."

He was not amused. Instead, he cleared his throat and turned away from the room, toward the staircase at the far end of the hallway.

She followed, unable to resist peeking into another room as she passed its open door. It was too dark inside, but she registered a great, hulking piece of furniture within. A pianoforte, perhaps? Then light was gone and Caleb with it. Sesily hurried to keep up, reaching him at the base of the staircase that rose to darkness above.

She lifted her skirts and followed him to the first floor and then the second, where he paused outside another open door, the only light inside from the embers of another banked fire.

A bedchamber.

Sesily's heart began to pound. He entered and she waited at the door as he busied himself with more light, wondering how to artfully present herself so that when he turned around, she appeared both innocent and tempting.

Come on, Sesily. You've done this before.

She'd broken her fair share of hearts. Surely she could make sure this American noticed her.

He never noticed her.

Wasn't that how he'd broken *her* heart? By not noticing her? By making it clear that he wanted nothing to do with her?

Memory came, summoned by darkness, as it always did.

They'd been outside her sister's country house, and Sesily had made every effort to tempt him with her winning smiles and clever retorts and magnificent curves, this impossible man, who'd refused her even as she'd known he wanted her.

I know better than to get anywhere near you, he'd said. *You want love.*

She'd resisted the words then, telling herself he was wrong. Love was for other women. Women who wanted marriage and children and large country houses with follies and lakes and things.

Sesily didn't want love. She wanted *him*, and nothing more. Nothing complicated. Except Caleb Calhoun was nothing *but* complicated.

If he was the only man she'd ever wanted, and couldn't have, so be it.

Sesily crossed her arms over her chest, memory and frustration flaring as she resisted the instinct to capture his interest again. She'd done that enough, and to no avail. And besides, even if she could interest this enormous American, tonight was not the night for it.

She was tired, and would likely be sore in the morning.

As he lit what seemed like the hundredth candle within the large room, it occurred to Sesily that this was a very nice bedchamber. Complete with a very nice bed, that she would happily sleep in.

Except, as she took in that very nice bed, the stack of books on a small table at the far side of it, and the fire in the hearth—it occurred to Sesily that this was not simply a very nice bedchamber.

"This is *your* bedchamber," she said.

He grunted a reply from where he fussed with a lantern, and her jaw went slightly slack. Surely he didn't mean for her to . . . for them to . . .

She put the thought—and the instant zing of response she had to it—away. Instead focusing on his work. "You have a lot of candles."

He held a match to a lantern at the far end of the room. "Doesn't everyone?"

Not like this. "Do you read a great deal in the evenings?"

"I like to see what I am doing."

"What? Or whom?" The bawdy question caught his attention, and he looked to her. *A hit.* "Ah. You finally noticed me."

His gaze narrowed, as though he had something choice to say, but he did not share it, because the lamp caught in that moment, and the flame singed his fingers. He hissed a curse that Sesily thought might have been for both her *and* the lamp, and snapped the glass door closed. "Believe it or not, Sesily, I am not elated at your presence here. It is a last resort."

Of course it was. But he didn't have to say it, did he? She swallowed the sting to her pride, came off the door, and entered the room. "You needn't rewrite history, American. I proposed a perfectly good alternative."

He didn't move, but he watched her carefully as she approached the bed. She set her fingers to the counterpane and said, "If you prefer me to be out of sight, I am happy to take a lesser chamber."

His gaze flickered to where she touched the bed, then back to her. "It is the only one in the house."

She tilted her head. "There is only one bedchamber."

He scowled. "I'm never here. I do not require guest quarters."

She smiled. "So, there is only one bed."

He moved to cross the room, for the door. "It is yours."

"Caleb," she said, when he was close—near enough to touch if she tried. Not that she did. "I cannot push you from your bed."

He looked to her, a retort on his tongue. She could see it, thanks to the lights all around the room making it impossible not to. But before he could speak, the lights made it impossible for her to hide from him as well— from his eyes focused on her cheek.

His brow furrowed, something like disgust flashing, and Sesily flinched. "I-is there something—" She put a hand to her cheek. "On my face?"

It took longer than it should have for him to answer, and she watched as a muscle flickered at his jaw, as though he were resisting saying precisely what he was thinking. "You're . . ." He trailed off, his gaze tracking over her face, to her neck, to the bare skin above the tight line of her dress.

It had been a long time since Sesily had dressed for anyone but herself, but now, here, she wished she had a looking glass, to see herself through his eyes.

Did she want that, really?

She pushed the thought aside. "What is it?"

The question seemed to pull him from his thoughts. He shook his head. "You should wash."

And with that, he left the room.

Chapter Seven

It was a mistake, of course. Nothing good would come of having Sesily at his home in the dead of night.

Caleb knew about bad decisions. He'd made more than a few in his lifetime—decisions that risked his life and rewrote his future. He knew that they came from unchecked emotions. And he made it his goal to keep emotion in check.

But Sesily was pure emotion. She was joy and anger and delight and sadness and frustration and a dozen others at any given moment, and that made her equal parts tempting and terrifying, like an inferno. Which was why Caleb had made himself a promise two years ago, when he'd first been singed by her fire, that he'd stay as far from her as possible. He was a man of sense, and he knew the score.

But as he'd watched Sesily go limp in the arms of a thug in The Place, as rage and panic raced through him without outlet, sense had disappeared. And Caleb, too, had been pure emotion. He couldn't remember the time between his coming to on the sticky tavern floor and carrying Sesily out of the fray, and that worried him more than a little. Without sense, fury had led. Followed by fear. And that combination, he knew from experience, was dangerous.

When sense had returned in the carriage, he should have returned it to the fore. But she'd opened her eyes and fear had been chased away by relief, and then, as she became enraged with what had happened and his plans for her, by guilt . . . which somehow, impossibly, made him more unhinged.

At least, he told himself it was emotion that unhinged him. The other possibility was not worth considering. That it was Sesily herself.

So. Whether it was guilt or relief or fury or fear . . . they'd careened toward his refuge, where he did not welcome guests. Where he certainly never intended to welcome her.

And then he'd led her to his bedchamber.

To his bed.

Telling himself that he was ignoring the rustling of her lush silk skirts, loud like gunshot. That he could not hear her soft breath barely-there and somehow all around him. That he did not detect the scent of her, wild and beautiful and making him think of warm sunshine and almonds.

That she wasn't soft and curved and warm and lush as a treat in a shop window, drawing him tighter and tighter on a string as he'd busied himself with light in the dark room, telling himself that it would chase away all the dark, sinful things he wished to do to her.

And then he'd turned and looked at her, and he realized the light had been a mistake, because it was suddenly easy to see the dark smudge at her cheek from the tavern floor and the one that matched it on the golden skin at the low neckline of her chest. And in between, the bruises on her neck—a reminder of how close she'd come to danger. To worse.

The rage had returned, and Caleb had left, not trusting himself to speak, let alone to stay.

Not trusting himself to remain distant and unmoved by this woman who always seemed too close. Too moving.

But leaving had been a mistake, too, because somehow, in the handful of minutes she'd been in the house, she'd filled it up, and there was nowhere to escape. Caleb had busied himself in the kitchens, making her warm milk—telling himself that if he treated her as he would a child, she'd leave his thoughts, and ignoring the fact that his housekeeper would almost certainly take him to task for using the wrong saucepan.

Perhaps she'd take him to task for all the sinful thoughts he could not put out of his head, as well.

The milk was another mistake, as when it was done, he had no choice but to return to her. Which he did, even as he told himself he didn't wish to. Even as he told himself that he should find his way to a comfortable chair on the ground floor and doze until morning, when he would return her to her home. Safe.

It would not be the least comfortable place he had spent an evening.

But what if she needed him?

What if she had trouble breathing in the night?

What if the men who'd attacked in Covent Garden found her here?

What if they'd been followed? Caleb hadn't been in his right mind; he should have paid closer attention. He could have put her in danger. Again.

So he returned, warm milk in hand, up the stairs. Telling himself that he was acting with nobility. Protecting the lady. Fucking gentlemanlike.

He knocked on the bedchamber door and she called out for him to enter. He did, immediately grateful that she'd extinguished a good half of the candles, making it easier to avoid looking at her.

Excellent. He'd simply set the milk on the bedside table and take his leave. The hallway beyond was perfectly comfortable for one night's sleep. It wasn't as though he was going to sleep, anyway.

As soon as he made sure she was breathing, he would leave.

As soon as he was certain she was comfortable.

Caleb was not a monster, and he was perfectly capable of avoiding this woman. He'd done it before. It had been from across an ocean, but it was fine.

He would barely notice her in his bed.

In fact, he could not notice her in his bed, as she wasn't in his bed.

She was behind the bathing screen.

Bathing.

And then all gentlemanliness was out the damned window.

Her dress—the color of temptation—was draped over a chair near the screen, which meant it wasn't on her body. Not that Caleb required superior powers of reasoning to discern that, as he could see her behind the screen. She'd brought a light with her, and so she was cast in shadow against the screen, a perfectly ordinary sailcloth that Caleb had never imagined was so revealing.

But with Sesily bent over the washbasin, it might as well have been a clear windowpane, her silhouette lush and fucking perfect as she straightened and ran a cloth lazily up her arm and behind her neck.

"You're washing," he said, because it was something to say. He should turn away.

It was Sesily who turned, the pretty swells of her curves stealing what was left of his breath. "You told me to," she said, continuing her lazy movements, as though it were all perfectly ordinary.

Christ. He had, hadn't he? And he'd meant it. He'd wanted her to erase the evening from her body. From her memory, just as he'd wanted to erase it from his own.

Except now, as he watched her, he couldn't imagine ever forgetting this evening.

"Caleb?" The word, curious and soft, returned him to sense.

Shit. He was still watching her. He coughed, his face suddenly burning at the idea that he'd been caught staring, and turned his back on her, setting the milk on the nearest surface. "Aye."

A smile in her voice. "Careful, American, you almost sounded like a Brit there."

He stilled at the words before grasping at them. "Never."

"It's not so bad here, is it?" she said, as though everything was perfectly aboveboard and he wasn't staring at his boots or the carpet or the molding on the ceiling or at anything but her shadow, flickering like pure temptation.

Was she nude back there?

"If you were in Boston less," she added, "you might enjoy it here more."

"I have to be in Boston," he said, the words low and forbidding, as though even his voice knew what was good for him. It was the truth. He had businesses in Boston. A home. A handful of decent friends. A life.

And every time he set foot in London, he risked it all.

He pretended not to notice as she continued her ablutions, not to hear the water swishing in the washbasin—it had to be cold if she'd used the clean water that had been left in the pitcher, but he wasn't about to offer to warm it, nor to wonder if she was using his soap, and what it would smell like on her.

"And yet here you are," she replied. "Why?"

"Your sister is having a baby." It wasn't the whole truth, but it wasn't a complete lie, either.

There was no mistaking the humor in the tone when she said, "I was not aware that you were a midwife."

He scowled and turned away, to the window where he stared out across the Marylebone rooftops. "Someone needs to keep the Sparrow in order while she . . . continues broodmaking."

"Broodmaking!"

Sesily's laugh warmed him from behind the screen, and he moved closer, knowing he shouldn't. Unable to stop himself. "Would you call it something else?"

"As I am one of five, Sera and Haven haven't quite hit the brood mark for me. Two seems a perfectly reasonable number of children if you like that sort of thing."

"Mmm," he said. "And do you? Like that sort of thing?"

"Children?"

"Mmm." Why on earth was he asking? Sesily Talbot's interest in children had no bearing on his life.

"I shall have you know, I am a superior aunt."

"Are you?"

"There are nine of them. Sera and Mal's newest will be number ten."

"Good God."

"I could not agree more," she said. "But I am excellent at the climbing of trees, the making of mud, and the annoying of parents . . . three things that are absolute requirements for decent aunts."

He couldn't help the half smile that came at the reply. "I thought aunts were supposed to be better behaved than children."

"As it is the children that define the role, I think it's only fair to let the children set the expectations for it."

He did laugh at that, a surprised bark that he bit back as soon as it released. "And you meet them."

"How insulting," she said. "I *exceed* them."

Of course she did. Sesily Talbot made a life by exceeding expectations.

Not that he was going to admit that.

"Well," she said after a while. "You are a good friend, coming when Sera asked. This time . . . and the last."

He was a terrible friend, lusting after Sera's sister in his bedchamber in the dead of night. "She made me godfather to her son. It's difficult to refuse to come for the christening."

He regretted the words the moment they were out of his mouth. The memory of the last time he'd been in London. The last time he'd seen Sesily, at little Oliver's christening, surrounded by her family, happy and beautiful.

Except when she looked at him.

Which hadn't been often. He'd noticed, because he'd found it impossible not to look at her.

He cleared his throat, knowing he ought to leave. Sesily was safe despite her trial, and his presence was not required. There was no reason for him to be there, in the chamber, while the woman washed. Not even with his back to her, not even studiously avoiding the mottled reflection of the privacy screen in the dark window.

"I don't suppose you have a dressing gown?"

He turned toward the question to find her peeking her head around the side of the screen, her dark hair coming loose from its moorings, her cheeks pink from the cold water, her blue eyes wide with the question.

The question . . . which was . . .

Did he have a dressing gown?

"A dressing gown," he said.

"My dress is quite filthy, and I'd rather not sleep in it."

"Of course not," he said. So, she wanted a piece of his clothing. Again, perfectly ordinary.

Clearly, he was being punished.

"I don't think you would like it if I popped out in my chemise," she added happily.

On the contrary, Caleb imagined he'd like that very much, but instead he clenched his teeth and said, "Right."

The whole fucking night was a mistake.

He went to the wardrobe and rustled around inside, looking for something suitable to give to the unmarried sister of his business partner whom he'd studiously avoided from across an ocean for the last two years before returning just in time to kiss her in a garden and see her attacked by ruffians in Covent Garden.

Something appropriate for a woman after whom he absolutely did not lust.

Sadly, the wardrobe lacked a suit of armor.

Grabbing the nearest thing he could find, he turned and shoved it around the edge of the screen, barely hesitating to make sure that she had received it before returning to the safety of the window.

A pause, and then, "So you do not have a dressing gown."

"I don't require one." When she did not reply, he felt compelled to elaborate—though he had no idea why. "I have three servants and no valet, and no one enters the room when I am abed or undressed."

"No one?"

He turned at the question. How could he not? The woman was asking him about lovers.

And yet, before he could answer, she was speaking, quick and clearly nervous. "I'm sorry. That was not . . ." She stepped out from behind the screen. "Appropriate."

Dear God, he was being tested.

She should have looked ridiculous. She was wearing one of his topcoats over her chemise, and everything about it was out of proportion. The whole thing was too long, the shoulders too broad, and the line of the lapels did nothing to hide the thin lawn beneath and, beneath that, the swell of her breasts.

And the chemise was so impossibly thin, he could *see* her. The curve of her midsection, her thighs, and between them—

Don't look. A gentleman wouldn't look.

A dark shadow that made his mouth water.

She shrugged. "I hope you're right."

What was she talking about?

"Hmm?" he replied, the sound like wheels on rough cobblestones.

Pull yourself together, man.

"That no one will enter," she replied, approaching. "I'm sure I look absurd."

She looked like land after a month at sea.

He resisted the urge to retreat. Not that retreat was an option with his back pressed to the window. He supposed leaping to the street below was an unreasonable course of action.

Though it was not the worst idea he'd ever heard as she drew nearer. "You really should have a dressing gown on hand."

"In case I find myself with another woman who refuses to go home?"

A light flashed in her eyes. "I expect you are no stranger to women who do not wish to go home."

"I am sorry to disappoint you."

She laughed, close enough for the sound to feel like a secret, and he liked it too much. He couldn't like her laugh. That way lay danger. That way, and all the other ways, it seemed. Her eyes, a rich, beautiful blue, ringed in black. Her heart-shaped face and her pink cheeks and her wide mouth and full lips that were all the more dangerous now that he knew the taste of them.

"How do you feel?" he asked, willing normalcy into this entirely abnormal moment.

She stopped her approach, setting a hand to the smooth skin of her neck, already shadowed with a blossoming bruise. "Not bad."

But not good, either. He gritted his teeth. He should have killed the man who'd touched her.

He'd wanted to kill him.

But even more, he'd wanted Sesily safe.

"Tomorrow it shall be sore," he said.

She smiled. "More importantly, tomorrow, it shall be an *eyesore*."

"No one will care about that." It would take more than a bruised neck to make Sesily Talbot an eyesore.

Before the words were even out, her brow was furrowing, her gaze focusing on him. She was reaching for him. "You're still bleeding."

He didn't think he could stand her touching him. Not like this. Here.

He turned his head. "It's nothing."

She frowned. "It's not nothing." She spun away from him, slipping behind the screen before reappearing with a strip of linen in her hand. "Let me—"

He ducked away from her touch. "No."

"Caleb—"

"No. I am fine. You should rest. Or do you need reminding that you were unconscious not an hour ago?"

"*You* were also unconscious."

"It was nothing."

"It was *not* nothing. You've taken a blow to the head, and you are bleeding."

"Leave it," he growled, catching her wrist in his grasp. "Sesily. Leave it."

She went still, her gaze hot on his, and he knew she had no intention of leaving it. But he did not imagine that she would say, "You have cared well for me; my sister will be grateful."

And he did not imagine how irritated he would be by the reference to Seraphina. "She is a good friend."

"And you have done right by your friend, caring for her sister." She paused. "Now, let me do right by my sister and care for her friend."

He put a hand to his brow, touching the place that stung. "It's not bleeding. Not any longer."

"It should be cleaned."

"I will do it when you sleep."

"Why not let me do it now, and we shall both sleep?"

As though he would sleep with her there.

Another impasse. Another silence, full of strong will. He sighed, releasing her. "You're incredibly stubborn."

"And you, so biddable," she retorted before smiling. "Anyway, it is part of my charm."

"Is that what it is? Charm?"

"You haven't noticed my charms?" He flinched at the sting of the cloth at his forehead, and she stilled, looking into his eyes. "You wound me."

"It's impossible not to notice you." Shit. He hadn't meant to say it.

Her lips curved in a barely-there smile and she returned her attention to her work. "Careful now, Mr. Calhoun . . . you'll turn my head."

Knowing he shouldn't, he watched her focused attention on his wound—her narrowed gaze and her furrowed brow, a tiny bit of her bottom lip caught between her teeth. He wanted to stroke his thumb over that furrow. Smooth that lip. Kiss it.

But she wasn't for stroking. Or kissing.

She wasn't for him.

That mouth wasn't for him. It didn't matter that he'd kissed it less than a week earlier.

"Do you remember the first time we ever spoke?" The soft question distracted him and he met her eyes, no longer on his wound, but now on him.

Heroically, he pulled away from her touch, putting space between them. "You were doing your best to scandalize a battalion of matchmaking mothers."

She smiled and shook her head. "I mean the first time we ever spoke *alone*, but I am impressed that you remember our first meeting."

He remembered every minute he'd ever spent in her company, unfortunately. And he knew what she was about to say. The memory she was about to invoke, even though he thought of it so often it barely felt like memory.

Sesily Talbot, inveterate flirt. Teasing him with a hint of what they might have if he gave in to temptation.

You see how good it would be. Like it was inevitable.

And it had been terrifying in its temptation.

But he couldn't admit that he remembered it. That way lay a path to destruction. So, instead, he said, "You set a feral cat on me."

"Brummell doesn't like men," she said offhandedly, as she finished her work at his brow. She tilted her head, and Caleb imagined she saw the truth and was disappointed in him. "Do you have a mistress?"

"What?"

"Am I keeping you from someone?"

Tell her yes.

It was an easy escape.

"No."

She studied him for a long moment, and he wondered what she would do. He'd spent a lifetime priding himself on his understanding of other people—on being able to predict their actions. And somehow, he could never see Sesily Talbot coming.

After a careful inspection, she seemed satisfied with his answer. She nodded once and turned, heading for the far side of the bed.

He took it as his cue, making his way around the room, extinguishing the candles she'd left burning, until there was only one left, on the table next to the bed. The bed she was now in.

Ignoring the way the realization sizzled through him, heightening each of his senses, Caleb found a chair by the dwindling fire, extending his legs before he said, "I shall be here if you need me."

"I'm sure it will be—"

"Nevertheless, I don't want you to have to search a strange house if you require assistance," he grumbled, crossing his arms over his chest. "The last thing I need to explain to your sister is how you broke your neck in my home in the dead of night."

He hated himself a bit as the irritated words hung in the silence.

An eternity passed before she said, "I am very grateful for your help this evening."

"It was—"

"Yes, I know," she cut him off, and it was impossible to miss the curt irritation in her words. "It was the least you could do for your friend." It was what he should have said, if not what he would have said, and so he stayed quiet until she added, "I don't suppose I could convince you not to tell my sister about tonight? I would appreciate being spared a lecture."

"I expect she'd have one for me, too."

"Maybe," she replied, and he thought he heard a smile in her tone. "But mine will be worse."

Her anger and frustration from earlier echoed, and he wanted to ease it even as he knew he shouldn't. "You weren't reckless."

The silence that stretched between them wasn't easy. It was full of awareness, as though she hovered in the low light, listening, waiting for more. He refused to look in her direction.

"You were . . ." He trailed off, regretting ever starting.

After a long moment—an age—she said, "What was I?"

He searched for the answer. Finally settled on, "You were Athena."

More silence. Easy this time.

"I won't tell your sister."

A long, slow breath from across the room, like a gift. Then a quiet, "Thank you."

He willed it to be the last thing she said that evening. He wasn't sure he could take more.

And then, in the darkness, "Why do you have so many candles?"

He shouldn't respond. Every question this woman asked brought them closer, when it was absolutely imperative that he keep them apart. When the answers to them threatened to reveal more than he'd ever shared with anyone.

And still, knowing all that, he said, "I don't like the dark."

She didn't reply for a long time, long enough for him to think she'd fallen asleep. And then, "I shall leave this one burning, then."

He sat in the dim light, the single candle flickering at her bedside, painting shadows on the ceiling, and he considered all the reasons he shouldn't be in that room. All the reasons he shouldn't be anywhere near Sesily Talbot ever again.

She was his friend's sister.

And she was unmarried.

And she was the purest form of temptation.

I know precisely what you want. But I am willing to wait for you to discover it yourself. The words she'd whispered outside the tavern earlier in the evening, a promise. A temptation. An invitation.

One he wanted to accept. One that promised another taste of her. A taste that maybe would be enough. A taste that—maybe—would clear her from his thoughts.

Because she would never, ever be for him.

Never.

"Caleb?"

He sighed. But did she have to say his name like that? In the darkness? Like it was just the two of them in the wide world? "Hmm?"

"You're not keeping me from anyone, either."

The words might have shocked another man, but they didn't shock him, and he didn't think they were meant to. She was a grown woman long off the marriage mart, and he didn't fool himself into believing that she'd never had a lover. But still—"Why would you tell me that?"

"I thought you might like to know."

It was an invitation, and it sizzled through him, making him ache with want. In all his life, he didn't think he'd ever heard anything he liked so much.

But he didn't wish to like it. And he certainly didn't wish to know that Sesily spent her nights alone, just as he did.

Knowing that made him want to rectify the situation.

And long ago, long before he'd known Sesily Talbot, he'd made choices that made a future with her—with anyone—impossible.

Still, he thought about her words all night long, playing them over and over in his head until the candle burned to its end, flickering out just before dawn streaked across the sky, and he vowed to be done with Sesily Talbot that very day.

Chapter Eight

"You're in a foul mood."

Caleb looked up from where he polished the ebony bar of The Singing Sparrow, to meet the eyes of Seraphina Bevingstoke, Duchess of Haven—his business partner and the only person he knew brave enough to comment on his foul mood.

Well, one of only two people.

The other one had put him in the foul mood, but he wasn't about to admit that. To Sera or to himself.

In fact, he'd spent the morning telling himself that his mood was because he'd fallen asleep in that uncomfortable chair in his bedchamber, resulting in a wicked crick in his neck, and not because when he'd woken with said crick in neck, Sesily had been gone.

Skulked out at the crack of dawn what must have been minutes after he finally slept, somehow collecting her dress and letting herself out of the house without notice.

Presumably to skulk into her own house sometime later.

It should have made him happy. After all, the only time worse than the dead of night to return an injured woman to her home on the most coveted block in Mayfair was first thing in the morning. And Sesily had saved Caleb the trouble.

It was sorted.

He never had to think of the woman again.

"I'm not in a foul mood," he said to her sister, returning his attention to the gleaming wood. "I'm busy."

She looked up from the crate of candles she was unpacking. "At half past nine in the morning."

"People are busy at half past nine in the morning."

"You don't have to tell me that," she retorted. "I have a business and a child. By half past nine in the morning, I'm ready for luncheon."

He sighed, then looked to her. "Then what is the problem?"

"You are never busy at half past nine in the morning. And if you are—it's for one of two reasons. One." She lifted an imperious finger. "You've not yet been to bed, or two"—a second snapped up to match the first—"you're in a foul mood."

His gaze narrowed on her. "You know, I am beginning to feel a mood coming on. I wonder why that would be."

She grinned. "Me, likely."

"I've never liked you."

"Watch it, Calhoun."

Caleb's gaze flickered over Seraphina's shoulder to land on her husband, seated where he always was when Sera was here—at the table by the door, spectacles on, poring over a pile of documents. "I've *really* never liked him."

The duke didn't look up. "The feeling is mutual, American."

Caleb turned away and headed for the stockroom at the far end of the tavern, intending to move a few dozen heavy boxes from one side of the room to the other in a bid to avoid conversation.

Sera had other plans, following him.

He opened the door to the stockroom to discover that it was not empty. Inside, Fetu Mamoe, The Singing Sparrow's second-in-command, looked up from where he was shifting crates of booze from one side of the room to the other. He turned and looked to Caleb, then Sera. "What's he doing here?"

"I own the place!" Caleb retorted.

The Samoan's brows rose.

"He's in a foul mood," Sera pointed out. "Which is why he appears to have forgotten that we, also, own the place."

When they'd opened the tavern two years earlier—Caleb's first and only business on British soil—he and Seraphina had done so as equal partners. Not soon after, they'd hired Fetu away from his cargo hook on the docks, and he'd made the place infinitely better. Within months, they'd offered him a percentage of The Singing Sparrow's take. And now, years later, the business thrived in large part to Fetu's calm presence and keen ability to keep it running like a well-oiled timepiece.

"He also appears to have forgotten that we own the place all year round, and not only when we feel like turning up in London."

"I turn up in London when you ask me to!" Caleb argued.

"Well, that doesn't mean it wouldn't be nice to see you more frequently," Sera quipped.

Caleb ignored her, turning to his other partner. "Alright, Fetu?"

Fetu nodded. "Alright." He handed Caleb a crate of gin before pointing to the far side of the room. "Over there."

Grateful for the distraction, Caleb did as he was told. But when he turned back, it was to discover that

Seraphina had taken up residence in the stockroom doorway. Accepting another crate from Fetu, Caleb did his best to ignore her.

Unfortunately, it seemed that one of the family traits of the Talbot sisters was an inability to be ignored. He moved two more crates before he gave in. "Goddammit, Sera. What?"

Dark brows rose, and she turned a knowing look on Fetu.

"Say I'm in a foul mood one more time," Caleb warned.

She rested her hands over her increasing midsection. "I can't watch you move things about like a brute? In shirtsleeves as well; we could sell tickets."

Fetu snorted a laugh.

Caleb clenched his teeth and headed for more crates. "If you hadn't married a duke, you could ask your husband to move things in shirtsleeves for your entertainment."

"The fact that he's a duke makes it all even more entertaining."

Caleb rolled his eyes and hefted a cask of whiskey onto his shoulder and approached, feeling irrationally pleased when she had to move out of the doorway to let him pass. "Funny how you say you're busy," he grumbled, returning to the bar and setting the oak barrel to the ground to work the cork out of its seat. "Feels like you've got nothing to do."

"Mmm," she replied noncommittally, installing herself at the edge of his vision, in the path of his escape. "What happened to your head?"

"Nothing." He resisted the urge to touch the wound that Sesily had tended the evening before. In his bedchamber. Where he'd resisted a different, baser urge to defile her.

He certainly wasn't telling her sister *that*.

"Looks like something," Fetu called from inside the stockroom.

The two of them were enjoying irritating him.

"It's nothing," Caleb said.

"Mmm," Sera said again. "Do you know, I heard something fascinating this morning."

He popped the cork and reached for an unused tap. "Scandal at the dressmaker's?"

"You know, you really are so droll, Caleb. I never tire at your endless amusement at the expense of my title."

"It's not your title I mock. It's the world it comes with."

"You like the way that world spends money here."

"Indeed, I do." Ensuring the tap was seated and sealed, he hefted the cask once more and slid it into place on the strong shelf behind the bar.

"Anyway, as I said, I heard something fascinating."

"Technically, *I* heard it," Fetu said from the doorway.

"Fair enough."

"And the two of you had a nice gossip this morning before I turned up?"

"Amazing that we exist when you are not on the page, isn't it?" Sera retorted, and if Caleb had been less in his head, he might have heard the edge in her words. She looked to Fetu. "Would you like to tell him?"

"Nah," he replied, looking very comfortable against the doorjamb. "I'll watch."

"Word is, The Bully Boys raided Maggie O'Tiernen's last night."

Caleb froze, his hands still on the front of the oak barrel.

"Word *also* is . . ." Here it was. "That *you* were at Maggie O'Tiernen's last night."

"Word from who?" He looked to Fetu.

The big man shrugged a heavy shoulder. "A woman I know."

"Biblically, no doubt."

"A gentleman never tells."

"He tells my business, though, don't he?" Caleb retorted.

That shrug again, as Sera added sweetly, "Not just your business though, because . . . and this is the really strange thing . . . I heard you carried *my unconscious sister out of there.*"

He looked to the ceiling. "Fucking hell."

And then Sera wasn't enjoying it. She was furious. "Fucking hell is right!" He turned to face her as she came for him, setting both her hands on his chest and shoving him backward.

He let her, but not without an aggrieved, "Hey! Watch it!"

"No, I don't think I will watch it! You're lucky I don't crack you over the head with one of these bottles!"

"Sera . . ." her husband said, from a distance, barely looking up from his work. "Gentle."

Caleb didn't imagine the Duke of Haven was suggesting she be gentle for his sake. He spread his hands wide as she kept coming for him. "Nothing happened."

She stilled, tall and beautiful as a queen, and looked at him like he'd grown a second head. "Nothing happened."

He shook his head. "Nothing."

"Mal?" She looked past Caleb toward her husband at the door. "If I murder him . . ."

"I know people," Haven said, unconcerned with their argument. He might not like Caleb personally, but he knew that Sera was safe with him.

"Please," Caleb replied. "She doesn't need your people. These two have a clear line to half the criminals in Covent Garden."

Sera returned her attention to him. "Any number of whom would happily see an American tossed into the Thames like tea, I'll remind you, so I'd be very careful with how you play this."

Fetu laughed again and Caleb threw him a look over his shoulder. "You're a traitor."

"I admit, I enjoy the theater."

Caleb rolled his eyes and Sera said, "Nothing happened?"

"Nothing," Caleb repeated.

"Caleb, was my sister unconscious at The Place?"

He froze. "Yes."

She nodded. "And when you carried her from there, she remained unconscious?"

"Yes."

"And that is when you packed her into a carriage and drove off with her."

He looked to Fetu. "Your girl really pays close attention."

"I'm thinking of keeping her."

"So you did drive off with her," Sera said, "because that was the bit that I found most fascinating, because at no point last night was I awakened by you turning up to deliver my injured sister into my care."

"Sera, I—"

"Mal?" she asked without looking away from Caleb.

"Yes, love?"

Caleb crossed his arms over his chest as Sera replied, "Were you awakened last night by Caleb turning up to deliver my injured sister into our care?"

"No, love."

"The two of you really ought to take this charming patter to the stage," Caleb said, dryly.

She looked to him. "I ought to punch you in the gob."

"Not in your condition," Haven warned.

"He has a point," Caleb pointed out. "You really shouldn't be exerting yourself, looking the way you do."

Fetu coughed.

Sera tilted her head. "Oh? How, exactly, do I look?"

The words were a warning Caleb didn't immediately understand. "As though you might produce a babe at any moment."

Haven looked up from his work then and said, happily, "Mistake, that, American."

Sera narrowed her gaze on him. "I assure you, Calhoun, I'm more than able to produce a babe *and* deliver you a facer for taking my sister to God knows where, unconscious—"

"She wasn't unconscious for long. She came to in the carriage."

"Ah, well," Sera said dramatically, "then you took my sister to God knows where, conscious, *after a recent bout of unconsciousness*."

"It wasn't God knows where."

A pause. "No? Then where was it?"

He hesitated.

She looked past him to Fetu, who said, "My information ends with the carriage door closing."

She returned her attention to Caleb. "You're telling me everything now, dammit. That's my sister! Where did you take her?"

She didn't know. For everything Seraphina knew, she didn't know the full truth of the prior evening. "I took her to Marylebone."

She blinked, surprise and confusion on her brow. "*Where* in Marylebone?"

"To my town house."

She snapped back at the words. "To your *what*?"

Silence fell, and Caleb was grateful for the shadows of the pub despite the full daylight outside, because they hid the hot wash of . . . embarrassment? Guilt? Something else? . . . that threatened.

"*I've* never even been to your town house."

He smirked. "Are you angling for an invitation?"

She ignored the retort, instead watching him for a long moment. "That's why you're in a foul mood."

"I'm not in a—"

"Caleb, did you seduce my sister?"

There was a shuffling of feet behind him, and Fetu coughed, apparently no longer feeling comfortable watching the theater, because he grumbled an excuse and the stockroom door closed with a snap.

Nevertheless, Caleb would wager the annual income of his other eleven taverns that the man had his ear pressed to the door at that very moment.

Sera stared him down. "Caleb."

"No. Christ, no." The truth. Thank God. She didn't need to know there were several moments when he'd been tempted to. "I carried her out of The Place after she'd been rendered unconscious. One would think your first question would be inquiring about her condition."

"I don't need to inquire about her condition," she said. "Even if I did not know that she returned home with the sun, I know you well enough to know you would have cared for her if she needed it."

Before he had a chance to ask how she would know Sesily had returned home that morning, the rest of Sera's words landed. He was both humbled and guilt-ridden at her easy, unwavering faith in his decency.

He'd watched Sesily bathe, for God's sake.

He'd catalogued the curves and shadows of her body.

He'd fallen asleep aching for her. Woken the same way. There'd been nothing decent about it.

Sera was still asking questions. "Did she seduce you?"

His brows rose. "No."

You're not keeping me from anyone, either.

"Did she offer to?"

The words shouldn't have bothered him. It shouldn't have mattered that Seraphina—like the rest of London— believed that Sesily would attempt to seduce him. What was it she'd said? *Scandalous Sesily, at best a vapid bright eyes, and at worst a tragic lightskirt.*

"You really aren't playing the doting older brother role well, Sera," he replied. "You ought to remember that generally they don't insult the honor of their sisters quite so readily."

"And again! So droll!" Seraphina said before adding, matter-of-factly, "I'm not playing some archaic role; Sesily can take care of her own honor."

It was Caleb's turn to be surprised.

"She's a grown woman and more than capable of taking a lover safely." She paused before adding, "Though I would most definitely take issue with *you* being that particular lover."

Later, he would hate how insulted he was at the observation, considering he had no intention of being Sesily Talbot's lover. "Why?"

Sera cut him a look. "You and I both know that you're emotionally . . . a problem."

"Excuse me?"

Haven snorted from his table in the distance and Caleb shot him a look. "Something to say, Duke? Shall we rehash your ridiculous love story? Spanning years, continents, and your own head up your—"

"Of course it's true, Caleb. You're the kind of problem that cannot help but ruin a love affair. You are so consumed by your inability to love—for reasons unknown and likely unreasonable—that you close yourself off from the whole world."

"They're not unreasonable, as a matter of fact."

"Oh, I'm sure not to you." She waved a hand in the air as though that bit was sorted, and went on. "What would you like me to say: if you harm my sister in any way, I shall have no choice but to destroy you?"

It wouldn't be entirely out of line. "Of course not."

"No, because we're all better than that," Sera said. "But you didn't bring her to me or any of my other sisters. And I know you well enough to know that you were absolutely not planning to take her home with you at the beginning of the evening. So why didn't she want to come to me?"

"I don't know."

"Presumably because she knew what I would say when I discovered her recklessness."

And there it was. That word Sesily had invoked in his carriage. *Reckless.*

It wasn't stupid and it wasn't reckless and I don't have to explain it to anyone.

"It wasn't reckless. She didn't start the row." He felt a responsibility to defend her. There wouldn't have been a row if not for him. He was the one who'd brought Peck to Maggie's doorstep.

His guilt from the night before returned, harsher now by light of day, when he wasn't hot with anger and wracked with worry. Crueler now that Sera was speaking the words Sesily had protested so vehemently in the carriage.

She hadn't been reckless.

I did what any decent person would do—what you did, I might add—I fought.

He came off the bar to his full height, and Sera backed up a few steps to give him space even as her gaze narrowed, as though she saw something curious on his face. He steeled himself for whatever she was about to say—preparing to deny whatever she thought she saw.

Whether or not it was true.

"She's damned lucky you were there," Sera said softly.

He'd thought so last night. But now, by the light of day, he wasn't so sure.

His friend sighed and turned away, making her way down the long bar and around it, her strides long and purposeful as she returned to the box of candles she'd been unpacking.

She lifted a handful of tapers and made for the chandelier on the stage at the far end of the room, and a lesser man would have thought she was through with the conversation.

Caleb knew better.

Not ten feet from the stage, she turned back. "She's up to something."

And with those four words, Caleb knew that Sesily wasn't at all lucky he had been with her the night before.

And he wasn't, either.

"She's out until all hours," Sera added, "routinely sneaking home at dawn."

"That could be anything," he said, knowing he shouldn't get involved. Telling himself not to get involved.

Sera shook her head. "Maybe, but she's avoiding the rest of us." The four other Talbot sisters. "Oh, she comes to luncheon or dinner or to the country house whenever she's invited. But when she's there . . . she's different. Distracted."

Caleb shouldn't be interested. He shouldn't care.

Sera looked to him. "On Wednesday evening—Thursday morning, I should say—she was supposed to attend some perfectly boring musicale, but somehow returned home long after it was over with blood on her skirts."

His brows rose at that. "Whose blood?"

She shook her head. "I don't know."

"How do you even know it happened?"

"The laundress at Talbot House told the housekeeper, who told me."

Caleb shook his head. "You've got the servants skulking about behind her back?"

Sera cut him a look. "If she weren't constantly giving us the slip, I might be less inclined to have her followed. Our parents are in France and she's spent the three months since they left telling one sister she's staying with a different one, leaving us all to discover that no one has seen her past six in the evening in a fortnight. It's maddening."

It sounded brilliant to Caleb. "Does she come here? To the Sparrow?"

"And risk my learning more about what she's up to? Never. I'm telling you, she's *up to something*. And it's not just carousing at Maggie O'Tiernen's."

That was clear, considering the knife she carried in her pocket, the way she'd fought in the brawl the night before—like she'd been trained in a ring—the fearless way she'd absolutely wrecked Totting in the Trevescan gardens.

Memory of that evening flashed, hot and unwelcome.

Sesily in the garden. In his arms.

I swore I'd never do this.

Unfortunately . . . circumstances dictate.

Totting tumbling from the gardens like a drunken ox. No. Not a drunken one. A drugged one. His sins inked on his face. Deservedly so . . . but dangerously, as well.

Haven't you noticed, American? I am trouble.

"She was caught up in a *raid*," Sera said, her voice wavering for the first time.

Haven heard it, too, and he was up and crossing the room in an instant, pulling her into his embrace, setting his lips to her temple. "She was fine. Caleb was there."

Don't make me a hero, Duke.

"It wasn't her fault," Caleb said again, softer. "She wasn't looking for trouble. That raid could have been anywhere."

Sera nodded. "Half the places in the Garden owned or frequented by women have increased security in the last six months." She grimaced. "A consequence of our new queen."

"Have we?"

"Fetu has four bodies on the front door and three on the back," she said, before looking up at her husband. "Mal has stationed men on the rooftops, and the Bastards have increased their watch as well." The Bareknuckle Bastards, protectors of the darkest corners of Covent Garden.

Haven pulled Sera tight to his side. "If they try it, they'll be taken care of."

Caleb nodded. He should go back to Maggie's today—help her sort out similar protection for The Place.

"And last night?" Sera interjected. "Who took care of them last night?"

He could tell her. He could name them. He'd seen them all working together, like they'd trained for just

such an evening as the one they'd had last night. The
Duchess of Trevescan, with money and power to spare.
Adelaide Frampton, whom the entire world seemed to
think was a simpering wallflower but was able to wield a
blade without trouble. Imogen Loveless, who'd knocked
a bruiser out with a concoction Caleb never wanted to
be on the receiving end of. Maggie, who had eyes every-
where. The others.

And Sesily, like a fucking goddess, up on the bar, red
skirts gleaming in the lanternlight, smile on her face
and quip on her tongue as she cracked a Bully Boy over
the head with a table leg like she was playing shuttlecock.

It was a crew if he'd ever seen one.

A revolution, clad in rouge and silk.

But he didn't say any of it.

Not only because he'd put those women in danger,
bringing Peck inside and summoning the raid. Not
only because he'd seen them stand together, shoulder to
shoulder. Not only because he'd fought alongside them.

He didn't say it, because he'd promised Sesily he
wouldn't.

And it was the only thing he could let himself give
her. So he stayed quiet, turning back to the row of bottles on the shelf behind the bar, busying himself with
them despite absolutely no need to do so.

"Caleb." Sera interrupted his thoughts, and he looked
to her—recognizing the hope in her gaze. Knowing
exactly what she was going to ask. Hating it. "I need
your help."

Shit.

"No."

Whatever she was asking, he wouldn't do it.

He couldn't. Not and keep his distance from Sesily.

Not and keep his friendship with Sera.

Not and keep his sanity.

"I would do it myself—"

"You absolutely will not do it yourself." Haven had put down his papers. "You're about to have a child."

"Did you not hear the bit where I told Caleb I could have a child and deliver a facer?"

"To Caleb, fine. But not to whomever Sesily is running with."

"That's just the point!" Sera said, her exasperation clear as she looked to Caleb. "Who is she running with?"

He moved from needlessly arranging gin bottles to needlessly arranging whiskey bottles and said, "Send one of the boys in the Garden to find out." The goodwill across Covent Garden for The Singing Sparrow afforded them access to any number of networks of informants.

"She's too smart for that. She'll sniff him out and, if I know Sesily, turn him into an ally. I need someone who is immune to her charms."

Good luck.

"Caleb . . . you're possibly the only man in the world who is immune to her charms."

Haven cleared his throat, and Caleb dearly wished a facer was a possibility for him, too.

"What makes you say that?" he asked, knowing he shouldn't. Knowing that giving Sera a single inch opened him up to be fleeced of a mile. He should know better than to fuss with the Talbot sisters.

"Well," Sera said, "she's wanted you for two years and you haven't taken her to bed, for one."

He stilled at the words. They weren't true, were they?

You're not keeping me from anyone.

"What?"

"I've lived with Sesily for thirty years. I know when she wants something. And honestly, I'm shocked you've resisted." She paused. "Of course, one might argue it is easy to resist from the other side of the world."

He knew from experience it was not.

She wanted him.

Fucking hell. It was impossible. It could never happen. "Sera. She is your sister."

And it had nothing to do with the fact that she was Sera's sister.

Unaware of the riot of thoughts in his head, Sera went on, "Even better. Perhaps you're not *immune* to Sesily's charms—is anyone really?—but you're absolutely unwilling to succumb to them."

He didn't reply, knowing that whatever he said would reveal too much.

The ideas he'd had. The things he'd imagined doing to Sesily . . .

"Let's be honest . . . if you did succumb . . . you'd be ruined."

His brows snapped together and he turned to face her, finally, discovering that she was closer than he'd expected. "Don't you mean *she'd* be ruined?"

She shot him an honest look. "No, Caleb. If the two of you had an affair, it might end with her heartsick . . . but it would end with you destroyed."

The words sent a thread of panic through him—something he'd never acknowledge—and he turned his back on her with something about needing to fetch more gin.

When he entered the stockroom, Fetu was crouching low in the corner, his back to the door, and Caleb willed him silent as he crossed to fetch one of the crates they'd just reorganized.

No luck there.

"You're always watching her, anyway," the other man said, keeping his focus on his work. "Might as well help Sera in the balance."

Caleb clutched the crate tight in both fists, bowing his head in frustration. "I'm not always watching her."

Lie. The woman was storm clouds at sea. Impossible not to watch.

"I'm never here." He couldn't be here. If he was here, it put them all in danger. He shouldn't be here now. He should never come back.

"I suppose," Fetu said, coming to his full height. "But you did when you were here. When she came here."

"Why did she stop?"

He'd wanted her to stop. When they'd opened, and he'd had to resist her for two months that stretched like an eternity. Last year when he'd been here for barely two weeks. Less time than he'd planned. *Because of her.*

"If you keep track of her, you can ask her."

It shouldn't have sweetened the pot, but it did. Lifting the crate, he returned to the main taproom, where Sera was waiting to play her final card. "You're the only person I can trust."

He gritted his teeth. "To keep your sister—who leaves mayhem in her wake—safe?"

Sera smiled—the smile of a beautiful woman who knew exactly how beautiful she was. The smile of a woman who knew that, eventually, she'd get her way.

"Don't smile at him," her husband grumbled with another kiss to her temple, returning to his table in the corner.

You shouldn't trust me. Not with her.

"You didn't trust me with her at the start of this conversation," he pointed out.

"In my experience, I have found it best to begin all conversations with men with severe mistrust."

He couldn't fault her that. "Your husband did a number on you."

"That he did," she said, "but he pays for it happily, do you not, Duke?"

Haven grunted in the distance, but Caleb knew the truth. There were few men on Earth who loved their wives more than the duke loved his duchess, and that was the only reason Caleb stomached the aristocrat in his tavern.

"Please, Caleb," she said, her hand stroking over the swell at her midsection. "Just until the babe is born."

"I'm only *here* until that babe is born," he said. "And then you'll have to deal with your sister yourself."

Sesily wanted him. She wanted him, and knowing it would slowly destroy him, because he could never have her.

Sera's brown eyes lit up. "You'll do it."

It was a mistake.

The words snaked through him, settling deep in his gut, gnawing at him. He sighed. "Once that babe is out, Sera . . ."

A triumphant smile broke across Sera's face. "You're a good man, Caleb Calhoun."

What a fucking lie that was.

Chapter Nine

"You slept in his *bed*?"

Sesily made a show of inspecting the detail on a particularly uninspired portrait of the Viscount Coleford, hanging in the man's drawing room, and whispered to her friend, "Adelaide. I would prefer all of London not be apprised of the situation."

Adelaide dismissed the words with a hand wave. "Please. No one pays any attention to us." She paused. "Well, no one pays attention to *me*."

"Yes, well, I think they might change their minds if they overhear your question, considering we are *at dinner*."

As the Duchess of Trevescan had promised, Adelaide and Sesily had received invitations to dine at the first dinner hosted by the new Viscountess Coleford, along with the duchess herself and a dozen other guests, ranging from moneyed commoners to a duke who was one of the dullest men Sesily had ever met. And when it came to dukes, that was saying something.

Nevertheless, the duo had accepted with pleasure and arrived that evening, ready to play their parts, and gather the information necessary to bring down Coleford—a likely murderer and an absolute bastard—whom Mayfair *should* have turned its back on years ago. But of course, men with money and title and power were never turned on. Not even when they should be.

Which was where Sesily, Adelaide, and the Duchess came in.

Earlier that afternoon, the trio had discussed the plan for the evening, each of the women prepared to play their best role: Sesily would divert the attention of the room with a raucous tale or a scandalous game while Adelaide disappeared from the room, found her way to Coleford's private study, and relieved him of the documents proving his involvement in defrauding the Foundling Hospital. The duchess would ensure all went smoothly.

It was a plan they'd run a dozen times, in a dozen different ways. More. Enough times that it was flawless. And on this particular evening, it would be in motion as soon as the men returned from whatever men did after dinner. Cigars? Scotch?

Ladies did sherry and pianoforte, which was injustice in itself, if you asked Sesily. Excruciating.

So Sesily and Adelaide stood shoulder to shoulder as the viscountess happily played the instrument in the corner, and considered the painting that dwarfed the rest of the art in the room. Finally, Adelaide said, "Dear me, this is hideous."

It was an enormous oil portrait, colors bright enough to suggest that the artist might require a physician to check his eyesight, set in a blindingly gilded frame. The only thing that prevented Sesily from believing the painter had been ill during the painting of it was the fact that it seemed to match the rest of the room— wild, brash colors that obviously had been chosen with no interest in the idea of their complementing each other.

The garish house was bested only by its garish owners on canvas, the aging viscount in a scarlet waistcoat
intricately embroidered with gold thread, and his newly
minted, third, extremely young viscountess in a wildly
patterned silk gown in canary yellow and a shade of
green that did not occur in nature.

"I cannot decide if it is a hideous painting or a hideous
subject." The pair stood there for a long while, taking in
the art, before Sesily added, "Perhaps both?"

"Absolutely both," Adelaide said, looking at their
hostess at her piano. "Poor thing. Imagine being married
to him."

"Awful," Sesily said, lifting a tiny glass of sherry to
her lips. "Worse than the portrait. But if she bides her
time, she might find herself free of it."

"If the man would hurry up," Adelaide said, frustrated, facing the door, on edge with the plan. Eager to
start. "Alright then. Tell me the rest. You were in his
bed. What happened?"

"Nothing happened." Sadly.

Her friend slid a disbelieving look in her direction.
"That's nonsense. We saw how he looked when he came
for you in the pub, Sesily."

Sesily's disbelief matched Adelaide's. "What does
that mean, how he looked? How did he look?"

Adelaide thought for a moment. "Terrifying."

In the wake of the matter-of-fact assessment, Sesily
looked back at the painting. "You're mistaking irritated
and annoyed with terrifying."

"No, I'm not. He became an absolute beast when
he saw what happened to you." A pause. "I like this
ensemble, by the way. Somehow both prim and scandalous. How's the throat?"

To cover the bruising at her neck from the events of three evenings before, Sesily wore a perfectly tailored black topcoat and a pristine white cravat over a stunning gown of sapphire silk. She expected that next week the scandal sheets would have something to say about Sexily Talbot making waves partially clad in gentleman's clothing, but she'd rather that than the questions about what happened to her neck. That, and she knew she looked fabulous.

But in that moment, she didn't want to discuss her appearance. She wanted to discuss Caleb's the evening before. Though she did not wish to admit it, she rather liked the idea of Caleb going beastly. "It's fine." Waving away Adelaide's concern, she said, "Tell me more about this beast."

Adelaide smiled. "You've turned men beastly before."

Not men like Caleb.

Not men she wished to be beastly.

"What would you like to hear?" Adelaide asked, quietly. "That I would have liked to see him fight a lion? That I'm fairly certain he would have won? That he came *tearing* across the place, tossing tables like they weighed nothing to get to you?"

Sesily's heart began to pound. Yes, all that was excellent information. "He wasn't terrifying in the carriage. He could not have been more put out when I woke."

"Well, he was not *put out* in the tavern. He was bleeding from the head and he smashed his fist into your attacker's face and felled the damn ruffian like a tree, then hefted you into his arms and carried you out. We tried to stop him. Told him that we'd see you to a physician if necessary, and home otherwise . . . but he was having none of it."

"Truly?" Sesily was having difficulty imagining any of it.

"Truly. It was exceedingly primitive," Adelaide said flatly before allowing, "And, I will admit, somewhat engaging. Come to think of it, considering how wild-eyed he was with you, we should have assumed that he'd take you somewhere to—*play croquet*."

Sesily barked a laugh, summoning the attention of the whole room and immediately regretting the way it aggravated her already sore throat. With a wide grin to the assembly, she turned back to her friend. "I'm sorry to disappoint . . . but there was no croquet played."

Adelaide looked positively affronted at the revelation. "None?"

"None."

"Not even a wicket?"

"Adelaide!"

"Sorry!" she said, shaking her head, her tightly moored red hair gleaming in the firelight. "It's just—I'm *so* perplexed!" Sesily cut her friend a look. "I mean, I cannot imagine how *you* must be feeling. It didn't seem like the evening would resolve itself with such . . . *boredom*."

Except it hadn't been boring.

For some reason, it had been immensely exciting, sleeping in his bed, the smell of him on the sheets, the even rhythm of his breath in the room. Even though he hadn't touched her. Even though he'd appeared utterly disinterested in her.

But he'd called her Athena.

Her chest tightened at the memory. In the carriage, he'd listened to her. He'd understood, or so it seemed. And he'd seen her for more than most did. Not reckless. Focused. Principled. He'd cared for her, seeming to understand what she needed before even she did.

And then, in the darkness, in the quiet, he'd called her Athena. A warrior. How many times had she played his words, low and dark and private, over and over like a secret in the three days since he'd said them? How many times had she considered taking herself to his tavern or his townhouse and asking him to repeat them?

"Perhaps he steered clear of you out of some sense of honor."

Sesily gave a little sigh. "Possibly. I was in no position to . . . but still . . ."

Adelaide's enormous brown eyes, which saw everything, softened with understanding. With pity. *How embarrassing.*

Sesily shrugged. "He slept in the same room as me. And it was difficult not to think of all the things . . . all the ways we might . . ."

"Play croquet?"

"Yes," Sesily said, exasperated. "And . . . nothing! I mean any other man in London would have happily played croquet. And . . ." She thought for a moment, lost in the memory. "It was as though he didn't even notice the field!"

Adelaide cut her a disbelieving look. "Sesily. It is impossible not to notice you."

It's impossible not to notice you.

Caleb had said the same thing, when she'd been tending to the wound on his head. When she'd been willing him to kiss her, the idiot man. And still . . .

"Well, he made a good show of it."

"I don't like it."

"Imagine how I feel," she said, slyly. Then she added, "At any rate, Caleb Calhoun is not here and I am not interested in letting thoughts of him ruin a perfectly good evening."

If Caleb were there, he'd no doubt involve himself in their well-laid plans and do something nonsensical, like toss her over his shoulder and remove her from the building.

And not for any of the reasons she'd be willing to be tossed over his shoulder.

Thankfully, at that moment, the door at the far end of the room opened, and the men returned, saving her from imagining just what it might be like to be tossed over Caleb Calhoun's shoulder.

"Ah," she said. "It begins."

Coleford crossed the room, tall and slim, his more than sixty years doing nothing to temper the unsettling look about him that women learned early to avoid. And that was when he was not in his cups, where Sesily would wager he was right now. Drunk and disgusting. His rheumy gaze slithered over the women in the room, lips curving in an unpleasant smile no doubt meant to be charming.

Next to her, Adelaide made a sound of disgust. "Are you sure you're up to keeping the man entertained?"

"A few rounds of faro shan't kill me," Sesily said as the viscount's eyes settled on the skin between her cravat and the line of her dress. She would require a bath later. "Just be quick about your work so I never have to sit face to face with him ever again."

Coleford turned to the far end of the room where his wife still played. "Do cease that racket," he said sharply, loud enough for all assembled to hear him.

The music stopped instantly, the too young viscountess's back going straight like steel as her chin lowered to her chest. Coleford turned to the men with whom he'd entered with a too loud laugh. "The chit thinks she's Mozart," he said, butchering the composer's name. "Apologies for the assault."

Adelaide stiffened next to her and whispered, "I should like to show him assault."

"The plan," Sesily replied softly as an uncomfortable silence fell, followed by a smattering of sniggers. She sipped at her sherry, surveying the room, cataloguing those who took pleasure in the man's cruel remarks.

"Come here, then," Coleford said, waving at his wife.

She did, standing in the deafening silence and walking to him, all grace—the product of a lifetime of lessons in poise and elocution, embroidery and menu-making and poetry—the kind of girl who was taught every skill required to succeed as an aristocratic wife.

And somehow never taught the skills that might be required to survive as one.

Adelaide was vibrating at Sesily's shoulder, and Sesily reached out to touch her friend's arm. To remind her that there was a plan for the evening. That, if it was well-executed, they would end the viscount and rescue the viscountess from her terrible marriage in one fell swoop.

But Adelaide was growing angry, and Sesily could see that the plan was not top of mind.

Out of the corner of her eye, Sesily noticed a gentleman step through the door—the boring dinner companion she'd had earlier in the evening. The Duke of Clayborn had missed the beginning of the scene, the lucky toff. He should have gone home.

Instead, he was there to see Lady Coleford draw close enough for her husband to reach out and take her chin in hand, lifting it to meet her eyes. "No one wants to hear you plonking about, girl. That's not what you're here for."

She lowered her gaze and said, softly, "Yes, my lord."

Coleford was much louder when he said, "Though I

suppose listening to your banging about is better than listening to your laugh. Like a wounded horse."

Sesily sucked in a breath at the words, unkind and unnecessary.

Adelaide's arm went to stone beneath her touch.

Not one person in the room moved, except to avert their eyes from the uncomfortable moment. Of course they didn't. It was the viscount with the power, not the viscountess. Just as it had been Totting with it, and not the girls they all knew he harmed.

Sesily had read the dossier on the viscount front to back, and she was certain he'd murdered two wives. The first, Fiona, died of "fever" at age forty-three, only months after the death of Mr. Bernard Palmer, Coleford's adult son and heir. The second, Primrose, had perished at twenty-two, two years into a childless marriage, in an "accident" at the lake on the Coleford estate in the West Midlands.

And still, this roomful of powerful people stood by and watched him mistreat his newest, youngest wife. Catherine, aged nineteen. And not one had anything to say.

Damn all of them to hell.

The young viscountess looked up at her husband. "Yes, my lord."

Perhaps if her voice hadn't cracked. Perhaps if she hadn't been facing them. Perhaps if they hadn't been able to see the tears in her eyes.

Perhaps then, Adelaide would have been able to stick to the plan.

Likely not, though, as when Adelaide was angry, plans were absolutely in the wind.

Unfortunately, Adelaide was furious. She shook off Sesily's hand and stepped into the room, toward the couple. "I, for one, enjoyed your playing, Lady Cole-ford."

Every eye in the room swung to Adelaide. Forgettable Adelaide Frampton, lifelong wallflower, known for her stern visage and her meekness . . . certainly not meek that evening.

Dammit.

Sesily looked across the room, finding the duchess's dark eyes already on her. So much for the plan.

Coleford turned on Adelaide, and Sesily registered the full heat of his loathing as he faced her. "I don't believe anyone asked you."

Ignoring their host in favor of their hostess, Adelaide continued, "In fact, I wonder about that tricky bit in the second movement. I've never been able to quite get the fingering right. Would you be willing to teach it to me at some point?"

Coleford stepped in front of his wife, putting himself between her and Adelaide, who did not waver. "My *wife*," he sneered, "will never be seen with you."

Adelaide met the man's eyes then. "Come now, old man, it shall surely be a step up from being seen with *you*."

Oh dear. Sesily's brows rose in shock.

Coleford's face went a shade of red she was not sure she'd ever seen before.

The whole room watched, agog. And still, no one moved, the cowards.

Well, no one but the Duke of Clayborn at the door, drawing closer, likely to get a better view. Sesily wrinkled her nose at the man and slid her hand into her skirts, finding the false pocket there—designed only to access the blade Sesily was never without, sheathed at her thigh.

Across the room, the duchess snapped open her fan, ruby silk over ebony.

If Coleford took one step toward Adelaide—they would not hesitate to defend her, and then they'd all have a larger problem than the plan going soft.

"Miss Frampton—" the viscountess said.

"Don't talk to her," Coleford replied. "I shall deal with this . . ." He stepped toward Adelaide, who did not move, holding her ground. A lioness. ". . . ugly . . . common . . . *nobody.*"

On the last, a titter spread through the room, and if she weren't so livid, so occupied by imagining how she would absolutely destroy this old man, Sesily would have laughed at the way the room chose the insult to be the thing they were offended by, as though the rest of the viscount's behavior was entirely aboveboard.

Of course, if she weren't so livid, she would have noticed the Duke of Clayborn had reached the trio, inserting himself between Adelaide and Coleford.

"That's enough." The words were full of smooth power, and Sesily shot a questioning look at Duchess, across the room, who lifted one shoulder in a tiny movement. A barely-there shrug, as if to say, *I've no idea.*

Neither did Sesily, but the Duke of Clayborn was about to have a file as thick as her thumb at Trevescan House. Thicker, when he shot a narrow look down at Adelaide and said, "It is time for you to leave, Miss Frampton."

Adelaide wouldn't like that.

She peeked her head around the broad shoulder of the duke and looked to the viscountess, who deliberately did not return the gaze.

"Now. It is not a request," Clayborn said to Adelaide. "You *overstep.*"

Who in hell did he think he was? Sesily would happily strip him down, too. She took a step toward them, stayed only by a cough from across the room.

The plan.

Was there still a plan?

She looked to the duchess, who was riveted to the scene.

"Have I made myself clear?" Clayborn asked, his cold, stern disdain raining over Adelaide. "You have forgotten your place."

What a proper ass.

Adelaide lifted her chin, fury pouring off her in waves. "On the contrary, Duke. It would seem I am the only one here who knows it."

For a long moment, the two stared into each other's eyes, and it occurred to Sesily that in that moment, Adelaide might do any number of things, including but definitely not limited to smashing a fist directly into that straight ducal nose.

At which point there surely would no longer be a plan.

But she didn't. Instead, Adelaide stepped back and nodded in the direction of Lady Coleford. "Thank you for the lovely evening, my lady," she said before she looked Lord Coleford dead in the eye and said, "And you, Viscount, I hope you get everything you deserve."

With a final, furious glance at the duke, she turned on her heel and left the room.

Silence fell, thick and unpleasant, as all assembled stood on the precipice of this unprecedented evening. Were they to go home? To pretend as though nothing had happened? To find some middle way?

And then, across the room, someone clapped her hands and called out, "Well, who is in for charades?"

The Duchess of Trevescan unlocked the room.

"Do play on my team, will you, Lord Coleford?"

Sesily met her friend's eyes as she crossed the room,

unable to miss the way she cast a look at the door where Adelaide had disappeared.

The plan remained in effect.

And Sesily was it.

Slipping from the room, she followed the discreet indications of a footman posted in the hallway beyond, aiming for a salon reserved as a ladies' retiring room nearby. A salon that, according to the map she'd been smart enough to study despite this *absolutely not being the plan*, was two doors away from a rear servants' staircase that led down one flight to a dimly lit corner of the ground floor, where Lord Coleford's study was dark and unlocked.

"Excellent," she whispered to herself as the latch turned easily in her hand. She could pick a lock, but it wasn't her preferred method of entering rooms. It was fiddly business, and best left to those who didn't prefer brute force.

Like putting a boot through a carriage window to procure fresh air.

Sesily resisted the thought—now was not the time to linger on the impressive strength of a man with whom she had no business being impressed.

Sliding into the dark room, footsteps silent, she shut the door with a barely-there click and paused, hoping that a shred of the moonlight beyond would make additional light unnecessary.

Apparently, her luck ran out with the unlocked door. The room was pitch-black, requiring her to collect a candle stub and flint from the pocket of her skirts and, once light was available, make her way to the heavy, forbidding desk that overpowered the rest of the room.

Moving quickly—imperative for searching an office during a dinner party and doubly so during a dinner party that had just gone sideways—she found a home for the candle, and set to work, opening and closing drawers with careful efficiency until she found what she was looking for.

A ledger, hidden beneath the false bottom of the lower drawer of the desk.

"Unoriginal as all the others," she muttered, opening it on the carpet, searching for the proof she needed that the Viscount Coleford, renowned for his work on the board of the Foundling Hospital, was skimming funds from the organization to which he was so publicly devoted. That, alongside being a half dozen terrible things—among them, an abuser, an adulterer, a rich man who refused to pay his debts, and a landowner who taxed his tenants to the teeth.

The monstrous man was literally taking money from orphans, siphoning donations from the rest of the aristocracy to a private account.

Sesily's heart began to pound as she turned the pages of the damning ledger, pages and pages of venerable titles and respected gentry, each paired with two deposits; the amount delivered to the hospital and the amount deposited into Coleford's private account.

And interspersed, lines marked *paid in full*, each with an obscure notation.

Her brow furrowed as she flipped through the ledger, searching for more information. And then she found it—a list of names and dates.

Women, Sesily was certain, who had given up their children to the hospital. Dates of surrender. Women who had nothing, and who were being shaken for additional funds.

"What a fucking monster," she whispered, rage coursing through her as she ripped the pages from the book. If they could find these women, they could find the men who preyed upon them.

And if she had the ledger, she could prove Coleford's part in the sickening scheme.

She cursed him as she replaced the heavy book in the false bottomed drawer. Cursed all like him—armed to the teeth with money, power, and title, and still cruel beyond words.

A score of them upstairs, standing silent as he mistreated his wife and Adelaide in front of them. For sport.

Her work complete, Sesily folded the papers into a rectangle small enough to tuck into the inside pocket of her topcoat, collected the scrap on the floor that had been trapping falling candle wax, and stood.

A scrape sounded from the hallway beyond.

There was someone outside the door.

Grabbing the candle from its place on the large desk, she extinguished it, ignoring the sting of the hot wax on her fingertips as she crouched in the darkness, tucking herself into the well of the desk, cursing skirts and tight fastenings as she collected yards of silk and prayed for dim light when whoever it was entered.

Best case? A servant, come to light a fire.

Worst? The viscount, who was supposed to be upstairs, delighted by the duchess's company.

She froze as the door opened and closed, winced as a key turned in the lock.

Gritted her teeth as footsteps approached, soft and steady on the carpet.

She considered her options. Though most of London would not blink at the idea of Sesily Talbot meeting a man in the dark, assignations did not typically occur in the homeowner's private offices. Moreover, they very rarely occurred under his desk.

And they would never, ever occur with a man as loathsome as Coleford.

She was not beyond braining whomever it was, but her only available weapon was the heeled shoe she wore, which would not carry nearly enough weight to fell a grown man.

She reached into her pocket, distaste running deep. She might have considered it earlier, but knifing a viscount wasn't the ideal activity that evening; even Duchess wouldn't be able to keep attention from skirts bloodied by a throat cutting. That, and Sesily had never cut a throat. She preferred not to begin tonight.

And still, as the footsteps neared, it occurred to her that she might not have a choice.

The footsteps stopped somewhere near the desk. Damn the darkness, which made it impossible to know exactly where the intruder was.

A flint sounded.

A soft golden glow lit the room.

A man stood directly in front of her. But it wasn't the viscount. The viscount had been wearing white breeches and hose. A waistcoat and topcoat that harkened back to a time when he was perhaps considered less odious.

This man wore dark trousers.

It was difficult to miss them as he crouched, his massive thighs coming into view—thighs that absolutely did not belong to the Viscount Coleford—followed by a wide torso covered with a black patterned waistcoat. Though his head remained above the desk, she was given a close-up view of the broadest shoulders she'd ever seen.

She knew they were, because she'd seen them before.

Recognition had her exhaling her panic on a long breath.

And then Caleb's head dipped below the edge of the desk, his jaw set in anger, his eyes flashing with fury, and she regretted the breath, because she couldn't seem to catch a new one.

"Fucking hell, Sesily."

Chapter Ten

Relief slammed through him when he found her under the desk.

In his wildest imaginings it had never occurred to Caleb that Sesily might land here, in the private study of the Viscount Coleford. It hadn't occurred to him that she'd ever end up anywhere near the Viscount Coleford.

When he'd watched her enter Coleford House, prettily situated on Bruton Street, just off Berkeley Square, he'd nearly gone wild with the revelation that things were about to go absolutely sideways on an evening when she'd emerged from her own house looking to all the world like a woman going to dinner.

Yes, she'd been wearing a topcoat and cravat—something that had somehow made him both furious for what he knew that cravat hid and riveted to the way the coat at once hid and accentuated her curves—but this was Sesily Talbot, and she did not leave the house looking ordinary. Ever.

He'd waited in the darkness, watching as she climbed into her carriage, and followed in a hired hack, expecting a dinner of staid aristocratic nonsense, which meant he could return to his life for a few hours before returning to follow her, hopefully, back to her house and see her tucked into bed.

But there was nothing staid about Coleford House.

There was nothing *safe* about Coleford House. For either of them.

Indeed, the idea of Sesily anywhere near Coleford House made Caleb's blood run hot with anger . . . and cold with fear.

But leaving her there was not an option, so, he'd exited the hack, releasing it back to the night, and watched as a half dozen other carriages had deposited additional aristocrats to the evening, the tight knot of panic in his chest easing a bit as he realized she wasn't there alone.

A bit.

Because he didn't believe for a moment that she was there by coincidence.

You are keeping truths of your own, she'd said to him outside The Place three nights earlier. *And if I have to learn them, I will.*

Goddammit. She had done as she'd promised. The woman was pure chaos.

So it was that, after he'd finished cursing her sister to hell for asking him to track Sesily around London, he'd spent half an hour skulking through a collection of dark gardens, and over stone walls, before sneaking his way into Coleford House—a place he'd studiously avoided when he was in London.

A place Sesily had no business being anywhere near—and even less business rifling through papers in the private study belonging to a man who was more dangerous than she could know.

She was going to get caught, dammit.

And somehow, instead of getting the hell out of her wake, Caleb had agreed to be her extremely mutton-headed savior.

She was going to get them both caught.

He was going back to Boston the second Sera whelped that babe, dammit. And he was never coming back.

If he didn't land at the gallows first.

When he'd entered the dark room, he could smell her, sun and wind and that hint of almond, barely-there over the lingering scent of recently extinguished candle wax. He'd followed it, like a dog on the hunt, to the viscount's enormous desk, and lit the lamp, knowing without hesitation that she was beneath the desk.

And when he'd crouched to face her, to find her pressed to the back of it, as though she wouldn't be found by anyone who entered the room, his worry and anger and panic had flared in a dangerous trio.

She threw oil on the flame with an easy smile. "Good evening, Caleb."

His teeth clenched until he felt physical pain. "What in hell are you doing?"

"I should think it was obvious," she said, the rasp in her words only serving to infuriate him more, as he knew how it had come to be there, the memory of her in the clutches of the brute at The Place.

"If you think I'm in the mood for your jokes, you have sorely misread this situation."

She had the sense not to reply, small favor.

He thought he'd calm down when he found her. He thought he'd be able, then, to imagine what to do. How to remove her from this house. From this situation.

He thought he'd return to sense.

But how had she known?

How had she found this place? How did she know the secrets it kept?

And how quickly would she discover his own secrets, locked away?

"Get out of there."

She waved a hand at him. "Bit difficult when you're looming."

He growled and stood, backing away as she emerged. "It's not even a good hiding place. I knew where you were the moment I walked in the room."

"Yes, well, I wasn't expecting to have to hide," she said, shaking out her skirts. "What are you doing here?"

He ignored the question, both because he was annoyed and because he wasn't sure how to answer it. "And if it hadn't been me? What were you going to do?"

"I am armed," she replied smartly. "Contrary to what you think, I am not without sense."

"And so, what, a bullet in the arm of the viscount?"

"A knife wound, as a matter of fact."

He looked to the ceiling and released a strangled laugh at the idea of Sesily knifing an aristocrat in his own home. "You'd be strung up faster than the man could bleed out, you madwoman. You're lucky I turned up."

"Oh, yes," she whispered. "I'm feeling extremely blessed at your appearance. Whoever would have sent me into hiding under a desk if you hadn't wandered in?" She pushed past him and rounded the desk to the lamp he'd lit.

"If I hadn't wandered in—"

"If you hadn't wandered in, nothing would have happened," she said. "Everyone else in the house is quite distracted."

"By what, charades with your friends?"

"In fact, yes."

He snorted his disbelief. "And that's supposed to keep Coleford distracted while you skulk about in his private study."

"You misjudge my friends."

"I absolutely do not misjudge them. I think they're all terrifying."

She smiled at that. "They shall be happy to hear it."

"Absolute misfits," he muttered. "It's time to go. You're going to get us both caught."

"I beg your pardon!" she said, the affront in the words clear. "The only times I have *ever* been *caught* have been by you!"

"I think you mean *rescued*, darling," he retorted. "The other night, when you leapt into battle despite being roundly outnumbered—"

"Oh, please."

He ignored the interjection. "—and the time before that, when you *vandalized* an earl—"

"Are you suggesting he did not deserve it?"

"He thoroughly deserved it, you absolute hurricane, but that doesn't mean it was your job to do it."

"No one else was doing it," she snapped. "I assure you, Caleb, if I thought a single *man* would stand up and deliver any one of these monsters their due—"

"Delivering the monsters their due doesn't eliminate monsters," he snapped.

"It reduces their numbers by one!"

"Goddammit, Sesily!" The protest unlocked him, and he couldn't help leaning down into her face, getting as close as possible to her, his heart pounding with frustration and a fear he had not felt in years. "You don't know what you're talking about. You don't know the repercussions of eliminating these men. You don't see what could come of it. What danger you are in. How they will stop at nothing to destroy you if they think you are a threat to their money or power or title." He paused. "You don't see how they will *end* you."

She blinked in the wake of his words, her beautiful blue eyes wide with surprise and confusion. Realization dawned. Whatever she was here for—it was not his secrets.

"Caleb, what—"

He shook his head. He certainly wasn't going to share them with her. "No. We're leaving. And you're going to give me your promise that you will never come back here. That you will never face down Coleford."

The sound she made was pure exasperation. "Truly, for someone who makes such a fuss about not having a thimbleful of interest in my person, you spend a fair lot of time following me about! *Which*, I might note, is categorically your own problem. I didn't invite you here."

"You shouldn't be here," he said, straightening his shoulders and approaching her, stopping only when she had to crane her head to meet his gaze. "Nothing here is your business."

"I believe I'm more than capable of divining what is and is not my business, American," she retorted, blue eyes flashing indignantly. She paused, the silence full of something Caleb didn't like. "Hang on."

She was too smart for her own good. Caleb gritted his teeth. "Time to go, Sesily."

"I didn't invite you here," she said, softly, as though everything were falling into place. "No one did. You *weren't* here. What are you doing—"

"No. We have to get out of here."

"Why *are* you here?"

"Following you." He reached for the knob on the lamp, intending to tip the room into darkness. Intending to hide in it.

"No." Her hand landed on his with surprising speed, the heat of her touch singeing him through the silk of her glove. "How do you know him?"

She didn't know.

He closed his eyes, relief and frustration warring within. "It's not important. What's important is that I know the kind of man he is. And I will lock you up myself if that's what it takes to keep you from him."

She searched his face. "Tell me."

Somehow, impossibly, he wanted to. What would it feel like to answer the question? To tell her everything? To unburden himself?

It would feel glorious.

And then it would wreck them both.

"I'm not—"

Her hand flew to cover his mouth. "Shh."

In the silence that stretched between them—which he was certain she would eventually fill—a bell rang. It was soft and distant, in the hallway beyond.

"Dammit," she whispered. Her head turned to the door. "I would have thought Duchess could keep him engaged a bit longer. For the record, Caleb, if you hadn't turned up, I'd be far from this room by now. So if we are caught . . . it shall be your fault."

His gaze narrowed on her. "Are we about to be caught?"

She reached into the folds of her skirts, a flash of metal—a knife?—winking up at him before she turned the knob on the lamp, extinguishing the light. "Quick," she whispered, claiming his hand and pulling him to the door, which she opened silently, barely. The flash again. Not a weapon. A mirror, slid carefully into the narrow space between door and jamb.

Clever.

"Now." Apparently satisfied that they would not be seen, she opened the door and tugged him into the empty hallway. "Quickly."

A man's voice sounded from a distance. "Coleford."

They both stilled, the rage thrumming through Caleb making him tighten his grip on her. "Now, Sesily."

"Ah, Clayborn," came the distant reply, the nasal voice sliding through Caleb, unwelcome. "Thank you for taking care of that dog-faced upstart. My *wife*"—Coleford spat the word—"should have known better than to invite her. They never know their place, these commoners."

"Your *wife*"—Clayborn's words were cool and stern—"deserves better from you."

Sesily's eyes went wide as Coleford began to sputter.

Not that it impacted the other man at all, who spoke with a calm threat in his voice that Caleb recognized because he'd used it himself on more than one occasion. "I shall be interested to see you turn over a new leaf on that front." The warning was unspoken, but clear as a bell. "And as for the *common upstart*, I expect you to steer clear of Miss Frampton. For good."

Sesily turned to Caleb and mouthed, "He's not a bastard?"

"Well, he's a duke, so the jury remains out," he whispered, "but we don't have time to sort it out. You can't go back that way."

"How lucky you are here, I hadn't considered that," she retorted in a tone indicating that she'd absolutely considered that. "Nor had I considered that *you* can't go anywhere, as *you should not be here at all*."

Caleb did not reply, instead running his fingers along the wall until he found what he was looking for. He threw a catch and opened a small cupboard, filled with rags and buckets. A servants' closet.

"He's coming," Sesily said, pushing Caleb into the tiny space and pulling the door shut behind her, throwing them into darkness. He retreated as far as he could without light, which wasn't far, his back immediately pressed to a row of shelving. His heel came up against a bucket on the floor, just enough to make a soft sound.

She covered his mouth again. "Shhh."

His arm snaked around her waist, keeping them both still, and he nipped her palm. She released him, pinching his arm almost instantly.

Another place, another time, he would have been amused. Delighted.

In that moment, however, he was preparing to protect her with all he had.

They waited, listening as heavy steps approached, and a door in the hallway beyond opened. The viscount's study.

"How did you know this was here?" she asked, the words barely-there.

He heard her. Of course. "Every house with money has a servants' cupboard."

A pause as she considered the words. As he willed her not to ask more. "And you make it your business to know where they are?"

"Aren't you glad I knew where this one was?"

"If you weren't here, I could have pretended to have been lost on my return from the retiring room."

"Lost on a different floor?"

"Do you doubt men's willingness to believe women are cabbageheaded?"

He didn't. But she wasn't cabbageheaded. "Sesily . . ." He chose his words carefully. "Coleford. He's not a decent man."

"I know," she said.

"You don't know—not all of it."

A pause. And then, soft, knowing, slightly pleading, "How do *you* know?"

He swallowed around the knot in his throat. "Whatever you're up to . . . you need to stop. If he catches you, if he counts you an enemy . . . he won't hesitate."

"You marched in here, uninvited, willing to be counted among his enemies. Why?"

Because I'm already counted among his enemies.

He would never say it; Sesily could never know it. She should never have even come close to it.

She wouldn't have, if he'd been able to stay away.

But he couldn't stay away from her. That was the problem, wasn't it? Had been, since the beginning.

Silence stretched between them, and in it, he began to think that perhaps he should release her. There was no *perhaps* about it. He absolutely *should* release her.

But he didn't want to.

So he didn't, leaving his arm around her waist, telling himself he was keeping her safe. She might trip over all manner of cleaning agents. Mops, buckets, piles of rags. Lye.

Lye was dangerous.

Best to hang on to her.

It had nothing to do with how she felt in his arms, soft and warm, her breasts rising and falling against him with every breath, her hands resting on his chest.

"So," she whispered, finally. "You followed me here. Into the fray."

He didn't reply.

The woman, however, was not to be ignored. "Caleb, if you're not careful, people will notice that you're following me and begin to get ideas."

His heart was pounding and he hated everything

about London and this house and still, he couldn't stop himself from holding her tight to him. "What kind of ideas?"

Where in hell had that question come from?

"The kind of ideas people have about any man who follows me."

"And what are those?"

The scent of her curled around him, like a lush treat in a shop window. Just out of reach. A heady tease. Her maddening fingers toyed at the edge of his waistcoat and he imagined her smiling one of her perfect smiles. "They don't call me Sexily for nothing."

He had no difficulty understanding why they called her Sexily. But now was not the time to discuss it. Did she not understand the seriousness of their predicament? "Not now, Sesily."

The teasing flirt in her tone increased. "I'm only saying that if you are so keen to be near me, you might consider escorting me somewhere proper."

"Oh? Is the servants' cupboard in the home of some viscount improper?" he asked.

"Some viscount," she said, and he could hear the smile in the words, as though they were anywhere but here, and they were doing anything but avoiding discovery. "You really should use titles with more reverence."

"I'm an American," he replied. "They confuse me."

A little, hoarse laugh sounded in the darkness and somehow, here, in this place, it loosened him. "They're very complex."

"For example?" He whispered the question, grateful for the distraction. For her.

"Everyone knows about dukes, of course," she whispered, those fingers still playing at the edge of his waistcoat, tracing longer and longer paths, slowly torturing him. "But I find Americans are easily confused just one step lower . . . with marquesses. Most of you pronounce it with that long e sound, and it's just atrocious."

"It's because of our debt of honor to the French," he quipped, and she laughed again, this time a bit louder— loud enough that it came out as a little bark. Not liking the sound and the pain she must be feeling after the events of the previous evening, Caleb tightened his arm, unable to stop himself from pulling her closer, as though he might be able to protect her. "I didn't mean examples of titles, Sesily."

She stilled, and he imagined her turning her face up to his, searching for his eyes in the darkness. As he searched for hers. "What then?"

"Where is a proper location for me to escort you?"

There wasn't one, of course. There was no scenario where he courted Sesily Talbot. No ices at Gunter's, no posies from a Covent Garden flower seller, no visits to her sister Sophie's bookshop. Courting meant a future. And a future with Sesily was impossible.

Even if she was the only woman who had ever tempted him with one.

But, here in the darkness, he wanted to hear what she imagined possible.

Before she could answer, noises came from the hallway beyond. Coleford, the bastard, closing the door to his office firmly, his footsteps retreating, slow and even, as he returned to the party abovestairs.

It was not the pace of a man who knew someone had just rifled through his belongings.

What had she been looking for?

What had she found?

As they were now safe from discovery, he could ask her. He could keep her here, in the darkness, until she told him the truth.

But before he did, she answered his earlier question. "You could escort me to Boston."

The words were a weapon, shattering through him, along with a vision of her in his tavern in Boston. In the bright sunny gardens of his Beacon Hill row house. On the shores of the Atlantic.

On the Atlantic . . . six weeks at sea with nothing but a private cabin to entertain them.

The things he would do to her in a private cabin.

"That's not a proper location at all," he said, softly.

"No, I suppose not," she said, "but maybe then . . ."

She trailed off, a thousand unsaid things in that pause. And Caleb was lost, because he wanted to know every one of them.

"Maybe then, what?"

"Maybe then, you'd tell me your secrets," she said, softly.

Never. He'd never burden her with them. And absolutely not here. In this house. Owned by this man.

As though he'd spoken the words aloud, she gave a little laugh and said, "You realize I shall learn them eventually. So that we're even."

A thread of unease whispered through him. "Who says we must be even?"

"I don't like an imbalance of power."

The woman was daughter to an earl, sister to a duchess, a future duchess, and a countess, stood to inherit a fortune, and had most of London in the palm of her hand. She could wave him away with one, pretty hand.

"I don't have any secrets," he lied.

"Why do you dislike the dark?" she asked, the question soft and pointed.

"I don't mind it now," he said, loving the darkness that had her pressing against him. When she didn't reply, he added, "When I was young, I was in a ship's hold for two months."

She inhaled sharply. "Two *months*."

"It was a long journey. Stormy. And . . ." *Awful*. There hadn't been money for rooms with windows. Or time above deck. "Dark."

"*Caleb* . . ." she whispered, her fingertips coming to his lips, soft like silk.

He cleared his throat and captured her hand in his. "As I said, I don't mind it now."

With you.

He pressed a kiss to one of those fingers, nipped it barely, enjoyed her intake of breath. "And you? What of your secrets?"

"You already know too many of them," she whispered, her free hand dancing up over his shoulder, up his neck, into his hair, as though it were perfectly ordinary for her to touch him. As though she owned him.

And what if she did? What if he let her, there, in the darkness, in the wake of the near miss with Coleford, relief rioting through Caleb for having found her. For having her in his arms. For keeping her safe.

Caleb felt the thread of his control slipping, unraveling beneath the play of her fingers. She was destroying him.

What if, just this once, he allowed it?

She wanted him.

"Can I trust you, Caleb? To keep my secrets?" Her fingers tightened, pulling his head down, until he could feel her lips *right there*, just waiting to be claimed. "Can I trust you, Caleb?"

No qualifiers.

Not that she needed them.

"Yes."

She kissed him.

Chapter Eleven

She should be more concerned about what was happening outside the cupboard—how she was going to find her way back to Duchess, how she was going to avoid discovery by the viscount, how she was going to get herself home if she were stuck inside that closet all night—but Sesily could find neither the interest nor the reason required to be concerned with much of anything beyond Caleb.

Something had changed there in the darkness, as he held her tight against him and let her explore him as she wished—as though he belonged to her, as though they belonged to each other. Somehow, everything had become more free and more dangerous, because as much as she wanted this man, the idea of having him . . . of touching him . . . of kissing him with abandon . . . threatened her future.

After all, once she knew what it was like to be in Caleb's arms, she might never wish to be out of them. And she didn't think she could bear it if he didn't feel the same way.

But now, in their dark, quiet spot, risk took on a new meaning. Here, as her fingers traced over his warm skin, as the scent of him surrounded her, amber and leather, as the rumble in his chest threatened to lay her low, Sesily realized that she was very likely lost.

Indeed, she'd been lost the moment his arm came tight around her, pulling her closer than she'd been, as that rumble became a growl, setting her aflame as he took over the kiss that she'd begun.

She gave herself up to it, sighing into his mouth as his lips opened over hers and his tongue dipped inside for a heartbeat, as though he couldn't resist the taste. She couldn't resist, either, and when he retreated, she followed, not ready to give him up.

That growl again, deep and delicious. His hand found its way into her hair, threatening to scatter hairpins across the floor.

And Sesily didn't care.

How many times had she dreamed of this kiss? How many times had she doubted it would happen because he'd made such a good show of telling her he didn't want it? That he didn't think of it?

He'd lied to her.

She knew it as surely as she knew his breath was ragged in his chest, just as hers was. She knew he'd been drawn tight as a string, just as she had. And she knew he wanted her, just as she wanted him.

She could taste it.

Triumph shot through her as he pulled her closer, his thumb tracing the arc of her cheek as he deepened the kiss, and Sesily was lost to the caress, to the feel of him, hard against her softness. A perfect fit, just as she'd always known he would be.

"Caleb," she whispered, unable to keep his name from her tongue—she'd been waiting for this forever.

He let her up for air even as he continued to pleasure her, pressing hot kisses to her cheek, to the underside of her jaw, to the soft skin of her neck above her cravat. "This," he whispered there, at the skin. "I hate this. God knows I loathe what it hides." He paused. "Does it hurt?"

The question stung. So caring. So sweet. So personal. "No."

"I'm sure that's a lie."

"Don't you dare use what happened the other night as an excuse to stop now," she whispered, tightening her fingers in his hair—how was his hair so impossibly soft?—holding his kiss to her skin.

He pulled away, just enough to speak, just enough for her to feel his breath against her. "You think I do not have enough excuses without it?"

They were hiding in a servants' cupboard after she'd rifled through the desk of a viscount—and there was a more than reasonable chance that they would be found, so she supposed there was plenty of excuse to stop.

And then, his words like sin in the darkness, he said, "Sesily . . . The reasons I should stop have nothing to do with our location."

Before she could ask him to elaborate, he licked over her skin to the lobe of her ear, sucking at it until she shivered her pleasure. "I should stop because you feel fucking glorious. Like a treasure to be thieved."

Oh. *Oh.* She liked that.

"I should stop, because you make me feel like a thief. Stealing your touch, your scent, your kiss—" He did just that, taking her mouth like a marauder, deep and thorough.

Except he wasn't stealing.

She gave it freely.

When he released her from his caress, he said, soft and hot at her ear, "I should stop because if I don't . . . I'm never going to want to."

She closed her eyes at the words, lost in them. In him. In the promise of him that she'd always wanted and that he finally, *finally* offered. "And if I didn't want you to stop?"

Another groan, this one tortured, sending pleasure pooling in her. "Don't tell me that."

She tightened her fingers in his hair as his lips lingered at the skin below her cravat, where she seemed to have more feeling than any one place on a person's body should. "What if I did tell you, though?" she asked, tilting her head to the side, making room for more of his delicious touch. "What if I told you everything I wished for you to do instead of stopping?" She sighed to the darkness. "What would happen? Would I be turned in for punishment?"

He flipped the lapel of her topcoat to the side, baring the skin beneath, above the line of her tightly fitted bodice, and scraped his teeth along the skin there, nipping gently. "I believe I can handle the punishment myself."

She arched against him. "Do you promise?"

A low growl was his reply, and he stripped her coat off her shoulders. She released him as he dispensed the garment, until he pulled her back in his arms, one hand tracing over her shoulder and down the broad, smooth expanse of skin he'd revealed.

Not that he could see it. He cursed his frustration. "Talk of punishment," he whispered. "If I'm only ever going to have this—a handful of stolen minutes . . . a smattering of kisses . . . a cupboard-full of pleasure—" She shivered as his fingers slipped beneath the silk of her bodice. "It seems special torture that I cannot see it."

She smiled in the darkness, a thrill coursing through her. "But you can feel it."

"That I can," he said, those wicked fingers teasing her despite the rigid binds of her dress. "You ache for me here." He pinched the tight tip of one breast, her gasp mingling with his delicious, low laugh.

"I do," she said, her lips at his ear.

In the wake of her words, he tightened his fist around the fabric where he toyed with her. He pulled the fabric down, lifting her breasts from their moorings. She sucked in a breath at the freedom from the tight bodice, and then released it in a long sigh at the stroke of his fingers, around and around the nipples that strained for his touch, hard and aching for him.

"Caleb." She sighed his name.

He did not reply, instead moving in the darkness, turning her, lifting her until she was balanced on a stack of crates in the rear corner of the closet. "Comfortable?"

She grew impossibly warmer at the question. At the care in it. "Very," she said, letting humor edge into her tone as she fisted the wool of his waistcoat, pulling him close again. "Remarkably accommodating for a cupboard. Do you think we are thieving someone's secret spot?"

His tongue traced the soft skin where her neck met her shoulder. "More than one someone, probably."

"When I was a girl, I once stumbled upon an upstairs maid and a stablehand."

His lips traced over her skin, from her shoulder to her breast, "And were you a good girl? Did you immediately take your leave?"

"I have never in my life been a good girl."

He rewarded the admission, dipping his head and taking her nipple into his mouth, slow and lush, scrambling her thoughts with the delicious caress. He lifted his head and blew a long stream of air over the tightening flesh. "Where were you?"

"At home. My parents had recently had a house party, and all the guests had left, and the maids were returning all the rooms to rights."

"Keep talking," he commanded, moving his attention to the other breast, licking over the tip before settling his warm lips to her, suckling in long, lovely tugs.

"I was . . ." She paused as his fingers touched her ankle, beneath her skirts, settled, still. She willed them to move. Wanted them higher.

He stopped the wonderful touch at her breast. "Sesily?" Her name like sin in his deep voice, spurring her to action.

"No," she whispered. "More."

His lips curved on her skin, smiling. "If you don't stop, I don't stop, sweet."

What was she saying? Oh. "I don't know why I was there," she said, "but it was the furthest room on the west wing of the house—as far from mine as possible. They hadn't closed the door all the way."

His fingers rose higher on her leg, pulling her skirts with them, tracing along her stockings in a slow, tempting slide. "Careless."

"Maybe," she whispered. "Maybe they hadn't thought about it, because they couldn't think of anything but—" The words turned into a little gasp as his fingers met the soft skin of her thigh.

"Maybe they wanted to be caught," he said, and the pure masculine arrogance in his voice sent want pooling through her. "Maybe you like the idea of that."

She opened her legs a little wider. "I do."

"Wicked girl," he whispered, his fingers reaching the leather strap and sheath that held her knife, stroking over it like it was a silk ribbon. "Wicked girl, with a blade at her thigh. Goddess of war."

She sighed at the words. At the way her secrets brought him closer.

But he didn't linger there. He was too interested in what else he might find. What else she might tell him. "What were they doing?"

She closed her eyes at the memory. "At first I couldn't tell . . . His back was to me. She was lifted onto the high, unmade bed, her legs wrapped about his waist. Her arms around his neck."

Those fingers, stroking carefully, ever closer to where she wanted him. "And?"

"She was making sounds . . . little soft sounds."

"Mmm," he said, as though they discussed a curious natural phenomenon. And then his fingers were there, playing in her downy hair, spreading her open, one finger parting the seam of her.

And then he stopped.

The wretched man *stopped*.

Sesily thought she'd go mad. She clenched her fingers in his hair. "*Caleb.*"

"You stopped talking. Tell me what they were doing. And I will continue."

She lifted her hips, hating the tease. Loving it. But he was ready, pulling away from her until he was just barely touching her. "Tell me," he insisted. "Tell me and I'll give you what you want." He stole her lips in the darkness, a sweet surprise, his tongue stroking deep.

When he released her, he pressed his forehead to hers and said, "Say it."

She didn't hesitate. "They were fucking."

He groaned his pleasure at the filthy words, and made good on his promise, sliding one finger deep into her softness, finding her wet and wanting, and then his thumb was where she ached for him, pressing firmly, circling with precision, as though he'd spent a lifetime learning how to pleasure her.

As though he was made to pleasure her.

She gasped his name and threw her head back, knocking it against a shelf behind her. "Yes," she whispered, knowing it was bold. Knowing he liked it.

And he did like it. "Yes," he repeated as a second finger joined the first. "And did you watch?"

She bit her lip as his thumb swirled, circling the tight center of her pleasure. "I did."

He tutted his disapproval—a blatant lie. "Naughty girl."

Sesily tightened her grip on his shoulders, this was the game they had always played—his censure, and her refusal to be censured. "I think *she* was the naughty girl," she said, his fingers moving in slow, deliberate thrusts, making her ache. "And she wasn't alone—he, too, was naughty."

"Lucky bastard." His lips were at her ear again, his breath hot on her skin like a brand. "And now?"

"Now," she said, turning to meet his kiss, slow and sinful, before she asked for what she wanted. "Now I would say you are not being naughty enough."

She heard the little hitch in his breath at the words. Barely-there and still, like gunshot in the silence. "Not naughty enough with my lips here?" He kissed her again. "With my tongue here?" He licked over her ear. "With my touch here?" He curled his fingers deep inside her, finding a spot that had her crying out for a heartbeat before he caught her lips again, drinking the sound. "Shhh, Sesily. You must be quiet, or we shall be caught."

The words sent pleasure pooling through her— pleasure she couldn't hide with him so close. With him inside her. He gave a little, low laugh at her ear. "Oh . . . You like that, too. You like my hands on you, bringing you pleasure, while you have to be quiet."

She did. She *did*. "Yes," she whispered. "I love it."

He shuddered at the words. "You're going to kill me."

She rocked her hips against him. "I could say the same."

He kissed her again, deep and delicious, before he whispered against her lips, "Can you stay quiet? Or do I have to stop?" The steel that edged into the words, like he *would* stop, threatened to end her there.

"I can," she promised, her fingers tight on his arm, in his hair. "I promise."

And then he was where she ached, his fingers and thumb slow and unyielding, following the movement of her hips, his words at her ear. "If you can't stay quiet, love, we shall be caught and that won't be the worst that happens . . ." he vowed. Everything fading except his heat and his muscles, and the magnificent way he touched her, like she was an instrument and he was a virtuoso. "If we're caught, I shall have to stop."

She stiffened at the words, rocketing through her as the wave of her pleasure threatened. "Don't you dare," she said, her hips working faster.

"Even if we're caught?" he asked, tempting, teasing, his fingers playing over her without stopping. "You'd want me to finish you even if the door opened and we were discovered?"

She was wild with it. With him. "Caleb. Please."

"You'd come against my fingers even then?"

"Yes," she promised, panting, lost to the fantasy.

"Show me now," he demanded. "Come."

The command was so imperious; she couldn't help but follow it, her mouth opening on a silent scream, turning to find him, needing to anchor herself to him. And he gave her that, too, pulling her tight to him with his free arm, stealing her lips as she came hard and fast around him, losing herself to the darkness and to this man who knew exactly how to give it to her.

She rocked against him, riding out the waves of her pleasure as he pressed soft kisses across her cheek, to her ear where he praised her in soft, dark whispers that made her want it all over again.

Not again. Still.

She'd wanted this man for years, and now that he was here, and it was in reach, Sesily didn't want to let go. "Caleb," she said softly, as he pulled free of her clasp. He was letting her go. They were going back to normal. But she didn't want normal. She wanted *him*. "Wait. Let me—"

She lost the end of the sentence when she realized he wasn't leaving her.

He was getting on his knees.

She blinked in the darkness. *Was he—*

Sesily was thirty years old and widely known as a proper London scandal. Once it had become clear that she was not for marriage, she'd had a handful of love affairs with artists and actors—never aristocrats, because that way lay more dramatics than even she was willing to tolerate. She knew pleasure, and wasn't afraid to ask for it.

But in the fifteen years since her first kiss and the decade since the first time she'd found pleasure with another, she'd never experienced one wildly satisfying orgasm only to be treated to another, instantly.

Confusion flared, and she stiffened as she realized what he was up to. "Caleb, you don't have to . . ." She trailed off.

"And if I want to?" he replied, casually, as he lifted her skirts up over her lap.

God, she wished she could see him. She clasped the fabric in one hand. "Well . . . I suppose that would be alright."

He nipped at the inside of her knee. "You suppose."

She smiled. He was so playful here in the darkness.

What would happen when they returned to the light?

No. She wouldn't think about that. "I mean, if you must," she retorted, teasing him.

He huffed a little laugh, tickling the inside of her thigh as he widened them. "Very kind of you."

"I do try to be accommodating," she quipped, threading her fingers through his curls again. They were so soft, impossibly so.

"Mmm," he said, lifting one of her legs over his shoulder. "What is the rule?"

She closed her eyes at the feel of his breath against her curls, as his fingers parted her again. She sighed her pleasure at the cool air against her flesh, still swollen from the pleasure he'd given her minutes earlier.

He growled. "I can smell you, love. Fucking mouthwatering."

"Caleb," she said, hearing the plea in her tone. Knowing she shouldn't beg. Knowing it was unladylike.

Unlike the rest of this. Exceedingly ladylike.

"What is the rule, Sesily."

Don't make this more than it is.

Don't fall in love with him.

She pushed the thoughts away, as he leaned closer, tempting her with the feel of him but not the touch she craved. "Sesily . . ."

That warning again, delicious.

"Stay quiet," she whispered.

He rewarded the answer with a single long, slow lick up her center. His low moan of pleasure was muffled by skirts and skin, but she felt it there, at her core, and she closed her eyes, growing wetter for him, wanton for him.

The wicked, wonderful man relished her response.

He licked over her, pressing his tongue into her softness, making love to her with slow, languid strokes that disappeared everything but this darkness, this heat, this man. His mouth was pure sin, like a gift.

She sighed again, louder, and he stopped, dammit.

"Quiet," he reminded her.

"I will be," she replied, instantly. "Do it again."

He laughed that wicked laugh again, the one she'd just discovered and suddenly had trouble imagining living without. "I have dreamed of this . . ."

He had?

She hated the darkness. She wanted to see him. Wanted to know if it was true.

Was it just a thing he said to women?

His tongue swirled at her center. "God, I have starved for you."

No. She couldn't bear thinking of him saying such a thing to other women.

She tilted her hips up to him. Insistent.

He did as he was told, the glorious man, returning his mouth to her as she bit her lip, trying to stay quiet, her fingers tight in his curls, holding him to her as she rocked against him, losing all control, unable to stop seeking more of him, claiming more of what he offered. And then it was Caleb making sounds, his hands releasing her thighs to wrap under her and clasp her bottom, pulling her to him as he found the tight bud of her desire and working it in ever tightening circles, until Sesily was reduced to nothing but the feel of him.

Her thighs began to tremble as he took what he wanted from her, as he gave her pure, unfettered pleasure in return. Her back bowed as she pressed herself to him—an offering at his altar—and came apart against him and still he did not release her, his magnificent mouth and his strong hands holding her in place as he delivered her to oblivion and stayed with her, softening as her movements slowed, as she found her breath once more, as she returned to the moment, to the small, dark space where they'd had no business finding such pleasure.

He turned his head and placed soft, lingering kisses over the inside of first one thigh and then the other, and she thought she heard him whisper, "Good girl," at her knee, before he lowered her skirts and smoothed them down her legs. The praise sent a flood of pride through her—knowing that she'd pleased him.

As well as he'd pleased her.

Impossible. It could not have been as well as he'd pleased her, because Sesily had never experienced anything like what he'd done. And she was terrified by what that would mean.

Before she could wrap her thoughts about this new reality, a soft rap came on the door, and they both froze. He stood, turning toward the door, putting his back to her. Sesily reached to stay his movement, fully intending to push past him, open the door, and talk her way out of whatever situation she was in. There was no reason whoever was outside would have to see him. He could escape without notice.

But when she touched him, she realized he'd turned to steel.

Gone was the soft, playful man who'd kissed and touched and teased her.

He was pure muscle now, strong and immovable.

Protecting her from whatever was to come.

And then she heard the bell. Short and light, the kind that summoned servants.

Or heralded friends.

"Open it," she whispered.

He did, his muscles rippled beneath her touch as he prepared for battle.

Instead, he found Duchess, a knowing look in her eye as she took in the scene in the cupboard, her gaze sliding over Caleb to the topcoat on the floor of the closet, then up to Sesily.

"Strange place for croquet, no?"

Chapter Twelve

"Aunt Sesily does not require additional maquillage, Lorna."

The only sign that Sesily's eldest niece, all of four years old, had heard her mother's warning was a slight flattening of her lips as she considered her aunt's face.

Sesily did her best not to smile at the little portrait of determination, so like Sophie, who had spent much of her life as the quiet, unassuming Talbot sister—without anyone realizing that she was an absolute battering ram when she needed to be.

Lorna's blue eyes, the exact color of her mother's, met Sesily's. "I'm not finished."

"Well then you absolutely must finish," Sesily said, leaning to one side from her spot on the carpet at the center of the Highley Manor library. "Sorry, Sophie, but she can't leave me half done. I shall look ridiculous."

Sophie, Marchioness of Eversley and future Duchess of Lyne, looked over, dandling her youngest babe, Emma, on her lap. Next to her, their sister Seleste, Countess of Clare, was busy adjusting the straps on her youngest son's trousers.

"We wouldn't want that," Sophie said. "You do not look at all ridiculous as it is."

Sesily grinned. "I like to look good for you lot."

"And we appreciate it," Sophie retorted.

For twenty years, it had been the five sisters against the rest of society, which regarded them with equal parts fascination and disdain.

The Soiled S's, so named for the way their father had built his fortune, were everything society loathed . . . but they made for good fun at a party, perfectly happy to be the center of attention—attending the events of the social season with elaborate, outlandish gowns paid for by their husbands, each richer than the last. But in recent years, four had married and chosen to have children.

As children were far less welcome at balls than scandals, the quintet now spent their time together in more domestic locales, along with the ever-expanding brood they'd produced.

Well, the brood that four of them had produced.

On nice days, the clan took over the northern edge of the Serpentine lake, loud and raucous and making an absolute scene to the disdain of London's society set (though, if any ever wandered over to say hello, they'd happily be welcomed into the fun). As November in Britain had a shortage of nice days, however, they often landed here, at Highley, two-hours' drive outside of London, at the country seat of the Duke and Duchess of Haven.

Here, the sisters, their husbands, and their children had the run of the massive manor house, which boasted more than a dozen bedchambers, making it perfect for large family gatherings that regularly became days-long affairs.

Though in the last two years, Sesily had made a point of coming with her own carriage, and leaving before the day turned into an overnight.

In the last two years, it had become more and more difficult to be with her sisters, with whom she had less and less in common as their lives diverged from her own.

Oh, they still loved her. They still found her amusing and teased her about her scandals and asked her to deliver the gossip from this ball and that tea and who was seen with whom in private boxes at the opera. And Sesily was always welcome at The Singing Sparrow— though Sera was rarely there in the evenings now that she was increasing, which meant that Sesily didn't see her near as much as usual.

Which was why she'd sought out The Place.

How she'd come to meet Duchess and Adelaide and Imogen.

Being at The Singing Sparrow had soon lost its appeal because it was so difficult to think of it as Sera's and not Sera's and Fetu's and Caleb's. And when he'd left without a goodbye two years earlier . . . one year earlier . . . Sesily had been forced to confront the simple reality that Caleb Calhoun was not interested in her.

Except . . .

He'd seemed exceedingly interested three nights earlier, when he'd delivered her a shattering amount of pleasure in the Viscount Coleford's servants' closet, with a not insignificant number of aristocrats in shouting distance.

Shhh, Sesily. You must be quiet.

The memory of Caleb's words thrummed through her, setting her skin aflame.

Caleb, whom she'd left in the closet, following Duchess up the servants' steps and back to the room where everything had gone pear-shaped to make her excuses and say her goodbyes, certain that when she returned to Talbot

House, he'd be there. She'd never admit it to anyone, but she'd held her breath as she entered her home that evening, imagining that he was already there. Imagining that he was waiting for her.

Imagining that they'd spend the evening repeating their actions in the dark . . . this time in a room awash in candlelight.

Imagination had not kept her warm that evening. Nor had it done the next day when she'd turned up at The Singing Sparrow ostensibly to deliver her sister a length of ribbon Sesily thought she'd like, but really just hoping to cross his path. To read his eyes. To steal another kiss.

Nor had it the following day, when she'd delivered the papers she'd stolen from Coleford to the Duchess of Trevescan, only to find Adelaide there, sprawled across a divan, reading the newspaper. The moment her friend had tipped the point of the newsprint down to look at her, Sesily had raised a finger in objection and said, "No."

Adelaide's only response was a raised brow.

Caleb Calhoun could return to Boston for all she cared. He probably was already on his way, the coward.

"Sesily." Her name, loud and firm, suggested that Sophie had been trying to get her attention for a bit.

She shook her head and smiled. "Sorry, lost in thought."

Sophie's brow furrowed just slightly in concern. "Are you well?"

Irritation flared at her sister's perceptive response, and Sesily knew it was unfair. Was that not what sisters were for? To see the truth and root it out? To pick at the scab until it revealed the wound beneath?

But this was not the kind of scab she felt comfortable discussing with her sisters any longer. Five years earlier—three years earlier—she might have told them everything. Might have disclosed every thought and every desire and every frustration she had with Caleb. But that was before, when there had still been a possibility that she'd walk their path.

Now, however, if she were to say anything about Caleb Calhoun and how he'd nearly had her in a servants' closet after she'd broken into the Viscount Coleford's desk during a dinner party, they would surely ask questions.

Which, if she were being honest, would not be entirely out of line. But she wasn't interested in answering them. Not today, and possibly not ever.

Her sisters loved her, but they didn't understand her.

And she wasn't sure they ever would.

Flashing a bright smile—the one made famous by the girls London used to call The Dangerous Daughters for how they threatened to steal hearts and titles—she said, "Perfectly well."

Before Sophie could probe, little Rose, Seline's daughter, a few months younger than Lorna and inseparable from her cousin, who'd spent the last thirty minutes removing all of Sesily's hairpins and then reinserting them so that they "were better," said in a voice full of awe, "You look *beautiful*."

The forced smile became real. Truly there were few things that puffed one up more than children's compliments. "Thank you very much, my sweet girl. I shall take that compliment, because it speaks to Lorna's superior talent with kohl and rouge, and to your own skill for hair, but I wonder, am I not also *clever*?"

The girls were distracted by adding additional red powder to her cheeks.

Seraphina, Duchess of Haven and mistress of the house in which the Talbot sisters had congregated, laughed from the far end of the room, where she returned a haphazard pile of books to a low shelf. "Girls, tell your aunt Sesily that she is clever," she said, standing up with more effort than appeared healthy.

"You're clever," the girls said in unison.

"It's not the same if you have to be told to say it, my loves."

Seraphina waddled toward her, big as a house, though Sesily knew better than to say such a thing after becoming an aunt nine previous times. The fruits of those many accomplishments were sprinkled about the library appearing very much like the Duke and Duchess of Haven had been delivered parcels of children that morning instead of the ordinary household goods.

Nine children: three belonging to Sophie and her marquess husband; two girls, wise beyond their years, belonging to Seline and Mr. Mark Landry, London's greatest horsebreeder; three boys under four belonging to Seleste and her husband, the Earl of Clare; and little Oliver, son to Sera and the Duke of Haven, one and a half, and his mother about to deliver another.

"Tell me something," Sesily said to the room at large. "Have the four of you been drinking some kind of tincture or tonic from the local midwife? Perhaps an incorrect dosage? How are you all so damned fertile?"

"What's fertile?" asked Adam, Seleste's eldest, from his place by the fire, where he and his middle brother were stacking books and toppling them to the ground.

"Nothing," his mother replied.

"Ask your father," Sesily said at the same time, flashing a grin at her sister. "Clare will love it."

"Oh, no doubt," Seleste agreed. The earl would absolutely not love it, but it would give him and Seleste something to argue about, which was their favorite pastime, and the act that had no doubt preceded the conception of each of their three sons.

Sesily grimaced at the prospect of another nephew. "There's no danger that the copious amounts of children in this room are . . . catching . . . is there?"

"Sometimes it does feel that way," Sophie said with a sigh, leaning back on the settee. "Best steer clear of Sera."

"Ten under five feels like some kind of biblical plague is all I'm saying," Sesily said. "Have we been so badly behaved that this might be punishment?"

"The aristocracy would surely think so," Seline replied, summoning a laugh from all assembled.

"Well, either way," Sesily said, "you're lucky you have a battalion of nursemaids. And one *very clever* aunt."

"Ah, *very* clever, now," Sera said, toddling her little boy over the carpet.

"Give him." Sesily waved her sister over.

He barreled into her arms. "Now, what's your name, then?"

"That's Oliver!" Lorna answered.

Oliver blinked up at Sesily, entranced by her paint. No one would blame him.

"Is it?" Sesily teased. "There are just so many of you, it's difficult to keep you all straight. Indeed, it would be much easier if I only saw you in batches of two or three."

"Us first!" Rose demanded.

"Clearly. And Oliver can stay." She bopped the child on the nose with an enormous powder puff, and was rewarded with a delighted giggle.

"And me!" Adam shouted from his book stacking.

"Who are you again?" Sesily asked.

"I'm Adam!" He wasn't amused.

"And are you new?"

"No!"

"I could swear we've never met."

He looked to his mother. "Mama, Aunt Sesily is being difficult."

"Imagine that," Seleste replied, pouring herself a cup of tea from the service in the corner of the room before looking to Sesily. "Are you quite finished riling them up? They do perfectly well on their own."

"I'm just doing my part. It's almost as though you shouldn't have had so many that they outnumber you," Sesily retorted, looking back to her minuscule ladies' maids and whispering, "So. Many. Babies."

The pair nodded with all seriousness.

"And they get *everything*," Rose replied.

"Tell me more."

"Papa bought Sissy a *pony* the other day. I didn't get one."

"Oh, for goodness' sake, Rose," Seline said from a distance. "Your sister is half your size and did not have a pony. You've three ponies, because your father gives you everything you ask, whenever you ask for it." Also because her father was one of the richest men in Britain and provided horseflesh to the entirety of Mayfair.

"Not when I asked for a new pony, he didn't," Rose said matter-of-factly before returning her short attention span to Lorna's work.

"Lord deliver me from spoiled children," Seline said to the ceiling.

"*I'm* not spoiled!" Lorna proclaimed with the braggadocio of someone who absolutely was, running a stick of kohl well past Sesily's eyelid. "*Ash* gets everything."

"I beg your pardon, young lady," Sophie said, warning in her tone. "What does your brother get that you do not?"

Lorna looked directly at her mother and said, "A title."

Sesily chuckled in the dead silence that fell. "A palpable hit, Lorna-roo."

"That's enough out of you, Sesily Talbot." Sophie came off the couch, setting the baby to her hip.

Sesily looked to her nieces. "I'm in trouble now."

They giggled.

"You are. For rousing this rabble." Sophie crouched next to them. "You are very right, Lorna. You don't get a title. And that is not at all fair."

Lorna's gaze narrowed. *Good girl*, thought Sesily. *That will serve you well in the future.* "Because I'm a girl."

"Because you are a girl. And it's terrible, and if we could, your father and I would give you all titles. We'd give you kingdoms." Lord knew the Marquess of Eversley would burn down Parliament if he thought it would get his girls treated with equity.

Sophie pushed on. "But look at all of us." She waved to the collection of women in the room. "Your aunt Seraphina and I both own businesses, your aunt Seline rides horses like she was born one, your aunt Seleste speaks more languages than most people can name. And we don't have titles, but we have ourselves, and we have each other. And that's better than any title, if you ask me."

Lorna was no longer listening, but Sesily was, and the words struck her more forcefully than she'd expected, tightening her throat. "That's a very good answer to a very difficult question," she said to Sophie.

Sophie smiled. "I have had practice."

"I am impressed."

"What about Aunt Sesily?" Lorna asked.

Everyone seemed to still in the wake of the unexpected question, and Sesily couldn't help but wait in the silence, wishing the little girl hadn't pointed out that Sophie had forgotten Sesily in her lovely list of her sisters' attributes.

Except Sophie, her youngest sister, who'd always been the one to surprise them, did not hesitate. "Aunt Sesily loves with her whole heart." The words sizzled through Sesily, tingling at the back of her throat. And then Sophie leaned in and said, softly, "And she keeps secrets better than anyone."

Sesily blinked and let out a little laugh that might have been called watery by someone who wished to be rude. "That's true, as a matter of fact."

Sophie looked to her and winked.

"You have always been my favorite sister," Sesily said.

"I know," said Sophie, happily, before plucking the stick of kohl from Lorna's hands. "That is enough now. Your aunt is going to have to return to the world eventually, and any more of this might become permanent."

Lorna's little face fell.

"Well, if your mother insists we are through, I am going to find a looking glass."

"And Lorna," Sophie said, "is going to find a washbasin."

In swooped one of the many nursemaids at hand and Lorna was whisked away, calling back, "Don't wash it off until Papa sees!"

Sesily turned her attention on her sister. "Do you think King would enjoy his daughter's masterpiece?"

Sophie's lips twitched. "I think he would send her directly to an artists' academy."

"In France."

"Nowhere else would do."

"Well, I won't wash it off, but I would like to see it." She turned to Oliver. "What do you think?" He reached out with the now rather gummy powder puff and powdered her chin. She shook her head. "Everyone in this whole family has a critique."

Propping him on her hip, she made for the hallway, where she found Seraphina speaking to the butler. Oliver, too, found his mother, reaching for her and making sounds that threatened to become unpleasant, so Sesily did what any intelligent aunt would do and headed for the parent in question.

". . . prepare a room for him, in case he decides to stay," Sera said, turning to catch a lunging Oliver. "Oof!"

"In case who decides to stay?" Sesily asked as the butler hurried off to do the duchess's bidding. But she knew the answer. It settled like a stone in her chest.

"Caleb," Sera said, distractedly, plucking the powder puff from her son's hand, one hand stroking over her midsection. "Have you let him eat this? It's . . . wet."

"He hasn't exactly ingested it," Sesily replied, trying to calm the rush of—whatever it was that was coursing through her. She didn't want to name it. She didn't like it well enough to name it. Instead, she redirected the conversation. "What's he doing here?"

"Oliver?"

"Sera. Pay attention. Caleb."

"I invited him," Sera said, as though it were perfectly normal. Which it wasn't.

Sesily's eyes went wide. She could name this feeling, despite loathing it. It was betrayal. *"Why?"*

"I thought he might enjoy himself," Sera said. "He likes the country. In Boston he has a large home on the water."

She didn't want to think about his home. She didn't want to think about *him*. "How nice for him."

Sera shook her head. "Sesily, what—"

"And who is running the tavern?"

Sera looked at her as though she'd gone mad. "Fetu. And our very competent staff."

"And if you have Fetu and a competent staff, tell me, why must Caleb be in England at all?"

Sera blinked, opened her mouth to reply, then closed it, confusion flashing in her brown eyes before it was chased away with something else. Suspicion. "Well. So much for being immune to your charms."

Sesily's brows snapped together. "What?"

"You and Caleb."

"What about us?" Sesily said, brazening it through.

Sera knew better. She tilted her head and said, "Sesily." And before Sesily could deny it. Or admit it. Or take a moment to find an additional possibility, her sister added, "How was it?"

Sesily's cheeks were instantly aflame.

"How was what?"

Sesily closed her eyes, grateful that her back was to him. Highley Manor was one of the largest estates in all of England, with more than one hundred and twenty rooms. And of course the man had arrived at the top of two flights of stairs, in the second-floor hallway, outside the manor's library at that *precise* moment, as though the whole thing were written in a novel. *Dammit.*

"Nothing," Sesily began, desperate for her sister not to say anything to make it worse.

No luck there.

"How were *you*," Sera said, rounding on him, babe in arms. "It's clear that you and Sesily have . . ."

"Have *what*?"

"It's also clear that you've hurt her, and I find I don't care for that," Sera added, ignoring his question. "On the continuum of annoyance, I'm not quite at furious older brother, but I'm most definitely at annoyed friend and business partner. Shall we give it time?"

"Sera—" They both said it. At the same time.

Sesily sighed and turned to face the man she'd last seen in the shadows of the closet where he'd spent the better part of an hour kissing various parts of her body.

Preparing for the absolute worst, she said, "Hello, Caleb."

His gaze found hers, deadly serious, and he stiffened with . . . regret.

Once, during her first season, Sesily had been in a ladies' retiring room fixing a stocking ribbon and eavesdropping, and she'd heard a young lady wish that the ground would open up and swallow her whole, so riddled she was with embarrassment.

At the time, Sesily had thought the woman dramatic.

No longer.

She looked to the floor and cursed the sturdiness of the marble there.

And then, matters got worse.

Because instead of returning the greeting, Caleb said, "What happened to your face?"

Chapter Thirteen

She looked like she'd been attacked by a mad painter. Covered in paint and rouge and what appeared to be eye kohl applied all around her eyes, out to her temples and above her eyebrows, her hair in wild disarray, pinned haphazardly and looking like at any moment it would all tumble down around her shoulders and tease at the edges of her perfectly fitted rose silk dress.

She looked all the ways women were told they should not look. Disheveled and untamed. An absolute mess.

Anyone would have asked her what happened to her face.

But when he gave voice to the question and it had landed in the foyer between him and Sesily and her sister, it struck Caleb that perhaps he should not have asked that particular thing in quite that particular way.

Because he found that however wild the paint on her face, however much her hair appeared to have been the result of a lady's maid who was part cyclone, he didn't like the way she responded to the question, too harsh, with too much of an edge.

He didn't like her closing herself off.

Even though he absolutely deserved it, and the biting tone in which she replied, "Have you never seen such a face, American? It's all the rage in Mayfair."

He couldn't help himself. "You know, I have recently been surprised by the things I've seen painted on faces in Mayfair."

A slight flare of her nostrils was the only sign Sesily caught the reference to what she'd done to the Earl of Totting in the Duchess of Trevescan's gardens, though Caleb would not have been surprised if she'd found a way to flay him for it, if only her sister hadn't decided to come for him first.

"Caleb Calhoun, you American menace!" Sera came toward Caleb, his godson in arms, and Caleb did his best to ignore the thread of guilt that coursed through him, instead focusing on the little boy, who clapped his hands. "You made me a promise."

He'd made one to himself, as well.

He resisted the thought, instead reaching into his pocket and extracting a paper sack of apple candies, procured from a sweet shop in St. James's before he'd driven out. He opened the sack and offered them to Sera. "I brought sweets."

She narrowed her gaze on him. "That is a paltry offering."

"Sera," he said, firmly. "Nothing happened."

Sesily made a sound from behind her, and Caleb realized that, too, might have been the wrong thing to say, considering she was *right there*. He looked to her. Had she told her sister they'd—

"He's right," Sesily said. Adding, "Not that it's any of your business."

"It may not be my business, *per se*," Sera insisted, swinging round toward Sesily, placing Oliver within striking distance of the sweets. Caleb reached into the bag and extracted a lolly. He needed as many friends here as possible. Sera looked back. "Excuse me, don't bribe my child."

Oliver popped the candy into his mouth.

"I don't see how it is your business at all, Sera," Sesily said. "I am a grown woman of thirty years with my own home, my own funds, and absolutely no need of protection. And whatever I do or do not do with"—she offered a dismissive hand in Caleb's direction—"whomever . . . is my business and mine alone."

Whomever?

He didn't care for that.

"Mine, as well, I hope," he said.

Both Talbot sisters turned wide eyes on him.

"So . . . something did happen," Sera said, triumphantly, as though she was London's greatest detective.

"Do you want something to have happened? Or not?" he asked.

Before Sera could answer, Sesily groaned and looked to the ceiling in frustration. "Remaining silent is always an option, American. *Nothing happened.*"

He'd said it first, of course. It wasn't Sera's business, and that was the easiest response to her questions. But damned if he didn't loathe the emphasis Sesily put on the response, as though nothing *at all* had happened. And damned if he didn't want to point out that while they might not have experienced the full scope of the act in question, he knew the feel of her full breasts in his hands, and she knew the feel of his tongue against her core, and he knew that she got hot when he asked her to be quiet, so *something* had occurred, dammit.

He'd thought that three days apart from her, resolving to put her out of his sight and thoughts, would have given him a chance to regain some strength when it came to her. Some sense. Some ability to resist her.

But no, here he was, wanting her all over again. Even as she looked . . .

And then a little girl with dark curls and bright blue eyes broke the awkward silence by running into the foyer with a shining silver platter calling, "Aunt Sesily! Mama said you could use *this* as a looking glass!" and presented it to her clearly favorite aunt like a tribute.

As though nothing at all was amiss, Sesily looked down into the shining silver, gasped her surprise, put a hand to her wild hair and said, without hesitation, "I look *beautiful*!"

And she did. She looked beautiful.

No good would come of thinking Sesily Talbot beautiful. Indeed, no good would come of him being here at all. Which was precisely what they were all about to agree on before he'd been distracted by Sesily and her general . . . Sesilyness.

He promised himself he'd sort out his return to London, just as soon as he was able to tear his attention from Sesily's laugh.

It was big and bold and perfect—the kind of laugh that welcomed all comers, making you feel like you'd been offered a glimpse at the sun after a voyage through the darkness. If only you were willing to take it.

Except, it wasn't for him. She'd just said as much.

And even if it were, he couldn't take it.

Not with any promise of the future.

The future.

Now, where in hell had that come from?

He should have stayed away. He'd known it would be a mistake. It was always a mistake to get too close to her. But the truth was, now he'd let himself get close. He'd let himself revel in her. And he wanted her now, more than ever, just as he'd always known he would.

So, he'd ignored all the clear, logical reasons why he shouldn't come, and he'd listened to the singular hope that if he did, he might see her. Even though he'd spent the last three days doing everything he could not to see her. He'd called in a favor from the brothers who provided the Sparrow with smuggled liquor—brothers who had eyes on every corner of Covent Garden and a wide swath of the rest of London—and asked them to keep eyes on Sesily, in part to keep his promise to Seraphina and in part to make sure that he could avoid her.

But an invitation to a family gathering—to a warm meal in a warm home full of people who cared for each other and welcomed him into their fold, one of whom was the woman whose taste still lingered in his memory—he hadn't been able to resist.

Of course he'd come. He'd wanted to see her.

He watched as she returned the platter to the little girl, and leaned down to point at him and stage whisper, "That man is Mr. Calhoun, Aunt Seraphina's very good friend. And if you ask him very nicely, he shall give you a whole bag of treats to share with the others."

The little girl's eyes went wide with excitement.

Caleb knew his role. He extended the sack of sweets as she inched closer and closer and then snatched it from him, as though he might change his mind. He might have been amused at the way she turned tail and ran off in the direction of the library, but instead, he was consumed with Sesily's description.

Aunt Seraphina's very good friend.

And what did that make him to her?

Nothing.

He was nothing to her. He would never be anything to her.

He couldn't be.

As the girl's footsteps faded away, Sera took a deep breath. "Well. One of you is my friend and one of you is my sister, and as I am not willing to sacrifice either of you to whatever *this* is, I highly suggest that you sort it out before dinner." She turned her brown eyes on him. "Do you understand?"

Caleb swallowed around the heavy knot in his throat at the words—Sera and he had been through enough battles for both of their lifetimes. "Yes."

She looked to Sesily, who flattened her lips into a defiant line.

Reading her sister's resistance, Sera said, "Or I'll tell the others everything."

Sesily narrowed her gaze at the threat. "You're going to tell them anyway."

"Of course I am, but it's your choice if I do it before or after dinner—and one of those choices will make the meal unbearable for you."

Sesily crossed her arms over her chest. "Fine."

Satisfied, the Duchess of Haven swept from the room, looking no less aristocratic for the babe on her hip. When she was gone, Caleb met Sesily's gaze for what felt like the first time that day, because suddenly, her mask was gone.

Her jaw was set, her chin was lifted, her eyes were flashing, and no amount of rouge or kohl or hair in a wild halo around her could make her look ridiculous. Not then.

Not when she was Athena, ready for battle.

Caleb wanted that battle. He wanted to tangle with her. He wanted to lift her off her feet and press her to the nearest wall and set his lips to the line of that jaw.

She was magnificent.

Too magnificent for the likes of him.

She deserved so much more than what he could give her. "I—"

"Don't," she cut him off. "Whatever you are about to say, don't. Don't tell me you're sorry, or tell me what you shouldn't have done, or what you wouldn't have done, if only. And whatever you do, don't tell me you . . ." She trailed off. "Just don't."

He hadn't intended to say any of those things. "Sesily—"

"Don't say my name, either," she said. "I love my sister and you love my sister and she wants us to be cordial, and we surely can do that."

"Cordial," he said, flatly.

"Yes. Cordial. Surely you've seen that done before. Tip of the hat and 'how do you do' and"—she dropped a little curtsy—"how pleasant to see you again, Mr. Calhoun."

Except it wasn't pleasant to see her. It was like looking into the sun.

"Cordial," she repeated, as though it was simple.

He didn't want to be cordial. He wanted to strip her naked in her sister's foyer. That was the problem.

"Now, if you don't mind, I need to find a washbasin. I'm sure I look ridiculous."

She didn't, but he didn't trust himself to say so.

Instead, he watched as she turned her back on him and headed for the east wing of the house, where the family kept its rooms. He watched her go, knowing he shouldn't. Knowing that if he were a gentleman, he wouldn't notice the wide curve of her hips, the full swell of her bottom beneath the dusky rose of her skirts. Knowing that no gentleman would linger on the thought of the pretty little bows at the front of her gown, imagining what it would be like to untie them. To watch the silk of her dress pool around her ankles. Knowing that no gentleman would wonder what she wore beneath. The color of her stockings. The design on her corset.

But then, he'd never been a gentleman, had he?

He had to get out of this house, which was suddenly too small, despite being able to sleep the entire population of Boston, and too hot, despite being in England in November.

He should leave.

Instead, he watched this woman who twisted him in knots until she reached the entrance to the east wing, and he could no longer stay quiet. He called out to her, knowing no good could come of it. "Lady Sesily."

She stilled at the honorific—one he never used, but she'd asked for cordial, had she not? Then she turned, just enough to look over her shoulder, covered by a little pelisse that he could dispatch with in an instant if the opportunity presented itself.

"Do you have a coat?"

What was he doing?

She turned to face him fully. "A coat?"

"They're traditionally worn out of doors to keep one warm," he said, ignoring the thrum of pleasure he received when one corner of her mouth tilted upward. "Do you have one?"

"I do."

"When you return, wear it. We're taking a walk."

Fuck cordial.

Chapter Fourteen

Whatever this was, it was a mistake.

But here they were, taking a walk, as though that were a perfectly normal thing to do. Which, of course, it was for most people. Most people enjoyed walks. They were full of things like fresh air and natural beauty and Sesily understood that many, many people enjoyed those things.

Highley Manor boasted some of the freshest air and the most natural beauty in all of Surrey, she suspected. Though, if someone sat her down and offered her access to the secrets of every man in Mayfair, she would not be able to tell them where the nearest tree was, as she was having difficulty paying attention to anything but her companion, who was several feet in front of her, and as *big* as a tree, his long stride eating up the ground.

Her companion who had unsettled her not a small amount by—instead of agreeing to civilly ignore her like any self-respecting man who'd decided he was done with a woman—inviting her for a walk. In November.

This was what she got for attempting to make a deal with an American.

She pulled her coat tighter around her and muttered into the collar, "This was a mistake."

"Hmm?" he asked, the sound perfectly cordial, as requested.

Another mistake. She *hated* cordial.

Sesily cleared her throat. "Did you have a destination in mind?"

"Some people believe the journey is the destination."

"Those people don't have things to do."

One side of his mouth kicked up in a half smile and Sesily resisted feeling pleased about it. He pointed to a nearby ridge. "There."

"Why there?"

"A nice view."

She looked over at him, sure she'd find him laughing at her. "You're taking me to see the view?"

"I am."

"On a cloudy day in November."

"It's England, my lady. If we waited for sun we'd never see it."

She winced. "Don't call me that."

"My lady?"

"Yes. It's . . ." *Awful.* Most people said it with a snide humor, as though there was nothing about Sesily that was worthy of the honorific. But it was worse from this man who'd served her whiskey and exchanged barbs with her and leveled her with heated glances, and who knew too many of her secrets, and who'd made love to her earlier in the week. "It's odd."

"Probably the accent," he said.

"Definitely the accent." She clung to the excuse.

"But you told me I couldn't call you Sesily."

"I didn't think an opportunity for conversation would present itself so quickly," she retorted.

"And yet, here we are."

"Fine. Call me Sesily." He was infuriating. "Why does it feel like you've just won a battle?"

"Because you view everything as a battle," he said, simply.

She pulled up short. "That's not true."

He stopped. "Isn't it?"

"No. How would you know how I view things?"

A muscle flinched in his jaw. "In the two years since we met, you think I haven't noticed?"

She ignored the thread of warmth that came at the knowledge that he, too, had been paying attention to the calendar. "You're never here."

"I don't have to be here. When I am here, you are always ready to fight. It's your natural state. You've battled your sisters and society and the rest of the world, never ceding an inch of turf. Claiming your space and your time for yourself. For your future. For your own path, whatever it may be."

Sesily's breath caught in her chest as she listened, as she watched this man who understood far more than he let on. Who understood far more than most people had ever even tried to understand about her. Most people saw her tight bodices and her generous curves, heard her loud laugh and her bawdy jests, and decided she was the most dangerous of The Dangerous Daughters.

But not Caleb. Oddly, never Caleb.

"And you think I haven't seen it." He turned away from her, continuing his march up the long, slow rise.

She followed, as though she was on a string. "You've never seemed to pay attention."

She almost didn't hear his reply, collected on the wind to be carried away from her. But this was Caleb, and in the two years she'd known him, in the handful of days she'd been allowed to watch him, she'd drunk him in. Memorized the sound of his voice, the tenor of his laugh. The scent of him. Been desperately jealous of the women he flirted with over the bar at The Singing Sparrow. Wondered about the women he flirted with in Boston. Wondered if he ever imagined taking her there.

So she heard his reply.

"I've paid attention."

Her heart began to pound. Before she could ask more, he repeated himself. "I've paid attention since the moment we met—every time I've been on English soil, I've watched your battles. I used to think it was for sport, and maybe it was, at some point. A way to resist the future the rest of the world insisted was mapped out for you. I—like everyone—thought you'd eventually settle. Take to the path."

Marriage. Children. Family.

"Domestication," she said, disliking the word.

He shook his head. "You want everyone to think you're wild."

"I am," she said, flashing her most Sesily smile. "The feral one. Unable to be tamed."

Something flashed behind his eyes. "Mmm. Maybe."

"Never say there's hope for me, yet?"

He ignored the teasing in the words. He wasn't interested in playing. And that alone made Sesily nervous. "You don't want there to be hope for you. You're not fighting for sport." He turned his back on her, as though the conversation was done.

Sesily followed, playfulness gone, replaced by frustration. Defensiveness. "So tell me, if you know so much about it. What am I fighting for?"

He looked back at her. "I used to think you were battling for yourself. Your own path. To keep on it as your sisters paired off and peeled away, and as they've pressured you to do the same. But I don't think that anymore."

"How do you know that?" She'd never said that to anyone.

He ignored the question. "I used to think that you would one day decide to follow them."

She shook her head. "I don't want that."

"I know. You're like no aunt I've ever met."

"Nine times over . . . it's the practice that makes the work perfect." He smiled at her, and she stepped toward him, unable to stop herself. Unwilling to. "Though I confess I am surprised you noticed. Have you met many aunts?"

"Are they so uncommon?"

"I mean, in their natural habitat. In my case, surrounded by altogether too many children under the age of five."

Another low rumble of laughter, like praise. "My own aunts count, don't they?"

Surprise flared. "I . . . suppose they do."

"I've shocked you with the presence of my aunts?"

"It's just . . . difficult to imagine you being a nephew."

"It's almost as common as being an aunt, no?"

"Surely. But now I'm wondering how it was that you were ever a child."

Something clouded his eyes. Something a little dark and a little sad and extremely curious, and Sesily bit her tongue, knowing that if she asked to see more of it, he would never allow it. So, instead, she said, "I would have wagered that you'd simply sprung, fully formed, from some place."

His amusement came in a little puff of air. "I thought we decided that Athena was reserved for you."

She grinned. "I could warm to the idea of being a goddess."

"I don't doubt it," he said.

"For a man who claims not to have secrets, this surprise aunt suggests otherwise," she quipped. "Never say there's more. An uncle. A grandparent."

"A sister."

She froze, the words truly feeling like a secret. "You have a sister?"

He looked away, across the immense estate, and took a deep breath. "I do."

"Is she—"

He cut her off immediately. "We haven't spoken in a long time."

There was something in the words—something like sorrow. Like there was more to the story. And of course there was. This was Caleb. Full of secrets. Every time she unearthed one, a dozen more appeared. She nodded. "I'm sorry," she said, meaning it.

"Thank you," he said, lifting his hand as though it was the most ordinary thing in the world, and stroking his thumb along the side of her face.

The air on the rise grew thin.

His thumb continued its path, down over the edge of her jaw, his touch becoming even more gentle on her neck. "There is a shadow here, still," he said, his voice low and graveled. "Does it pain you?"

"No." She shook her head. "I had covered it with paint, but . . ."

He smiled. "It washed off with the rest."

"The downside of aunting."

"Risk of revealing your other work." A pause. "Tell me about it."

That thumb, warm and rough—he wasn't wearing gloves—lingered at her pulse for a moment, and she worried that he might feel the way it raced, divining its truth.

Making her want to tell him everything.

Which would be a mistake, because the more of herself she gave to Caleb Calhoun, the more she wanted him to claim. And Caleb had no interest in claiming her.

But still, she answered him. "There isn't much to say that you don't already see." She paused. "Everyone thought I would take one path. I took another."

"That easy, hmm?"

She smiled at the dry words. "When you're a person who wants something different than what society offers you . . . than what society tells you is the only correct path . . . you are grateful when a different one is illuminated. Even more so when it becomes clear that others are on the path. And that they will walk it with you."

"The Duchess, Miss Frampton, Lady Imogen."

She inclined her head. "Three of many."

"How many?"

Maggie, Nik and Nora, Mithra, a dozen other women from all walks who'd found their way to Trevescan House. Ladies with titles and husbands and children. Mistresses, women of pleasure, business owners. Actresses. *Magicians.* And beyond them, scores of others who lived their truth and fought for their place and blazed new paths. Ones that suited them.

"More every day," she replied. "It turns out that when you've spent a lifetime held under one thumb and then the next, there is power in helping others escape them. Especially when those who have capacity to help . . ." She trailed off, thinking of the evening with Viscountess Coleford.

"Won't."

She met his eyes, warming at the way he saw her. At the way he understood. "Most people would say *can't.*"

He tilted his head. "It's not can't though, is it?"

"No."

"Which makes it more dangerous," he said, softly. "You're in danger."

"We were in danger before, too. But before we didn't fight."

He saw the truth in the words, understood them. And it was then, in that moment, that Sesily realized Caleb Calhoun hadn't broken her heart two years earlier, when he'd rebuffed her advances and left for America.

Because it was then, as he saw her, as he *understood* her, that she realized he might break her heart in earnest this time.

Dammit.

"These aren't small battles, though," he said, an edge in his tone, something urgent. "They're bigger foes. More dangerous ones. Totting, The Bully Boys, Coleford . . . these are battles that have reason and reach beyond the personal."

Caleb Calhoun is not stupid. The Duchess's words from the night at The Place, before Calhoun and Peck arrived and The Bully Boys came knocking. *It won't take him very long to put it together.*

"Do they not seem personal?" she asked. "They feel personal." She cleared her throat and moved away from his touch, feeling for a moment like Athena, because it took an actual feat of strength to slide past him and walk away from his touch, leading the way up to the rise. "It's not far now," she tossed back, pretending as though she wasn't a riotous tangle of emotion. "I hope the view is worth it."

He followed in silence, his much longer stride easily catching up to her, but this time he didn't overtake her. He walked next to her, in silence, and Sesily did her very best not to look at him, even when he said, "I was right, wasn't I?"

"About what?"

"These fights put your life in danger," he said, and she could hear the frustration in his words.

"And the others didn't?"

His brow furrowed as he considered the question, and she saw the answer reveal itself. Of course they had. It had just been a different kind of danger. The kind that lasted for a lifetime.

These battles were the kind that made a lifetime.

They'd reached the top of the rise, where the northern half of the Highley estate spread out before them like an oil painting, the sky swirling in the distance with greys so deep they edged into purples over a land that was lush and green in the summer but had gone to autumn browns, crossed with handsome stone walls and dotted with white sheep.

"I will admit, this is stunning," she said, pulling her cloak tighter around her to combat the brisk wind whipping over the ledge.

"England shows in the winter better than anywhere else."

She pointed to the folly tower that stood at a distance, rising forty feet into the air like a perfect castle turret. "That's where Haven told Sera that he loved her."

"Which time?"

"The time he ruined everything."

"Which time he ruined everything?" Haven had been an ass on several occasions before he'd realized that Sera was his entire world.

She laughed. "The time before he fixed everything." She turned her attention to the little copse of trees just at the bottom of the rear side of the ridge. "Is there a building there?"

"Mmm," he said. "A groundskeeper's cottage."

She looked to him. "How do you know that?"

He grinned. "I take a lot of walks when I am here."

"For your constitution?"

"Yes . . ." he said. "And your brother-in-law is insufferable."

She laughed. "He is that."

"We settled a truce when he and Sera reconciled," he said. "And I guess he's an alright sort."

"The faintest of praise. But he loves my sister madly."

"And he's got a hell of an estate."

She looked back at the land. "That much is true."

They stood shoulder to shoulder for a moment, taking in the view, and Sesily became consumed with the feel of him there, tall and warm and steady next to her, as though he'd stand there and look at the grey storm clouds in the distance forever.

Unable to resist, she turned to look at him, his profile strong and stark against the grey sky. He hadn't worn a hat, and his hair, tousled by the November wind, fell in soft curls over his brow. How many times had she watched her sisters touch their husbands with casual pleasure—dusting a sleeve or straightening a cravat or pushing an errant curl back into place? In all the years since she'd come out, Sesily had never lingered on the idea of one day having those pleasures. Of the natural ease of them.

Until now, as she stared up into this beautiful man's untouchable face.

Sesily loves with her whole heart.

Sophie's words from earlier. Unwelcome. She looked away, disliking the uncomfortable tightening in her chest, made worse by the fact that, at that exact moment, in her periphery, she saw him turn to look at her. As though he'd heard the words.

Don't say anything. She willed herself quiet. *Let him speak next.*

She waited, aware that he was staring at her, no doubt having found a bit of kohl or something that she'd missed. Rouge in her ear.

Don't touch your ear.

Dammit. She was Sesily Talbot. She'd spent the last decade being looked at. And by remarkable people! She'd had poetry composed for her! Some of it had been bearable! She'd been an artist's muse! The fact that he'd been an absolute ass was irrelevant.

In 1834, she'd been the reason London dressmakers couldn't keep peacock feathers on the shelf! She routinely had men and women salivating over her! She could have her pick of admirers! *Had* had her pick of them!

She could certainly handle being looked at. So why did Caleb's gaze feel so hot?

"I'm not like them." Where had that come from?

Wherever it was, he did not hesitate to reply. "I know."

"I don't have Sera's tavern or Sophie's bookshop or Seline's knack for horses or Seleste's ear for languages."

"You have something else."

"Yes," she said, softly, oddly grateful that he'd noticed. More so when he continued.

"Your loyalty—lord knows I would do crime to have someone give a fraction as much to me."

I could give it to you.

She pushed the reply aside. "You give the same kind of loyalty. You might not wish for others to see it. But I do. I see it."

He stopped at the words, and she did, too. The air shifted, thickening between them, and Sesily watched him, taking in the tightening of his jaw and the flattening of his lips, as though she'd said something wrong.

His beautiful eyes flashed with something like anger. "What makes you say that?"

"I've seen you stand for my sister. I've seen you help her get everything she wished, without an ounce of self-ishness."

He shook his head. "Most days, I am all selfishness."

"No, you're not. You forget that all the times you've noticed my battles, I've noticed yours. You've protected Sera's business from the Houses of Parliament, her reputation from the aristocracy, and her identity from Haven when she needed it."

He didn't move.

"You own a dozen pubs in America, and if you wanted to, you could have built an empire here. But you've never shown a bit of interest in anything other than helping Sera make The Singing Sparrow legendary." She paused, because he'd looked away, like he couldn't hear the words. Like he didn't like them. He really wasn't going to like the rest. "Because you are a good man."

He looked up at the sky for a long moment, the muscles in his jaw and neck working as he considered his next words. "I hear you stopped coming to the Sparrow."

"No, I didn't."

It was a lie and they both knew it. "When we first opened it, two years ago, we couldn't keep you away."

"You mean *you* couldn't keep me away," she said, defensively.

"What does that mean?"

"Only that Sera was not the one who was telling me to go home all the time, Caleb. You were." She paused, then added, "You say I view everything as a battle? You started a fair lot of them with me."

It was his turn to say it. "That's not true."

"Of course it is. You pushed me away so much you left the country."

"That's not why I left."

She didn't believe him. "Then why?"

Silence fell, long and heavy, and Sesily added, "All we do is fight battles. I am tired of them. I'd be done with them if I could."

"Then let's be done with them," he said.

"The battles are how I get a piece of you."

His head snapped around, his gaze rapt on her.

Where had *that* come from? And why did it feel so good to say it? It was out now, and she couldn't take it back, so she went on. "I'm tired of wanting you, Caleb. I'm tired of thinking maybe you want me. Of thinking that our kisses are as heady for you as they are for me. Of thinking that my touch singes you the way yours does me. Of imagining that the pleasure we find together is something out of the ordinary."

She looked away from him, because she was hot with embarrassment and frustration and she didn't want to face it or him. But the words kept coming, and she couldn't stop them. "You're right. I don't go to the Sparrow anymore. Because I am tired of it. I am tired of the memory of you there. I'm tired of the way my heart races every time I think of you. Here is the truth. I stopped going to the Sparrow because I stopped begging for scraps from people who could not see me."

She didn't want to stand there any longer, waiting for whatever it was she always waited for with him. Knowing that it wouldn't come.

She began to descend the rise, toward the trees at the base of the hill, telling herself she didn't care if he followed her.

Wanting him to follow her.

He did.

"What's that supposed to mean?" he called out, following her down the hill. "You think I cannot see you?"

She didn't look back. Refused to.

He kept talking, his words carrying to her on the wind. "You think I don't see you? You think you don't shine like the fucking sun every time you're in a room?"

She did turn then. "I think you see me because you feel you must. Because I am the reckless, outrageous sister of your dearest friend. Because to stand with Seraphina, you must stand with me. Your loyalty to her has extended to me, her wild sister. You think I didn't notice how you leapt to help in the Trevescan gardens? When The Bully Boys knocked over The Place? How you pulled me from the fight to keep me safe? How you followed me into Coleford's—which was absolutely out of line, by the way—to protect me?"

The last had him coming down the hill faster, toward her. "I didn't protect you at Coleford's. I took advantage of you at Coleford's."

She hated the words, and the way they stripped the event of anything like passion—making it seem as though she'd had no choice but to be swept along for his pleasure, like she hadn't found her own, twice. Swallowing around the weight in her chest, she said, "Well, while my pride could do without the reminder, I think there's an argument to be made that your regret for the events of the evening comes from the same place as all the rest."

He came up short. Still. "What did you say?"

"It's clear you were acting out of your unbending loyalty for my sister." Only after the words had left her did she realize that his eyes had gone stormy themselves—wild enough to rival the clouds that suddenly seemed less ominous by comparison.

She took a step back, down the hill.

He advanced, and when he finally spoke, the words were low and dark, and somehow loud as gunshot. "You think I regret it?"

"I—You disappeared."

He advanced again. She stepped back again. "And you think it was because I wish it had not happened."

The words were a curling, searing heat inside her, driving away the cold wind that swirled around them. "Was it not?"

"No, Sesily," he said, closing the distance between them. This time she did not retreat. This time she relished his advance. "Christ. No. Don't you see? That's the problem . . ."

He reached for her, his big hand cupping her cheek, his fingers sliding into her hair, scattering hairpins, threatening the quick work she'd done to put it to rights earlier. She didn't care. Let them fall. Let them rust in the soil to be found two hundred years from now.

She didn't care, not as long as he finished what he was saying.

And then he pulled her close and bent his head, pressing his forehead to hers and said, "I *don't* regret it, Sesily. I want it again. I want more. I want it all. And if I take it, it won't be cordial."

She clasped his wrist, warm and strong in her grip, and lifted her mouth to his, stealing his kiss, quick and soft and barely-there, like the words she whispered. "Hang cordial."

He groaned, rewarding her kiss with one of his own, wild like his eyes. Wild like her pulse.

Wild like the late-autumn sky, that opened with a crash of thunder and a torrent of rain.

Chapter Fifteen

This woman kissed like a goddess.

The rain could have been snow or hail or a plague of frogs, and Caleb wouldn't have cared. He would have stood halfway up that rise and kissed her until they were up to their knees in ice or amphibians, because he'd never had such a straight shot of pleasure like the one Sesily Talbot delivered with her devastating kisses.

And it didn't matter that the freezing rain coming down in sheets was soaking them to the bone. Not when she was soft and lush and sinful in his arms.

Not when her arms were wrapped around his neck, her fingers tangled in his hair, holding him to her as they kissed.

Not when she sighed that small, perfect sigh, drew her tongue over his bottom lip, and sucked it, slow and languid, as though they weren't in torrential rain.

She kissed him like the rain was all part of the plan.

Eventually, though, she released him, pulling back just enough to open her gorgeous eyes, her long lashes spiked with the rain, her hair weighed down with it. The look of her, tousled and bedraggled and fucking perfect, brought a tightness to his chest, made worse when she smiled and said, "That kiss was so perfect, I could swear I heard thunder."

He laughed. He knew he shouldn't. Shouldn't let himself be amused by her. Shouldn't let himself be any more drawn to her than he already was. Shouldn't risk being any closer to her.

But she was everything Caleb had always refused himself. She was bright where his world was dark, beautiful where it was ugly, welcome where he'd never found it. And that made her more tempting than anything he'd ever experienced.

She was the treat in the shop window, the coin in the rich man's purse.

She was better.

So he let himself laugh.

He knew he didn't deserve her, but it was raining and it was cold, and while he did not care about his own comfort, he found he cared a great deal about Sesily's, and it had nothing to do with loyalty to her sister.

It had to do with keeping her warm and dry and safe. With pretending she was *his* for a heartbeat. With pretending a heartbeat would be enough.

It had to do with the fact that he would never regret it. Not even if he should.

After stealing another kiss from her pretty pink lips, Caleb peeled off his coat and held it up over both of their heads, loving the way she instinctively tucked herself beneath it, inside the crook of his arm, flashing him a bright white smile. "Cozy."

Pleasure thrummed through him at the word, along with a keen desire to make her feel that way for longer than it would take to walk the brief distance to the closest shelter.

When they got to the trees, they were slightly more protected from the rain, and he pulled the coat back on, leaving it unbuttoned and taking her hand, guiding her over fallen branches and the soggy leaf cover on the ground—surely soaking her shoes. He didn't like that idea.

He increased his speed, eager to get her inside.

When the door to the groundskeeper's cottage came into view, tucked away behind a grouping of high shrubbery that looked as though it had been left to its own growth for several years, Sesily came up short, tightening her grip in his. "Should we be concerned about . . . a groundskeeper?"

"I guess we'll find out," he said, knocking sharply before peering in the window. It was difficult to see much, but considering the stillness of the place, the way ivy had run riot over its roof and along its windows, Caleb doubted it was inhabited.

He tried the knob. Locked.

Sesily made a noise behind him, and he spun toward her, not liking the sound of it, like she'd been surprised and not pleasantly. Caleb was prepared to discover a foe—ogre, large wolf, woodsman with an axe—but instead found Sesily, eyes closed, shoulders up by her ears, and a stream of cold rain coursing down one side of her face, directly into the collar of her coat.

"So cold!" she announced when she opened her eyes, and while later he was certain that he would look back and think the moment charming, he found he didn't care for it one bit. He didn't like her cold or uncomfortable. And he didn't like her in the rain.

So he did the only thing he could think to do . . . he turned back to the door of the cottage and kicked it in.

Another gasp from Sesily, and he threw a look over his shoulder to find that she didn't appear to be cold anymore. Instead, she was staring wide-eyed at the place where the door had once been, her mouth hanging open in a surprised half smile. Her gaze flew to his. "You really shouldn't get in the habit of that," she said, though from her tone it sounded like she didn't mind it.

It sounded like she liked it.

Which made Caleb want to kick in another dozen or so.

"Have I done it more than once?"

"Cottage doors . . . carriage windows . . . it's terribly destructive."

For her comfort. For her well-being. "Would you believe that until I met you, I'd never kicked in a window or a door?"

"Careful," she said with a smile, sliding past him, filling him with the scent of her, wind and rain and sugared almonds, looking back at him before disappearing into the dark house. "You shall turn my head with such flattery."

He followed her inside, the sound of the storm immediately muffled by the quiet space, where the only noise was the sound of her skirts swishing against the floorboards.

He closed the door behind him, jamming it shut with a chair nearby.

Her skirts weren't swishing any longer. "You're going to have to pay for that damage, Mr. Calhoun."

"The duke knows where to find me," he said, turning back to the room. It was reasonably appointed, a small table and chairs sat to one side, what looked like a chaise and two more comfortable chairs underneath cloth to the other. Between them was an enormous fireplace, complete with a stack of dry firewood.

And there, at the center of it all, was Sesily, wet hair loosed from its moorings in a number of places, dripping onto her coat, which was soaked through. Her cheeks were pink from the cold, her lashes spiked with raindrops.

She was perfect.

"Well," she said, turning her attention to the fireplace, placing her hands on her hips, emphasizing their pretty swell. "I suppose we ought to get this thing going." She paused, considering it, before looking back over her shoulder. "Can you light a fire?"

"Have you mistaken me for a duke?"

She laughed at his affront. "I do apologize. What a terrible insult *that* must be."

"As a grown man with work, it most definitely is."

"I should never have doubted you," she said, stepping back from the hearth. "Please, sir, showcase your skill."

He'd like to showcase a series of different, much more interesting skills, if he was honest, but he'd settle for lighting a fire. The storm had kept them in check, stopping them before they could start, and he would do well to remember that that had been the best course of action.

Otherwise, he would have laid her down in the grass and made love to her until she cried her pleasure to the wind and sky.

Moving past her, he crouched at the fire, keenly aware of her there, filling the room with her smile and her scent as he laid the hearth, grateful for something else to consider, rather than the softness of her skin, or the sweetness of her lips, or the sound of her cries when she came in his arms. Against his tongue.

He cleared his throat.

Being in close quarters with her was going to drive him mad.

And then she started taking her clothes off.

He'd just begun to strike the flint and steel to light the fire when he heard the heavy slide of wet fabric, indicating that she'd removed it, and he stopped, unable to avoid looking. She'd turned away to drape her coat over one of the chairs in the corner.

"You'll get cold," he said, the words coming out more like a warning than he expected.

"I'm already cold," she said, simply. "I needn't be wet, as well."

With a low grumble, he returned to his task, doing his best to ignore her as she removed the dust cloths from the more comfortable furniture, finishing her task as the fire took hold.

She rewarded his success with a wide smile. "I should never have doubted you."

His face warmed at the words, as though he was a schoolboy, and he left the room to investigate the small house, finding a kettle, a tin of what smelled like ancient tea, and a chest full of woolen blankets. He collected them and returned to the main room, already markedly warmer, depositing them on the divan she'd uncovered.

Sesily had returned to the table where she'd deposited her coat, and was now working at the buttons on her gloves. He watched as she slid them off and lay them on the table.

Running a finger through the thin layer of dust there, she said, "As inns go, this one requires some care."

"I shall alert the owner."

She looked to him. "You know, I believe you would, if this were an inn."

"I wouldn't like you to be displeased." It was the truth, though he hoped she heard a jest.

She took a step toward him. "You shouldn't say such things to me, Mr. Calhoun. You'll spoil me."

"And what then?" he said softly, letting her come even closer. Loving it.

"I fear I would become incorrigible."

."You?" His brows rose. "Unimaginable."

She smiled. "Some find it part of my charm, you know."

"Do they?"

Another step toward him. She was close enough to touch, now. He wouldn't even have to try. He could reach his hand out and wrap it around her waist and pull her close. "You are welcome to spoil me."

He wanted that. To spoil her. To give her everything she wished. Forever.

"Alright then, Lady Incorrigible," he said, barely recognizing the low edge to his voice—the result of her being so close. Of wanting her so much. "What would you ask of me?"

Her eyes lit as though he'd offered her a sack of her favorite sweets. She lifted a finger to her chin and tapped it thoughtfully.

It was a game.

How long had it been since Caleb had played a game? Had he ever?

Had he ever enjoyed one?

No matter the answer, he knew one thing in that moment: he was going to enjoy this one.

"Well, first, I would insist that you remove your coat, Mr. Calhoun. You're dripping all over the floor."

It was gone in an instant, without hesitation, deposited over another chair.

"Much better," she said, softly. "But you see the problem with doing my bidding is that I begin to enjoy the power."

He lifted his chin at that, the pleasure of the words rioting through him, leaving his chest tight and his cock hard. "Incorrigible, after all."

"After all," she agreed, setting a hand to his chest, the heat of her touch finding its way through his waistcoat and shirt. It was gone before he had a chance to enjoy it, however, and she said, "The rain has soaked you through."

He did reach for her then, capturing a long dark lock of hair, wet and loose from the storm, sending a rivulet of rainwater down the slope of her breast, where it disappeared beneath the soaked silk of her dress. "Not only me."

"No," she said, following his gaze and giving a little laugh, raising her hands to her hair, lifting the heavy mass and letting it drop, the teasing light in her eyes making his mouth water. "But this does not seem the kind of establishment that has a lady's maid on hand."

The game again. "Mmm," he said. "A problem."

She stepped closer. Or maybe he did.

He definitely slid his fingers into her hair. And he absolutely said, softly, "Perhaps I can help, my lady." The words weren't an honorific. They were a claiming.

"Please," she said softly.

Caleb was lost. He began to remove her hairpins, setting them to the table with slow, deliberate movements, some part of him fearing that she might stop him.

She didn't. Instead, she closed her eyes and let him work his fingers through her heavy, sable curls, leaning into his touch as he ministered to her, removing a dozen hairpins, more, and freeing the mane of hair that he'd only ever imagined she had.

Lie. He'd never imagined it.

He'd known better than to imagine it.

Because as they stood in that quiet cottage, the only sound the crackling of the fire and the heavy rhythm of their breath, and the regular click of the pins on the table, Caleb realized that when he took his last breath, it would be this image in his mind—Sesily, tall and lush and beautiful, her hair pouring down around her shoulders like a silken promise.

When he removed the last pin and set it to the table, she opened her eyes, and he saw the truth in them—she wanted him. "Thank you," she said as she took over, shaking out the mane of curls. "That feels wonderful."

He wanted to lay her down in front of the fire and spread that hair around her and watch the flames play golden tricks with it as it dried, and in that moment, Caleb knew he was past being able to stop this. There was no return to the reality of an hour earlier, when she was a beautiful aristocratic lady and the sister of his friend, with the world laid out before her, and he was a man who had spent a lifetime running from his past, knowing that things like happiness and love and a future were not for him.

Of course, he hadn't been able to stop it an hour earlier, either.

Or a day earlier.

Or a year earlier.

They'd been on this path since the first time they'd met.

And now, they'd arrived at the cottage in the woods.

And it would have to be enough.

Because when she reached for him and slipped a finger beneath the edge of his waistcoat, and tugged, pulling him closer, and saying, softly, "And what of you, Caleb? May I help you with your wet things?"

He did not have the strength to say no.

She worked the buttons of his waistcoat until he tossed it to the table, to join their coats, and then she spread her hands wide and warm over the cotton shirt beneath, setting him on fire. "And this?" she said. "May I—"

"Sesily," he said, reaching for her, cupping her jaw in his hands and tilting her face to his. "You may do whatever you wish. You may have whatever you wish."

I am yours.

The words flashed, but he did not say them.

He was not a fool.

And Sesily was not waiting for them. Instead, she was tugging the shirt from the waist of his trousers, and then he was helping her, and the shirt joined the rest, and she was staring at him with that look in her eyes again—the one when he'd offered her her favorite sweets.

"You . . ." She looked to him. "You're beautiful."

And it was Caleb who was spoiled.

He kissed her, because he couldn't wait another moment to have his mouth on her, claiming her, owning some small part of her in some small way.

Of course, it wasn't Caleb who owned. It was Sesily.

Sesily who claimed, her fingers trailing up over his bare chest, leaving fire in their wake until he couldn't bear the teasing anymore and he pulled her tight to him.

"Ah!" He pulled back from the kiss.

"What?"

"Your dress," he said. "It's freezing."

"And here I thought Americans were made of sterner stuff." She shook her head with a pretty pout that made him want to suck her lower lip until she begged him to suck other things.

"Mmm," he said, reaching to pull her close again. "Give me another chance."

She danced away, out of reach. More of her delicious play. "No, I'm afraid now I'm quite concerned."

"I shall endeavor to persevere."

"Well, that's very noble of you," she said, "but I do worry that if we find ourselves in such close proximity again, you might catch cold."

"I am willing to risk it," he said, stalking her backward, across the room, toward the now uncovered furniture, imagining a dozen ways they might find it of use.

"No, no. I'm afraid I can't allow that," she teased, slowing down, letting him get close. Close enough to touch her. Close enough to get down on his knees and worship her. Close enough to hear her whisper, "There's only one solution."

"And what is that?" he asked, his fingers on her chin, tilting her face up to his for another kiss.

She let him linger there, at her lips, before she said, "The dress—it has to go."

The words hummed through him, and he couldn't help his smile, his fingers tracing the edge of the gown against her soft skin, until they reached the dusky rose ribbon tied in a little bow right at the center of her bodice. "Does it?"

"Oh, most definitely," she said. "It would be beneficial, I think. To our health."

He fingered the bow, slowly and deliberately, teasing them both with anticipation until a harsh breath shuddered through her and he was absolutely certain she wanted him. "Caleb," she whispered, and the need in the word was enough to make him wild.

"Shh," he replied to the exposed skin just above the silk, rising and falling in a wild rhythm. "You are the prettiest present I've ever received . . ." He pressed a soft row of kisses along the edge of the dress as he untied the bow. "I'm going to take my time unwrapping you."

And he did, untying the line of bows down the front of her dress in between slow kisses that threatened to make them both wild. But Caleb had been waiting for this for two years, since the first moment he met this dark-haired, olive-skinned beauty, and he was going to savor it.

But when the dress finally fell away, pooling at her feet, along with a pile of petticoats decorated with silk ribbons to match, everything changed. There was no more going slowly.

She was wearing a corset in the same rich rose as her dress, and a pair of stockings tied with elaborate ribbons in a matching silk . . . and nothing between. No chemise, no undergarments—just stays and stockings against smooth, supple skin.

Caleb's mouth went dry as he took her in, absolutely stunning, as though she'd stepped out of his dreams. And when he raked his gaze back to hers, finding her watching him with something like nervousness, something exploded in his chest, like cannon fire. "My God, Sesily," he said. "You're fucking perfect."

She smiled at the words, a wash of pink darkening her cheeks. "I didn't know if you would—"

He didn't let her finish. He closed the distance between them and kissed the rest of the sentence away. "I would," he whispered, before he kissed her again, longer and deeper. "I would." And again. "I *will*."

She shivered in his arms, and he cursed himself for not taking better care of her. Stealing a quick, final kiss, he said, "Don't move," and turned away to fetch the blankets he'd found, laying them out like a pallet before the fire, now burning in earnest. He crouched to throw another log on the flames, but before he could return to her, she came to him, her fingers combing through his hair.

He looked up over her beautiful body to find her staring down at him, her eyes gleaming with heat that had nothing to do with the fire.

"I moved," she whispered.

"Mmm," he said, sliding a hand up her leg, over her thigh, to the swell of her full, bare bottom. "Ever incorrigible."

"Whatever shall be done with me?"

He didn't deserve this. He didn't deserve her.

But he was going to take it, nonetheless.

And hope it was enough for a lifetime.

"I've some ideas," he said, and he pulled her down to the blankets before the fire, reveling in her laughter.

Chapter Sixteen

In all the times Sesily had imagined this—and there had been many, many times she'd imagined this—she'd never imagined that it would be on the floor of a groundskeeper's cottage on her sister's country estate.

But she was warming to the idea.

When Caleb lifted her clear off her feet and onto the pile of soft woolen blankets he'd carefully arranged in front of the fire, she couldn't stop herself from squealing her delight, and then when he followed her down, broad and warm and beautiful, delight hadn't been the word at all.

It had been absolute pleasure, as he tucked himself against her side—blocking the path to the door, to the cold, to the rain, to the rest of the world—closing out everything but this, the fire, them. She watched him for long moments, her hands stroking over his wide chest, playing with the dusting of dark hair there, stroking over his arm—thick and strong from his work, now painted with flickering golden shadows in the grey afternoon.

She pressed a kiss to the muscle of his biceps, then to his shoulder, and the soft skin of his neck, swirling her tongue beneath his jaw and loving the low growl of pleasure he released.

"You like that," she said.

"I like *you*."

She blinked, the words heavier than she expected between them. "Do you?"

"Sesily," he said, so soft, like breath. He lifted her hand and pressed a kiss to her fingers. "Yes. I like you too much."

"Is there such a thing?" she asked, injecting a teasing into her tone that she didn't quite feel.

"There is for me. There is when it comes to you." Another kiss, a little suck at the tip of her index finger. "I've liked you from the moment I met you. From the moment you looked at me with those beautiful, teasing eyes, and flashed me that smile that makes promises I want you to absolutely keep."

She gave him that smile. "I'm going to keep them today."

He leaned forward to kiss her, stopping just before their lips met. "I'm going to keep mine, too."

Another kiss, like wine.

"Turn toward the fire," he said, softly, and she followed the instruction, not understanding it even as she knew that whatever was to happen, it would be perfect.

And it was. He pressed a soft kiss to her shoulder and another to the back of her neck, and removed her corset with quick movements. "These are torture devices," he said. "I loathe them."

"You, and every woman in Britain."

"Then why wear them?"

She turned back, one arm crossed over her now bare breasts. "I'm not wearing one, as a matter of fact."

The words unlocked him, his gaze tracing over her hands. "Show me," he said, the command a different kind of silk and steel, and she did, without hesitation, removing her hands and letting him look his fill.

And he did look, his gaze like a touch. Her nipples hardened, and he noticed, looking up at her with a wicked gleam in his eye and saying, "You want me."

She didn't hesitate. "Yes."

But instead of taking her, of rising over her and setting his mouth to her and easing the ache that was making her desperate, he touched her in a way no one ever had. With reverence, like she was treasure.

And it made her ache more.

She arched up to meet his finger as it traced circles around her full breasts, the touch soft and firm and soothing after they'd been caged for the day. "Sore?"

"Not there," she said in a near pant, aching for him to tighten the circle.

And then he did, spiraling his touch tighter and tighter, until he found the straining tip of her breast, and painted over it with that slow, wicked finger. She hissed in a breath. "There."

"Mmm," he said. "You're so hard here. For me."

"Yes," she whispered. "Please."

"Please what?" He pinched the tip, just enough to send a spark of pleasure directly to her core, and then eased off, gone before she could bask in his touch.

"Again," she said.

He didn't do it again. He did better.

He used his mouth, licking over the straining, aching flesh with the firm flat of his tongue before sucking gently in lush, lovely strokes, making her wish he'd never stop. "I've wanted to do this for so long," he whispered. "Since you bathed in my bedchamber."

She hissed a breath, her fingers threading through his curls. "You watched."

"I couldn't resist," he said with another perfect, slow suck.

Her grip on him tightened and she arched up to him. "I wanted you to," she confessed. "I wanted you to ache for it."

He stilled and lifted his head, his green eyes hot on hers. "I ached for it."

She lifted her chin, desire pooling deep. "What did you do?" He lowered his mouth and sucked the tip of her breast once more, his eyes on hers like sin. She gasped. "Tell me."

"You want me to tell you how I eased the ache? How I have eased it every day since then? Lying in the dark and stroking myself and imagining you until I can't bear it anymore?"

"Yes," she said, rubbing against him. "God, yes." The room was no longer cold. It was an inferno, everything disappearing but his words and the heat of his mouth and the way he worshipped her.

And it did feel like worship when he finally released her to lavish similar attention on the other breast, long, slow tugs that stole every thought except the singular desire for him to never stop.

She begged him not to stop, holding him firm to her breast, her body bowing toward him, an offering.

When he finally pulled back to look at her, she strained for more, and that sinful finger traced her curves, around her breasts again and over the swell of her belly and hips, and she followed that touch as though it had summoned her, as though he'd given her no choice.

And maybe he hadn't, because the pleasure he offered was too good.

Too right.

And maybe she knew, even then, that it would not be forever.

That finger became his whole hand as he stroked down her thigh, lingering at the ribbons of her stockings, and she parted for him, whispering his name.

He gave her what she wanted, lifting himself up and over her, planting one thick thigh between hers like a gift. She wrapped her arms around his neck and rose to meet him, pressing her chest to his, and rocking against him, the soft wool of his trousers rough against her softest skin.

"Now you are aching for it," he said, the words rough at her ear, threatening to make her wild.

She answered first with her body, rocking against him, the hard muscle of his thigh pure pleasure. Planting one hand on the floor, he wrapped the other around her waist, bracing her against him.

"Yes," she whispered. "Please."

"You could find it here, couldn't you? Just like this?" He growled the words, and the hitch in them—the thin thread of control there—unraveled her. He wanted it.

She met his gaze, so close, those beautiful green eyes refusing to let her go. She moved again, slow and languid, and his pupils dilated, his arm tightening around her, keeping her rhythm, lifting them both upright. "You could come like this," he said, stealing her kiss, licking deep. "Using me for your pleasure."

"Mmm," she agreed, lost in the feeling of him as her arms wound around his neck and she moved again, slow and sinful, the pleasure of his thick thigh against her almost impossible to bear. "But I don't want to."

"Liar," he said, hot at her ear before taking the lobe between his teeth. "You're hot for it."

"Not it," she said. "You." She leaned back and reached for the band of his trousers, sliding her fingers beneath the button at his waistband.

He grabbed her hand. "No."

She met his eyes. "I want to see you."

A shake of his head. "This is not for me, love. It is for you."

She smiled. "Have you not heard of me? I am terribly selfish." She rocked against his thigh again and they both sucked in a breath. "Caleb . . . it *is* for me. Take them off."

He cursed, dark and hot in the quiet room. "Sesily, if I take them off . . ."

When he trailed off, she filled the silence, hating the self-doubt that made her ask, "Will you regret it?"

Another curse. This one harsher. "No. No." His hands were on her, stroking up her back, digging into her hair. He kissed her, deep and intense. "I won't regret a minute of this."

And still, she couldn't imagine how he wouldn't, this man who had spent two years avoiding her. Two years ignoring her. Resisting her absolute best attempts to seduce him. "Are you certain?"

"Christ, Sesily," he said, softly, his gaze not leaving hers. "I've never been more certain of anything. I shall never regret this. I shall never regret kissing you in the rain, and unwrapping you here, before the fire."

Her hands spread over the ridged plane of his stomach, tight and muscled, and he sucked in a breath at her touch. "I shall never regret you above me, your hair like mahogany fire. I shall never regret the taste of you, the feel of you."

He kissed her again, and finished his vow. "I shall never regret you. This. Us. Here."

There was such reverence in the words that Sesily feared what they did, cracking her open with desire and something more.

Her sister's words echoed from earlier in the day. *Sesily loves with her whole heart.*

If she wasn't careful, she would love this man, this man who saw her the way no one else did. Who understood her the way few could. Who kissed her the way no one else had.

This man who'd never let her seduce him . . . because she'd never had to. He was here, and he wanted her, no seduction required.

Of course, a little seduction never hurt anyone.

"Shall I tell you what I would regret?" she asked, her hands stroking over his chest, loving the rattle of his breath as she pleased him.

"By all means," he replied, hissing as she leaned forward and licked one of his nipples, scraping the puckered skin with her teeth before turning to give the same treatment to the other.

Her fingers found the waist of his trousers, stroking over the crisp hair there, just for a moment, before exploring further, finding the heavy ridge of him hard and straining against the fabric. "I would very much regret not seeing this." She leaned up and kissed the point at his neck, where his pulse pounded. Triumph flared at the knowledge that he wanted her as much as she wanted him. She stroked over him, firm and sure, and he pressed his hips into her touch. "I would very much regret not touching this."

Another low growl was her reward.

"Wouldn't you?" she teased.

He laughed, the magnificent man, low and delicious. "I would, as a matter of fact."

"Take them off," she ordered.

"But then I have to stop touching you."

She climbed off him, sitting back on the blankets, watching him as he stood and dispensed with his shoes and trousers. When he turned back, he was nude, and he was coming for her, his muscles rippling as he approached, bunching as he prepared to lower himself to the pallet—hopefully not to rise for a very long time.

Before he did, however, she raised a hand. "Wait."

He did, as though he was hers to command. And she wanted to command him. "I only . . ." She trailed off, her gaze tracking over his body, muscle and bone and flesh, wide shoulders and narrow hips and thighs . . . and between them, the heavy length of him, thick and proud.

"In two years . . ." she started again, marveling at him, at the way he let her watch him. "I have imagined this . . . you . . . so many times."

She raked her gaze over him, lingering on his hard cock, which seemed to grow harder as she watched. "Show me."

He knew what she wanted, and gave it to her. He touched himself, taking himself in hand, rough and firm, stroking in long, lovely pulls. She could have watched him for hours, her mouth watering and her body drawn tight like a bow, aching for him to stop and make love to her, and somehow, equally desperate for him not to stop.

She tore her gaze away from him, meeting his eyes, heavy lidded with desire. And she said the only thing she could think to say. "Caleb, you're so beautiful."

"What have you imagined, love?"

She shook her head. "A thousand things."

"Start with the ones you liked best." He was moving, coming for her, and excitement coursed through her.

She leaned back as he loomed over her, sliding one thick thigh between hers, the muscles in his arms rippling beneath her touch. "I've imagined this. Imagined touching you. Imagined looking at you." Her gaze flickered down over him, her touch following. She sighed. "I've imagined you so much, touching you seems like a fantasy."

A low sound rumbled in his chest as she found the straining length of him. "You're so hot," she said. "So hard."

He thrust into her grip, the movement sinful and wicked and lewd and perfect, and he bent his head and whispered at her ear, "I've seen you looking."

"I'm sorry," she said, not feeling at all sorry. "I couldn't help it."

Another thrust. A scrape of his teeth at her neck. "I've tried so hard not to look in return."

She turned her head, met his eyes. Tightened her grip, loving the way the muscle in his jaw worked through his pleasure. "Why?"

"Because I don't deserve to look at you," he said, softly. "Because if I look at you, just once, just for a moment . . . I will want more."

How could she resist smiling at that? "I think that would be alright."

He parted her thighs and settled between them, and she released him, stroking up his arms and over his shoulders once more. "If I look at you," he said, softly, moving his hips, "just once, just for a moment . . . I will want to kiss you."

She lifted her head to meet his lips, but he was already slipping away, down her body, pressing kisses to her breasts and down over her torso. "If I look at you, just once . . . just for a moment"—he lingered there, at the soft swell of her body, and whispered—"I will want to taste you."

"I will want that, too." She arched toward him. "Caleb."

He did look at her then, his gaze tracking over her, hungry. Claiming. "This is the prettiest thing I've ever seen," he said, one finger sliding over her, parting her folds.

If he didn't kiss her, she was going to go mad. "You're looking now."

His green gaze found hers, and she loved the smile in his eyes, hot and delicious. "I am, in fact."

She lifted herself toward him again. An offering.

"The other night, I couldn't see it," he said, the low words rumbling against her as he stroked that single finger over her, up and down, until she was moving against him. He watched her for a long, lush moment, and added, "Imagining what it looked like threatened my sanity. And here it is . . . and it's so pretty . . ." He slipped a finger inside her. ". . . and it's so wet . . ." Slow and steady and delicious and perfect. ". . . and it's mine."

The truth. "It is."

It always will be.

And then his mouth was on her, and she was gasping his name in the quiet room, and her fingers were in his hair, fisting tight as he feasted on her. "Oh, yes," she said as his big hands slid beneath her, lifting her up to him like a chalice. Like he was a god and she was his to do with as he pleased.

He did do as he pleased—and as she pleased as well—his broad shoulders tucking between her lush thighs as he settled in, licking her in long, lovely strokes with the flat of his tongue, slowly, rhythmically stripping her of thought, and replacing it with sheer pleasure.

"It is," she repeated on a sigh. "It is. It's yours."

I am yours. She barely resisted speaking the words aloud, instead rocking against him, taking her pleasure even as he lifted her to gain better access, to give her more. Everything she asked.

Everything he wanted.

"I've been wild for this taste since the other night." He spoke to her core, the words making her ache for him. "I've been desperate to get you somewhere alone, where I could lick you until you scream."

He didn't wait for her to reply—best, as his filthy words had stolen hers—instead returning his mouth to her, seeking and then finding the perfect spot, the perfect rhythm, making her tighten her fingers once more and hold him close. "There," she panted, and he growled against her, the vibration sending her even higher, giving her even more pleasure as his tongue worked in time to the rhythm of her hips, circling, pressing, stroking, again and again. "Oh, Caleb. Don't stop. Don't you dare stop."

He didn't. She was coming apart. He was destroying her. She'd never felt anything like this. And she didn't care, as he worked her with his mouth and his hands, so strong, holding her so tight, and his shoulders refusing her quarter until she gave him what he wanted.

Until she took what she wanted, screaming his name as she found her climax.

And the magnificent man stayed there, guiding her down from her pleasure, his tongue and fingers still against her as she pulsed against him, her hold on him loosening as she fell back into the blankets, her body loose and languid and sated.

She sighed and opened her eyes as he lifted his head, and looked up over the length of her body, those green eyes burning with wicked satisfaction—as though he knew what he'd given her was like nothing she'd ever experienced.

Like that, she was no longer sated.

Not when she might give him the same. Like nothing she'd ever experienced.

Like nothing *they* had ever experienced.

Energized, Sesily came to her knees, meeting him as he rose to lie with her and pushing him to his back. "It's my turn," she whispered, straddling his thighs, stroking over his beautiful chest, staring down at him. "You're my prize," she said. "Let me look my fill."

And he did, his big hands stroking up and down her legs as she explored him, scraping her nails over his flat, copper nipples, over his ridged torso. How did one man have so much muscle? She stroked over the skin, marveling at his heat and strength, stilling when she found the puckered skin at his side.

She stroked her thumb over the circular scar gently, and he caught her wrist in one strong hand, stopping her.

Her gaze flew to his. "What happened?"

He shook his head. "Nothing that is important now."

Her brow furrowed and for a moment, she considered pushing him on it, but he recognized the thought. He shook his head and lifted her hand to his lips, pressing a kiss to the pad of her thumb, then biting it softly, just enough to send a straight shot of delight through her. "I thought you were looking."

Yes. She was.

Continuing her exploration, she found the hard length of him once again, and once again took him in hand, stroking slowly, now using that thumb he had nibbled to rub over the tip of him, back and forth, soft and steady, until he exhaled a curse.

She did it again, feeling utterly triumphant, until he was working himself in her hand, her name on his lips like a prayer. She answered it, leaning down and pressing a kiss to his rigid flesh, licking over the salty sweet tip of him, loving the deep groan of pleasure she summoned.

Releasing him, she rose up over his beautiful body and said, "Caleb?"

"Mmm . . ."

"You asked me once if I liked children."

He stilled. "I did."

"I've no interest in having them," she said.

"I see," he said, the words tentative. Exploratory.

Her lips curved. "I don't think you do, actually. What I mean to say is—I do not have any interest in having them . . . not now, and not ever. I do, however, have a great deal of interest in . . . this." She stroked him again, reveling in his hard length.

He gritted his teeth at the pleasure. "I shall take care."

She had no doubt he would. He would always take care with her. "You don't have to," she said. "There are ways—and I use them." She paused, feeling it necessary to say, "Though I have not had need for them in . . . a while."

Two years.

Not since she'd met Caleb.

He nodded, watching her. "Nor have I."

"No women in Boston, on their widows' walks, awaiting your return?"

"Nary a one. And you . . . no men on the rooftops of Covent Garden, keeping watch?"

"Nary a one. And no women, neither." She paused, then confessed, "Though, sometimes I wonder what it would be like if you were there . . . watching over me."

He reached for her, pulling her down and pressing his lips to hers. "I'm watching over you tonight."

What if it wasn't enough?

No. She pushed the thought aside. There wasn't time for it. Not now, not when he was big and warm and hard beneath her. Not with the broad head of his cock parting her folds, notching against her. Not while she was sighing her pleasure, lifting herself up until he was there, at her entrance, pressing into her, slowly, barely moving, making her wild.

Not with his hands on her hips, guiding her as she sank down on him, holding her still for tiny, impossible moments as she stretched to welcome him, making it possible to memorize every inch of him as he filled her, until they were pressed together, sealed to each other, and she wrapped herself around him and gave herself up to the pleasure of him. Of them.

Like nothing she'd ever felt before.

She sighed his name at his ear, the word coming on a ragged breath. "I've never . . ."

"Neither have I," he replied, the words sounding devastated. "It's fucking paradise. You're fucking heaven."

She moved, slowly, up and then down, and they groaned together. "Are you sure it is not you, who is fucking heaven?"

He laughed, the movement trembling through them. "I am, indeed, fucking heaven."

This wonderful man, finally, *finally* playing with her.

And then playtime was over, and he was moving, thrusting into her, hot and perfect, and she was filled with something like pleasure and something else, something that, if she lingered on it, would feel like fear.

Because she was certain, in that moment, that she would never experience anything like this again.

But she couldn't linger on that emotion, because he began to move her, to move himself, slow and smooth, like he'd been made to hold her and she'd been made to hold him, and they'd been made for this . . . which of course they had. It was the only explanation for how they fit together, and how they moved together, and how they loved each other.

And it felt like love then, as he moved deep within her, with slow, languid thrusts, short and perfect, layering pleasure inside her over and over, until she was panting against him and begging him for . . . she didn't know what.

He did, though. Because he was Caleb, and of course he did, moving deeper, faster, with more power, his hand firm at her back, ensuring that every thrust knocked him against the spot that drove her wild, over and over until she was lost to sizzling, impossible pleasure, her eyes sliding closed. She was going to—

"Look at me," he whispered, one hand sliding into her curls, tightening in a glorious sting. "Sesily, look at me, love."

How could she resist one last look?

How could he?

They moved together, perfect. Like they were made for each other.

She'd known they would be.

She'd known they were.

"Now, love," he whispered. Commanded. Rocking up into her. "Take it."

She did, coming hard around him, falling into pleasure with his name on her lips as he came inside her with beautiful, heavy thrusts that made her wish he was closer.

Losing her strength, she fell into his arms, against him, and he caught her. Of course he did. Because that was where she belonged . . . in his arms. Sesily, who had spent her whole life in motion, restless, searching for more, for different, for better . . . found peace.

She sighed against his chest, where his heart beat in a wild rhythm that matched her own, and his hands never left her, stroking over her skin, tracing patterns with his touch, leaving tingling pleasure in his wake.

He pressed a kiss to the top of her head, and whispered her name into her hair. *"Sesily . . ."*

She warmed. No one had ever said her name like that. Like it was more than her. Like it was the wide world.

Like it was all he'd ever wanted.

They lay there, tangled in each other, for an age, heartbeats slowing, breath evening, the fire painting their skin in light and heat, the storm outside making it seem like there was nothing beyond this cottage.

Just the two of them.

A pair . . .

Caleb held her as she fell asleep in his arms, warm and soft and wonderful, her skin like silk against his rough palms. Glorying in all the ways she was his opposite. Soft where he was rough, lush where he was firm. Lingering on the ways she offered him pleasure, the way he took it, greedy for more.

He marveled at her.

Marveled at this—the closest he would ever come to paradise.

The closest he would ever be to free.

He wrapped his arms around her, loving the way she sighed and curled into him, the way she claimed him, even in sleep. For the rest of his life, this day—these stolen hours in the rain, in this place that tempted him with the impossible—would be the memory he held closest. On the darkest nights, he would imagine her here, in his arms, and he would remember that, for a heartbeat, he'd known peace. He'd known home.

Home. What a strange, impossible word.

A word he'd never allowed himself to think before then.

A word that came with dangerous companions—companions like hope. Like joy. Like the future.

Like love.

He loved her.

The thought shattered through him, tightening his chest until it ached, and he had to release her to rub a hand over his heart, willing away the pain.

Wondering if it would ever go away, now that he knew what he might have had in another world. A different past. A different future.

Sesily Talbot was not the kind of woman who let the future slip through her fingers. She was the kind of woman who claimed it, and everything that came with it—beauty and hope and laughter and love. And Caleb.

Christ, he wanted to be claimed by her.

He'd had a glimpse of what it could be to be claimed by this magnificent woman, and he wanted it beyond words.

But it was impossible.

Guilt and something else swirled through him—something he'd sworn to her he wouldn't feel. *Regret.*

He loved her.

He loved her, and because of it, he had to get out of England.

And never return.

Chapter Seventeen

The next evening, doing her very best to put the events of the previous day out of her mind, Sesily entered the Duchess of Trevescan's home on South Audley Street through the servants' entrance to discover the regular ball in full swing.

When it was said that everyone who was anyone attended parties at Trevescan House, few understood the full truth of that statement.

Every second Tuesday, in the same room where the duchess had hosted the brightest stars in London for the ball that ended the Earl of Totting, she hosted the stars of a different constellation. Just as bright. Just as brilliant. Just as powerful, refracted through a different lens.

Tonight, she hosted the maids.

The difference in the evenings could not be more stark—gone were the powdered, liveried footmen, the staid orchestra, the bland food, the tepid punch, the ridiculous gowns, and the icy, disapproving gaze of the *ton*'s most respected titles. Tonight, the room was filled with raucous laughter and loud conversation, cakes and tarts piled high and ale and wine liberally poured by . . . well, there were footmen, but they weren't required to remain barely seen and never heard.

The attendees came dressed for their pleasure, some in simple, every day dress, some in trousers, and some clad in frocks far prettier than the fashions of the day for which their mistresses paid Bond Street handsomely. Whether in simple lawn or castoff silk, ladies' maids knew how to wield a needle and thread, and Tuesday nights were the proof.

The orchestra had been replaced by a collection of musicians who played music meant for real dancing— no simpering steps for this lot, and the ballroom was packed full of dozens of women, many of whom were employed by Mayfair's most revered titles.

One would think that the most powerful homes in London would easily discover that they were lacking in female servants on particular Tuesday evenings, but that would require the residents of those homes to pay attention to their servants when they were out of view. Which rarely happened.

Suffice to say, if any of the duchess's Park Lane neighbors wandered in, they'd be shocked to their shoes and most definitely require smelling salts.

Every second Tuesday on South Audley was an absolute delight. And if Sesily were telling the truth, Mayfair maids were far more interesting than their employers.

In the two years since Sesily and the duchess had come to know each other, Sesily had attended this particular soiree countless times, and continued to marvel at it being the absolute best kept secret in London.

It shouldn't have been a surprise, of course, as no one kept secrets better than aristocratic servants.

Or, rather, no one kept secrets from aristocrats better than aristocratic servants.

And every woman in attendance knew that this party was to be kept secret. The duchess ensured it, by mak-

ing sure every woman in attendance had access to more
than the party. Every guest had access to freedom.

On these evenings, just inside the rear entrance to
Trevescan House, accessible to all who passed, was an
ancient, chipped soup tureen, dug out from the dark
corners of the Trevescan kitchen and filled with money.
There were no rules for borrowing from the tureen—
there were no limits to the amount that could be taken,
nor was it required that funds be returned. Instead, the
money was available to any guest who needed it. To escape a horrid employer, to help a friend in need, to find
passage out of London. No questions asked.

Once, Sesily had praised the duchess's cleverness in
adding payment of sorts to the women who attended
her soirees, and the other woman had corrected her instantly. The money was to help, not to barter. It was not
for quid pro quo, but to ease the ever-present worry that
so many women had when money was not available and
they were in over their heads.

The duchess knew the truth: money was power. And
on these evenings, she did what she could to put power
into the hands of women who too often had too little.

Take what you need, the duchess would tell her guests
when asked. *And if someday, you've something to spare,
you may always return.*

The Tuesday night group rarely had guineas to spare . . .
but they knew the value of what they did have.

Gossip. Worth far more than coin.

Weaving in and out of the jovial crowd, Sesily made
her way to the far end of the ballroom, where the duchess held court over the revelers. Missing nothing, she
caught Sesily's eye and waved her through the crush,
which took longer than expected, for all the stopping
Sesily did to chat with women she recognized.

Apprentice seamstresses from Bond Street and ladies' maids from Park Lane, a beloved cook from a club on St. James's who always had something interesting to say—gentlemen were quick to show their entire arse at their clubs, Sesily found.

Turning away from a group of laughing women, she collected a glass of wine from a passing tray and returned to her path, getting no more than a few steps before recognizing a new face in the crowd—familiar because she'd seen her just the day before, at a different aristocratic house. One of the battalion of nursemaids who worked for Seleste.

Sesily smiled. "Eve, isn't it?"

The young Black woman's eyes went wide as she recognized her employer's sister, and she started to drop a little curtsy before Sesily shook her head, staying the movement. She put a finger to her lips. "Tonight, we keep each other's secrets."

Eve nodded. "Of course, my lady."

"Sesily, please."

Eve hesitated, obviously perplexed by the extraordinary situation before apparently remembering that there was nothing ordinary about this place or this party. She nodded once, firmly, and offered a small smile. "Sesily."

"Don't tell my sister?"

The woman's smile broadened. "Tell her what?"

Sesily laughed and winked at her co-conspirator before they both spun off in different directions. Pushing through the crowd, she reached the duchess, raised up on the dais at the edge of the ballroom, keeping watch over the festivities.

Collapsing next to her friend on the divan upholstered in brilliant emerald velvet, Sesily drank her wine, considered the crush below, and said, "You're inviting the girls who work for my sisters now?"

"Your sisters have money and title, don't they?"

"As do I."

"Yes, but I know your secrets."

Sesily shook her head, impressed. No one was out of Duchess's reach. "Ruthless. Really."

The duchess waved a dismissive hand. "You know it would take something truly catastrophic to use whatever I've got on your family."

"Ruthless, nevertheless."

The duchess inclined her head. "Probably. But your sisters' employees deserve a good party, too, don't they?"

"Considering my hellion nephews, that girl deserves every party she can find." She forced herself to survey the rest of the room, disliking the way the reference to her nephews, to her sister, brought with it an echo of the previous day. A shadow of it.

Of him.

She pushed it away. She wasn't here for him.

She was here for the opposite.

"Anything of interest tonight?"

"Everything is of interest at one point or another," their hostess said, summoning a passing footman to claim a fresh glass of champagne. "In fact . . ." She trailed off, her gaze falling to a gathering of young women nearby, several of whom appeared absolutely terrified.

It wasn't uncommon for newcomers to the event to be nervous about meeting the Duchess of Trevescan—but no one made a body feel more welcome than she. Sesily smiled as her friend came off the divan and approached the girls, taking their hands and leaning close to introduce herself. Tonight might be a party for the women who came, but it was work for their hostess. Though she never made it seem as such.

Sesily returned her attention to the room. There, at the center of the crowd, Adelaide spun and spun in a wild reel. She was joined by Lady Nora and her partner, Nik, apparently free that evening of her duties as lieutenant to the Bareknuckle Bastards, Covent Garden's king smugglers.

As she watched Adelaide's skirts rise up like a silken parachute in a children's game, Sesily considered a dance herself . . . until the tempo of the music whirled faster and faster and Nora tipped into Nik's arms, and the two shared a laughing, gasping kiss that made Sesily's stomach flip with something she didn't wish to identify.

There was nothing at all attractive about envy.

And there certainly wasn't anything appealing about wondering at the whereabouts of Caleb Calhoun, cad, scoundrel, bounder, and now . . . ghost.

He'd left her.

She ignored the thought, deliberately looking away from the joyful embrace, searching for Imogen. Imogen wouldn't be dancing. She'd be talking. And sure enough, Sesily found her in the corner of the room, gesticulating wildly to an audience that hung on her every word.

As she watched, Imogen spread her arms wide in the universal sign for *boom*.

Surely this was the only party in Mayfair where young women were discussing explosives.

Nearby, the duchess nodded to the women she was speaking with and said, "You take what you need for now. Leave your names with Mr. Singh." She indicated the tall, handsome Punjabi man on the balcony above, a fixture at these events.

To all of Mayfair, Lashkar Singh was the Duke of Trevescan's London man of affairs, proxy for the duke himself, keeping the duchess from spending Trevescan funds on frocks and frivolities. Of course, nothing related to Trevescan House was quite what it seemed. Mr. Singh was a brilliant mind and worked closely with the *duchess*, keeping all of her secrets and a few of his own. He'd have letters of reference prepared for these women within minutes.

"We shall find you new positions. In better houses. With decent employers. Understand?" The girls nodded seriously, several dashing away tears. "And you come see me if you need anything else, yes?"

Satisfied with their response, the duchess found Mr. Singh above, and the two shared a look. *Sorted.*

Sesily considered her friend. "Alright?"

The duchess sat next to her. "Totting's closing the London house. Running to the country. Refuses to pay any of the servants' severance."

"Bastard," Sesily said. "Can't even turn tail with decency."

"Yes, well, as long as he turns tail, I'm happy to help with the decency part," the duchess said. "We'll find a list of his country servants and do what we can for them. And once he's gone, we cross another off our list."

Another terrible man, dispatched.

"And for every head that rolls, two grow in its place," Sesily replied. "Truthfully, I'm beginning to think they are all bad."

The duchess slid her a look.

"Except for your duke, of course. Bless him and his fat bank accounts and his absolute disinterest in London."

Duchess lifted her champagne in a toast. "I shall drink to it."

"But only him," Sesily said.

"Sesily, darling, it seems you have had a difficult day."

"What would make you think that?"

"Well, your Medusa-like loathing for the men of the species did give me a clue."

Sesily sulked. "I wish everyone would stop comparing me to goddesses."

"Technically, she's a Gorgon," the duchess said, "and to be fair, you're the one who brought mythology into it. But do tell—who else is comparing you to goddesses?"

"Sesily is a goddess now?" The music had paused and Adelaide arrived, out of breath and ready for a break. She collapsed onto the steps at Sesily's feet. "I mean, of course you are."

"Thank you."

"But who is calling you one?"

"It's not important."

Adelaide and the duchess looked to each other. "The American," they said in unison.

"He didn't. Well, he *did*, but I don't think he meant it to be a compliment."

Two sets of brows rose.

"He called me Athena."

"Ah. Slayer of Medusa," the duchess said.

"Perseus slayed Medusa," Adelaide retorted.

"Perseus was the muscle; Athena was the brains."

"Would the two of you stop!" Sesily said.

They did, thankfully, two sets of enormous eyes wide on her.

Unfortunately, Imogen had arrived. "What's going on?"

"It's unclear," Adelaide replied. "But it seems the American has likened Sesily to Athena, and she doesn't care for it."

"Athena was a virgin, you know," Imogen reported, happily.

And like that, Sesily reached the end of her tether. "I did not know that, as a matter of fact, Imogen, but thank you so much for underscoring all the ways the American is wrong about me, as he fully confirmed my lack of virginity yesterday."

Two sets of enormous eyes became three.

And then, Imogen said, "I *told* you he wanted to . . ."

"We all knew that. Impossible not to, really, after the events in Coleford's cupboard," the duchess added, as though they'd all been privy to that particular thirty minutes. Which they clearly had.

Sesily narrowed her gaze. "I really don't know what I would do without you all to play town crier throughout Mayfair."

"Oh, please. It's not the town. It's *us*." Ordinarily, Sesily would agree. But tonight she wasn't exactly feeling magnanimous. She was feeling embarrassed.

She *loathed* feeling embarrassed.

"Sesily," Adelaide said, softly. "I don't understand. Isn't this what you've wanted for two years?"

Yes. Yes. Of course.

The response caught in her throat, tight and uncomfortable. And worse—horrifyingly—it came with the hot sting of tears. Dear God. Was she going to *cry*?

"Oh no," Imogen said.

"Oh dear," Adelaide chimed in.

"More wine," the duchess instructed a passing footman. "Quickly." She turned back to Sesily and said, "You cannot cry. You shall run your kohl, and then think of what everyone will say."

Sesily gave a little laugh. "Terrifying."

"Precisely. Now. You'd best tell us everything before Imogen decides to poison your American."

The tightness returned to her throat. "He's not my American."

"Was it terrible?" Adelaide asked. "If it was terrible, Imogen doesn't have to poison him. We'll simply tell a half dozen of the women in attendance tonight. And Maggie. And like that." She snapped her fingers. "In a month, it will be in all the papers in Boston."

"Good plan," Imogen said with admiration in her tone. "Lord knows Maggie will make sure no one ever goes near him again."

Sesily shook her head. "It wasn't terrible."

"It wasn't?"

"No," she said, softly. "It was really . . . good."

A pause. Then, Imogen said, "Good."

It was a ridiculous descriptor, that. Good. Like the way someone might describe a pasty purchased from a cart in Covent Garden Market, or praise a child's drawing, or report on a debutante's accomplishments at the pianoforte.

It was not the way anyone should describe the experience of having Caleb Calhoun make love to them. She winced at the thought. At the words *make love*. Sesily Talbot was thirty years old and was more than capable of separating pleasure from emotion when necessary, and in all those years she'd never once fooled herself into believing that she'd been made love to.

Until yesterday.

When it had felt really . . . really . . .

Don't say good.

Special.

Oh no. That was worse.

"I love him."

Her friends exchanged alarmed and confused looks, and Sesily couldn't blame them. There was much to be alarmed and confused by, if she were being honest.

"But that's . . . *good*, right?" Adelaide ventured.

Sesily looked down at her lap, studying the steel blue of her skirts, not wanting to tell them the whole story and wanting to tell them absolutely everything. Knowing that Caleb might have deserted her in that little house in the middle of nowhere, but these three women . . . they would never do the same.

So she did, on that dais on one end of the Duchess of Trevescan's ballroom, as a raucous party swirled around them. Sesily poured out the whole story—the rouge and the kohl and the walk and the way he seemed to understand the joy and purpose she received from her work with them, even as he was concerned about her being in danger.

And then she told them about the kiss and the rain and the way he kicked in the door, and built a fire and found them warm blankets and made her laugh . . . and made her believe that she might finally, *finally* have a chance to feel some kind of way about this man who'd made her feel some kind of way for years.

And when she was done, she said, "But . . . the long story turned very short, it was all perfect and exactly as I had dreamed, and I thought it was the beginning of something new. Except, when I woke, the rain was finished, night had fallen, the fire had burned to nothing, and he was gone."

Sesily knocked back her wine, and the duchess handed her another, which she accepted without hesitation.

"He *left*." Imogen, this time.

She nodded. "His carriage was gone when I got back to the house. I couldn't bear to look at Sera, so I left a note with the nearest footman and came home."

Home. She hesitated over the word, disliking how it felt to call that enormous house on Park Lane where she had happily rattled about in the last few months *home*, when a day earlier, she'd had a glimpse of what home could be.

She pressed her lips together, hating the silence that settled between them as the music swirled through the room, the women in attendance dancing wilder, drinking deeper, laughing louder.

But the quartet on the dais remained quiet, the duchess reaching out to take Sesily's hand, and squeeze it tight. Adelaide set her own hand on the toe of Sesily's slipper, the weight there welcome in a strange way.

And Imogen, dark eyes blazing with indignation. "Poisoning is too good for him."

Tears threatened again. "You three are excellent friends."

It was the truth. How many times had she worked beside these women, fought beside them, trusted them with her secrets and been trusted with theirs? They'd given Sesily a road to travel when her journey had been solitary. And now, even as she nursed the worst of wounds from the day prior, she was grateful for their comfort.

Even Imogen was a comfort, despite the unsettling gleam in her eye, as though all Sesily had to do was ask nicely, and she would toss Caleb into the Thames without a second thought.

Except, Sesily would have second thoughts.

She sighed. "Do you know what is the worst part?"

Her friends shared a look before the duchess said, "You still want him."

"More than before!" she replied, turning her face to the pretty gilded ceiling, glittering with massive candelabras. "How is that possible?! He left me on the floor of my sister's groundskeeper's cottage, the absolute rogue! To walk back to my sister's home through a *sopping wet field*!" She didn't know why the field was the most offensive bit at this point, but it was too late to rethink it.

"Monstrous."

"Absolutely abhorrent."

"Poisoning is back on the table!"

Sesily couldn't help a little huff of laughter at the immediate response in triplicate.

"And if he turned up here? Right now?" the duchess asked, all casual. "What then?"

Sesily scowled. "A facer would not be out of the question."

"A good start," Adelaide pointed out. "And *then* we let Imogen poison him."

Sesily did laugh then, the light in Imogen's gaze impossible not to enjoy.

"Well, while I cannot deliver the facer . . ." The duchess reached for the notebook she kept close at hand—the one with the silver bell embossed on the cover. "I can offer you something else."

Sesily's gaze fell to the book—filled with pages and pages of names and notations and business and information—and her heart began to pound. "What is it?"

The other woman held the book in a tight grip. "Tell me the truth. What do you want?"

The truth. She hadn't even let herself consider the truth. She wanted Caleb. And that meant . . . "I want . . . to know."

Her friend nodded. "You're sure?"

"Yes." She wanted to know, so that she could move forward. Without him.

Lie.

"He's hiding something," the duchess said.

"He's hiding everything," Sesily replied, irritated.

"Yes, but I'm speaking literally. He's hiding something, and whatever it is, it has to do with Coleford."

Sesily went hot.

"Now I want to know, too," Adelaide said, icy anger in her throat. "I want that man's head on a pike."

The duchess raised a brow in her direction. "Coleford's? Or Clayborn's?"

"I am able to hold two thoughts at the same time," Adelaide pointed out. "I want Coleford destroyed, *and* I require personal vengeance on the Duke of Clayborn, that cold bastard."

Later, Sesily would have to tell Adelaide about the conversation she overheard at Coleford House. But now . . .

Coleford. He's not a decent man.

Caleb's whisper in the dark.

"He knows him," she said, softly. She looked up at the duchess. "He knows him. And not in passing. He knows more of him than most."

Duchess's gaze narrowed. "So the other evening, he was not there for you?"

He'd found her in Coleford's study. He'd known where to look for her. Where to hide. "I don't know why he was there. But he knows Coleford and he warned me about him."

The duchess opened her book, flipping through copious notes as the rest of them looked on. Sesily knew what was coming. Wanted it, even as irritation flared. "You went looking for this. The relationship."

The duchess did not look up. "Of course I did."

"I told you I'd get his secrets."

"Yes, but we couldn't be sure you'd be willing to look at them, not once you had him in reach."

We. Sesily looked to Imogen and Adelaide, who both had the grace to at least pretend sheepishness, even as Imogen shrugged her shoulders. "We weren't wrong. You knew he was connected to Coleford, and you didn't tell us. It became personal."

"Adelaide is about to bring down a duke for being rude to her!" Sesily argued. "Is that not personal?"

Her friends were silent in the wake of her replay. And then, finally, Adelaide said, "It's different, Sesily."

Of course it was. It was, and the duchess had something that Sesily didn't. She wanted it. "Give it to me."

The duchess closed the notebook for a moment. "He's bought passage back to America."

"I know. He's only here until Sera has the babe." Still, the reminder that he intended to leave stung.

"No, Sesily. He leaves on Friday morning."

She blinked. "What? Which Friday?"

"This Friday."

He was leaving the country. He'd left her, and now he was leaving the country.

And still, she asked, hating the question and how much she wanted the answer, "When did he make the booking?"

"This morning."

She'd known it, but it struck like a blow to the chest nonetheless, sending her back against the divan. She swallowed around the disappointment.

He was leaving the country. He'd knocked down a door and made love to her in a dusty cottage and left her alone and cold to walk back through a wet pasture and he was so thoroughly opposed to facing her again that he had to *leave the country*.

Again.

She looked from one friend to the next—no words of comfort from Adelaide. No threat to sink his boat from Imogen. But that was fine. Sesily did not need either. Because her disappointment and disbelief had dissipated nearly as quickly as it had come. Seared away by the heat of something much more powerful.

Anger.

"That *coward*," she said, sending three sets of brows rising into hairlines before she leveled the duchess with a stern look. "Tell me the rest."

The duchess tilted her head, and Sesily found she was not interested in game playing. "His leaving has nothing to do with Coleford, and you're a brilliant mind, so you didn't require your book to recall the information. So that's not all, *is it*?"

Her friend's lips curved in admiration. "No. It's not. I needed the book to give you this." She tore a page from it, passing it to Sesily. "The ledger pages from Coleford's revealed several interesting pieces of data."

Sesily took the paper and considered the address scrawled across it as the duchess continued. "The funds the viscount is skimming off the Foundling Hospital are not simply going to aid The Bully Boys. They're also going to *pay* The Bully Boys. For services rendered."

"What kind of services?"

"To keep watch over *that*." The duchess's finger, wrapped in aubergine silk, pointed to the paper.

Sesily looked, surprise and satisfaction coursing through her. They grew closer to understanding the scope of Coleford's theft. She had no doubt that whatever was at the address in Brixton was the key to ensuring justice was served to the viscount. "What is it?"

"I don't know," the duchess said. "But I know it's not just Coleford who is interested in it."

The pieces fell into place. "Caleb."

The duchess nodded. "Calhoun is sending money to the same address."

"Why?"

"Again, I don't know. But your American—"

"Not mine."

"Well, whatever his secret," the duchess said, "it is there."

Anger and frustration and curiosity and something else she didn't care to name flooded through Sesily as she considered the paper.

"You shouldn't go alone," Imogen said. "Not if The Bully Boys are watching it. I shall go with you."

"No." Even now, even furious with Caleb, Sesily knew that wherever this trail led, she didn't wish to betray his secrets. Even if he'd rather leave the country than share them with her.

"You at least shouldn't go unarmed," Adelaide said. "Half those boys will recognize you. You knocked Johnny Crouch in the head with a table leg last week."

Caleb had been there, too, at The Place. By her side. Fighting.

He'd pulled her out of there. Protected her.

Who would protect him?

"Sesily?" Adelaide prompted, pulling her back to the present.

"I am always armed."

Chapter Eighteen

Though Sesily delivered on her promise to arrive armed at the mysterious address an hour's drive south, over the river, in Brixton, it became clear that the knife strapped to her thigh and accessible via secret pocket of her skirts was not necessary for this particular outing.

During the sleepless night and the hour carriage ride, Sesily had had a fair amount of time to consider what might be housed at number three Bermond Lane. Considering the fact that it was being watched by absolute thugs, on payment of an absolute monster, and had something to do with an American tavern owner who would rather leave the country than face her, Sesily had imagined all manner of things—a well-guarded warehouse, a tavern, a brothel, any number of dodgy shows in dodgy parts of town.

It had never occurred to her that it would be a home.

The carriage stopped at the end of the pretty lane lined with holly bushes not five minutes from the Brixton town center, where streets and shops bustled. The last stop on the post road before London, this little town afforded many travelers a final opportunity to prepare for a city debut.

It wasn't the kind of place one expected to find in the ledger book of Lord Coleford. Nor was it the kind of place one expected to be known to The Bully Boys.

And as for whatever Caleb was involved with out here . . . well, Brixton simply didn't seem like the kind of place that made for secrets in dire need of keeping.

She stepped down, confusion furrowing her brow as she looked to her driver, Abraham, who'd been with her for two years and knew the South Bank like his own face. "You're sure this is right?"

The young man's look indicated that he was affronted by the mere suggestion that he might have delivered her to the wrong location. She gave a little laugh. "Fair enough," she said. "I don't think this will take long, but why don't you head down the road and find a bit of cake?"

Abraham's sweet tooth did not require additional encouragement. Parting ways with her driver, Sesily headed up the narrow path toward a charming, well-tended collection of modest, thatched roofed houses, four in a small half circle, each with a gate and well-tended garden that Sesily imagined bloomed beautifully in the spring and summer.

Stopping in the little cul-de-sac, she considered the slip of paper she'd committed to memory the night before, knowing that she was looking for number three—the quaint house with the blue door almost directly in front of her.

Now what?

"You're here for the dressmaker?"

Sesily turned, meeting the curious gaze of a middle-aged Black man, crossing a small, tidy garden toward her. "Pardon?"

He smiled in full then, his expression matching his kind eyes. "The only time we get ladies we don't know down here, it's to see the dressmaker. Mrs. Berry." He indicated the house with the blue door. "Number three."

A dressmaker.

Well, it wasn't what she'd been expecting, but Sesily knew her way around dressmakers. At best, she'd sort out whatever secrets were kept within and at worst . . . well, she'd order herself a new frock.

"Thank you," she said to the man, who waved from the other side of the fence and turned back to his business.

Entering the gate for number three, Sesily approached the door and, having made her decision, knocked.

It opened within seconds, as though the woman on the other side had been waiting for her arrival. She was tall and dark-haired, laughing at something outside of Sesily's view—the kind of laugh that felt free and safe. But when she looked at Sesily, she grew serious—smoothing her hair and shaking out her moss green skirts. "Hello," she said, her posture shifting. Making way for performance.

For business.

"Hello. I'm Sesily Talbot—"

The woman's blue eyes went wide and her mouth dropped open. "I've heard of you!"

Sesily tilted her head. That was unexpected. "Oh?"

The woman nodded, the black ringlets framing her face bouncing happily. "I read the gossip pages and you and your sisters are always—" She cut herself off, the wide eyes going horrified. "I'm so sorry. I shouldn't have—I mean to say . . ."

She trailed off and Sesily couldn't help her laugh. "Oh, please don't stop on my account. When we were young, my sisters and I used to count the words devoted to each of our scandals and compete for the most." She leaned in. "I am proud to say that I won the most often."

The other woman laughed. "Is it wrong for me to say that I always thought your scandals were the most fun?"

"Not at all," Sesily said, happily. "In fact, you were right."

The woman's eyes lit up. "Is it true you sat for a nude painting?"

Sesily laughed. "That was my friend, as a matter of fact. But I did know a sculptor for a while."

The woman opened the door wider. "Miss Talbot— Lady Sesily—" she corrected herself with a half curtsy. "I don't know what brought you to Brixton, but I'm Jane Berry, and I'm at your service. Would you like to come in for tea?"

Like that, Sesily knew there was no possible way this dressmaker in this pretty house down this pretty lane was the person she was looking for. No matter what Abraham said, they were in the wrong place. New frock it was.

Perhaps Mrs. Berry could produce one in the same moss green as the one she was wearing. "I would, indeed," Sesily said, stepping over the threshold.

"What does bring you to Brixton?" Mrs. Berry asked.

Sesily shook her head. "Would you believe, I had the wrong address?"

"Well, it strikes me that you have the right address!"

Sesily smiled. "You are a dressmaker?"

"I am!" Mrs. Berry looked around Sesily to see her neighbor, standing by his fence, watching. She waved. "Hello, Mr. Green!"

Mr. Green returned the wave, and Jane closed the door, shaking her head. "He's a wonderful neighbor, but adores being in all available business."

The words settled between them, and the back of Sesily's neck began to tingle with awareness. Perhaps she didn't have the wrong address, after all.

Perhaps Mr. Green was correct.

But it didn't explain who this woman was, or why so many people were interested in her.

"Tea!" Jane pronounced, leading the way into a charming sitting room appointed for business with fabric swatches and a handful of dress forms in various states of design.

"Thank you," Sesily said, distracted, looking around the room, feeling as though she had been handed a box full of puzzle pieces with no indication as to what the final product should look like.

"I shall put the kettle on," Jane said, turning to leave the room, just as a boy came bursting in. "Peter! Manners, please!"

The boy immediately came to a stop, giving Sesily a chance to look at him. He was eight, perhaps nine, and he had an open, easy smile like his mother, which he gifted to Sesily.

"Hello," he said happily, his green eyes flashing. Familiar.

Recognition flared. Sesily's heart stopped.

She had the right address.

This boy was Caleb's son.

Tall for his age, with the whisper of the handsome man he'd become in his young face. Green eyes, dark curls. The same smile. The absolute image of Caleb.

She swallowed, suddenly cold in the warm house, her palms sweating. "Hello."

"Alright then. Outside, please. The lady is here to discuss a dress." Jane's words came from a distance. From miles away. And then Peter was gone, through the door and into the garden without a care in the world, and Jane was saying more. Apologizing for the interruption.

And Sesily was shaking her head and replying—whatever was the appropriate thing to say in this situation. Waving away the apology.

And Jane—

Pretty, laughing Jane.

Peter's mother.

Which made her . . . what to Caleb?

Mrs. Berry. Not Calhoun. Sesily's gaze dropped to the other woman's hands and the thin gold band on her finger. She was married.

Sesily thought she might be sick.

Was this his secret? Was this his *wife*?

Jane disappeared into the back of the house, toward the kitchens to put a kettle on, and Sesily stood in the middle of that pretty sitting room, a roar in her ears as she realized she absolutely could not remain one more minute in the middle of that pretty sitting room.

She had to get out.

"So sorry—" she said to the empty room, as though it might pass the message along to its inhabitant.

She left, moving as quickly as possible, out the door and through the now empty garden—Peter had disappeared to wherever boys went when they were sent outside. Thankfully. She hurried down the path and through the gate, then down the lane, the holly bushes suddenly less idyllic. The sun had slipped behind cloud cover and the wind had picked up, a reminder that winter was round the corner.

She pulled her cloak tightly around her.

Caleb had a child. A Peter.

Caleb had a Jane.

A beautiful family, out here in Brixton, hidden from view as he lived . . . *where*? Marylebone? Boston? Neither? *Here?*

Questions roared through her, as fast as her heartbeat. As quickly as she made for her carriage. The horses had been properly hitched and there was no sign of Abraham—of course. That would be too easy, wouldn't it? Passing the carriage, she turned toward the town, prepared to go find her driver and drag him back to take her home.

She'd buy him a hundred cakes when they were back in Mayfair. She'd buy him a whole bakery if he'd return.

But if she never returned to Brixton, it would be too soon. Brixton, where Caleb had a pretty wife and a beautiful son . . . a family.

No wonder he'd left her.

Did Sera know?

Had she kept this from Sesily on purpose?

And what of Caleb keeping it from her?

He didn't owe her this secret. They hadn't made promises to each other. But she'd thought they were more than this. She'd thought he would at least . . .

She tucked her chin to her chest, the biting cold of the wind nearly unbearable.

She'd known he kept secrets, but she'd never imagined him a liar.

That moment on the hill at Highley flashed, when she'd thought he saw her. Understood her. When she'd feared he'd break her heart.

She'd been right.

All that time, he'd had this. A little house. A kind woman. A sweet child, with his own winning smile. With his beautiful green eyes.

Her breath caught in her chest, and her throat grew tight. Dammit. She wouldn't let this man make her cry twice in two days. She wouldn't cry. At least, not until she was in the carriage. She had her pride, after all.

Her pride, and a seed of anger, taking root. Because he hadn't just lied to her.

He'd made her something she'd sworn she'd never be.

He'd made her reckless.

And therein was the problem. Because she was so consumed with Caleb, she'd forgotten that there were others interested in this particular address.

The reason she'd come armed.

Someone grabbed her from behind, lifting her off her feet and pulling her into a grove of trees at the side of the road. She shouted her surprise, and a filthy hand came to smother the sound.

"Well, well. Sesily Talbot. Who'd 'ave guessed a lady like you would find 'er way south of the river?"

Of course. She closed her eyes for a heartbeat, frustration and irritation and no small amount of fury coursing through her at the familiar voice.

She'd forgotten The Bully Boys.

Johnny Crouch tightened his grip on her. "But then again, you ain't a lady, are ya?" She struggled against him, twisting and squirming until he moved his hand, his hot acrid breath at her ear. "No screaming. If you bring the locals coming, I'll gut them in front of you. The boy first."

There was no risk of Sesily screaming. She knew better than to bring others into her fight. She worked best alone. "Your manners are atrocious, Johnny."

"They get worse when you're around."

"Careful, you'll turn my head." She fought the tight grip he had on her, his arms like a vise around her midsection, keeping hers locked to her sides. She cursed the way she'd allowed herself to get distracted earlier. Johnny was a big brute, but easy to fell if one relieved him of his strength.

She'd been so lost in thought, she'd lost the upper hand. *Reckless.*

Which meant she had to use her own brute force, and hope he didn't see it coming.

"Why don't you tell me what you want with the dressmaker?" he said.

"Truth be told, Johnny, after you put your filthy hands all over one of them, it shouldn't be so difficult to imagine that I want a dress. You should try bathing," she added, deliberately attempting to rile him. "It's all the rage."

"You're awful bold for a lass about to be delivered to the enemy," Johnny said. "Coleford won't like the idea of one of you lot lurkin' about here."

Fear thrummed through her. If Coleford got wind of her here, he'd peg the others—Imogen, Adelaide, Duchess. Worse. Maybe her sisters, who had nothing to do with this. Who wouldn't expect retribution.

Caleb. What did Coleford want with Caleb? With his family?

She swallowed around her nerves and brazened it through. "Coleford is opposed to new frocks?"

"You ain't here for a dress. Which means Coleford is going to want to know why you *are* here. And I'll tell you what—he don't treat ladies well."

She feigned a little laugh around his tight grip. "Coming from you, that's something."

With a grunt, he lifted her clear off her feet and started down the empty lane, toward a small, run-down cottage tucked into an overgrown cluster of trees. Sesily's heart began to pound and she struggled again. If he got her inside a building, she'd have less chance of escape. "Wait. Wait. Johnny," she said. "You've got me too tight. You've broken a rib."

"That's not the only thing I'll be breaking if you don't shut yer gob," he warned, not hesitating. Of course he didn't hesitate. She'd smashed his face with a table leg at The Place. Turnabout was fair play on the London streets—a lesson she'd had to learn when she'd fallen in with the duchess.

They drew nearer to the building, and Sesily knew she had less than a minute to gain ground. "Fair enough," she said, as brightly as possible, knowing her fear would only feed his brutishness. And then she went limp in his arms, the shift of her weight enough to make him stumble.

She closed her eyes and threw her head back as hard as she could, hoping she'd calculated the correct angle.

A wild screech sounded, followed by the foulest curse she'd ever heard.

She'd calculated the correct angle.

In the heartbeat during which he loosened his hold on her, she spun away from him, reaching into her false pocket even as she turned to face him. Apparently she did require a weapon, after all.

Johnny was hunched over, his hand to his nose, profusely bleeding. For the second time in just over a week. "Goddammit! You bitch! You broke my nose! Again!"

"Would we say *again* if it hasn't healed from the first time?" she asked, the hilt of her blade cool and welcome in her hand.

Johnny did not care for the question. He looked up and came for her as she backed away with speed, toward the main road, hoping that Abraham had returned and that he knew how to use the pistol she kept inside the driver's block of the carriage.

He lunged and she swerved out of reach with a flick of her wrist, the point of her blade slicing the palm of his hand when he got too close.

A hiss of pain sounded and he found the last bit of strength and agility necessary to grab her with his unharmed hand, his grip tight on her wrist, twisting her arm until she dropped the knife in the mud with a muffled cry of pain.

He smiled, rotting teeth flashing. "Not so brave without yer weapon, are ya?"

She bit back another shout as his hold grew even tighter, willing herself to stay quiet. She couldn't risk Jane or Peter. Or that nice man who enjoyed others' business. This business was not for him.

And she had to stay conscious if Johnny broke her wrist . . . which was likely to happen if she couldn't fight him back.

There was one chance left.

Using all her remaining strength, she swung toward him, her free hand reaching up, palm flat, to crack his nose one final time, knowing there would be no time to linger if he let her go. Knowing she would have to run, as fast as she could, and pray her carriage was ready when she got to it.

The blow struck true.

And she was turning, in motion before Johnny's wicked howl sounded.

Running. Straight into a brick wall.

Or, rather, the brick wall ran straight into her, catching her, turning her and shoving her behind it as it put itself between her and Johnny Crouch—The Bully Boys' biggest fist.

Not as big as Caleb Calhoun, though, who put his own fist directly into Crouch's face and knocked him out cold. Sesily blinked and looked down at the unconscious man, sprawled out on this dirt path in Brixton, gratitude and frustration and something she did not wish to identify coursing through her.

Breathlessness.

Because even now, even after the horrid events of the last thirty-six hours, even with his hat low over his brow, shadowing his face, she still responded to Caleb.

Not that she would ever, ever show it again.

Refusing to look at him, she turned on her heel and started for the carriage, stopping to collect her blade from the mud.

"No thanks?" he called after her, and she thought she exercised remarkable control in not replying by settling the filthy knife directly into his side.

"I had it under control," she tossed over her shoulder, refusing to look back.

He caught up with her. "He nearly broke your wrist."

"And I broke his nose," she said, ignoring the ache in her wrist. "Three times, by my count. So I think we were even."

"You were not even," he said, anger broadening his accent. Good. Let him be angry. Let him come for her. She would enjoy it. "You are lucky I was here." He paused. "Fucking hell, Sesily—you shouldn't be here. What were you thinking?"

And that was when Sesily reached the end of her rope.

"Don't you dare," she said, spinning back toward him. "Don't you dare even think of scolding me, as though I'm not a grown woman. As though you have some sort of claim over me—some responsibility to protect me from being roughed up in a deserted lane in *Brixton*." Her voice was ragged with her own anger. "You don't. You don't have claim or sway or responsibility for me. I've never asked you to protect me. Not in the two years I've known you, not the other night at The Place, not in Coleford's study, and not today . . . minutes after being surprised by the existence of your *wife and child* barely a day after you left me naked and alone on the floor of a country cottage like a damned . . ." She searched for the proper word. Nothing seemed right. Nothing seemed bad enough. Nothing seemed like it would hurt him enough.

And she wanted to hurt him.

But he'd hurt her so much more. And suddenly all the clever quips and the scathing barbs that Sesily had never struggled to find in her arsenal were gone.

He'd taken those, too.

"I thought you were decent. I thought you were good." A little, humorless laugh bubbled out of her. "I thought that whatever I found here would prove it. That I would fight alongside you to keep your secrets. To make them right."

Silence fell, full and aching, between them, and Sesily realized that even then, even with everything crashing down around them, she'd hoped she was wrong. That he would defend himself. That he would wave this away with some explanation—some proof that he was all the things she'd thought. The things she'd loved.

But he didn't.

"I never imagined you were as bad as all the rest," she said, sorrow rolling through her. And still, he said nothing. So she straightened her spine, and continued. "So, no. I feel neither gratitude nor luck that you were here. I would have rather taken my chances with Johnny Crouch." She paused, rubbing her thumb over her bruised wrist. "At least I know what I'm getting with him."

She turned to leave, to find her carriage and her way home, and console herself with wine and her cat and perhaps summon her friends to her side. They would come. Duchess would bring wine, and Adelaide would bring sympathy, and Imogen would bring fantasies of revenge.

The idea was already making her feel better when the carriage came into view, Abraham seated on the block, waiting. Thank heavens for small favors.

Except the heavens weren't watching. Not when Caleb caught up with her, his hand at her elbow, guiding her around to the far side of the carriage—out of view of anyone who might come down the lane.

She snatched her elbow from his touch, hating the way awareness thrummed through her. "Don't touch me."

He didn't. Of course he didn't. He wouldn't. Instead, he opened the door to the carriage. "Get in," he growled.

She narrowed her gaze up into the shadows of his face, the brim of his hat low enough to make it impossible to see his eyes. Good. She didn't want to see his eyes. She didn't want anything to do with him. "You needn't worry I'll linger."

"You are lingering," he said.

"I would never—" She stopped. *He couldn't believe* . . . She started again, quiet and firm. "As much as I would enjoy ruining your day, American, you cannot think I would ever make trouble here."

"You have no idea what trouble you have made here. Get in. Now."

She'd taken on The Bully Boys again. Johnny Crouch would come to, and she'd have to deal with him. But she had proof of his crimes, and proof of Coleford's as well, and it was time to see them both to justice.

But Caleb did not mean that trouble. He meant something else. Something that she'd likely never understand, because he'd never tell her. And it no longer mattered, because now, she'd do all she could to avoid him. Forever.

This wasn't like the other times, when he'd leave and she'd hold her breath hoping for the kind of return that made him hers.

Now, she knew the truth. He would never be hers.

And so, this might well be the last time she would see him. It would certainly be the last time she ever spoke with him.

She got in the carriage, refusing to look at him. Knowing that if she did, she'd say something that she'd regret forever. Something like, *I loved you.*

And even that would be a lie.

But she would go to the grave with the truth.

Sesily turned back to close the door behind her, to discover him climbing up behind her, filling the space inside the carriage with his enormous body, quickly closing the door behind him and thumping the roof of the vehicle without hesitation.

"No," she said, sharply. "Get out."

The carriage lurched into motion, and Caleb ignored her, turning to look out the rear window, as though checking to see if they were being followed.

Irritated that she hadn't done it first, Sesily let her anger fly. "Did I not make it clear that I have no interest in being confined with you? That I certainly have no intention of *going anywhere* with you?"

He spun to face her, and she sat back against the seat—shocked by the frustration on his face. The wild fury in his eyes. The fear there. "This isn't a fucking choice, Sesily. This isn't painting naughty words on some man's face in the gardens. You're in *danger*. And now they are, too."

Jane. Peter.

He might have said the words a dozen other ways at a dozen other times, and she would have ignored him. Would have fought him. But here, now, there was something in his tone, in the way he held himself, that unsettled her.

He was afraid.

"And you?" she asked. "Are you in danger?"

"I'm always in danger."

"In danger of what? Discovery by The Bully Boys? They're aware of me, Caleb. Discovery by Coleford? What does he have to do with this place? With that house? With your—" She swallowed the words.

Wife. Child.

Betrayal came hot and unbidden. She shook her head. She wouldn't say it.

She didn't have to.

He turned to face her, and she looked out the window, feeling sick to her stomach and, for the first time in her life, not because of the motion of the carriage.

"Sesily." Her name on his lips, soft and insistent. Neither contrite nor angry.

She shook her head. Refusing to look.

"*Sesily,*" he said again, urgent.

How many times had she dreamed of him saying her name like that? Like he wanted her attention more than anything in the world?

She looked at him, his hat now off, his mahogany curls in disarray over his brow, his green eyes fairly glowing in the late afternoon light. She crossed her arms over her chest, pressing her lips together, and waited.

He sat forward, elbows on his knees, and covered his head with his hands, rubbing them through his hair once. Twice. A third time.

And then he looked up and found her eyes. Sesily caught her breath.

"Jane—" he began, his voice hitching with emotion. The name was reverent. Precious. Sesily braced herself, ready for the blow.

He finished, "She's not my wife. She's my *sister*."

Chapter Nineteen

He shouldn't have told her.

Jane's existence—his existence—was the kind of secret a man took to his grave. It was the kind of secret that put anyone who knew it in danger. It was not the kind of secret a man told the woman he loved. But when a man had been put through the wringer worrying about the woman he loved, he wasn't exactly in his right mind.

When Fetu had turned up on his doorstep two hours earlier, concern in his eyes, Caleb had known, instantly, that something had happened to Sesily.

A message, delivered to Caleb at The Singing Sparrow. Collected by his partner because he hadn't been there, because he'd been at home, packing to leave again. Once more, for the same reason he'd always left. To keep them all safe.

To keep her safe.

"Your girl—she's headed to Brixton."

Fetu hadn't minced words, and neither had Caleb. He hadn't pretended not to know who his friend referenced. Hadn't denied the descriptor, even though he knew it wasn't accurate.

She wasn't his. She would never be.

But that didn't mean he wouldn't do everything he could to keep her safe.

He'd driven hell-for-leather over the river, southwest of London, making the hour-long journey in half the time, not knowing what he would find when he got there.

A singular thought in his head.

Keeping Sesily safe.

He'd loved her for an age, and he would love her for an age, and though he knew that seeing her, being near her, touching her—all of it—would make everything to come worse, he knew that he would do everything in his power, forever, to protect her.

But first, he had to get to her.

When he'd found her in Crouch's grasp, in obvious pain and struggling for freedom, Caleb had gone mad with fear and anger that someone—anyone—would dare touch her, let alone threaten her.

He didn't remember what came next—everything blurred until he was staring down at the other man unconscious in the dirt, Sesily looking at him, frustration in her eyes along with pain—not caused by her wrist. Caused by him.

He should have let her leave without him. Let her believe what she wished. Followed at a distance. Seen her home. Safe.

Packed his things. Found passage to Southampton.

He should have let her go then. It's what a decent man would have done. But Caleb had never been decent. Wasn't that the point? Wasn't the proof of it that he'd followed her there and dragged her further into his past? Put her in further danger?

Wasn't the proof of it that he didn't regret it, even then? That he would never regret following her. Never regret vanquishing her enemies. Never regret tying Crouch up and leaving him to be found by the next of Coleford's henchmen . . . or never at all.

But he knew, without question, that he would regret telling her the truth about what she had found there. Because once the truth was out, he wanted to tell her everything. And it would only make him love her more.

Silence fell in the wake of his words in the quiet carriage, the importance of the statement heavy between them even as he willed her not to understand the full impact of the truth.

"Your sister," she said, finally, uncertain.

"Yes."

"But . . . she's English."

"Yes."

"You're American."

Secrets. "No."

She shook her head. "How is that . . ."

He didn't reply. Was afraid that if he did, he'd reveal more. Too much.

But he didn't have to reveal it. Sesily was brilliant, and it took her no time to put the pieces together. "She's your sister. And you're English. And Coleford is watching her." Her eyes, clear and bright, met his. "And you knew his house. When I was there in his study, you knew where the servants' closet was. You've been there before."

Caleb lifted his chin, hating the way the words brought the feeling of being there again, with too little muscle and too little power and far too little understanding of the world. "Go on, then." When he spoke, Boston was gone, replaced by the West Midlands.

Her eyes went wide at the accent. "I—" She shook her head.

He gave it to her. "His son."

Her brow furrowed. "The one who died?" And then, understanding. His brilliant, beautiful girl. Of course she'd put it together in an instant. "No, not died."

He nodded. "Killed."

She shook her head. "No. Wait. The son—Bernard Palmer—he died. A riding accident. Years ago." Of course she would know something about what had happened. Sesily Talbot was not a fool and she was not reckless, and she would not have ransacked Coleford's study without knowing something of the man she investigated. Of his past.

But she did not know everything. Only two people in the world knew everything. "Bernard Palmer, heir to the Viscounty of Coleford, died eighteen years ago," he conceded. "But it was not a riding accident. Nothing about it was an accident."

"He deserved it."

He tilted his head. "How do you know that?"

She met his eyes. "Because I know you."

She did.

"The Honorable Bernard Palmer," he said, a humorless laugh in the words. "It wasn't an accident, and he wasn't honorable."

"You were so young," she said, and he could hear the understanding in her voice. *Seventeen.* "It was so long ago."

"Not long enough. Coleford was still watching. Waiting for me to make a mistake."

The words landed, and he regretted them instantly. Regretted the guilt that shadowed her eyes. "I was it. The mistake."

"No." She would never be a mistake. Not one moment with her would be. "No. Sesily. Listen to me. Whatever happens. However this ends. . . . you were not the mistake. You were—"

Athena.

Ready to go to war for him. With him.

"—perfect," he finished.

She watched him for a long moment, the rocking motion of the carriage and the sound of the wheels all there was between them. He came off his seat, leaning across the space to yank open the window next to her. "You need the air."

"I'm not going to be sick," she said. "Tell me what happened."

"No."

"Why not?"

"Because some things are not for knowing."

"What if I can help?" He started to answer, but she held up a hand, irritation flashing in her eyes. "Don't tell me I cannot help. Have I not proven how useful I can be?"

God, she was magnificent. "I know how useful you are, Sesily. I've seen you go head-to-head with earls in Mayfair and brutes in Covent Garden. I've seen you break a man's nose twice."

"Three times."

"I was only there for two of them." Her lips curved just barely, and he realized he would have given anything to see her smile. But she wasn't having it. So he finished. "This is not a problem that you and your gang of brilliant ladies can solve. Not every tragedy can be righted with a pretty smile and a vial of laudanum."

"You don't know that if you haven't tried it."

He did, in this case, but as she stared him down, this stunning woman, he realized that he wanted her to know some of it. That he wanted to, for a moment, share it with someone.

With her.

He'd stop before he put her in danger. *More* danger.

Before he could change his mind, he spoke. "I was born Peter Whitacre, raised in the stables on the Coleford estate in Warwickshire. My parents worked there, and their parents before them, and my father was a respected stable worker, so we lived in a small cottage on the land."

"Your parents and you, and . . ."

"And my sister Jane, a year younger than me," he said, softly. "We were servants' children and so we grew to be servants ourselves. Me in the stables and Jane in the main house. My mother was a maid and good with a needle, and Jane learned to sew before she could talk."

"She loved it," Sesily said, sad and nostalgic, as though it was her memory, and Caleb liked that—the idea that she might know his past—even as he knew it was a luxury he should not claim.

"She did," he said. "And that made her good at it. But she wasn't old enough to mend for work, so when she was eight, she became a scullery maid."

"Eight," Sesily said, softly.

"No one was a layabout at the Coleford estate," he said, lost to the memory. "The old man wanted every penny he paid us."

Her gaze shadowed and she moved, crossing to sit next to him. He shouldn't like it. But then she took one of his hands in hers and he forgot about should, because her warm, firm grip was too tempting to resist. "The man deserves a cold, cruel death. In Newgate."

He met her eyes, fierce and beautiful. "I think he would prefer it to meeting you on a dark street."

"I guarantee he would, and I have not even heard the meat of your story."

"Goddess of War. I wish we'd had you."

Her gaze softened. "I wish the same."

He leaned over and dropped the window next to him, the crosswind in the carriage pulling tendrils of her sable hair loose from their moorings, making her more beautiful—and when she smiled . . . Caleb resisted the urge to rub the ache from his chest. For a moment, he let himself dream of her. "I wonder what it would have been like, if we'd been at your father's estate instead of Coleford's."

She smiled. "You would have hated it. You think I am mayhem *alone*. We were five girls born outside of the aristocracy and delivered to it untamed and untrained when my father won his title."

"I wouldn't have hated it," Caleb said. "I promise you I would have done everything I could to turn your head whenever you came near the stables."

She laughed and tucked herself into the crook of his arm, and he knew he shouldn't notice the way she felt there, in that space that suddenly felt made for her. "I am sorry to say, good sir, I never went to the stables. Seline would have been the object of your affection."

The scent of her was making him wild. There was no other explanation for why he replied, "No, Sesily. One look at you, and I would have been done for."

"I would have liked that," she said, tilting her face up to look at him—full and lush and beautiful, like she belonged on a swing in a painting by a French master, her skirts blown up to her waist, showing pantalets and stockings and ribbons. Waiting for him to kiss her.

God, he wanted to kiss her.

It would only make it harder to do what needed to be done, but he wanted it like he wanted his next breath. Resisting the desire, he refocused, returning to his story, but retaining his hold on her. Not wanting to let her go— especially not then. Not while he resurrected the past. "The winter of 1819 was terrible. Coleford had raised the rents and there wasn't enough firewood or food on the estate, and we all struggled. My parents . . ." He trailed off.

"Caleb," she whispered, lifting his hand to her lips. "I'm so sorry."

He swallowed around the tightness in his throat, and focused on the feel of her lips against his skin. "You mean that."

"Of course I do," she said, surprised. "How old were you?"

"Sixteen."

"And what happened?"

"We were given pallets with the other servants. Me in the stables, her in the house. It was warm—mostly— and dry, and it seemed like we had more food than before. And I began to feel like all might be well." He paused, then said, "Almost a year went by before Palmer returned home from university and discovered Jane."

Sesily swore, angry and vicious, her fingers tight on his, as though she could protect them through time. He took the grip and the words as a sign that he did not have to elaborate. She knew what was to come.

"We all knew about Coleford. We knew he was cruel to the servants and the tenants and his wife. But Jane didn't tell me that his son was the same."

She nodded. "She didn't want you to be punished; she wanted to keep you safe."

Of course Sesily knew it. But he hadn't. "Palmer hounded her. She did her best to stay away from him, and the other servants at the estate all did their best to make sure she was never alone." But it wasn't enough. It couldn't be. And Sesily knew that as well as anyone. Better, for all she'd seen of the world beyond her drawing room.

"A few months later, it was decided that Jane would be sent to the house in Mayfair, where Palmer was to live as he entered society and took up the mantle of future viscount." He paused, then spat, "He'd requested her. As a *gift*."

Sesily cursed.

"That's when she told me everything, because she was scared, and she knew she couldn't keep it a secret any longer. She knew that once she was in Mayfair, he'd have access to her."

Sesily nodded. "She wouldn't be protected there. The servants in Mayfair wouldn't know her. They wouldn't help."

"For someone who's never been a servant you know more than you should about how we worry." He met her eyes and couldn't resist putting his own hand on hers, warm and firm. "I traded six months' pay to switch places with a stablehand who'd been slated to outride to London with the family when they moved to town for the season."

"That's how you knew the house."

No reason to keep the secret any longer. Not now, with the story pouring out of him. "Jane sewed a pocket in her skirts. Lined it with leather."

"For a blade."

He slid a look to her. "I wondered how your blades come and go so quickly."

"Reticules are not handy in a pinch," she explained. "But the leather . . . inspired."

"The story goes the way all stories go."

"Except it doesn't," she pointed out.

"No, I suppose it doesn't."

He'd never told anyone this story, and there was something about telling this woman, in this rocking carriage, the air from outside blowing past them, carrying his secrets away after he'd spoken them, that set him free.

"It was the two of us against the whole world. And we did all we could to keep her from him." He stopped. The memory of the evening playing out in his mind. Jane, shaken, but unharmed. The pair of them, suddenly on the run. "I did what I had to to keep her safe."

She didn't push him, and he was grateful for the way she understood, even though she could not possibly understand. "She was lucky to have you."

He met her eyes, so blue and so honest. "She didn't have me for long. I ran."

"What other option did you have?"

It sounded so simple on her lips. As though it were what anyone would do. Leave their sister. Alone. Go make a fortune across the sea.

"She didn't go with you."

"No. I knew we were more likely to be caught if we were traveling together. And I knew that if we were caught, I'd be hanged, and she'd be alone with no one to protect her."

She nodded, understanding in her eyes. No judgment. Nothing like what he felt every day for the choices he'd made a lifetime earlier.

"There was a house in Yorkshire—a place the girls at the estate whispered about. A place that would take Jane in if she could get there. And so I gave her every-thing I had—every penny I'd saved—and put her on a mail coach."

"And what of you?" She touched his leg, her grip on his thigh strong and sure. Certain.

"I went the other way," he said. "I knew that if Coleford ever found me . . . it wouldn't only be me at the end of a rope. The things I'd seen him do . . . I knew he'd take Jane, too. Within months, he'd killed his wife to marry another. To secure a new heir."

She shivered in his hold, and he pulled her closer. Loving the feel of her, safe with him after the afternoon's events. "But you escaped."

Barely. "I was sure he would have screamed murder and gone straight to Bow Street. Poured money into runners' pockets to ensure they found me."

Sesily nodded. "Difficult to scream murder when you're planning one yourself. So he announced a tragic accident and . . ."

"And vowed to hunt me," he finished for her. This brilliant woman who always saw the whole field. "Peter Whitacre stowed away on the ship. Caleb Calhoun disembarked in Boston. I knew that to survive . . . I had to start fresh. I sent money and a letter to the house in Yorkshire when I'd found a position. Scrubbing pots at a tavern for Yanks."

Sesily smiled at that. "And look at you now, a Yank yourself."

"Boston was a good place to get lost. And I was lucky enough that there were people there who found me."

"Brilliant boy," she whispered, and he warmed at the praise, so welcome even now, decades later. "So brave. Now Caleb Calhoun, owner of a dozen of the most successful taverns between Baltimore and Boston. Wealthy American businessman with all his teeth and a full head of hair and legs that go all the way down to the floor."

His brows rose. "Is that what they do?"

"You've a lovely set of legs. I always wondered if that was just how they came in America. Imagine my excitement to discover they are home grown." He couldn't help a small laugh. "And how long before you came back to see Jane and Peter?"

The smile disappeared.

Sesily looked up when he turned to stone. "What is it?"

"You know his name."

"Peter? Yes. He looks like you. He has your eyes. Your smile."

"You . . . spoke with them?"

"I . . . did . . ." The words came out cautious, as though she knew something was happening, but couldn't sort it out. A dozen emotions flashed across her face, her brow furrowing as she attempted to understand what was happening. "Caleb—are you saying—have you never—" She sat up and turned to face him. "When was the last time you saw her?"

"I've seen her," he said. "Peter, too."

But it wasn't everything and she knew it. "How long since they've seen you?"

"Eighteen years."

The sadness that filled her eyes was almost unbearable to watch, the tears that turned them liquid, like the sea. "Caleb," she whispered, and the ache in the word matched the one in his chest.

"Coleford has been watching her since she returned to London. When she married Peter's father the banns were posted. He's watched her since then."

"Waiting for you."

He nodded. "But as long as he sought me, she was safe."

"His only hope of finding you."

He nodded. "Coleford has poured every penny he has into hunting me, and watching this house, in the hope I would slip up. Return."

And he had.

"But vengeance is expensive. Watchmen cost money, and a viscount who mistreats his tenants cannot find enough of it in the estate," she said. "So he sinks himself into debt and, to get himself out of it, steals from

the Foundling Hospital . . . adding yet another reason
why he can't get near Scotland Yard. Because if he did,
they'd discover his fraud."

"Enter Sesily Talbot," he said, softly.

"They're going to discover his fraud either way, I'll
have you know."

He looked out the window to keep himself from
kissing her. They were on the bridge, the sunset in the
distance setting the Thames aflame. "He was certain I
would make a mistake."

"You went as far away as you could to avoid it," she
said. "I cannot imagine how difficult that must have
been. How you have lived a lifetime to protect them."

Nearly impossible.

No. Absolutely impossible.

"He knew I cared. Knew I was sending money when I
could. Making sure that she and her husband and Peter
had everything they needed. I covered my tracks. The
funds come via a half dozen accounts, none of which
can be traced to me. And still . . . he knew I would slip
up and show my face, eventually." He reached for her,
running the backs of his fingers over her cheek. "And he
was right. I couldn't stay away forever."

Her brow furrowed. "Why would you ever set foot in
Brixton? Knowing what would happen if they saw you?
When they reported back to him? Why would you put
yourself in danger?"

Don't admit it. Some secrets weren't meant to be
discovered.

Too late. She was already there. "Because of me."

"You changed everything by coming here."

"So you followed me. You showed your hand."

"I knew Jane was safe. But you"—his thumb stroked
over her bottom lip—"you'd go to war."

She clasped his wrist in her hand, holding him tight. "Caleb. He cannot have this. He cannot take it from you. Your sister. Your nephew. The people you love."

"He has done," he said. "After what he lost—"

"A wretched son who deserved what happened to him a dozen times over?"

This woman, full of rage and fire. He adored her. And still, "*This* is his punishment. And only because he could not find a way to mete out anything worse."

But now, Coleford could mete out something worse. He could come for Sesily. And that meant everything had changed. It meant Caleb could no longer run.

Sesily stiffened, seeing the whole play. That Crouch would report that she'd been in Brixton. With Caleb. That, after the dinner earlier in the week, after the scene Adelaide had made, after the *enemy* she'd made, Coleford would know that Sesily's presence was not coincidence. She'd be suspect. And so would Caleb.

And everything would unravel.

"You cannot turn yourself in." She grasped for something. A way out. "He might not find you."

Of course he would. "Sesily—"

"No! He might not make the connection between you then and you now." She was speaking so fast, her mind turning over the facts. Considering the outcomes. Planning. He couldn't believe he'd once thought her reckless. She was brilliant. Calculating every possible scenario.

But he'd been calculating them for eighteen years. And this one ended in only one way. "Sesily."

"No! Listen. Johnny saw you at The Place. You were with me. You carried me out of there. You protected me."

Of course he had. And he would again. He would do everything he could to keep her safe. Forever. "Sesily."

He didn't want to plan. He wanted to hold her.

He wanted to love her for just a little bit.

Just a taste of it. Maybe it would be enough.

But she was frantic. "There's no reason for them to believe that you had anything to do with Jane."

"Shh." He reached for her, taking her hand in his and pressing a kiss to her knuckles. "You're not wearing gloves."

"I don't like them when I'm working." The words were clipped, distracted. Her mind was turning over and over, trying to find another end to this journey that had begun long before she'd been a part of it. "Caleb, you cannot—"

He ignored her, placing another kiss at her knuckle, red from her blow. "Does this hurt? You delivered one of the Talbot sisters' famous facers?"

"I taught them all how to deliver a facer, I'll have you know."

His brows rose. "Impressive."

Her other hand came to clasp his. "Caleb," she said, the words urgent. "Listen to me. They don't have to know about you. You didn't see her. You didn't go to the house. This doesn't change anything."

He lingered at her knuckles, pressing little soft kisses along them, knowing the truth. "Of course it does. Johnny Crouch saw me."

"Johnny Crouch is a cabbagehead good for nothing but muscle. The Bully Boys aren't welcome at the Sparrow. There's no guarantee he even recognized you."

It wasn't true. Crouch was a respected lieutenant of The Bully Boys. Had come up through the gang running pickpockets and now managing bruisers for money. "Sesily. A minute ago, you were passing me off as your savior because he did recognize me. He knocked over

The Place. I watched you crack his skull. I was there. And even if I hadn't been . . . he recognized me."

"Fine. But it's been eighteen years," she argued. "There's no guarantee Coleford will."

That much was true, but Coleford had been waiting for this for eighteen years. And he might be a monster, but he knew the score. Caleb and Sesily in Brixton on the same day was too much of a coincidence to do anything but ring the viscount's bell.

It was over.

Caleb didn't stop the soft kisses. Didn't want to. Didn't want to sacrifice even a moment of time at her skin now that he saw the way the end would play out. He pulled her closer, across his lap. Wanting her close. "Even if he didn't recognize me, Coleford will come after you. Now. Not later. The moment he hears you were here. He is ruthless and relentless and he will scent me on you, even if Crouch never whispers my name. He will destroy you to get to me. To get his vengeance."

She hesitated.

"How did you find the house?"

She was still lost in thought, half answering. "He's running a scheme—people are taking money from mothers looking for the children they left long ago at the Foundling Hospital. Promising to find the lost children and pocketing the cash. A percentage is going to Coleford."

Caleb swore. Taking money from women who left their children because they couldn't care for them. Like father like son. A fucking monster.

"He's using the funds he steals from children and the desperate mothers who've surrendered them to pay The Bully Boys to watch Jane. To watch for you. It's all in the ledger pages I stole."

"And so you took yourself to investigate. Put yourself in danger." He hated it.

"Not for him," she whispered to the fast dimming carriage. "For you."

Christ, he hated that more. Hated that he'd been the reason she was in danger now. "Sesily—Johnny Crouch might be stupid, but he's not stupid, you understand? It will take him no time to get word to Coleford that you were there. At Jane's. And that I was there, too."

"So, we fight them."

Alone, he might have. But not now. Not with her safety at risk. "No, love. We can't. There's no winning on this front."

"Because you killed a man who needed killing twenty years ago?"

"Not just any man. Son of a viscount. A viscount with enough power and madness to make sure that justice is served."

"Justice *was* served," she said, the words urgent. Familiar. Furious.

"Gorgeous girl," he whispered to her curls, unmoored in the wind. "So angry."

"I am angry. This isn't how it goes, Caleb. This isn't how it ends. He's not the only one with power. I have it, too. And money. And friends." She turned her fierce gaze on him, unwilling to free him from the conversation. "Whatever you think Coleford can do—to me, to you, to Jane . . . The world is changing and these men—wealthy and titled and privileged and monstrous—they do not always win."

"And what of me? Am I not a monster?"

Had he not endangered her? His sister? His nephew? Had he not demolished the structure built of spun sugar, protecting them all? Was it not smashed to dust?

She set her hands to either side of his face, staring into

his eyes. "No. *No*. There is nothing bad about you. You are good and kind and so decent and I . . ."

She was killing him. Destroying him with her words and her passion and he knew what she was about to say, and he wanted it. Caleb had lived a life of want, and never wanted anything like he wanted to hear Sesily complete that sentence.

But he knew that if she did, he'd never be able to leave her.

And that was the only way he could keep her safe.

"Caleb, I—"

He kissed her to stop her from telling him that she loved him. Pulled her tight against him, loving the way her hands slid beneath his coat, flat and warm against his chest as though she owned him.

Which of course she did.

She owned him even as he pulled her close, reveling in the feel of her, soft and lush and beautiful as she opened for him, and he licked into her, long and slow and reverent, as though they were anywhere but there, in her carriage, and he were anything but racing the clock, and they had forever to explore each other.

And for a moment, he let himself believe they did. He let himself think that he might spend a year investigating the swell of her lip and the taste of her tongue and the curve of her hip in his hand, and the softness of her hair in his fingers.

She sighed, and he deepened the kiss.

Loving her. Silently.

And when he lifted his lips from hers, and she opened her eyes, slow and sinful, he reveled in her beauty, in the way it promised him an eternity when all they had was a carriage ride.

She pressed her forehead to his, and he tightened his fingers in her hair and closed his eyes, breathing her in, tempting and perfect. "Why did you come back?" she whispered. "To London?"

His heart pounded, and he bit back the truth. "Your sister wanted to open the Sparrow."

He should have known it wouldn't work. Sesily would never allow falsehood here. Not between them in this carriage full of truth. "And after that?"

He closed his eyes.

Don't tell her.

"Oliver's christening."

She nodded. "And this time, for the babe."

It would hurt them both.

"Yes." *No.*

"Liar."

No good would come of it.

And even knowing that, he couldn't stop himself. He looked at her, her gorgeous eyes on his, refusing him escape. The carriage had slowed, and Caleb knew that their time was nearly up. That when the vehicle stopped, and they parted, it would be the end.

Maybe because of that, it mattered very much that she hear the truth. "I come back because I cannot stay away."

She was close enough that he could feel the way her breath hitched in her throat. "Stay away from what?"

He brushed a curl from her face, tucking it behind her ear. Marveling at her. At the fact that, for a moment, he'd had her, perfect and his. He whispered her name, and it was the closest thing he'd ever spoken to a prayer. "From you."

She went still in his arms, and the words hung between them, heavy and honest. She raised a hand and touched his lips, her fingers like a kiss. "You put yourself in danger for me."

"Sesily." He took her hand in his, holding her firm. Needing her to understand. "I would walk into fire if it meant seeing you one last time. And I would not hesitate."

Her eyes slid closed, her forehead bowing to his lips as the carriage came to a stop. And then he couldn't say more. Couldn't tell her all the ways he was tethered to her. All the ways she consumed his thoughts. All the ways he adored her.

The drive was over.

It was all over.

Except it wasn't, because she whispered, "Come inside." And then, before he could say no, she whispered, "Please. I—"

He could have kissed her again. Stopped the words. But he wanted them too much. And though he knew that hearing them would wreck them both, the knowledge was not enough to stop him.

He wanted them. Almost as much as he wanted her.

But she didn't give them to him. Instead, she said, soft and perfect, "Caleb . . . I need you."

Somehow, it was worse than he'd expected. Because love might have reminded him that he should leave her. That he should keep her safe. But need . . . need made leaving her impossible.

Because he needed, too. He ached with it. And he was hers. He always had been. From the moment he'd laid eyes on her.

And what she needed, he would give her.

Chapter Twenty

They didn't speak when they exited the carriage, nor when they entered the house—Abraham knew enough about Mayfair and the way the neighbors gawked and gossiped to bring them to the rear, where they could enter past the mews and into the kitchens.

They cut through the room, empty of staff despite the lovely smell of freshly baked bread filling the room, and a pot happily bubbling on the stove. Good luck—the best of the day to be sure—as Sesily feared disrupting the quiet agreement she and Caleb had made in the carriage.

Still, he did not touch her. Not in the kitchens and not when they slipped through the narrow doorway leading to the dimly lit servants' passage. Not as they climbed the stairs to the first floor, and then the second. And not when they made their way through the hallways, no longer bright with the day's light, but not yet lit for the evening.

With every step, the absence of his touch and his voice made Sesily more and more desperate for both.

In the carriage, he'd resisted her. She'd sensed the way he pulled back from her desire, from her openness. She hadn't missed the moment he'd kissed her . . . just as she was about to tell him she loved him.

Perhaps he didn't want her love, but he wanted her. That much was clear in the way he touched her and kissed her . . . the way he explored her body and held her tight and said her name, like it meant something.

The way he'd unraveled.

The way his words had unraveled her.

And he'd followed her inside, had he not?

But it wasn't forever.

She'd sensed it in the carriage—the shift in him. The certainty in him, as though he'd been on the edge of a decision that would impact them all and then . . . he'd made it. And that's when he'd changed, touching her and kissing her and telling her the things she'd always dreamed he'd say.

I cannot stay away.

And somehow, it had all felt like the end.

But he was here now and he was hers for the moment . . . and she didn't want to think about how long that moment would be or how short it would feel when it was over.

She only wanted to live it.

And dammit, she wanted him to touch her. With every step, the desire grew headier and more consuming, until she could think of nothing else but the way he would set her aflame.

He didn't touch her until they reached her bedchamber, and she set her hand to the door handle. Before she turned it, his enormous warm hand came over hers, staying the movement for a heartbeat. Just long enough for him to draw impossibly close and whisper, "Are you certain?"

If she hadn't wanted him so much, she might have laughed at the question. Did this man not know that she belonged to him? That whatever he wished, whatever he dreamed, she wanted to give it to him?

She turned, and his lips brushed over her temple, leaving fire in their wake. "I am certain."

He turned the knob and opened the door, and she stepped in, turning back to face him as he pulled the door closed. "Will we be disturbed?"

"No," she said, marveling at the size of him. His broad shoulders and the sharp angles of his jaw.

"How do you know?"

She smiled. "Because my driver is a terrible gossip. And my staff knows how the world works."

One dark brow rose. "And how is that?"

"Is your memory failing you?" she teased. "Do you not recall what happened the last time we were alone together?"

He turned the key in the lock and set it on the small table next to the door. "I might require a reminder."

"It can be arranged." The end of the word lost its sound as he stalked toward her. He was big and broad and the handsomest thing she'd ever seen, and he came at her with purpose, like he'd spent his whole life waiting for this moment. For this room. For her.

She was breathless from it, backing away, loving his watchful gaze and the quirk of his lips. He liked this. He liked it and after the carriage ride . . . the day . . . a lifetime . . . she wanted to give him what he liked. "You enjoy the chase."

"I enjoy the catch," he replied, low and sinful, his arm snaking around her waist and pulling her tight to him.

She laughed. This was perfect. He was perfect. "Oh," she said, softly, wrapping her arms about his neck. "Look at me . . . caught."

His chest rumbled against hers, and she delighted in the feel of it. In the way he tilted her chin up to bare the column of her neck. The way his lips pressed to the soft skin just beneath her ear. "I think, my lady . . ." he said there, soft and sinful, the honorific doing impossible, wonderful things to her, ". . . that I am the one who is caught."

It wasn't true, she knew. If he were caught, she wouldn't be so terrified of what was to come when they left this quiet, dark room and returned to the world. But she put it out of her mind, and came up on her toes to kiss him.

He met her caress with his own, stroking over her slow and languid and lush, tasting of wickedness. She pressed herself against him, wanting him closer. Wanting their clothes gone.

As though he'd read her mind, he broke the kiss and turned her around, his fingers finding the buttons at the back of her bodice like an expert ladies' maid, working them deftly until the dress loosened into her hands.

She held it tight to her while he stroked over her bared skin with warm fingertips and warmer kisses, sending shivers of pleasure through her. They'd only just begun and she already ached with need.

And then he was working at the laces of her corset, releasing her from silk and bone and she caught that, too, as he painted soothing patterns over her bare skin. "You're so warm," he whispered at her ear, the words more breath than sound. "So warm, and so soft, and so fucking beautiful."

The curse sent a thrill through her and, desire pooling, she turned to face him, teasing, "What language."

His eyes flashed, dark and delicious. "I'm a simple man. No poetry to be found."

"Mmm," she said. "I've never had much use for poets."

She let go of the dress and the corset, letting them fall to her feet.

His gaze tracked down her body, bare, except for stockings, lingering at her breasts, at the curve of her hips, her full thighs, the dark curls between them.

In her lifetime, Sesily had been thoroughly admired by men and women both, but never like this. Never with this kind of intensity. Never with this kind of . . . hunger. Caleb lifted a hand to his lips, rubbing over his mouth like he didn't know where to begin, and Sesily's knees went weak at the picture—a man absolutely consumed with desire.

The man she loved, consumed with desire for her.

And when he dragged his attention back to her face, she wanted to throw herself into his arms. "Earlier, you said that if you had known me when we were young . . ." She paused. "You said, one look at me and you would have been done for."

He nodded. "Aye."

The word was rough, like broken glass, and Sesily had never loved a sound more. She lifted her chin and met his eyes, emboldened. "And now? What if you look at me now?"

The look he gave her was hot as the sun. "Now, I've got plans."

"Show me."

He moved even as she spoke the words, coming for her, lifting her up and carrying her across the room to the bed, setting her down at the edge as he came to his knees before her, his great height putting him level with her body.

His hands slid down her thighs to her knees and pressed her open, leaning forward to take the tip of one breast between his lips as he stroked the other, the softness of his tongue combined with the rough callus of his thumb—evidence of a lifetime of work—making her sigh with pleasure.

Her hands came to his hair as he worked her over, sending desire curling through her as he licked and sucked and worked her into a frenzy, his name on her lips. When he finally released her and looked up into her eyes and said, "You're aching for it, aren't you?" she thought she might dissolve into pleasure.

"I am," she whispered. "I want you. All of you. Everything you'll give me."

Forever.

She didn't say it. That wasn't the game they played. Even though it was the truth.

"Then I shall give you everything," he said, leaning up to steal a wicked kiss before lifting one of her thighs over his broad shoulder. "Lean back."

Yes.

Except, "No."

He stilled, his eyes on hers, the muscle in his jaw ticking with effort. Sesily threaded her fingers through his soft curls, tilting his face up to her. "I want to give you pleasure."

He closed his eyes at the words, and she felt their impact in the shudder of his muscles at her thigh. Another delicious curse. "This gives me pleasure," he whispered, pressing a kiss to the swell of her stomach. "The feel of you." He turned and licked along the length of her thigh. "The sight of you." He gently spread her core open. "The taste of you." He leaned forward and licked up the seam of her, long and slow and lingering, and she thought she might scream.

"God," he groaned. "The taste of you. I could stay here forever."

She could let him, she realized as he came up over her to pin her to the mattress with his caress. Working her over with his tongue, licking and sucking as though there was no need to ever stop. His thumb found her opening and stroked in slow, languid circles, until she was out of her mind with the pleasure and she fell apart in his arms, fingers so tight in his hair that it must have hurt—not that he stopped.

He didn't stop—not when she rode out the climax against his lips and tongue, not when she rocked against him and claimed every bit of pleasure he offered, not when she collapsed to the bed, boneless. Instead, he pressed soft kisses to her thighs and praised her. "Fucking perfect," he whispered, his breath coming as harshly as hers. "Gorgeous girl."

When she stopped trembling, he said, soft and sinful, "Do you think you can do it again?" She gasped at the question, and then sighed when he growled against her, "I think you can do it again," and then he pressed his mouth to the center and proved himself right, making love to her with his beautiful mouth and his wicked tongue, in slow, sinful strokes until she was arching against the bed, serving herself up to him.

He took her offering, and Sesily realized that she'd never felt more treasured, more worshipped, more pleasured than she did now, coming hard against him—this man who'd somehow become the center of her world.

And she wondered, even as she slipped into pleasure, turning thoughts over to feeling, if she'd ever survive the way she loved him.

She didn't know how long they stayed that way, her hands tangled in his hair, his stroking over her too-sensitive skin, his lips soft and reverent against the swell of her belly as he whispered his praise, but when she returned to the present, she knew she could not wait any longer to touch him. To learn him. To reciprocate.

He stayed silent as she guided him to his feet, as she came to her knees on the bed and undressed him in smooth, methodical movements, reveling in the hard planes of him, in the ridges of his muscles and the dusting of hair across his chest and finally, in the length of his cock, like steel, aching for her touch.

She touched, loving the ragged breaths he took as she worked him, exploring his pleasure. Loving the way his eyes went dark and hooded as she learned how he liked it. "Yes," he whispered as she stroked him, "like that."

She kissed him, her lips sliding over his chest, her tongue painting little circles along the magnificent ridges of his torso. And, as she teased him, inching closer to the place he wanted her—the place she wanted to be—he whispered her name and slid his hand into her hair, so gently.

God, she loved how he held himself in check, not wanting to push her.

Which meant she could do the pushing. She could push him right over the edge.

She pulled away when she reached him, leaning back to consider the size and strength of him. *He was* there. He was there and he was hers to do with as she wished.

"Sesily." Her name was ragged on his lips, and then lost to a groan as she licked up the hard, straining length of him. He reached for the bedpost, holding himself steady even as she could feel the tremor in his hand at her hair. "Fuck," he whispered. "You like it."

She did. She loved the way he turned himself over to her. The way he relinquished himself to her. Ceding power even as he oozed strength.

"I love it," she whispered at the tip of him before she opened for him, taking him in, the salty musk of him making her mouth water.

He groaned her name at the confession, his fingers flexing against her as she parted her lips and took him slow and deep, loving the sounds of his desire and the way they matched to hers—not only what he'd given her earlier, but what he gave her now.

She gave herself up to Caleb's pleasure, licking and sucking and drawing him as deep as she could, playing with speed and sensation, finding the places that seemed to drive him wild and trying—desperately—to send him over the edge.

And when he reached the edge, he cursed again. God, she loved his filthy mouth. "Sesily . . . If you don't . . . I won't be able to hold back."

"Don't hold back," she whispered, releasing him for a heartbeat. "Don't you dare keep this from me. I want it. I want this."

He gave it to her, his hands impossibly gentle in her hair, the muscles of his thighs hard and straining beneath her touch, the thrusts of his hips short and careful even as he could not resist them. And Sesily, sucking deeper, finding a rhythm that made him curse and groan and urge her on, until he couldn't resist any longer, and he came, strong and beautiful, against her.

As he had worshipped her with lingering kisses and stroking touches, Sesily did the same for him even as he leaned over and kissed her, stroking deep as he hefted her up into the bed, leaning over her, spreading her legs and settling between them, turning the tables, stroking over her body, worshipping her curves, whispering her name and praising her with soft, lingering kisses, until she was writhing against him and he was once again hard.

When he entered her, it was in a long, smooth stroke, deep and devastating, filling her beautifully, perfectly, as though they were made for this moment. For each other. They moved in unison for minutes . . . hours . . . losing track of time and place . . . lost to everything but each other until she was begging for release and he was driving her toward it, and they tumbled into pleasure like it was their purpose.

Together.

It was like nothing she'd ever experienced. Perfect. And terrifying.

Because she didn't think she'd ever recover from it.

She would never recover from him.

He turned to his back, pulling her over him, stroking along her skin, sending licks of pleasure through her as she set her ear to his chest and listened to the hammer of his heart, heavy and quick—matched to her own.

"I love you."

The words were out before she could stop them. Before she could predict that he would go stiff beneath her. That his touch would stutter over her skin.

She closed her eyes, her throat full, her eyes suddenly hot with tears, "I'm sorry," she whispered. "I know that you don't want it. I know it's not why you're here. But I love you, and I cannot keep quiet any longer." She kept her head on his chest, refusing to look at him. Not wanting to see the rejection in his eyes. Knowing she couldn't bear it, and still, knowing she couldn't bear the other. The not ever having said it. "I cannot hold it in any longer. I don't wish to wait to love you. To tell you."

And once she began to speak, it was suddenly impossible to stop. So she spoke to her hand, playing at the soft hair on this chest even as she felt that she was stealing the touch—what might be the last. "You said you can't stay away from me and . . . I hate how I love that, even as I hate that you *wish* to stay away from me."

His caught her hand in his then, tight and firm, holding her still. "Sesily."

Her name rumbled in his chest and she ached at the feel of it, wishing she could commit it to the ordinary—that it was just the way Caleb said her name at night. When they were together.

But she could not take it for granted.

She held her breath, desperate for him to say more. And then he did.

"No one has ever loved me out loud."

It couldn't be true. This magnificent noble man, who had spent a lifetime fiercely standing with the people he loved . . . he deserved a company of people who loved him back. A battalion of them.

She lifted her head. How could she not? Met his beautiful gaze, and saw the truth in it. "Let me do it. Let me love you. Please."

The last came out honest and ragged and Sesily might have been horrified by it if she didn't know this was her last chance. Because whatever came next, when they left this room, she knew it would change everything.

He tightened his grip on her, pulling her impossibly closer, sliding his hand into her hair and holding her still as he kissed her, deep and thorough and with such longing that she lost track of herself. Of him.

It was them. And it was perfect.

And then he ended the kiss and met her eyes, and whispered her name. "Say it again. Please."

She'd never refuse him the request, but she couldn't look at him. Not when she knew that tomorrow the sun would rise and he would return to the role of noble protector, and he would convince himself that this had all been a mistake.

She couldn't look at him. But she could put her ear to his chest and memorize the steady beat of his heart and say, "I love you."

And then she could revel in the heavy heat of his arm at her back, and the breath of her name, barely-there in the even rise and fall of his chest, and imagine that tonight was forever.

"Stay with me," she whispered.

A deep breath. Her name again, the ache in the sound an echo of the one in her heart. "I cannot. If I stay, he'll come for you."

"He will come for me anyway!" she said, pushing up to look at him. "He will come for me, just as he will come for you."

"Not if I stop him."

This infuriating man! "Not you, Caleb. *Us.* You are not alone."

"In this, I am," he said, the words like steel. "You want to know why I leave London? Why I stay in Boston? Why I have always pushed you away? Because of this. Because this is a battle I must fight alone . . . or I will put you in danger." He sat up and swung his legs over the edge of the bed, and Sesily stared at his back, his head bowed to his chest. "Sesily. If anything happens to you . . ."

He trailed off and she waited, her heart pounding, aching in her chest.

"If anything happens to you," he tried again. "That's what will destroy me."

"Caleb," she whispered, frustration and fury bringing tears to her eyes and a knot to her throat as she felt it all slipping through her fingers. She crawled over the bed toward him, desperate to hang on. To hang on to him.

She wrapped herself around him, pressing her cheek to his shoulder. "Please."

Don't do this.

Don't leave me.

Love me.

She didn't say any of it, and neither did he, but he didn't leave, either, instead, turning to pull her into his arms and kiss her, again and again, soft and slow and sweet, his hands trailing over her body and her name on his lips like he was trying to remember her. Like he might forget her.

She let him, glorying in his touch and kiss until his heart slowed and his breath deepened, and he slept, as though he knew he might never sleep again.

And once he slept, she found she could not.

Instead, she pressed a kiss to his warm, wide chest and slipped from the bed, pulling her dressing gown on and heading to the window to draw circles on the glass and look down at Hyde Park spread out before her, dark as midnight.

But there, in the street below, were a half dozen men, big as houses.

Security.

Which meant Sesily was about to receive a visitor.

She dressed carefully in dark colors—a deep hunter green that felt appropriate for what was to come. Tight in the bodice, with trousers beneath split skirts designed for ease of movement. And a quarter of an hour later, she opened the front door onto Park Lane as a carriage came to a halt in front of the house, the insignia on the door ancient and venerable.

The Duchess of Trevescan did not like to be kept waiting.

The duchess's brows rose when she discovered Sesily waiting. "You realize I could have been anyone."

"Most people don't come with bruisers big as yours." Sesily lifted a chin in the direction of the men beyond. "You don't think I can take care of myself?"

"I think you've your work cut out for you already," the other woman replied. "So what say you let me share a bit of the load?"

Relief shattered through Sesily, and she opened the door wide.

The other woman stepped inside, peering around the darkened foyer. "Where is he?"

"Who?" Sesily replied, feeling obstinate. Knowing it was unfair.

The duchess ignored it. Which was what friends were for, Sesily supposed. "I understand you had a run-in with The Bully Boys."

"News travels fast from Brixton."

"Straight to Coleford House."

She'd known it. The watchmen outside were not for show. Still, Sesily sucked in a breath. "So. He knows."

The duchess nodded. "He has your name and Calhoun's. Crouch couldn't have come screaming any faster." She paused. "If ever there were a man who needed killing, Sesily."

She would have laughed if it all wasn't so awful. "I shall endeavor to do better next time."

"See that you do." The duchess looked about the Talbot House foyer. "There is a great deal of gold in this room."

"Duchess," Sesily prompted.

"Yes. Well. It's only a matter of time until the viscount puts it all together."

"And you? Have you put it together?"

A head tilt. "Why not save me the trouble."

Sesily did, leaving out the things that were not hers to tell, and her friend listened, patiently, finally saying, "I told you there was a reason he never took what you offered."

Sesily's heart pounded. "It was possible he did not want it, you know."

Except he had.

I cannot stay away.

"Mmm. And he knew he could not hide forever, and that tying himself to you would only serve to put you in danger."

"I'm in danger every day."

"And at some point your gallant knight will have to understand that."

"He's not my gallant knight."

The duchess cut her a disbelieving look. "For someone who is not your gallant knight, he certainly turns up to protect you a great deal."

I would walk into fire if it meant seeing you.

She swallowed around the lump in her throat and crossed her arms over her chest.

Her friend watched her for a moment, and then said, "Your man is in danger, Sesily. And he's no longer alone in it. You were there. Your name is attached to it. And that's before we bring the sister into play. The boy. Calhoun can no longer hide."

Sesily nodded. "He knows."

"Well? Does he have a plan?"

She took a deep breath. "No doubt something truly noble."

"No doubt something deeply stupid," the duchess said, irritation in her tone. "Which ordinarily would be none of my concern. But you love him, which means that when he does something deeply stupid, you are likely to do something deeply stupid as well."

Sesily's brows shot up. "I beg your pardon?"

"Oh, did you mishear? Love is nonsense, and you are going to need your girls with you to survive whatever it brings next."

It was not the easiest thing to dispute.

"But the truth is," the duchess added, reaching for Sesily, "I stand with you, Sesily Talbot, stupid or not. Though I would like very much for whatever plan you devise to be . . . *not stupid*."

"He won't let me help him," Sesily said. "He's already made it clear, he chooses this fight on his own."

The duchess raised a dark brow. "Has he. And how do you feel about that?"

Sesily met her friend's eyes—this woman whom she had stood with, shoulder to shoulder, for two years. This woman whom she had followed into battle. Whom she had led there. Sisters-in-arms. "I don't care for it, honestly."

"Then you are going to need a plan."

A light flashed in Sesily's eyes. "Isn't it lucky that I've already got one."

Chapter Twenty-One

In the two years he'd known her, Caleb Calhoun had witnessed Sesily Talbot do any number of scandalous things—including but not limited to, gambling, drinking, frequenting pleasure houses, stealing from a viscount, going head-to-head with some of London's most notorious criminals, and breaking a man's nose twice—but he'd never imagined this.

And yet, here she was, on Thames Walk, a dead body at her feet.

He approached in the darkness as she paused, waving a nearby carriage forward. It was made to look like a hired cab, but absolutely not a hired cab. In Caleb's experience, hack drivers hesitated to get involved with women in possession of corpses.

Hack drivers were smarter than Caleb, apparently.

Caleb, who'd fallen in love with the only woman in London who wouldn't think twice about moving a dead body in the moonlight on the banks of the River Thames, where any number of people could see her.

Stepping out of the shadows, he made his way down the steep inclined street toward the place where Sesily stood, back to him now as she spoke to the driver, her words carried away from him on the wild wind that lifted her cloak, revealing silk skirts dark as the night beyond.

Of course Sesily was dumping a body in a gown at three o'clock in the morning, as though she'd just slipped away after the midnight waltz, telling all the world that she needed to fix a hem or whatever women told people to escape cloying ballrooms, and was just going to quickly dispose of this poor blighter before sneaking back in for the next quadrille, the whole world none the wiser.

Except she hadn't slipped away from a ball.

She'd slipped away from him. Left him in her bed, to wake up in the dead of night to discover her gone, the sheets cold, a hastily scribbled note where he'd expected to find her.

Back soon. Don't worry.

Like she'd gone to the dressmaker, except it was the dead of night and she'd also left a little oval portrait with the note—a gift.

Something that felt suspiciously, awfully, like a parting gift.

Which had him damn well worried, so it was now in his breast pocket, against his heart, like if he kept it there, he could keep her close.

He approached from behind, making sure he could be heard—not wanting to unsettle her. She didn't move. Didn't stiffen or turn or give any indication that she'd heard him.

Of course she heard him. "How did you find me?"

The driver snapped to attention, hat low on his brow, shielding his identity.

Irritation flared at the curious words, made worse by the next. "Don't tell me. Duchess."

The Duchess of Trevescan, who'd been calmly reading on a seat outside of Sesily's bedchamber, Sesily's cat happily nestled on her lap, when he'd ripped the door open, shirt untucked, coat in hand. He'd pulled up short when she'd turned a page and said, calm as ever, "I don't suppose I can convince you to let her handle this?"

He'd made it clear he'd allow that over his dead body. It had not occurred to him that there was an actual dead body in play.

"She wasn't supposed to tell you where I was," Sesily said. "I told her you wouldn't be able to resist following me." Caleb hesitated at the words, and the tone in which they were spoken, cool and calm, as though she hadn't come apart in his arms the night before. As though she hadn't told him she loved him.

As though she hadn't slipped from her bed and his arms and left him to wake alone and worried.

Of course he followed her. And still, he said, "Do I follow you?"

Sesily turned and moved toward the rear of the carriage, not looking at him. "You followed me here. To Coleford's. To Brixton. To The Place."

Of course he followed her. He'd always follow her if it meant keeping her safe. "I didn't follow you to The Place. I stumbled upon you at The Place. And I only followed you to Coleford's because—" He stopped himself.

She turned toward him, the hood of her cloak keeping her in shadows. "Because what?"

"Because your sister asked me to follow you."

"My sister—what?" Sesily went still, and Caleb likely should have regretted the confession. But he wouldn't regret a single word spoken to Sesily Talbot tonight. "Sera asked you to follow me? For what?"

"She was concerned that you were in trouble."

"Amazing," she retorted, and he heard the irritation in her words. "One would have thought she'd consider asking me if I was in trouble."

"Perhaps she thought you would take affront."

The dry humor in his tone was a mistake. She cut him a look. "Oh, I most *definitely* take affront. And I shall have words with my sister. But first, I shall have words with you."

The reply should have felt like a threat, but instead felt like a gift.

More words.

More time.

More of her.

He continued his advance. "I believe it is my time for words with you, Sesily. After all, you skulked from my bed, and I told you . . . I like the chase."

She caught her breath. He liked that. Even as he grew more frustrated with her. With this madcap plan she'd concocted. "First, it was *my* bed."

As though he didn't know that. As though he hadn't woken hard and wanting, cloaked in the scent of her. Almonds and sunshine.

"And second, you didn't tell me you like the chase. You told me you like the catch."

He liked all of it with her.

She stepped toward him, the carriage's exterior lantern illuminating her face.

"It doesn't matter why I followed you before," he said as she pulled the carriage door open, leaning in to fiddle with whatever was within. "Tonight I follow you for me."

She turned to face him at that. "Why?"

The ache was back in his chest. *To say goodbye.*

And it wasn't as simple as sailing back to Boston. That play was gone now, the route closed off. And the next move was the only one left if he wished to keep them all safe. Jane and Peter. Sesily.

What used to be as simple as removing himself from his world once more, running, finding a new name. A new city. A new life, had become exponentially more complicated because Coleford knew the truth—that Sesily was on the table.

And that threw every well-laid plan into chaos.

Because Caleb loved her, and he could see that at another time, in another place, he might have had her. He might have lived out his days with this magnificent woman by his side.

He'd spent two years searching for that play. That path. Two years, imagining all the outcomes if he let himself take the one thing he wanted. Sesily.

He'd never been able to find it. And now, with Coleford knowing everything, there was no hope of finding it. That place, that time, that life, this woman . . . he could not have it. Not without taking her away from everything she loved. From her friends and her family and her world— and the work she did with power and passion to change the world in which they all lived.

Even if he left on the boat to Boston, swearing never to return, he could not keep Sesily safe.

Which was the only goal now.

And so, there was one path.

He would turn himself in.

He'd dashed off a letter there in her rooms, making sure Jane and Peter were cared for. Making sure Fetu and Sera had access to everything on both sides of the Atlantic.

Making sure Sesily had everything she would ever need.

Secured the Duchess of Trevescan's promise that she would see it delivered.

And he told himself it would be enough. That he could walk into Scotland Yard and give himself up to Thomas Peck without seeing Sesily again, because it would be enough that she was cared for.

And then the duchess had asked, as though they discussed sport or weather or the latest bill in the House of Lords, "Don't you wish to say goodbye in person?"

As though he could avoid it once it was offered. The chance to see her once more. He wasn't a fool. He had an opportunity to look into her beautiful face once more . . . and he took it, heading for the address in an unsavory part of London, wondering the whole time what he would find when he got there. What he would say when he got there.

And somehow, after all he'd known Sesily to get into, he still hadn't expected the corpse. But he certainly wasn't going to say goodbye before he understood it.

"What are you up to?"

"Your favorite question."

"If you ever gave me a straight answer, perhaps I'd find another."

"In my experience," she said, stepping back from the carriage and waving the driver forward a few yards. "The more people know what I'm up to, the less likely they are to support it."

"I cannot imagine why anyone would be unlikely to support you," he said, drawing closer to her. "This all seems perfectly ordinary."

She looked over her shoulder, and he resented the shadows of the carriage for the way it cast her face in darkness, making it impossible to see her eyes as she said, "Are you here to help? Or not?"

She stepped into the carriage's wake, and Caleb's instincts about the vehicle were proven right. It wasn't a hack. It wasn't even an ordinary carriage. It was small and black, and clearly made to move easily through London's narrow streets, but it had a rear door. Two of them, which Sesily opened on easy, well-oiled hinges.

The kind of conveyance that was designed to move things quickly and quietly.

He moved behind her, so that he, too, could see into the gaping dark space, the blackness within absolutely impenetrable. Instead, he turned to the dark shadows of the buildings facing the river, a mass of shadows that made for excellent hiding places if someone were interested in watching the activities of a wild woman as she dragged a body into the tide.

"Whatever you're about to do, you know you're going to be seen by at least a dozen tide pickers."

"It's not low tide," Sesily replied, moving several boxes out of the way in the dark carriage.

"Oh, well. You're right then. In that case, anyone watching from the shadows will find this endeavor to be absolutely unremarkable."

"Tell me something," she said, all casual, as though the moment wasn't heavy with awareness of what had happened earlier that evening. Of what would come next. "In your experience, do people who lurk in shadows spend a great deal of time involving themselves in the questionable activity of others?"

"I was in the shadows. And here I am."

"Of all the shadows in all of London, you had to lurk in mine?" she quipped.

"The stars aligned."

She turned at the words, the movement sharp and angled, devoid of her easy grace. He cursed the darkness and the way it hid her eyes, leaving him with nothing but her words. "Stars have nothing to do with it, Mr.

Calhoun," she said. "Tonight, I make my own luck. And yours, too, if you play your cards right."

His pulse began to pound. *What was she up to?*

"At least let me help you dump it."

"Shows how useful you are. I'm not dumping it; I'm collecting it," she replied dryly before poking her head around the side of the carriage and calling up to the driver on the block, "Ready."

In response, the driver knotted the reins and stood, turning to face the vehicle. A scraping sound came from within, and Caleb watched as the back wall of the carriage opened, allowing for the driver to scramble inside.

"You're *keeping* it?"

"In a manner of speaking."

"Fucking hell, Sesily." *Didn't they have enough problems already without adding a dead body to the mix?*

"You know, the rest of London somehow finds a way to use my name without profanity."

"I imagine you don't test the rest of London the way you test me. Who is this?"

"I believe you mean *was*." This, from the driver, now inside the carriage, followed by a low feminine grunt as something slid across the darkness, stopping with a thud against one side of the now gently rocking vehicle. Something heavy. And unwieldy.

Caleb's eyes widened and he looked to Sesily. "How many bodies are inside this thing?"

"None, yet." She did not look away as she reached inside the yawning blackness and found what she was searching for, grasping the latch on a sliding ramp that was attached to the floor of the carriage and hinged in such a way that it easily dropped to the ground.

"Alright," he said, "how many bodies *have been* inside this thing?"

"A few," she said casually, as though it were perfectly reasonable.

"And how many of them have been dead?"

She lifted a shoulder in a small shrug. "Not all of them." She turned away and stepped back from the shadows and into the moonlight that finally gave Caleb a chance to look at her, her beautiful face like air. He itched to reach for her, to pull her close and press his face to her neck and breathe her in, rich and lush and perfect.

Caleb could not resist cataloguing the rest of her—all strength and shape—lush curves and soft lines and temptation that he knew better than to linger with. Because if he allowed himself to linger on Sesily Talbot's temptations, he'd be lost for good.

And she, with him.

So, instead, he committed her to memory, suddenly desperate to have her close.

One last time.

When that was done, his gaze tracked to her toes, peeking out from beneath her skirts, and he found himself staring at the body on the ground.

"Did you kill him?"

"Really, Caleb. I should be offended. I was with you not three hours ago."

He raised a brow in her direction. "Never say you'd need longer than that."

"Are you going to help? Or not?"

He leaned down and hefted the heavy body under the arms. A man, nearly his age, nearly his size. "This isn't an old body." If Caleb had to guess, the man had been dead no longer than six hours.

"Of course it isn't," she said, as though he'd offended her. "I don't deal with graverobbers." She reconsidered. "Not tonight, at least."

"And to think," he said, hefting the weight. "For a moment, I wondered if you might be involved in something nefarious."

She gave a little laugh as though they were at ladies' tea, and she was indicating a plate full of tea cakes rather than a mysterious ramp attached to a custom-made carriage.

He hated that sound, light and airy, as though she weren't in danger. "What are you up to? Tell me the truth."

She looked directly at him, then, her eyes glittering like starlight. "Tell me something, Caleb Calhoun," she whispered, and the sound of her soft, curious voice twisted through him like sin. "What are *you* up to?"

He shook his head. "Nothing."

It was a lie, and she knew it. She could see it in him, somehow, even as the rest of the world had never seen his lies. Never heard them. She could.

She nodded, and he imagined it was sad. She pushed past him, around the corner of the carriage, toward the driver's block.

Caleb resisted the urge to say something, to defend himself, instead moving the body as easily as one could, placing the head at the uppermost portion of the board as Sesily leaned down to shift two booted ankles onto the ramp.

He rubbed his palms on his trousers and redirected the conversation away from the whisper of guilt that ran through him. "At least tell me what you did to him."

"I told you. He's not mine."

"Odd, then, how you seem to be the only one with any semblance of interest in the poor bastard."

"Suffice to say," she replied, "he's the kind of man who is more useful after death than he was in life." She nodded into the darkness within. "He's on."

A nod from the driver, and Sesily reached down to lift the ramp, which went flat with ease, and slid without hesitation back into the conveyance. Once it was inside, Sesily threw three latches, presumably locking the ramp into place. "Right then," she said, with two short raps on the metal floor.

Three soft clicks from within the carriage indicated that the driver had done the same thing at the head end of the ramp, and then she was out onto the driving block, sliding her secret door closed as Sesily closed and latched the rear doors.

"And you've got the driver in on whatever trouble you're causing?"

"She's not just a driver, and she'd never dream of missing out on trouble," she replied, raising her voice. "Alright, Adelaide?"

"As ever," came the happy reply from the driver's block, as though Miss Adelaide Frampton dealt with dead bodies on a regular basis.

He looked to Sesily. "Truly, your gang's unique skill-set grows more fearsome by the hour."

"Caleb is afraid of you, Adelaide," Sesily said happily, as though they were somewhere brighter. With fewer corpses.

"If there's a happier sentence, I've never heard it," Miss Frampton quipped, poking a head around the edge of the carriage. "Are you coming?"

Don't go.

He knew he couldn't say it. Knew he didn't have the right to ask her to stay. Especially not here. On the banks of the river, where anyone could stumble upon them.

"Give me a moment," she called to her friend, taking a step toward him.

Caleb held his breath, the air between them shifting, throwing him off balance. What had been frustration was now anticipation. What had been concern was now desire. What had been fear was now need.

She was close enough to touch, her presence almost overwhelming for what a gift it was. For how he ached for her—to reach for her, pull her close, and breathe her in, sunlight and almonds, sweet like her tongue.

But he had to resist the temptation if he was going to do right by her.

He had to survive this—the last moment with her. Cloaked in darkness and the silence of a city that passed them by, Sesily coming toward him, unbridled, like fire.

When she pressed herself to him, her curves a welcome memory, what could he do? He touched her, his arm snaking into her cloak, where it should not be, wrapping about her waist. Tightening, pulling her close as her arms came around his neck, making him forget all of it, everything he should not do. Everything he should not want. Everything but her, this woman, the most luxurious temptation he'd ever faced.

Irresistible.

How was he to resist her? How was he to walk away from her, this woman who was more than he'd ever imagined. Whom he'd watched for years, for whom he'd ached for years and now, finally, claimed.

Only to have her stolen from him, by his past. By the knowledge that they had no chance at a future. That she had no chance at one as long as Caleb was free.

"Sesily—"

"Shh," she said, softly, tipping her face up to him.

She was going to kiss him, and he was going to let her, and then he would stop this madness and leave. But he wasn't a fool. She was soft and strong and lush and perfect in his arms, and she would taste of spice and sunshine and he wanted her.

He'd never wanted anything so much.

Kiss me, he willed her. *One last time.*

She did, and it was as magnificent as the first time. No. It was better. Because it was not simply soft and hot and sweet and sinful. It was full of her. Of them. Of the two years they'd ached for each other and the last few days, when they'd finally given in to that longing. It was full of knowledge.

It was full of love.

He pulled her close and poured himself into it, knowing it was the last time he'd ever be able to kiss her. Knowing it was goodbye.

When she ended it, pulling away from him, Caleb resisted the urge to roar his frustration. He didn't want it to be the end. They didn't deserve this to be the end.

They deserved a beginning.

His gaze flew to her eyes—the night disappearing their uniqueness—the ring of black around deep blue, and there, in her gaze, he saw that she'd felt it all. All his love and frustration and desire . . . and sorrow. A bone-deep sorrow that he would carry for the rest of his days.

Regret. That he hadn't had more time to love her.

But there was something else in her eyes. Something light. Like a secret. Like hope.

"Caleb," she whispered, "don't you recognize him?"

Who?

The body. He'd forgotten that she had a dead body in the carriage.

He pulled away, her little dissatisfied sigh nearly—
nearly—succeeding in summoning him back to her. But
he was a man who had control, dammit.

Caleb stepped back and gave her his sternest look.
"Who is it?"

She tilted her head, considering him, and for a moment
he thought she might not tell him. And then she smiled—
full and honest and . . . happy. As though he should have
known the answer. As though the truth would set them
all free.

That smile—Christ. Wide and winning and dazzling—
like a blow to the head.

"Sesily," he repeated, her name tight on his lips, his
blood roaring in his ears. "Who is that man?"

"Caleb," she said, simply, as though he should already
know the answer. "He's you."

Chapter Twenty-Two

Poor man. He didn't know what had hit him.

"I swear, I didn't kill him."

His brow furrowed as he stared down at her. "What do you mean, he is me?"

"He isn't, of course." She waved a hand in the air. "He *was* the brother-in-law of one of the boys who works at Maggie's." A boy who'd come to the duchess for help getting his sister out of a marriage that too many women would understand. The duchess and Adelaide had formed a plan to relocate the girl to a trusted estate, owned and managed by a mistress willing to employ women without verifying letters of reference.

"But, fortunately for everyone," she added, "the brute turned out to have a bad heart, which gave out mere hours ago in"—she waved a hand in the direction of a dark building in the distance—"that absolutely disgusting tavern. And so, we collect the body, the wife stays in London, and the husband, well . . . perhaps this final act will keep him from the deepest level of hell."

"You stole his body."

"I beg your pardon," she said, feigning affront. "I paid handsomely for it."

Now, all she had to do was convince Caleb to let her finish the job, and they could live happily ever after. She'd never gone in for a fairy-tale ending, but if it meant loving this decent man until the end of her days, she'd take it.

He watched her for a moment, his jaw set, his eyes unreadable.

"Caleb," she said. "Don't you see? This is the solution. No matter what happens. Peter Whitacre, turned up dead in the Scotland Yard morgue, a hastily written confession in his pocket. Caleb Calhoun, innocent of everything except putting Johnny Crouch into the dirt . . . and everyone knows Crouch deserved it."

"And what, we just hope no one ever notices that this man isn't me?"

"No one *will* notice." She looked away, frustration etched on her pretty face. "It's been eighteen years. You've been in hiding, afraid to see your sister. To know your family. To—"

To love.

She held it back.

"And what of Coleford?" he asked. "He won't believe it."

"He'll be in Newgate after the whole world discovers he's taken tens of thousands from rich aristocrats and orphans." She laughed. "Don't you see? It's time for you to be free."

He went quiet, thinking, and for a moment, she thought she might have convinced him. She *did*. There was a light in his eyes. Something like hope. Something like *relief*. Silly man. Didn't he know what it was like to be part of a team? He would. She'd show him.

For the rest of their lives.

He shook his head. "It's too easy."

Panic flared, and frustration. She forced a little high-pitched laugh. "I realize I made it seem like a dead body is easily turned up, Caleb, but I wouldn't exactly call it eas—"

"Stop," he said. "You know that's not what I mean." He shook his head. "This . . . if it worked tonight, tomorrow . . . a week. A year . . ." He paused and looked out at the boats again. "It's a week, a year, that I am on the run, constantly looking behind me. Waiting to be found." He reached for her, his fingers tracing over her cheek. "And what, love, you come with me?"

She hated the endearment she so desperately wanted to hear in his beautiful voice, a word that should have been full of adoration, of wonder—now full of regret and sorrow and disappointment. "Yes," she said. "Wherever you want to go. Back to Boston. Around the world. Whatever you want. You did it before, and with less power. Less money. Fewer connections."

"I didn't have you."

She nodded. "You would have me. That's a week, a year, that we can be together. Maybe a lifetime."

Those fingers, stroking over her cheek, back and forth, the pad of his thumb rough and wonderful, making her want to grab his hand and hold her close. "We leave your family? Your friends? The work—the world—you are building? What kind of man would I be if I took that from you?"

She swallowed around the frustration in her chest. "The kind of man who knows it should be my choice."

He smiled, sad and so handsome, that dimple flashing in his cheek like a lie. "You're right. It should be. But you forget, I know this life. I have lived it for as long as I remember. I have run and looked over my shoulder and dreamed of the day when I could stop and have what I wanted."

He was looking at her like he'd never seen her before. Like he'd never seen anything so beautiful as she was. Like she was the sun. "Me?"

His touch changed, cupping her cheek, tilting her face into the light. "You." A pause. And then, "You wouldn't love me if I let you choose that life."

Sesily did grab his hand then. "Caleb—"

"No." He cut her off. "For two years I have watched you. I have ached for you. I have basked in your sun for the handful of days I was with you, and savored the warmth of it for all the others. And that's the thing— you are made for full sun. Not a woman for a life lived in the shadows. And perhaps it's selfish, but I could not bear to see that light in you dimmed by life on the run. I would hate myself, and one day, you would hate me, too. And that, Sesily, is a fate worse than all the rest."

Tears came, hot and angry and devastating. "No—"

"Yes," he said softly. The words barely there. "Yes. If I take what you offer . . . Christ, Sesily. I've never wanted anything the way I want what you offer. But if I let you love me—"

"*Let?*" She let the word fly. "You cannot *stop* me from loving you."

"You think I do not know that? You think I have not watched you love others for two years? You think I have not burned with envy for the same? You think I would be able to let you go if I let myself feel the full force of your love?"

Sesily loves with her whole heart.

What an idiotic thing to do.

He was still talking. "If I take what you offer . . . Sesily . . . you will be dragged into the muck with me."

"I don't care about the muck." Her temper snapped and she pushed his hand from her cheek, storming past him to the stone wall that blocked them from the swirling water below. She looked down into the inky blackness for a moment before spinning back around to face him. "So there is muck. In my thirty years on this Earth I have discovered that we all find ourselves in it at one point or another. My God, Caleb, for my entire life, people have called my sisters and me The Soiled S's. Because we were born in muck."

His words were like steel. "I'll destroy anyone who calls you that."

"Well we're going to need a bigger carriage for all the bodies, because it's half of Mayfair," she retorted, turning back to face him, the lantern light from the carriage beyond casting him into shadow. "You idiot man, I don't care what they call me. I don't belong to them. They cannot touch me. Not when I am here. Not when I am with you."

He shoved a hand through his hair, frustrated. "Dammit, Sesily. Every minute with me puts you in danger." The other hand slid down his chest to the place she'd found at the cottage at Highley—the puckered skin of a healed wound. "He put a bullet in me before we ran. I won't think about what he might do to you."

"So, what . . . you leave and I live a half life? Having loved you, but no longer able to do it out loud, as you asked? So I spend a lifetime a widow at heart . . . wondering what happened to you? If you'll ever turn up again?"

He closed his eyes. "You won't wonder." He turned toward the carriage, the lantern light illuminating his resolve, and she wanted to scream. He was giving up. He was giving *them* up. Before they'd even had a chance.

"Tell me."

"There is only one solution."

She knew it. From the moment she left him in her bed, she'd known she was in a race against time, with only a few hours to make ready before Caleb woke and did something noble and foolish and irrevocable. "You're going to turn yourself in."

He looked away from her, toward the river, where the tide was rising and with it, an enormous number of boats. Lanterns swinging like floating lights, casting the world on the Thames into golden shadows.

"Since I was seventeen, I have done everything in my power to keep the people I love safe. But Coleford will not stop until he has his revenge. And I cannot protect you. I cannot keep you safe. Not now, not ever." He looked to her. "You think I have not spent the last eighteen years thinking about how to return to this life? To this world? You think I have not spent the last two years thinking about how I might be able to have you?"

She caught her breath.

"You think I have not woken every night in my empty bed and wished that you were there? By my side? That I have not lain awake every night in that same bed, aching for you? Loving you? Christ, Sesily, I went back to Boston last time, intending it to be for good, because the only way I could stop myself from touching you was to put an ocean between us."

Her eyes went wide. "I didn't know."

"Of course you didn't. How could you? How could you know that I dreamed of purchasing return passage the moment I got off the fucking boat because six weeks was already too long without seeing your face? Your smile? Your eyes? Because I already missed you teasing me and taunting and running me ragged? And for a year, I tortured myself with it. Because I can't bear to not be close to you, even as I know you are better off without me."

"I am not better off without you!"

"You are *safe* without me!"

The words came on a shout, and Sesily matched it, turning to the water and screaming her own frustrated anger, letting the sound roar around them, reverberating against the buildings, before she turned back to face him. "Who cares about safe? I spend my days plotting the demise of men who take advantage of those weaker than them. It is not safe work. But it is mine. And I choose it." She paused. "In the last two weeks, I have drugged an earl, broken the nose of a thug *thrice*, and robbed a viscount—three events where you have been by my side and I have been safe, I might add. I carry a blade in my pocket and my dearest friends are a spymaster, a con artist, and a woman who is *extremely* fond of explosives. I am recklessness personified."

"You are not," he snapped, his tone clipped and full of his own anger. Good. Let him match her. "Every one of those events was the result of timing, training, and planning. Every one of them perfected. You are not *reckless* and anyone who spends a moment in your presence should see it. Anyone who doesn't see it, doesn't deserve to be in your presence."

He came for her then, setting his hands to her arms and holding her in a firm grip, as though he could will her to his way of thinking. Her heart pounded. "You are not reckless, Sesily Talbot; you are *regal*. You're a damn queen."

Pride burst at the words. Pride, and pleasure, that he *saw* her. That he understood.

She loved him beyond measure.

She lifted her chin. "I won't take a demotion. I was a goddess before."

He pulled her to him then, claiming her mouth in a wild kiss, and she met it, eager and frantic and desperate for him in case this was it . . . the last time. His arms were around her, lifting her high to sit on the stone wall, and he was licking into her, claiming her mouth with long, lush sweeps, and her hands were in his hair, her fingers knocking his hat off his head, lost forever to the wind off the river.

Neither of them cared.

Sesily was drunk with the feel of him, with the scent of him. With the wildness in him. *Hers.*

But in moments, the kiss changed. Fading from wild to something else. Something not so frantic and still, no less intense. No less important.

It was goodbye.

She pushed at his shoulders the moment she recognized it, and he released her instantly. "No," she said. "Caleb."

He backed away, shaking his head. "I can't. This is how it ends."

"No," she said again, and tears came. Hot and angry and devastating. How could he end it here? Just as it began? "No. I need more time. There is another—"

"There is no other way. This is how it ends. You promised me a boon. In the Trevescan gardens. Another outside The Place."

She shook her head again. "No."

"You did, though. And I am calling them in." He reached for her, his hands coming to her face, tipping her up to face him, and she closed her eyes, not wanting to look at him. He waited for what seemed like an age, until she opened them again, and pressed a kiss to her forehead. "You are so beautiful."

She hated him, this man she loved.

"This is my request: go home. Or go to Maggie's, or wherever Sesily Talbot, walking scandal and absolute delight, spends her nights. Live your life."

The tears came in earnest now, his hands warm and firm at her cheeks, his words like wheels against cobblestones. "Love out loud."

"No."

"I've had eighteen years of freedom, Sesily. And tonight, I had the woman I love in my arms."

"No," she whispered through her tears. "There is another way."

"Look at me." She did, his gaze clear and beautiful on hers. "You asked me once why I do not like the dark."

She closed her eyes at the memory of his response, knowing the full story now. Alone and scared and on the run without his sister. In the darkness.

"It wasn't just the ship all those years ago, love. It was a lifetime in the darkness. In the shadows. On the run." He was so handsome. So certain. "It is time for light."

She gripped his hands at her cheeks, her heart breaking.

"There is no other way. This is how it ends. With me loving you more than I ever imagined possible. And you walking away."

"Fuck your boon," she said, the words without heat. "I renege."

"You can't," he said. "I need this. I need to know you're safe. Jane. Peter. Sera. Fetu. All of you."

"Caleb, if you do this . . . they will *hang* you."

Instead, he leaned in and kissed her, one last time. Slow and sweet, like they had a lifetime together. Like they'd had a lifetime together.

And he said the words she'd dreamed of him saying for two years.

Except, he said them all wrong.

"I love you, Sesily Talbot."

Chapter Twenty-Three

Detective Inspector Thomas Peck was having a bad day. It had begun with the knock at the door of his residence, a modest flat in Holborn let from a landlady who *did not care for disturbances before breakfast or after tea*, which was a particular challenge when her tenant was a detective inspector at Scotland Yard. When things went wrong at Whitehall, sergeants were sent round to rouse Peck. That was simply how it went.

That morning, after making his apologies to Mrs. Edwards, who was quick to remind him that she had not yet had her breakfast, he exited the building to find that the sergeant had been instructed to wait, which was the detective inspector's first clue that his day was going to go sideways, and quickly.

Which it had, the moment he arrived at No. 4 Whitehall Place, to discover that Caleb Calhoun had turned himself in for murder. And not just any murder. The murder of Mr. Bernard Palmer, the only son and heir of the Viscount Coleford.

Which was a surprise to everyone, as there was no record of the son and heir of the Viscount Coleford being murdered.

Peck listened patiently to the American, asking a handful of pointed questions before finally leaning back in his chair, rubbing a hand over his smooth, dark beard, and saying, "You're turning yourself in for a murder committed eighteen years ago."

Calhoun looked annoyed. "That's what I've been saying, yes."

"And you're doing it because . . ."

"Because I did it."

Peck's gaze narrowed on the other man, who in different circumstances might have been a friend. "Scotland Yard didn't even exist when this happened."

Caleb paused. "I assume that might cause a problem."

"Indeed. Largely, that I'm going to have to summon the viscount and half of Parliament to dig up the protocol on decades-old murders, and that's going to take some time."

Caleb nodded. "I shall wait."

Peck watched Calhoun for a long moment, feeling no small amount as though something was happening just outside his understanding. "We've known each other for what, two years?"

Caleb nodded. "Sounds right."

"And you've been a decent bloke. Helped once or twice. Just last week, you identified three of The Bully Boys who tossed over The Place. I've got two of them in custody."

"That's good news."

Peck grunted. "And now you're here, in my office, confessing to a case in which Scotland Yard has taken no interest."

"I would think you'd have a bit of interest in the murder of an aristocratic heir."

"I'll be honest, mate, I didn't even know this particular aristocratic heir existed until now."

Certain that there was more to the story than Calhoun had shared, Peck had found him a bench in one of the overnight cells that had just been cleared of the drunks from the evening before. He'd returned to his office to pen a missive to the Viscount Coleford—truly there was nothing worse than a day that required interacting with the aristocracy.

He'd barely set pen to paper when the second knock of the day came at his door, equally unwelcome.

Over the next ten hours, there would be fourteen knocks at the door—each one revealing a sergeant on duty, each one heralding the arrival of a lady, there to report a crime.

Fourteen women from some of the most powerful families in London—many titled, most rich, all powerful in their own way, and not one of them willing to speak to anyone but Detective Inspector Peck.

Mrs. Mark Landry came to file a complaint about foul language on the public horse trails in Hyde Park—a complaint Peck found odd, considering he'd met Mr. Mark Landry once three years earlier, and the man had cursed no fewer than a dozen times in as many minutes.

Three duchesses appeared in succession, which was more duchesses than Peck had met in a lifetime. The Duchess of Haven began the parade, reporting a stolen reticule. She'd left it on a bench outside Gunter's Tea Shop six days earlier.

The Duchess of Warnick came with information about a carriage accident in Regent Street, Tuesday, one week earlier. After Peck had spent a half an hour looking for evidence that this particular accident had occurred, she remembered that, no, it must have been Wednesday.

The Duchess of Trevescan arrived to report a missing diamond necklace. She'd left it in the bed of her lover, you see, but couldn't possibly name him—think of the scandal.

The Marchioness of Eversley reported three books shoplifted from the bookstore she owned with her husband. Mrs. Felicity Culm of Covent Garden was bereft over her missing carriage blanket. Mrs. Henrietta Whittington arrived with her to file a report on a missing dog—a stray from the docks who hadn't come round for his morning offal three days running.

After insisting that he call her Nora—something he absolutely would never do—Lady Eleanora Madewell, daughter to some duke, filed a wildly elaborate report about a carriage wheel that had been stolen, only to return ten minutes later, not two minutes after he'd completed the damn paperwork, to report that no, in fact, no wheel had been stolen after all.

Maggie O'Tiernen even turned up, which Peck had hoped was something . . . until it turned out that she was reporting an empty ale keg thieved from the alleyway behind The Place the night before.

And so it went, one woman after another, for a full day, and not one of the crimes a worthy report. Over the hours, Peck had attempted to send the missive to Coleford a half dozen times, but without fail, the moment he began to write, another knock would come.

Until, finally, knock number fifteen.

"No more," he said, standing up from his desk and marching across his office. "I've honest work to do. I don't have time for women," he called out, pulling open the door.

There was no sergeant on the other side.

Instead, there was a woman. Short and plump with a pretty round face, enormous dark eyes, and a wild mane of black hair. He recognized her instantly. Lady Imogen Loveless, the youngest child and only daughter of a baron or earl or something. More importantly, she was a regular frequenter of The Place, and had been inside when The Bully Boys tossed it over the week earlier.

He remembered her. She was not the type of woman one forgot.

He looked out into the empty hallway. "How did you get here?"

"You've terrible security," she said, happily.

"I do not," he replied.

She shrugged. "You're right. I was escorted direct to your door by a handsome and now invisible policeman."

He considered her for a long moment, noting her deep purple cloak and the large carpetbag in one gloved hand.

"Are you taking up residence, my lady?"

"I like to be prepared." With a nod into his office, she said, "May I?"

He followed her gaze to his desk, piled high with files and paper—much of which had accumulated that day—and said, "I don't have—"

"Time for women," she finished for him. "Yes. So you said."

Well. Now he felt like an ass. He stepped back from the door and waved her in. "How may I help you, ma'am?"

She entered and approached the desk, setting her bag at her feet and considering the piles of folders. "You've a great deal of work here."

"Yes. It's been a busy day," he said, rounding the desk to put it between them. Feeling somehow as though it was important to keep a distance from her. "May I help you?"

She looked up at that and smiled, and he was struck again by how pretty she was. He recalled her giving him a thorough once-over at The Place. What had she called him? Strapping?

Not that it mattered.

"You may, in fact."

"You are here to file a police report."

She looked at him as though he was mad. "Good God, no. I find there's rarely a need to involve the police when one can handle a problem oneself. You tend to overcomplicate everything." She sat. Which meant he could sit. But he didn't want to sit. He wanted this woman out of his office. He had work to do. Real work. "Please, Detective Inspector. You needn't stand on my account."

He sat, annoyed at the long history of chivalry that made it impossible for him to boot this woman from his office. And the long history of aristocracy that made it *very* impossible for him to boot this woman from his office.

"Now," she said, folding her hands primly in her lap, which shouldn't have amused him as it did, but truly the woman did not strike him as at all prim. "I am here because you have Caleb Calhoun in custody, and I think you should release him."

Well. He wasn't expecting that.

"I beg your pardon, Lady Imogen." He leaned in. "How would you know who I have in custody?"

She sighed and picked at a little piece of lint on her skirt. "Detective Inspector Peck, you have Caleb Calhoun in your holding cell one floor below us. You've had him there for just over . . ." She pulled a tiny watch chain from beneath the cuff of her frock. "Ten hours. He arrived this morning just after dawn and confessed to the murder of Bernard Palmer, the only son and heir of the Viscount Coleford. After waiting a surprising length of time for you to arrive, I might add."

"I arrived within the hour of being apprised of the situation, ma'am." Not that he owed her the clarification.

She did not seem interested in it. "Mr. Calhoun gave his confession at half-eight, at which point you plonked him in a holding cell. And you've been dragging your feet on the situation all day, because you think there is something strange about it." She looked up, her wide eyes finding his. "It's now half-six. That's ten hours."

Well, there absolutely was something strange about it now.

If Lady Imogen Loveless had stripped nude in his office and stretched herself across his desk, Peck could not have been more surprised. It was only fifteen years of training as a Bow Street Runner and Scotland Yardsman that kept him from falling directly out of the chair he instead leaned back in, before tenting his fingers at his lips.

She met his eyes again.

The woman wasn't pretty; she was mayhem.

"Now that we all agree on the facts," she added, as though it was a perfectly ordinary conversation, "I believe you should let him go."

"Why?"

"Because Viscount Coleford's heir deserved killing."

Peck exhaled on a shocked laugh. "Ma'am . . . that's not how it works."

A pause, and then, "Well. Certainly you can admire the effort." While he considered the possibility that she was, in fact, mad, the lady leaned forward and reached down to the bag at her feet. He couldn't see what was inside for the angle of the desk, but after a moment's rifling, she brandished a folder.

He narrowed his gaze on it, light blue, with an indigo bell painted on it.

"I brought you a gift."

"I don't want a gift."

"Are you sure? You could consider it an olive branch."

"For what?"

She stood and set it atop one of the many piles on his desk. "My ruining your day."

"Alright. That's enough, then." He'd had enough of this woman, who clearly delighted in leaving chaos in her wake. He stood and came around the desk, pausing while she collected her carpetbag, and he found himself wondering what was inside.

Standing, she collected the file. "I'm taking this back. I'm not sure you deserve it."

"I don't know how I will go on," he said, guiding her across the room. He set a hand to the door handle. "Thank you for your visit."

He opened the door to his office to discover another woman standing in the doorway, pretty and dark-haired, with a rosy-cheeked round face and laugh lines at the corner of eyes that were not smiling. "Detective Inspector Peck?"

He bit his tongue. Of course there was another woman at his door.

He forced a pleasant smile despite wanting to do the very opposite, and looked down at Lady Imogen. "I assume the parade of ladies reporting nonsensical crimes today has something to do with you?"

"Really, Detective Inspector," she said, "you are lucky I do not take offense at being called a criminal mastermind."

"I didn't call you a criminal mastermind."

"Ah. Well. Now I *am* offended."

Absolute mayhem.

She leaned forward and, in a stage whisper, said, "The others were just for fun. This one is real." And then she dipped a little curtsy to him—one he absolutely should not have enjoyed considering the way he simmered with frustration at being toyed with for a full day—and slipped beneath his arm, turning back to face him once she was in the hallway.

"Warm in here, don't you think?"

Scotland Yard could be called many things, but warm was not one of them.

Before he could reply, she'd turned away. He watched her go, her full hips swaying beneath the cloak she wore.

His visitor cleared her throat in the doorway. "Detective Inspector Peck?"

He tore his gaze from the wild woman, not altogether certain that she could be trusted in the building on her own, and looked down at the newcomer. "Yes, please. Come in, miss."

He backed away, holding the door as the woman entered, hands clasped tightly together.

"How can I help you?" he asked, sure he was about to receive another time wasting report.

Missing embroidery hoop, lost on Bond Street. Might it be recovered? Could the police help?

Except . . . *This one is real*, Lady Imogen had said.

And the woman looked it. She looked serious. "My brother did not kill Viscount Coleford's son."

Chapter Twenty-Four

Ten hours after he'd confessed to murder, Caleb sat on a hard stone slab in a dimly lit, dank holding cell at Scotland Yard, thinking about Sesily.

He'd stopped waiting for Peck to turn up hours earlier. As the time passed, it became clear that he wasn't of much interest; a handful of policemen had wandered by to have a look—he'd recognized two of them from Covent Garden. But eventually, news of his presence in Scotland Yard had traveled far enough that he was left alone, which gave him more time to think than he'd like, because thinking about Sesily was almost too much to bear.

There were a dozen thoughts he might have summoned when it came to her. The softness of her skin, the wild fall of her sable curls when her hair was loose around her bare shoulders. The curve of her lips. The taste of her, sweet and sinful.

But he didn't think of all that. Instead, he sat, her portrait in hand, brushing his thumb over the silver frame, and thought about her laugh. The way it echoed through a room, loud and carefree. The way it rolled through him, filling up all his dark places. The way it lit her eyes and reddened her cheeks, and became more than just amusement.

Watching Sesily laugh was a revelation.

And whatever was to come—prison, the gallows, passage to Australia—he'd carry the warmth and the hope that filled him every time she laughed forever. When he breathed his last, it would be with that sound in his thoughts and her name on his lips.

And if he never heard it again, never saw her again, never heard her voice, it would be enough. Because she would be safe.

But Christ, he'd give everything he had to hear her voice again.

"Fucking hell, Caleb."

He came off the slab of concrete at the sound, wondering if he'd conjured it, even as he knew that if he were conjuring anything, it wouldn't be her cursing his name.

Or, maybe it would be. Maybe it was perfect.

Perfect or not, he hadn't conjured her. She was there, on the other side of the cell bars, looking glorious in a dress of shining silk the color of the summer sky, even as she crouched, inspecting the lock on the cell door.

He was at the bars in a heartbeat, hands gripping them tight until his knuckles went white. "What in hell are you doing here?"

"Not now," she said, not looking up from her work. "I'm really very annoyed with you."

None of this was as he'd planned. How had she gained access to Scotland Yard? How had she gained access to his cell? "You can't be here," he said. "Jesus, Sesily. This is a jail."

"Please," she scoffed. "This is Whitehall. It's not exactly Newgate."

"It's crawling with police officers."

"Not one of whom appears to be interested in you. You've been in here for ten hours, and Peck hasn't even sent word to Coleford."

"How do you know that?"

She did look up at him then, her beautiful blue eyes like a gift. "At what point in our story do you think you will realize that I'm fairly good at knowing things?"

He would have laughed at that if he wasn't in a jail cell. But he was, and he didn't want her knowing things about that. He didn't want her anywhere near that. *She'd* be locked in a jail cell if she was discovered doing . . . whatever it was she was doing.

"Whether or not they've taken interest in me, Sesily, I'm locked in here for a reason."

"Yes. A misplaced sense of responsibility. We're going to discuss that just as soon as I'm through." With a little, frustrated growl, she stood up and stomped her feet. "Dammit. We shall have to wait for Imogen."

He didn't like the sound of that. "Why is Imogen here?"

Sesily cut him a look, as though he was a child. "Because I know better than to stage a prison break without reinforcements, Caleb."

"I thought it was just Whitehall."

"Yes, well, they've upgraded the locks since I was in here last."

He blinked. "You've done this before?"

She waved away the question as though it weren't important. "The point is, tonight I am breaking you out, you idiot man. You are not allowed to just leave me."

"Sesily," he began, hating that they were to have this conversation again. "I told you. If I am not here, you are not—"

"Safe. Yes. I heard you the first dozen times you said it."

"Goddammit!" he whispered, not wanting to be heard. Not wanting to get her caught. "It matters!"

She smiled at him, soft and loving, as though they were at a horse race, or walking in Hyde Park, or meeting eyes across his tavern. The look made him want to reach through the bars and pull her close. And then she said, "Tell me, Caleb, has it occurred to you that it might also matter that *you* be safe?"

This woman. "Sesily, I don't get to be safe. I—" He paused. "I killed the heir to a viscounty!"

She shook her head. "You magnificent man. Full of protective instincts and a need to sacrifice your happiness. Truly, someone should put you in a novel."

The words sent a thread of cold through him. "What does that mean?"

"It means," she said, her tone firmer than before, accusatory, "that you *did not* kill The Absolutely Not-Honorable Bernard Palmer, and no one is going to jail for a crime they didn't commit today. Not if I have anything to say about it."

His heart stopped. "How do you know that?"

There was only one way. She had to have spoken to Jane.

"You will find, Mr. Calhoun, that I have an immense network of very skilled people at my disposal. A network I am not afraid to use if it means ensuring that I get what I want. Which, tonight, requires stopping the man I love from committing this very noble and exceedingly stupid act."

The room was growing warm as Caleb's panic began to rise. "Sesily—" he warned. "Jane is—"

"Jane isn't going to jail for any crime, either," she said. "I told you there was another way, didn't I?"

Except there wasn't. There was no other way, except Caleb here, and Coleford knowing it. "Where is she?"

"She is safe. Peter, too. And his father," Sesily said. "And all very eager to see you, I might add. Not quite as annoyed with you as I am. Though I understand why you didn't tell me the truth. Some stories are not for you to tell."

"She told you?"

"She did," Sesily said. "She told me the whole story. The terrible Mr. Palmer, the way he came for her. How she had no choice but to defend herself. And how you, you gorgeous man, did what you do best—what you have done best, apparently, since you were a child. You protected her. Just as I've seen you protect every person you've ever loved. Your sister. Your nephew. Seraphina."

"You," he said. "*You*."

"Me." She reached for his hands on the bar, her fingers warm and firm on his skin, and aching for her touch, he threaded his own through them. "You're quite brilliant, you know. It turned out that your plan was the one all along."

"What plan?"

"No more darkness." She smiled. "We're lighting the lights."

He couldn't get to her and it was making him wild. "Goddammit, Sesily. You shouldn't have come."

"There's no use getting angry with me," she said. "Aside from the plan being already in motion—"

"What plan?"

"The one where I save you," she replied. "Aside from us being well down that path, you're locked in there and these bars are quite strong." She leaned away from them, turning to look down a darkened corridor. "I do wish Imogen would hurry, on that note."

"What's Imogen up to?" He paused. "What have you all done?"

"I could answer that any number of ways," she said. "I've had a very busy time of it since you left me—did I mention I do not like it when you leave me?"

"You did, yes." Christ. It had ripped his heart out to leave her there, on the river. To walk away without looking back.

"I thought I might never touch you again," she said, squeezing his fingers in her own. "I didn't like that."

"I'm sorry," he whispered.

"I thought I might never see you again. I didn't like that, either."

"I'm sorry."

She met his gaze. "And you told me you loved me. I didn't like that, either."

His brows shot together. "You didn't?"

"I didn't. You said it the way you say it to someone you're intending to never see again. You said it the way you say it to someone whose heart you're about to break. You said it like an end, instead of a beginning."

Christ, he wanted it to be a beginning.

He reached for her through the bars, his fingers brushing across her cheek, sliding into her hair. "I'm sorry. Shall I try it again?"

"I'm not sure you'll do it right this time, either," she said, anger in her words for the first time since she'd appeared at the bars of his cell. "I need you, Caleb. I don't need you in prison, protecting me. I need you out here, shoulder to shoulder. With me."

He needed it, too.

"Has it occurred to you that I am a great deal of trouble?" she added.

"Only every day since the day we met."

"And do you think I will be less trouble once you are gone? Because I shan't be. I assure you, I will not take your death well. I've no intention of withering gracefully in silent despair, like some widow wearing black and reading sad poetry."

Widow. He lingered on the word. On the way it made it sound like they'd had a lifetime together. On the way it made him ache.

But Sesily was just beginning. "Let me be clear, you arrogant man. You know nothing of what I will do if you die. If you die, I will *detonate*. They will have to invent new words for the havoc I will wreak."

Her blue eyes flashed, full of furious promise. Good lord, she was magnificent.

"So you are not allowed to die on some silly hill and claim it is *for* me, Caleb Calhoun. I don't want it and I certainly don't need it."

Magnificent, and his.

"You think I am reckless now—"

"I don't think you are reckless. I think you are fearless. That's not the same thing." He reached through the bars and pulled her closer. "You are making a very big promise, Lady Sesily. Are you sure you mean it?"

She narrowed her gaze on him. "What kind of promise?"

"If we stand together . . . if we fight together . . . if we go with your plan and light all the lights, tell all the truths . . ."

"It was your plan."

"You make it sound more fun."

She lifted her chin. "I do, don't I?"

"I want it."

She blinked. "You do?"

More than anything he'd ever wanted. And he'd wanted many many things in his lifetime. "I want it, and I want you." He paused. "You have a plan?"

She nodded, understanding lighting her eyes. "Yes."

Shoulder to shoulder. That was the promise.

"Then lead the way."

She grinned and reached for him, her hand coming to his face through the bars. "I love you."

"I love you," he said, softly.

She met his gaze with a watery smile. "That was better."

"You see?" he replied. "I just need practice."

"Try it again," she said.

"I love you," he replied.

"Good," she said. "I'm absolutely furious that you came barreling in here like some kind of hero, instead of letting me do what I do best."

"Which is?"

"Win."

"Does it involve viscount vandalism?"

She grinned. "Don't tempt me with a delicious challenge. But no, I've more skills than a steady hand with kohl."

A bell rang at a distance, distracting Sesily. She looked down the corridor and released a little breath. "Honestly, Imogen, it took you long enough."

"I would have been here sooner if you'd let me do it my way from the start," Lady Imogen said to Sesily before looking to Caleb. "Good evening, Mr. Calhoun."

Sesily had brought chaotic reinforcements. "Is it?"

"It's about to be," the woman replied.

"I assume the detective inspector refused the request."

"Indeed. The whole thing was a real disappointment." She paused. "Except the man's beard. That isn't disappointing."

Sesily laughed.

Caleb attempted to keep the conversation on track. "What request?"

"The request to release you," Sesily said offhandedly, looking down at Imogen, who was rifling through her bag, passing items for Sesily to hold. A narrow silver spoon. A tapered candle.

"Did you expect him to release me upon request?"

"No," Imogen said, happily, removing a heavy blanket from her bag and unwrapping it carefully to reveal a glass jar within. "And if I'm being honest? I'm happy he didn't."

She passed the jar up to Sesily.

"What is that?" he asked, suspicious.

"No need to worry," Sesily and Imogen said together.

Which immediately made him worry. "What in hell is that?" he repeated, suddenly keenly aware of what, in hell, it was. His voice rose. "Christ, Sesily . . ."

"Best not to yell," Imogen said, digging deep in the dark bag. "Being caught with a jar of gunpowder in Scotland Yard is not the most ideal scenario at this point."

He looked to Imogen. "Is there a less ideal scenario?"

"There is," she said, now distracted by the lock.

"Which is?"

"I could drop it," Sesily said, matter-of-factly.

Caleb's heart began to pound, and he spoke through his teeth. "What happens if you drop it?"

Lady Imogen looked up at that. "The odds are not insignificant that she would explode us all."

He stuck his hand through the cell bars. "Give it to me."

"Really, Caleb," Sesily said. "I'm not going to drop it."

He was coming unhinged. "How is it that in this situation, *you* are the one who is exasperated?"

"Because you are the one requiring this production. No one is here breaking *me* out of prison, are they?" She tutted in his direction, passing the jar to Imogen, who was now crouched by the lock on the cell door. When that was done, Sesily winked at him, as though this were all a game. "If I had my way, we'd be at my home in my bed right now."

An image flashed at the words, Sesily, rising over him, beautiful and bold, with that playful light in her eyes that never failed to draw him to her like a dog on a lead. He wanted it. And for the first time in a lifetime, this woman made him realize that it might not be an impossibility.

He narrowed his gaze on her. "When I get out of here . . ."

She smiled then, broad and bright and beautiful, and he was struck by how fucking perfect she was— or, at least, how perfect she *would be* if she were not holding a jar of gunpowder as though it were a cup of tea. "I'm very happy to hear that you intend to get out of there."

"I haven't a choice," he said. "You can't be trusted on your own."

"It's true," she said. "That . . . and you love me."

"I do," he said, softly, his fingers coming to hers through the bars of the cell.

"If you two are through?" Imogen asked as she quickly repacked her large bag and moved it out of view of the cell bars. She looked to Caleb. "Is there is a far-off corner in there?"

His brows rose and he looked around the cell. "I wouldn't say *far*."

"Least close?"

Caleb looked to Sesily. "Is she going to blow me up?"

"We thought about having you kick the cell door down, but . . ." She trailed off with a grin, and Caleb imagined all the ways he'd kiss it off her if she were in the cell with him.

No. If he were out there in the world with her.

"So, she might blow me up," he replied.

"He worries a great deal," Imogen said, tossing a look at him. "There was a time when I did consider blowing you up, you know."

His brows snapped together. "Why?"

"You'd broken Sesily's heart."

"Imogen!" Sesily said, as the air left Caleb's lungs. "He didn't break my heart." She looked to him, and he imagined a flush on her cheeks. Embarrassment. "And even if he had, he's mended it now, so do try not to blow him up."

"It's alright if I blow *something* up, though, isn't it?"

He looked to Sesily. "Is it going to be Scotland Yard?"

"With Imogen one never knows."

"I would never dream of blowing up that nice man," Imogen said, casually, focused on her project. "It would be a waste of those thighs."

Caleb looked to Sesily. "Does she mean Tommy Peck?"

"Is that what his friends call him?" Imogen asked. "Tommy?"

"Considering he's put Caleb in a holding cell for a full day, I'm not sure we would call them friends," Sesily said as Imogen approached, wiping her hands on her skirts.

"Right. Out of the way, Sesily."

She nodded and looked to Caleb, reaching through the bars and pulling his face down toward her. "I'd rather do this without the barrier, but needs must." She kissed him, quick and intense. "Best find a corner."

"You, too."

They retreated and a flint sparked in the dark hallway, setting smoke billowing and a trail of gunpowder sizzling, igniting the tail end of oiled linen jammed into the lock of the cell door. Caleb turned away, shielding his eyes against the stonework cell, and counted the interminable seconds, hoping that Lady Imogen, mad genius, was more genius than mad.

The explosion rocked Scotland Yard.

Caleb turned around, heart in his throat, already headed for the cell door, calling Sesily's name into the thick cloud of smoke, the silence that followed the explosion threatening to destroy him.

The cell door remained closed, so he did the first thing that occurred and put his boot to it, kicking it wide with unnecessary force, as Imogen had broken the lock. He was in the hallway in an instant. "Sesily!"

"Here!" she said, appearing at his side, breathless.

He had her in his arms before the word had even left her tongue, pulling her tight to him and lifting her, walking her back into the wall across from the cell they'd just destroyed, and kissing her, wild and thorough, licking into her until she sighed her pleasure and went loose in his arms.

When he broke the kiss and opened his eyes, it was to find her with a happy, dazed smile on her lips. "Am I back to being a goddess now?"

"Mmm," he said, kissing her once more, fierce and quick. "I didn't think I'd be able to do that again."

She wiggled in his grasp. "Let's spend the rest of the night doing it."

"Now is not the time for croquet, you two," Imogen said from somewhere in the smoke as shouts sounded down the hallway. "It's time to go."

Sesily stiffened. "I don't imagine that detective inspector with the nice beard is going to care much for what you've done to his jail, Imogen."

"Nonsense," Imogen replied as they made their way away from the approaching police. "With the attention the papers will give him? He ought to send me a gift of some sort. Fruit."

Caleb snorted his laughter and tightened his grip on Sesily as they ran. "Is it always like this with you lot?"

Sesily smiled up at him when they reached the end of the corridor. "Aren't you excited to throw yourself in with us?"

He was, actually.

Something strange thrummed through him at the idea, something akin to relief, but more complex. In his lifetime, he'd never known the pleasure of the support of others. He'd never known what it was to be cared for.

To be thought of.

But now . . . Sesily thought of him. Cared for him. *Loved him.*

"You go that way," Imogen said, pointing to a far staircase. "It will lead you out the side door. The duchess is waiting."

"And you?" he asked, turning to Sesily's friend, who had put herself in danger for him.

"I've a gift to leave for the detective inspector."

He shook his head. "You can't stay inside. They'll be looking for you."

"Why on earth would they be looking for me?" she scoffed, heading back toward the cell she'd destroyed. "A *woman*? Breaking a prisoner out of Scotland Yard? Absolutely laughable. Just the kind of thing an American would dream up."

He opened his mouth to argue, only to realize Lady Imogen was right. No one here would ever believe it.

The trio parted ways, Caleb refusing to let go of Sesily, pulling her along the corridor toward the promised exit. They were free of the smoke here, but the hallway was dark in the evening light—no one had lit the lamps that hung on the wall yet. Scotland Yard was, apparently, busy with other things.

"What's the gift?" he asked Sesily as they hurried down the corridor.

"A file. Thick as your thumb." He shot her a curious look. "Suffice to say, I expect the Viscount Coleford will be receiving a visit from Scotland Yard sometime very soon. In my experience, the aristocracy has a poor view of those who thieve from them and their favorite charities. Which the viscount has been doing for years. He'll be headed to prison, most definitely."

"He won't do well in prison," Caleb said as they came upon the farthest door in the place, marked WHITEHALL MEWS in jagged white paint.

"That much is true," the words came from behind them, and Caleb's blood ran cold as Sesily stiffened next to him. He turned, mind already working, knowing what he would find.

Coleford, pistol in hand.

Chapter Twenty-Five

He wasn't supposed to be there.

They'd sent enough women to keep Peck so busy that he couldn't notify Coleford all day long, and they'd had servants watching for missives to and from Scotland Yard all day. As of an hour earlier, when Imogen had knocked on the detective inspector's door, Peck hadn't notified Coleford, and still, here was the viscount, not upstairs in an office, but here, pistol in hand, pointing it at the man she loved, and Sesily found she did not care for that at all.

She cared for it even less when Caleb moved to put himself in front of her. Ever looking to keep her safe at his own expense.

Coleford swung the pistol toward Caleb. "I wouldn't, if I were you, American." A pause. "But you're not an American, are you?" He shook the pistol. *"Are you?!"*

Don't answer that, she willed.

"No, I'm not."

Damn this man and his unwillingness to lie.

"You killed my son. I know you did. You're the right age. The right height."

Caleb shook his head. "No, I didn't."

Bless this man and his unwillingness to lie.

"Well then you're lying prettily to someone, because I'm hearing you've confessed to it. No doubt to prevent my dogs from coming to get you. And your sister. And the whelp." He looked to Sesily, who resisted the urge to spit in the man's face she loathed him so well. "There's time still for them, I suppose. And for your lightskirt."

"Truly, you grow ever more charming, Lord Coleford," she said, not hiding her disdain for this man who had for so long ruined so many lives.

Caleb hissed a warning, his fingers tightening on hers, making it impossible for her to move.

"You think I don't know who you are?" the viscount spat. "You, who came into my home with your common bitch of a friend who thought to tell me how to treat what's mine?" His eyes narrowed with pure hate. "Embarrassing me in front of my own guests?"

"That's not all we did," Sesily said smartly, smoothing her skirts.

"Sesily." Another warning from Caleb.

She ignored it. "But I would not worry, my lord. You were an embarrassment long before my friend decided to help you along. And you've far more coming."

Coleford grimaced in her direction. "I suppose you think you're one of these new, clever girls. Coarse and sharp tongued, whoring yourself out to anyone who will have you now that there's a queen on the throne."

Caleb took a step toward him, a low growl in his throat, hard as steel with leashed anger. With an obvious desire to take this man down if not for the pistol in his hand. "Watch it, old man."

The viscount continued, spewing his poison. "Ruining England. Everything we worked for. You think I don't know who your family is? Your father, who made a mockery of the aristocracy? And you—the lightest skirts in London."

"I am surprised to hear you speak so highly for the sanctity of venerable institutions. What with the fact that you never reported your son's murder to the police." She paused. "Or your wife's. Either of them."

He turned a murderous look on her. "That's slander."

She raised a brow. "Only if it's false, though, right?"

The man's ruddy cheeks went impossibly redder, and the pistol swung toward her. "I'm going to take great pleasure in killing you both. I'd hoped the boys I had watching the Brixton house would make it a private affair, but if it has to happen here, I suppose it will do."

"Your boys?" she asked. "The ones who swindle mothers searching for their orphaned babes?"

"Sesily . . ."

"You know about that, do you?" said the old man. "Well, let's be honest, it's not as though the silly women have any hope of finding them otherwise."

Caleb swore, harsh and angry, unable to keep the loathing from his voice. "I look forward to you rotting in prison for a long while."

Until that moment, Sesily had imagined prison and devastation for this man to be the perfect revenge. Revenge for raising a son as monstrous as he was, for what she was sure he'd done to his wives, for stealing Caleb and Jane's happiness, for stealing from the Foundling Hospital, for stealing hope from women who had nothing but hope left. But listening to him speak of the crimes he'd committed, she realized that prison would never be enough for this man.

"Your boys won't take initiative when you've stopped paying them. Indeed," she added, "I imagine they'll happily sing when it becomes clear that you cannot pay

your debts. Your wife, too. I don't think the new viscountess cares much for you. You should have treated
her more nicely."

"Sesily." Caleb, warning her again, even as she kept
going, eager to unsettle Coleford. Knowing that unsettling him was their best chance at escaping this unharmed.

"And you *will* go to Newgate. Your title won't save
you—not when the public gets hold of everything you've
done. You know it, and we know it, and now, Scotland
Yard knows it, and it's a bold choice to threaten to open
fire here, when your name is surely the newest on the list
of wanted criminals."

Something flickered in the man's gaze—something
like fear, and he gripped the pistol more tightly.

"You *bitch*," the viscount said. "You know nothing of
this. Every penny I have—every penny I have spent—
it's been to find *him*." He waved the pistol in Caleb's
direction, but his hate was directed at Sesily.

Good. Keep it there.

She would never let him have Caleb.

Except Caleb had other plans. "You're right."

She turned to him. "What are you doing?"

Caleb took a step toward Coleford. "I was there,"
Caleb said. "Your boys found me. And your fight—it
is with me."

Sesily realized what he was doing. Redirecting the
viscount's attention. Buying time.

It worked, and soon Coleford's pistol was pointed at
him.

"No. Caleb." It was Sesily's turn to hold him back,
but Caleb shook her off, taking another step, to the side,
blocking her view.

Blocking Coleford's shot.

Protecting her.

Once again, putting himself in harm's way to keep her safe.

"I suppose you thought that by coming here, you could protect yourself. You were caught, and you thought you'd surrender to justice." Coleford waved the weapon in a circle, and Sesily couldn't stop watching his eyes, unfocused and wild. "But you made a mistake, you see. I never wanted justice. I didn't report the boy's murder, because I don't want it."

"You want vengeance." Sesily sucked in a breath, and Caleb moved again, releasing her hand, stepping squarely in front of her. Infuriating man.

Respect flared in the older man's gaze. "Indeed."

"I understand that. I want it, too." He stilled, slipping one hand into his trouser pocket, leaving the other free at his side.

And that's when Sesily remembered she, too, had pockets.

And what she kept in them.

Infuriating, brilliant man. Fighting alongside her after all.

"Only one of us is going to get it, though," Coleford said, leveling the pistol directly at Caleb's heart.

Within seconds, the hilt of her knife was in his hand, and he was moving like lightning, the blade flying through the air as Sesily leapt to knock him out of the way of the gunshot that sounded in the darkness.

Sesily's scream sounded alongside Coleford's high-pitched whine and Caleb's wicked curse. The viscount dropped to the ground, the hilt of Sesily's blade protruding from his shoulder even as Caleb lunged for the pistol, kicking it into the darkness, far out of reach.

He turned to face her then, her name like a breath, over and over, soft and full of worry, his hands stroking over her arms, up to her face. "Are you alright? Are you safe?"

She nodded, her own hands coming to his cheeks, his arms. "Yes. Yes. I'm fine. Are you? He fired the gun—the bullet?"

"Fucking hell, Sesily. You could have been killed. Next time, you let me take the damn bullet."

"We'll discuss it."

He pulled her close, planting a quick, firm kiss on her lips. "We will not, dammit." Releasing her, he said, "I don't suppose you're willing to part with any of those pretty petticoats in service of tying up an absolute rotter?"

She gave him her brightest smile. "Did you think the ribbons sewn into them were merely for show?"

She'd just lifted her skirts to fetch the bindings when behind them, an irritated voice said, "Goddammit, this is just what the day needs."

Thomas Peck stood at a distance, lantern in hand, the golden light illuminating his extreme annoyance as he took in the scene. Coleford writhing in the darkness, Caleb and Sesily fussing with her skirts.

Smoothing them down over her ankles, Sesily took Caleb's hand and stood. "With all due respect, Detective Inspector, you would have been immensely helpful a few minutes earlier."

"Well, my lady," Peck said, the honorific sounding more like epithet on his tongue. "As my hallways were teeming with women at the exact moment of the explosion, it was rather difficult to move with any deliberate speed."

She nodded. "Ah. No need to worry. As you can see, Mr. Calhoun had things well in hand."

"The amount of paperwork you people have caused me today." He looked down at the viscount, writhing on the ground. "I gather this is Coleford?"

"In the flesh," Calhoun said.

"Mmm," Peck said, looking down and addressing the viscount. "Well, you turning up here certainly saves me having to come round and arrest you for attempted murder in Scotland Yard, but I could have done without a knife wound." He raised his voice to an unseen aide. "Someone get a damn surgeon, please?"

Sesily resisted the urge to laugh at the man's demeanor. No wonder Imogen liked him.

He seemed to sense her attention. "And you, Lady Sesily, I suppose you just happened by? Out for a carriage ride with your friend Lady Imogen?"

She flashed a bright smile at him. "I heard there was an explosion. You couldn't expect me to stay away from a thing like that."

"Mmm. Lucky that Mr. Calhoun survived it, considering there turned out to be no reason for him to be in custody to begin with. Thank heavens for small favors, I suppose. All I needed was a dead man in my jail cell to make this day perfect." He nudged Coleford with his toe. "Oy. Don't die on me, toff."

Coleford whimpered from his prone position.

"Hang on." Caleb's brows rose, and Sesily delighted in the surprise on his face. "No reason for me to be here?"

Peck sighed. "Not considering the fact that the body of one"—he removed a slip of paper from his breast pocket—"Peter Whitacre was delivered to the morgue this afternoon, along with a confession for the *eighteen-year-gone* murder of the viscount's son." He paused, returning the paper to his pocket. "A fact I would have known sooner, if your friend hadn't been attempting to drive me mad, Lady Sesily."

"I shall have a stern talk with her," she said.

"If you would, please," he replied. "And also, I understand you've plans to donate the funds to repair one cell door."

Her smile widened. "I am nothing if not a staunch supporter of the law."

"Mmm," said the detective inspector. "I cannot see how anyone would think otherwise." He looked down at Coleford on the ground for a moment before turning an irritated gaze back on them. "A *great deal* of paperwork, in light of which, I believe I will not be entering into the record *either* of the conversations I had today regarding the murder of a man who can only be described as out-and-out villain. Especially considering we now have a confessed perpetrator in the morgue."

Beside her, Caleb went taut with shock. Sesily could've kissed Thomas Peck right on the mouth, but somehow she didn't think Caleb would like that.

"Thank you," he said, the rough gravel of his voice hinting at the wild relief he felt. They both felt. She slipped her hand into his, loved the way his grip tightened on hers. Like he'd never let her go.

Like he'd never have to.

Peck nodded, his eyes glittering with the light of a man who followed his own code of honor. "Someday, American, I shall ask you to remember it."

The message was clear. It was no longer Peck who owed Caleb, but the other way around. And one day, the inspector would call in the chit.

Caleb didn't hesitate. With a nod, he agreed to the terms.

Satisfied, Peck turned his stern gaze on her. "And now, I think we've all played enough 'Visit Scotland Yard and Toy with the Detective Inspector' for the day."

She resisted the smile that threatened. "Yes, sir."

"Then you'd best see to your man, my lady. And quickly."

Her man.

The words sent a shiver of pleasure through her.

Her man. Free and clear.

Wait. What?

"See to him? Why?" She turned a worried gaze on Caleb. "What's happened?"

"He's bleeding."

Her eyes went wide and she reached for his waistcoat, ripping it open to discover a bloom of red over the white shirt beneath.

"You're bleeding!"

"It's not serious," Caleb said, pulling her close. "Come here."

"Now is not the time, Caleb," she snapped.

"Yes it is," he said. "It is."

"Really? Because it appears you are *bleeding*!"

"And I'm free."

She stilled, looking up at him, meeting his gorgeous green gaze. "You are," she said, going up on her toes to press a kiss to his full, beautiful mouth. "You are also, however, bleeding. And we must go."

AFTER THEY DISAPPEARED through the exit to the Whitehall Mews, Peck turned back to the day's mess. Instructing the nearest officer to take the still whinge-ing viscount into custody and find him an *unexploded* location from which he could await his solicitor, Peck picked his way through the still smoky hallway to the cell where Calhoun had been all day.

Stepping through the now destroyed door, the detec-tive inspector made his way to the center of the small space, the rubble crunching beneath his once shined boots. They, like everything else in this area of Scotland Yard, were now covered in a thick film of dust.

Almost *everything*.

He stilled, his gaze falling to a light blue file, set carefully on the low bench that had somehow survived the blast. On it, an indigo bell. And not a speck of dust.

Lady Imogen Loveless's gift, from earlier. The one she'd taken back.

Apparently, he deserved it after all.

Opening it, he began to read—pages and pages on the viscount he already had in custody. Proof of a dozen crimes. Possibly more.

When he spoke to the empty room, it was with shock, and disbelief, and no small amount of admiration.

"Hell's bells."

NIGHT HAD FALLEN, and outside, a carriage waited, the Duchess of Trevescan and Adelaide deep in conversation next to it. When Sesily and Caleb came through the door, the pair looked up and hurried forward, worry on their faces.

"Is everything alright? We heard a gunshot." The duchess looked to Caleb, her attention immediately on his hand at his bloody side. "Let's have a look." Before he could think to refuse, she was moving his hand, considering the wound.

"Your Grace—" he said, feeling like he ought to at least acknowledge her position.

She shook her head and chuckled. "Not in that American accent, Mr. Calhoun. Call me Duchess." Her brow furrowed as she completed her inspection. "No bullet. A graze."

Sesily released a breath. "Good."

The duchess's concern turned to anger. "Was it police?"

"No."

"Imogen?" Adelaide guessed.

"I beg your pardon!" Imogen said, appearing alongside the carriage, having returned from wherever it was she'd been. "I've been very well behaved. Followed the plan *to the letter*."

"It was Coleford."

Imogen scowled. "Did you do him in?"

"No. He's currently under arrest," Sesily said. "Turns out, they don't like it when you nearly kill two people in Scotland Yard."

"Explosions are fine, though," Caleb said, dryly.

"Explosions have style," Imogen replied.

With a smile, Duchess turned to Caleb. "And you? Are you in hiding?"

"I am not, as a matter of fact. You'll never believe the coincidence—" Caleb said, cutting Sesily a look. "The killer's body turned up. Hard to imagine how that happened."

Her brows rose. "You didn't think I would start listening to you just as you were breaking my heart, did you?"

He stilled at that, hating it. Reaching for her, his fingers stroking over her impossibly soft skin. "I didn't mean to break your heart."

"Then you are lucky it is easily mended," she said, leaning into him. "I forgive you."

"I'm not sure I do, for the record," Imogen said.

"Nor I," the duchess chimed in.

Caleb's brows rose and his green eyes lit with equal parts trepidation and humor. Sesily smiled. "Sod off, you two. I love him."

They did sod off, thankfully, at least, to the rear of the carriage, where they pretended not to notice him snaking an arm around her waist and pulling her close for a long, lingering kiss.

"You love me," he whispered, when they finally broke for air.

"I do," she said, happily.

"You saved me."

She smiled. "Someone had to."

"You're the most beautiful thing I've ever seen, Sesily Talbot."

"You can tell me that any time you like."

"What if I tell you I love you?"

"You can tell me that, too." She leaned up to kiss him again, her fingers stroking down over his chest to his waist. He sucked in a breath at the sting when she found the damp spot on his shirt. His wound.

Sesily pulled back quickly. "You need a surgeon."

"I don't need a surgeon," he protested. He needed her. "I need soap and water and a needle and thread."

"I can help with that." The words, on a soft, unfamiliar English lilt, somehow, impossibly familiar.

Sesily caught her breath at the words, releasing him as he turned to face the woman who'd spoken them.

Jane.

His sister. Something burst in his chest, years of worry and sorrow replaced with relief and joy. She was older, and she looked so much like their mother. He'd missed her so much.

They approached each other with slow movements, as though they feared the meeting might not be real. And when they finally reached each other, the embrace they shared was long and emotional, their eyes closed, their faces full of awe and sorrow and regret and hope.

And then they began to laugh, because there was nothing else to be done, and the sound was infectious, and soon everyone was laughing, reveling in the knowledge that Caleb and Jane, after all the years apart, finally had each other once again.

When they released each other, it was Jane who remembered the task at hand. "I would very much like to stitch you up, brother."

"Into the carriage!" Adelaide replied. "Do try not to bleed on it, American. This is the nice one, not the one we use for corpses."

Jane's eyes went wide and Caleb couldn't help his laugh before he turned back to Jane. "Wait. Before we go anywhere . . . what are you doing here?" Worry came, on a rush of heat. "Why are you here?"

His sister set her hand on his wrist. "For you."

He didn't understand, looking to the rest of the assembly, each face more delighted than the next, and then to Sesily—beautiful, perfect Sesily, happy tears on her face.

As it had been Sesily's plan, it was Sesily who explained. "There was no use delivering proof of Coleford's crimes without delivering the man himself. Too much of a risk of him fleeing, and we couldn't risk it. Obviously." She smiled at him. "The goal was your freedom, and there was no way of having it without Coleford under arrest."

Caleb shook his head, confused. "I still don't—what does it have to do with Jane? Peck was to summon Coleford this morning when I confessed."

"Yes, well, that timing didn't work well for us," Sesily said. "Adelaide needed to make the confession look legitimate, and Imogen needed time for . . ."

"Concoctions," Imogen provided happily, brandishing her bagful of weaponry with what Caleb thought was an unsettling disregard for safety.

"So, we had to keep Peck busy *and* make certain Coleford came to Scotland Yard before we broke you out, or else we couldn't be certain he wouldn't harm us all in the balance. While Duchess sorted out occupying Peck, I went to see Jane," Sesily explained, looking to his sister. "Who agreed to lead the watchdogs here."

"Adelaide fetched me and The Bully Boys followed just as we expected they would," Jane said simply, as though she'd been a part of the group from the start.

"And once we arrived, Jane was a star," Imogen added.

"A whisper in a Bully Boy's ear that you and Sesily were *also* at Scotland Yard . . ." the duchess pointed out, "and Coleford couldn't stay away."

"Lamb to slaughter, really," Sesily said simply. "Though we had intended for him to land in Peck's office. The shooting you bit was . . . unplanned."

"But it is lovely to see a plan come together, nonetheless," the duchess announced. "Into carriages, everyone. Mr. Calhoun continues to bleed."

And then the whole team was in motion, and Caleb, left to wonder at Sesily's plan. He pulled her close, tight to his good side. "I should have believed you from the start."

She nodded, serious once more. "Will you believe me in the future? This is how we love. Out loud. With truth. This is how we fight. Together, or not at all."

That ache in his chest was back.

He loved this woman with all he had.

She was up on her toes again, pressing a kiss to his cheek before whispering in his ear. "Let's go home."

Home. A word he'd never allowed himself to think. To claim.

Now his once more. With Sesily. With Jane and Peter. With this crew of wild women.

"Do ride with me, Mrs. Berry," the duchess said from far off. "I am told you are an excellent seamstress."

"She specializes in designs with leather-lined pockets," Sesily called after them.

"Clever," Adelaide said from her seat on the block, all admiration.

Jane's brows rose in surprise before she found her voice. "I find pockets of all sizes and fabrics can be useful in a pinch."

The duchess smiled at Jane, and Caleb imagined he could see the plans already forming behind the woman's eyes. "How do you feel about specialty knickers?"

His sister did not hesitate. "I believe I can meet the challenge, Your Grace."

It was Caleb's turn to be surprised, and Sesily couldn't help a little laugh. Approaching him, she asked, "Have we embarrassed you, American?"

He laughed, pulling her tight. "Imagine, in all I've witnessed among you lot, it's the undergarments that did me in."

She came up on her toes to whisper in his ear, "And here I am, not wearing them at all."

It didn't matter that he was bleeding then, because all he could think of was what he intended to do the moment he had this woman alone. With a low rumble of pleasure, he kissed her again, slow and lush, ignoring the collective groans around them, punctuated by Jane's happy laugh.

Sesily broke the kiss. "We can do that anytime now," she whispered. "No more longing."

"I think I shall long for you forever," he said.

She smiled. "I will allow it."

He tried to kiss her again and she dodged out of the way. "No. You need to be stitched up. And then you can kiss me all you like."

"Kissing you *is* all I like."

She laughed, and turned for the carriage, looking back only when she realized that he hadn't followed her; instead, he stood in the lantern light from the exterior of the vehicle, watching her.

Wanting her.

Wanting to claim her as his, forever.

Her brow furrowed. "What is it?"

He lifted his chin in her direction. "You still owe me a boon, Sesily Talbot. And this time, I won't take no for an answer."

She couldn't help her smile. "Fair enough. Name it."

He approached, unbothered by the wound in his side, by the day he'd spent in jail, by the past he'd just overcome. Thinking only of the future, for the first time in a lifetime. "Marry me."

She tilted her head. "Maybe."

"Fucking hell, Sesily," he growled.

She grinned and reached for him, fisting the fine lawn of his shirt and pulling him close. "Are you sure? Marriage to me won't look like my sisters' marriages."

"I don't imagine it will, considering it comes with broken noses and break-ins and explosions and corpses." He paused. "Are the corpses negotiable?"

"We can discuss it," she laughed.

He leaned close. "If our marriage were like the others, I wouldn't be married to *you*. You, who I've wanted from the first moment I saw you. You, who I've ached to make mine from the start. Marry me, love."

She answered him with a kiss.

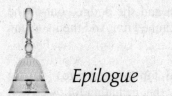

Epilogue

One Year Later

The house was quiet when Caleb entered after a long evening at The Athena—his new tavern in Marylebone, one of three he and Fetu had opened in the year since everything had changed.

Since he'd been set free to move through the world without fear of discovery or punishment, to start new businesses, to claim an enormous family full of sisters and sisters-in-arms, nephews and nieces and brothers-in-law.

To love his wife. Out loud.

Sesily and Caleb had married only weeks after the explosion at Scotland Yard, in the quiet parish church near Highley, the ceremony attended by their families and closest friends. Sera and Haven hadn't blinked when the newlyweds had requested the groundskeeper's cottage on the estate for their wedding night. Caleb had filled it with hothouse roses and lavish cushions before the roaring fire, and one lingering night had stretched into three, until they'd remembered that they had a home of their own in London perfect for every lingering night thereafter.

Of course, there was less lingering in London.

Between the taverns, Sesily's work, their families, and their friends, the evenings were full of joy and pleasure, of happiness and purpose. Sesily no longer avoided his pubs and Caleb realized quickly that he didn't mind a society ball if there was a possibility that his beautiful wife was going to scandalize the attendees.

Which was an important realization, as it was clear Sesily had no intention of stopping. And Caleb had every intention of following her into the fray.

Together, or not at all.

Sesily had spent that particular evening at The Place, and Caleb was eager to get home, to see her. To hold her. To love her.

After their wedding, Sesily had turned Caleb's Marylebone house into a home—full of lush furnishings and beautiful art and a thousand other comforts that he'd never allowed himself to imagine before he met her, when he'd lived holding his breath.

Before she taught him to breathe.

A single lantern happily flickered on the table just inside the door. *She was home.* Caleb picked it up without stopping, taking the stairs two at a time to reach her. As he rounded the corner to their bedchamber, he wondered if he would ever make this journey without speed. Without aching desire. Without a near desperate need to be near her.

Never.

She was not in the bed cast into darkness on one side of the room. Nor was she in the chair by the fire that cast dancing orange shadows around the dimly lit space.

She was bathing, behind the bathing screen, where it seemed she'd lit every candle they owned, ensuring that her silhouette was clear and sinful on the sailcloth.

Caleb's mouth was instantly dry, his cock hard.

The bedchamber door closed with force.

She raised one long arm and he was riveted to the movement, to the slow slide of her other hand as she ran a strip of linen over her skin.

"You're home," she said, the words quiet, the little breathless hitch in them barely noticeable.

He noticed.

Pleasure thrummed through him, and he slipped out of his coat. "So are you."

"Quiet night at The Place," she replied, switching arms. Stealing his breath.

He cleared his throat. "It's never quiet at The Place."

She paused in her slow strokes. Tilted her head. "Quieter. All trouble was delightful trouble." Resumed her bathing. "And you? How was the crowd?"

"Rowdy," he said. "Raucous." The ideal crowd for a new tavern. "Fetu was happy."

"And you?" She smiled. "Were you happy?"

I am now. It seemed impossible that he was so happy. "I wanted to come home," he said. "I wanted to see you."

Another pause. "I wanted to see you, too."

His heartbeat went heavier with the promise in the words. "Have you been waiting long?"

"I've kept myself busy."

The words sizzled through him as she lowered her arm, slow and languid, and leaned back against the high wall of the copper bathtub—too high, if you asked Caleb, considering how little of her he could see. Her hair, piled high and haphazard on her head. Her beautiful profile.

"Tell me how," he said, the words coming like gravel. He worked the buttons of his waistcoat with rough urgency, unable to take his eyes off her. *Show me.*

She raised her leg out of the bath.

Yes.

"We've had several invitations to Christmas," she said, leaning forward to stroke a length of linen over the lush curves of her calf to her pretty ankle.

Caleb cast off the waistcoat, imagining all the ways he might make that clean limb dirty again.

"Caleb?" she asked, bringing him back from his thoughts.

"Hmm?"

The leg disappeared. "Do you have an opinion?"

"About?"

"Where you would like to spend the holiday." He didn't miss the dry amusement in the words. She knew what she was doing to him. She was enjoying it.

"With you," he said, simply.

She sat up and turned her head, her arms coming up on the edge of the bathtub, the silhouette of her shoulders soft and curved and perfect. "Besides me."

"Doesn't matter," he replied, pulling his shirt over his head, letting it sail across the room.

"I think Jane's then," she said.

He'd missed eighteen years of Christmases with his sister. A decade of them with Peter. The promise of a family Christmas with them was wonderful. And of course, Sesily knew that.

But he did not want to talk about his sister. "Sesily . . ."

She shifted, the water around her making lush promises that he hoped his wife intended to keep.

"We can plan for Boxing Day at Highley," she said.

"I honestly don't care, love," he said, running a hand across his bare chest, down to the buttons of his trousers. Lower, stroking over his straining length. "Tell me more about what you've been doing while you waited for me."

A pause, and then she straightened, turning back to profile. Tilting her face up to the ceiling. Giving him more of a view. Her breasts, full and perfect. She stroked over them with her cloth, and he did not hold back his groan. "Are you sure you'd like me to tell you?"

She stood, the sound of the water sluicing off her body like sin as her full silhouette came into view, the curves and swells and dips and valleys. Her lush hips and round bottom. Her hands lifted to her hair, and she fiddled with the tower of it, pulling it down in heavy rich waves. "Or would you rather I show you?"

He was across the room and around the screen in seconds, pulling her to him as she squealed her delight. "Caleb! I am still wet!"

"And I'm going to make sure you stay that way," he growled, lifting her out of the bath and up into his arms. "You're a tease."

She shook her head. "I'm not!"

"No? Then what was all this? Talk of The Place and my tavern and where we shall spend Christmas . . . with no awareness of how you were making me wild with need?"

Her blue eyes flashed with pleasure and her fingers tangled in his hair, pulling him down for a kiss. "A little awareness."

He groaned, licking deep, sucking on her full bottom lip until she sighed with pleasure. "A lot of it."

"Wild with need, are you?"

"Always, when it comes to you, wife." He carried her around the screen, crossing the room in long strides, to drop her, nude on the edge of the bed.

She parted her thighs and he stepped between them, grateful that when she'd redecorated this particular room, she'd thought to raise the bed on a platform. When he pressed himself to her, her heat searing him through the rough fabric of his trousers, they both groaned their pleasure.

And then his magnificent wife pulled him down for a kiss, deep and lush and perfect, releasing him only to whisper, like sin, "Whatever will you do with me?"

"I have some ideas," he promised, tipping her back onto the bed and following her down. "Would you like to hear the best one?"

"Please," she sighed, arching up to him, making him ache.

"I'm going to love you, Sesily Talbot. Every day . . . for the rest of our lives."

Her eyes met his, blue and beautiful. "Out loud?"

She was perfect. And his.

"Out loud."

And he set about doing just that.

Author's Note

The joy of writing historical romance is this: while the stories are always about the way we experience the world and ourselves and love in present day, every book begins with a little truth from the past. Often, those truths are wilder than anything I could imagine on my own.

Several years ago, while staring at Twitter instead of working on what would become *Brazen and the Beast*, I stumbled upon a tweet referencing the Forty Elephants, the women's branch of the Elephant and Castle Gang— the largest gang in Victorian London. While the Elephant Boys were into all the things gangs are usually into, the Forty Elephants were a less overtly violent bunch. The women worked as bookies and ran the largest shoplifting ring the United Kingdom had ever seen, wearing enormous skirts over specialty undergarments that could carry anything that wasn't bolted down in the department stores of the late 1800s. The stories about the Forty Elephants are wild, and I became fascinated by this gang of women who ran their own network.

Let me say now, the Hell's Belles are not the Forty Elephants. If the Hell's Belles are a martini, the Forty Elephants are the bottle of vermouth waved over the glass. Without them, however, I would not have imagined this group of women, with them a far-reaching whisper network and specialty undergarments, who know their way around a locked prison cell, a tavern brawl, and a bottle of chloroform. So, here's to Alice Diamond, aka Agnes Ross, aka Diamond Annie, and to her girls, for the inspiration. For the record, I think Alice would hate this book. It's far too soft for a woman who falsified papers to find work in a munitions factory and secure a line to explosives. I firmly believe, however, that she would make a lewd comment about Caleb's thighs, and I respect that. For more on the Forty Elephants, do not miss Brian McDonald's terrific *Alice Diamond and the Forty Elephants*.

Speaking of chloroform—the mixture that Imogen has invented in her own laboratory is the same mixture invented simultaneously in Germany and the United States in 1831. More on that in her book, I'm sure!

I also can't say enough about London's Foundling Museum, which has stayed with me for years, since my first visit. As always, I owe a tremendous debt to the Museum of London, the British Library, and the New York Public Library for endless rabbit holes of research . . . even during a global pandemic. Hug your closest research librarian.

By now, my friend Dan Medel is used to late-night texts asking strange questions like, "If someone gets choked to the point of passing out, what would happen to them?" Thanks to him, as always, for patient answers which now usually begin with, "If death isn't an option, then . . ." The fact that he tolerated my nonsense this time while being a doctor during a pandemic . . . if that isn't friendship, I don't know what is.

I spent 2020 feeling immensely grateful for my own girl gang—a community of women who I honestly don't think I could have survived endless 2020 without: my ride-or-dies Louisa Edwards and Sophie Jordan; my dear friends Jen Prokop and Kate Clayborn; everyone in the Writers Room text chain; and Kennedy Ryan and Meghan Tierney, for keeping me honest until the very end.

The Duchess's soup tureen is inspired by a similar setup in the home of a long-ago friend of my mother's. So thanks to Venturi—for the idea and for introducing my parents at one of your great parties.

To the amazing team at Avon Books, number fourteen is in the books! Thank you to: brilliant Carrie Feron, who never blinks when I pitch her a bananas idea; Asanté Simons, who never blinks when I ask her a silly question; Brittani DiMare, who makes me look so much better than I am; Brittani Hilles, who jumped into the pool with both feet; Jennifer Hart, Kristine Macrides, Christine Edwards, Ronnie Kutys, Andy LeCount, Josh Marwell, Carla Parker, Rachel Levenberg, Donna Waikus, Carolyn Bodkin, and the entire Sales team, who all come with big excitement; and Jeanne Reina and everyone in the art department, who saw what *Bombshell* could be and made sure it had a cover to match.

Rounding out this gang of very excellent girls are Holly Root, Kristin Dwyer, Alice Lawson, Eva Moore, and Linda Watson—I'm so grateful for each of you.

Thank you to my loves: V, who turned the tables and left her mom notes at the beginning of the day; Kahlo, for hours lying on my feet under my desk; and Eric, for everything you do, even when you think I'm mayhem.

And this is all before I get to you, dear reader! Thank you for waiting so patiently for Sesily and Caleb. I hope I made it worth the wait. I hope you see now why it took so long . . . I had plans! I can't wait for you to see what I've got cooking for Adelaide, coming next year.